Dark Beneath the Moon

Sherry D. Ramsey

Dark Beneath the Moon

Sherry D. Ramsey

TYCHE BOOKS LTD.

Dark Beneath the Moon
Published by Tyche Books Ltd.
www.TycheBooks.com

Cover Art by Ashley Walters
Cover Layout by Lucia Starkey
Interior Layout by Ryah Deines
Editorial by M. L. D. Curelas

Author photograph: John Ratchford

This book was funded in part by a grant from the Alberta Media Fund.

Dedication

For Emily and Mark
because it's not always easy to have a mom
who spends almost as much time with her characters
as she does with you.

Contents

Away! the moor is dark beneath the moon,
Rapid clouds have drunk the last pale beam of even:
Away! the gathering winds will call the darkness soon,
And profoundest midnight shroud the serene lights of heaven.

~ "Remorse," Percy Bysshe Shelley

Prologue — Jahelia

Planet Quma, 227b

THE SMALL, DINGY room where my father lay had taken on the cloying scent of death. It clung to the yellowed lampshade on the night table, to the blue and green embroidered coverlet my mother had once smoothed so meticulously, to the curtains he'd insisted on keeping closed for weeks now. He would not leave this room alive, and he and the room—and I—knew it.

He'd been dying by inches for months. The tiny machines that had toiled vigorously inside his body for decades had finally begun to fail, and there was no-one in Nearspace who could fix them.

At least, that was what he had told me. I'd asked him over and over, and his answer was always the same. Until the last time.

"It's my own damn fault," he wheezed as I held the glass of water close to his lips, waiting for him to take a sip. It wasn't cold any longer, but he preferred it this way. It might calm the cough and it might make it worse: every swallow was a toss-up.

"Shhh, *paĉjo*. Just take a little drink, now."

He pushed the glass away with a hand that shook more every day, but was still strong enough to make his will known. His mind had flown into the past, still retracing old regrets. "I should have waited until we were further along. Until we knew for sure that we had it right. I jumped the gun. But PrimeCorp—"

He launched into a fit of coughing that wracked his entire body, from his sunken chest right down to the thin, mottled sticks his legs had become beneath the coverlet. I rubbed his back, feeling the bones sharp through his thin pyjamas and fragile skin. When the cough released him, he dropped against the pillows and lay still, panting.

"There's no-one else from your old team who might know something? Anything that might help?" I prodded again, although I was convinced by now that it was useless. He hadn't contacted anyone for help when Mamma was dying—he wouldn't do it for himself. But I had to ask. I was sure he was holding out on me, and equally sure that he would take his secrets to the grave with him.

He lay staring at the ceiling, unmoving for so long that I was tempted to put my ear to his chest to make sure his heart still beat. If I watched closely, though, I could make out the shallow rise and fall of his breathing.

"How are you feeling, Lia?" he asked finally. The change of subject, and the sudden use of my childhood nickname, threw me for a moment.

"Me? I'm fine, Dad."

He turned his gaze to me, his rheumy eyes red-rimmed and watery from the coughing fit, yet still piercing. He nodded. "You've got the next generation. Not the same as mine. Not the same as your mother's. You should be fine. I don't want you worrying."

I shifted uncomfortably on the hard wooden chair next to the bed. "I know. It's *okej*."

His eyes found the ceiling again, focused as if he were trying to count every crack in the aging plaster. His next words were barely louder than a whisper. "But I don't know for sure. Not for *sure*."

I tried to keep my voice light. "Well, no-one knows much for sure, right? We all have to take it one day at a time. We've already had more than most. And anyway, once you feel better—"

He shook his head, slowly. "We should have known for sure."

I patted his hand, my unlined one a stark contrast to his newly age-spotted skin and deeply grooved lines. The changes had come on suddenly, alarmingly. "I've had a good run so far. I've got no complaints."

He twitched his hand out from under mine as if my touch were hot. "I made a promise," he said, his voice stronger than I'd heard it in days. "I made a promise and I kept it, goddamn it, but I'm not taking it to my grave. I've done some things I'm not proud of, but they don't matter now."

I wondered if he was starting to ramble, and bit my lip. I itched to get up and open the curtains, let some light in to the stifling room. Instead I straightened the things on the night-table. His water glass and datapad and glasses. He'd only started wearing them two months ago and resented them heartily.

"At least your mother never knew." His voice was lazy, distant.

I'd been worried for weeks now that his mind would start to break, not sure how I would handle that. "Shhh, Dad," I tried. "It's *okej*. You should rest, not worry yourself about the past."

He reached out and grabbed my hand again, squeezing it. "But this does matter. It matters to you, and your future. It will matter if your bioscavs ever start to fail, too."

His hand squeezed mine painfully, but I didn't pull away. *If your bioscavs ever start to fail.* The one thing I feared the most, now. Now that I'd seen it happen to both my parents.

"There is someone. One person in all of Nearspace who could help. A woman. My old team leader. In spite of—in spite of me, she'd help you, I think."

Something dark clutched at my heart. "What? I've asked and asked you this! Why didn't you say—"

"I wouldn't ask. Not for myself." He shook his head vehemently.

"She might have been able to help you!"

"No. She doesn't even know—but for you . . . she had a daughter, too. She'd understand."

"Could she still be alive?"

He laughed, a short sharp bark that held no humour. "Oh, she's still alive, I'm sure. She'd have used the bioscavs, no doubt—

probably better, newer ones than mine."

"What's her name? I'll get in touch with her. I'll ask her to help you, if you won't ask yourself."

He shook his head mutely again, and I snatched my hand away from his. I stood, knocking the chair over. It hit the floor with a dull thud. "I'll get her here. I'll make her help you—"

He'd closed his eyes and eased back against the pillows again. "No, Jahelia. Not for me. But I'll make sure you know . . . if you need her. Only if you need her . . ."

His voice trailed away as he fell asleep, quickly, in mid-thought, as he was prone to do lately. I stood staring down at him for a few long moments, shaking, damping down the anger. *He didn't have to be dying! He'd lied to me!* There was someone out there—somewhere in Nearspace—who might have been able to help him. But he'd been too stubborn to ask. Not for Mamma, either.

I ran a hand through my hair and blew out a long breath. That was him all over.

Slowly I righted the chair and took the glass of water to freshen it up for when he woke later. My eyes strayed to his datapad, dust-covered on the nightstand since he hadn't bothered with it for weeks now. I picked it up, glancing over to make sure he hadn't woken up as suddenly as he'd fallen asleep. He wouldn't like me snooping around in his data. But his eyes were still closed, the thin, blue-veined lids twitching slightly.

I weighed the datapad in my hand, considering. There might be nothing on it, no clues to this woman he'd mentioned. I licked my lips. But if there was a chance . . . I'd risk his anger. Tech was my thing, and I doubted the old man could have a pass-encryption on his data that I couldn't break. I was going crazy sitting in this tiny walk-up, anyway.

I took the datapad with me out to the pallid kitchen and set to work.

I'D UNDERESTIMATED MY father. He must have paid some techdog a pile of credits to pass-encrypt that datapad. He could have simply asked me to do it, but then I'd know the way in. It was obvious that I was one of the people he'd been keeping secrets from for a long, long time. I cracked it, ironically, the day he died, and later found the key scrawled on a paper he'd hidden under his mattress for me to find. That assuaged my guilt at breaking into his datapad.

There was no news for me in the fact that he'd worked for PrimeCorp as a genetics researcher, searching for ways to extend the human lifespan. Searching for the fountain of youth, or at least for the nanobioscavengers of immortality. He'd apparently found them, too, as my youthful appearance attested. I'd known that for a long time, and known what he'd done with them just before the project had come to a mysterious end. Some people might think it unethical to inject your two-year-old daughter with barely-tested nanotechnology, but I couldn't fault him, not really. Not when I looked—and felt—twenty-eight instead of seventy-seven. Not when the same technology had kept him and Mamma alive and healthy too, letting us travel the reaches of Nearspace together—until the day it all started to go wrong. I'd blamed him for the choices he'd made. Still did. But there were things I hadn't known.

That my father had been blackmailed, a coercion that dictated how he and my mother and I had lived the rest of our lives together. That the woman responsible had also made herself the self-appointed gatekeeper of immortality for the entire human race, and shut down the project. I realized now, as I read the files, hands trembling with repressed anger, that if the project had been allowed to continue, my parents would probably still be alive. The name of the woman responsible was there, too. And the way that everything circled back to PrimeCorp, and ethics, and money, the way that everything always comes down to the money.

That even now, my father had died when he could have been saved.

Those were the things he'd kept from me.

Those were the things I vowed to do something about.

Chapter 1 — Luta
Homecoming Delayed

Nearspace, 2284

I WAS ALONE on the bridge, enjoying a mug of hot, sweet double caff and a few minutes of uncommon solitude, when the comm signaled a message from my brother the *Admiralo*. My far trader, the *Tane Ikai*, plied the spacelanes about halfway between Mars and Earth. It had been a long and difficult few weeks since Lanar and I had left our mother behind again on Kiando after an all-too-brief reunion, and I hadn't expected to hear from him at least until we'd arrived Earthside.

"*Salut, Kapitano,*" he said in Esper, grey eyes twinkling as I opened the comm screen. "How are things aboard my favourite far trader?"

"Don't even ask," I told him, shaking my head. But I smiled at him. "It's good to see you again, little brother."

His eyes narrowed immediately. "What's wrong?"

I sighed and shrugged. "How long have you got?"

He sat back in his chair and folded his arms across his steel-blue Protectorate uniform. Behind him, a viewport opened to an endless starfield, so he was certainly aboard his own ship, the

Nearspace Protectorate vessel *S. Cheswick.* The *Cheswick* was a Pegasus-class ship, with a hundred and seventy-five crew aboard, but Lanar seemed to manage them with ease. "I've got time, Luta. Spill it."

Well, with such a large crew under him, maybe he could give me some pointers. I relaxed in my own chair, ticking items off on my fingers. "I'll give you the condensed version. Viss won't speak to Yuskeya, and he's grimly overhauling every system on board to keep busy. Yuskeya, or Commander Blue to you, hardly pokes her nose out of her quarters unless she has a duty shift." I gave Lanar a look to remind him that I still hadn't entirely forgiven him for secretly installing an undercover Protectorate officer on my bridge, then went on.

"Rei got a message the other day that she refuses to talk about, even to me, and she's spending every off-duty minute practicing some kind of Erian martial art down in an empty cargo pod. It seems to involve considerable amounts of screaming." I rubbed my temples. My nanobioscavengers were probably the only thing keeping my blood pressure from spiking merely talking about it.

"And Hirin has decided that he hates PrimeCorp so much, he's planning to research everything they've ever done until he uncovers enough dirt to bury them. The only ones who aren't miserable are Baden and Maja, and watching them gaze at each other all starry-eyed is making everyone else crankier. Is that enough?"

I took a sip of the smooth, creamy liquid, hoping Lanar wouldn't notice I was leaving something out—the tension between my husband, Hirin, and me. Or what had been bothering me ever since Lanar and I had finally found our long-lost mother. Sisters have to keep some secrets, after all.

Lanar raised his eyebrows. "Well, everyone hates PrimeCorp, so I can't fault Hirin for that. But it does sound like you've got your hands full." A slight frown creased his smooth forehead. "I'd wondered why Commander Blue's reports were slow, but I thought things were just—quiet."

I chuckled mirthlessly. "Oh, they're quiet, all right. Unless you go down to the cargo pod with Rei. Frankly, I can't wait to get Earthside for a little shore leave."

Lanar broke eye contact with me, glancing down at his desk. "Um, about that, Luta . . ."

"*Dio*, Lanar, don't tell me there's some reason we can't go to Earth now?"

It was his turn to sigh, and he glanced up, grey eyes apologetic. "Remember when we were on Vele, and you wondered how long Yuskeya would be staying on board your ship?"

"Yes," I said cautiously.

"I said there was something I'd talk to you about when you got back to Sol system."

"I thought it would be when we got *Earthside*, and that it actually had something to do with Yuskeya," I said, "but go on."

He leaned toward his comm screen. "How's your encryption level?"

"If I know Baden, better than yours," I told him with a grin. My comm officer was a techdog, and he liked to have the latest—everything. "He upgraded it when we were on Kiando."

Lanar quirked a half-smile. "Maybe I should borrow him sometime. Anyone there with you?"

I started to shake my head, but footsteps sounded in the corridor outside the bridge and I turned to see Yuskeya crossing toward me, carrying a steaming mug and a plate of cinnamon *pano*. It was still early morning, shiptime, and her duty shift wasn't set to start for a while yet, but her long dark hair was neatly plaited and her shipsuit fresh and crisp. Only the creases at the top of the suit's legs betrayed the fact that she'd been up and dressed and probably sitting and reading for a while now. We'd all taken refuge in something to ease the tension aboard the ship, and Yuskeya's escape, like mine, was books.

She halted far enough away that she couldn't see the comm screen and raised her eyebrows.

"Yuskeya just came in," I told Lanar. "I think everyone else is still asleep."

"Well, actually, that's *perfekta*," he said. "It will save me briefing her later. Ask her to sit in, would you, Luta?"

"Your boss," I told Yuskeya, tilting my head toward the comm screen. "He wants to talk to both of us. Extra encryption level, so I'm sure we can both guess what that means."

"Trouble?" Yuskeya said, grinning. She set the mugs down with the plate of *pano* between us, and pulled an extra skimchair over before saluting Lanar and sitting down.

I took a slice of cinnamon bread as Lanar and Yuskeya exchanged greetings. It was crumbly and delicious, as I knew it would be; Yuskeya had been pampering me a little on this trip. Her way of making up for keeping the secret of her identity as a Protectorate officer from me for the last year or so.

"So what's happening to keep us from Earth?" I asked, before they could get too involved in Protectorate gossip and forget all about me.

Lanar held up a hand. "Now, it's only a favour. You're not under any obligation to act for the Protectorate if you'd rather not."

I waved that away, the cinnamon bread sprinkling crumbs across the comm panel. "Sure. But I know you wouldn't be asking if you didn't really need help, and if you really need help you know I'll do it. So tell me."

He grinned again, and I knew he'd been counting on that. "*Okej*, here's the situation. A new wormhole's been discovered in the Delta Pavonis system."

"Really?" Yuskeya narrowed her eyes. "I hadn't heard that." As navigator, she made it her business to keep informed about new wormhole discoveries.

"Almost no-one has," Lanar said to placate her. "The Protectorate is keeping it pretty quiet. It's not the wormhole itself, but what's on the other side."

"Which is?" I prompted, when he didn't continue.

"Are you sure about that encryption?"

"*Dio*, Lanar," I said in exasperation. "If you don't trust it, then come and meet me, and we'll talk in person. *After* I've had a nice long vacation Earthside."

"All right, all right." He leaned in toward the comm screen again, grey eyes earnest. "Beyond that wormhole is an unknown system. And in that system, there's a moon."

Yuskeya and I glanced at each other. This was like slow torture. I'd never known Lanar to be so reticent.

"*Hola*, a moon. How unusual," I said.

He didn't smile. "It's no ordinary moon. It's an artifact, and they think . . . they think it's a Chron artifact."

I almost choked on the sip of double caff I'd just taken. A Chron artifact? No wonder the Protectorate was keeping it quiet. The Chron had come close to eliminating the human race, along with our allies, the Vilisians and the Lobors, in a war a century and a half ago. A war for which we'd never learned a reason or explanation. The Chron had made no attempt to communicate with us, simply showed up in Nearspace and started attacking. Nearspace wasn't even very big then—a handful of systems linked by a few wormholes. The war had gone on for three years, and on the cusp of a Chron victory, they disappeared without a trace.

Yuskeya leaned forward, resting her elbows on her knees. "When you say artifact, do you mean—"

Lanar nodded. "Not naturally occurring. Man-made. Well, Chron-made."

"An entire fabricated moon? What was it for?"

Lanar's eyes were bright with curiosity. "That's what everyone wants to know. And that's where the *Tane Ikai* comes in. Look, here's the way it is. The Protectorate is very interested in keeping this completely quiet for a while, as you can imagine. We know we're being watched by any number of the corporations, including PrimeCorp—especially PrimeCorp—as well as a half-dozen other groups who don't trust any kind of power or authority and want to keep tabs on us. A rush of Protectorate ships into the Delta Pavonis system will attract unwanted attention."

I nodded. That made sense. The power balance in Nearspace, among the various governments, corporations, and Protectorate authorities, was complex, esoteric, and delicate.

"There's a Lobor historian on Nanear who's willing to come and assess the moon, see if they can help understand it," Lanar continued.

"Historian? Why wouldn't you be bringing in scientists?" I asked.

Lanar shrugged. "There are scientists there already—a xenobiologist, a cryptographer, I don't know what else. But the Chron war was a hundred and fifty years ago. No-one's really studying Chron technology—what little we have of it—anymore. There were no real breakthroughs with it, and with the Chron out of the picture there was really nothing else left. This historian is the best bet we've got, besides the Protectorate science team that's already on-site."

"So let me guess. You want us to collect this historian and deliver him to Delta Pavonis?"

Lanar winked. "Got it in one. Except, it's a *she*. She'll get herself from Nanear to Anar in the Lambda Saggitae system, and you can pick her up there. Then it's only four skips out to Pavonis. You'll be fully compensated at double the usual passenger rates."

"*Only* four skips! Couldn't she get passage as far as Sol system? Then the crew could have a little break while we wait for her, restock and refuel on Earth and set out from there."

Lanar shook his head. "We don't want her coming into Sol system on a commercial shuttle. Someone might pick up on it. Better if you pick her up on Anar. I also don't want you coming Earthside and getting into a scuffle with PrimeCorp. You just finished sticking it to them on Vele, and—"

"I know, I know," I broke in. "Don't go looking for trouble. *Okej*, Lanar, we'll do it, just like you knew we would. But we're stopping on Mars for supplies. I'm not making another wormhole skip until we've restocked."

"Understood. PrimeCorp doesn't have the influence on Mars that they do on Earth, and the Schulyer Group keeps a pretty close rein on everybody else. But keep this quiet, all right?"

I sat back in my chair and folded my arms across my chest. "Yes, Lanar, I get it. Got any other dirty work you'd like me to do for you while I'm at it?"

"I think that's it for now," he said with a satisfied smile. "I'll send along the details of when you should be on Anar, and a full briefing for Yuskeya, and the rest is up to you. And good luck," he added with a smirk, "with those other problems you mentioned."

"Thanks a bunch. Always nice to talk to you, little brother," I said wryly, but I winked at him before I broke the connection.

"Well, *that* was interesting," Yuskeya said, cradling her own mug. Hers would be filled with hot, spicy chai. "And what problems did he mean?"

"What was interesting? What problems?" Hirin asked, coming onto the bridge. He'd dressed for the day in dark cotton pants and a faded Ivan Mecha Band t-shirt he'd picked up in a thrift shop on Kiando; he disliked shipsuits as much as I did. He hadn't brought a lot with him when he left the nursing home on Earth to rejoin me on the *Tane Ikai* for what he thought would be his last journey, so he was building a new wardrobe with bits and pieces.

The nanobioscavengers my mother had given him had continued to shave years off his appearance, so that now he resembled a hearty sixty-year-old instead of a nonagenarian. Which he was, of course. He simply no longer looked or felt like one, just as I looked about thirty, not my chronological eighty-four. He wore his salt-and-pepper hair slightly longer than military length, and his face was freshly shaved and smooth.

He strode in, hesitated slightly, then headed over to the pilot's skimchair and sat. I knew that long habit would have taken him to the chair I occupied, had it been empty. The captain's chair. He hadn't said a word about it . . . yet. But it had been his chair for decades, until he'd taken ill, and now that he was better, I knew without a doubt that he must want it back. But he wouldn't ask me, his wife of sixty years, to give it up for him. And frankly, I didn't really want to.

In the ten years he'd been in the nursing home, I'd discovered that I liked running the ship.

That was one of the problems I hadn't mentioned to Lanar.

"Oh, nothing much," I said, ignoring the second of Hirin's questions. "We've been drafted by the Nearspace Protectorate, that's all, and we won't be landing Earthside anytime soon."

Hirin's eyebrows shot up, and I shook my head wearily. "Let's wake everybody up and I'll only have to tell it once," I said, and shuddered at the thought of everyone having to be in the same room together. The amiable crew I'd left Earth with a scant couple of months ago had turned into the surliest bunch of spacers this side of the Split, and I was still trying to figure out how to deal with them.

I only hoped they wouldn't mutiny when I told them shore leave had been curtailed.

Chapter 2 — Luta
Cats in a Blanket

IF IT HADN'T been so annoying, it might have been an interesting psychological study to observe how the crew arranged themselves in the galley for our meeting. Yuskeya and Viss, my engineer, sat as far apart as possible. They'd had some romantic interludes over the year since Yuskeya had joined the crew of the *Tane Ikai*, but since the recent revelations about their Protectorate involvement, they weren't even speaking to each other unless it was a life-or-death situation. Fortunately, those were rare.

Baden, the communications officer, and my daughter Maja, on the other hand, were still in that new-relationship honeymoon period, and sat close together, his dark head bent to her blonde one. They were so taken up with each other I wondered if they even noticed the various palls hanging over everyone else on board. Maja and I had been—not quite estranged, but close to it, for years, and our recent reconciliation and her presence on the ship made me ridiculously happy.

Rei, my best friend and the ship's pilot of record, didn't even sit. She'd pulled a triple caff from the machine when she first came into the galley, and now she leaned against the counter and ignored it while it cooled, arms folded across the jacket of her dark green shipsuit, face completely neutral behind her *pridattii*. Some people thought the face tattoos worn by Erian women concealed their expressions; after knowing Rei for five years, I thought they made her face easier to read. Now they spilled a dark beauty over a face set in unyielding anger. I'd have to talk to her, and soon. This behaviour wasn't like her at all, and it was making everyone else nervous.

Hirin sat in one of the big armchairs, studiously trying not to look like he'd rather be sitting where I was, leading the briefing. I sighed. Wrangling this crew was beginning to feel like carrying cats in a blanket. Well, maybe a little shock treatment would nudge them out of it.

"*Okej*, folks. I have bad news and bad news. Which would you like first?"

No-one laughed at my weak attempt at humour, so I carried on. "We won't make it Earthside for a while yet. In fact we're turned around and heading back to Mars right now on autopilot."

Maja's face fell a little at that, and I felt a twinge of conscience. I remembered that she and Baden had booked in at a little resort on the NorthAm east coast for a few days. Well, they'd have to reschedule.

"We've also been drafted into the service of the Nearspace Protectorate for a little while, so you're all going to have to take a pay cut."

"They can't do that," Viss said quietly. "Drafting of commercial vessels is prohibited except in times of war or planetary emergency."

I grinned, but no-one else was laughing. "I know, I know. That part was a joke. But it's true that I've agreed to take on a job at the request of the Protectorate. Money's not an issue, since this is a paying job. But there is one problem."

"Of course there is," Rei muttered.

"If you want out, you have to decide before I tell you anything about it, because it's one of those top-secret things the Protectorate likes to do." I mentally bit my tongue and deliberately didn't look at Viss or Yuskeya. Shouldn't have poked my finger into that sore spot. "Anyway, since my brother Lanar has asked me to do it, I won't let him down. If you don't want to participate, I can leave you on Mars for some shore leave and collect you afterwards. You'll get your standard leave pay."

"Is it dangerous?" Maja asked, her voice testy. She'd been on board for a few weeks now, and although she wasn't technically part of the crew, she'd confided in me that she'd like to learn navigation. We'd been estranged as mother and daughter for so many years that I was just happy she wanted to spend time with me again, and that we were figuring out how to be friends. Not that her prickly side didn't surface now and again, but it was less frequent.

I shrugged. "Lanar didn't mention any risks, and I'm sure he would have if there were obvious ones. It's only a passenger delivery run, but it involves things the Protectorate wants to keep quiet."

"Makes no difference to me where we go," Viss rumbled. "I'll stay aboard. Think I'll clean out the plasma intakes and overhaul the Krasnikov generator if we're planning many skips."

I stopped myself from rolling my eyes. I found it hard to imagine there was a major system on board that Viss hadn't already stripped down and rebuilt since we'd dropped Mother off on Kiando, but if it gave him something to do and kept him from moping around the galley then I wouldn't complain.

"Nowhere else for me to go," Rei said expressionlessly. "Never was that keen on Mars."

Baden and Maja shared a glance, and Baden drawled, "I guess we're in, too. Frankly, the curiosity would keep me on board, if nothing else. We can change our leave plans."

Maja nodded. "But what does the Protectorate need from a far trader? They've got lots of passenger shuttles."

Yuskeya had her orders from Lanar to participate in the job, so the only other one I needed to hear from was Hirin. I realized too late that I really shouldn't have said yes to Lanar without at least checking with my husband, but when I glanced at him, he gave me a slight nod. I felt a wave of relief wash over me. At least he wasn't angry that I'd bypassed him.

"*Okej* then, here's the situation." I filled them in on what Lanar had told me about the new wormhole, the artifact moon, the Chron connection, and our mission.

Baden whistled long and low. "A Chron artifact? How do they know?"

"Lanar didn't say. But they must be pretty certain."

"The Protectorate has a reasonably large database on the Chron," Yuskeya offered. "It doesn't get used much, but I guess they'd send people who were familiar with it."

"Can't be too large," Viss said, his eyes on his steaming mug. "As I recall my history lessons, we couldn't find out enough about them to help us stop them. None of us would even be here if they hadn't disappeared on their own."

"It's pretty meagre, but it's comprehensive." The hint of defiance in Yuskeya's voice was clear.

Hirin spoke in the awkward silence that followed. "Wonder why they think a Lobor historian will be able to help out?"

"I wondered that, too," I said. "I guess we'll find out when we meet her on Anar."

"That moon must be worth a pile of credits," Baden mused with a grin. He'd put an arm around Maja's shoulders. "Think they'll let us take away souvenirs?"

"Somehow I doubt it." I yawned and stretched. "All right, everybody, it's time for me to catch some shut-eye since I had the night duty shift. Rei, the course is laid in for Mars; wake me when we get close. Yuskeya, plot the shortest course to get us to Anar, and Baden, compile everything we have on our Lobor passenger, would you? Her name is Cerevare Brindlepaw."

What else needed doing? "Maja, do you want to dig up anything we have about the Chron wars? We might as well be as well-informed as possible when we get there, and we have to make conversation with our Lobor guest. Viss, start whatever maintenance you want, and Hirin, you've got the chair. We could take cargo on Mars if there's any going our way, if you want to check the job boards."

I left them pulling hot drinks out of the machine and fixing breakfast, and headed to my quarters. Once I got some sleep, I promised myself, I would tackle some of the crew problems I'd been avoiding. I wasn't taking this bunch of soreheads on any kind of a mission, least of all one where I'd have to answer to the

Protectorate.

As I opened the door to my quarters, I allowed myself a smile. I was secretly excited to have this mission. Although I hadn't said anything to anyone else—and this was the other thing I'd kept from Lanar—I'd been feeling rather . . . adrift, since we'd left my mother on Kiando. I'd spent decades searching Nearspace for her, following leads, wondering whether she was even still alive. Searching for the answers to my apparent agelessness, why Lanar and I stayed physically and mentally in our thirties while everyone else around us aged normally. It had been my driving force, my focus, for almost fifty years. Once I'd found Mother and got my answers—the nanobioscavengers she'd introduced into our bodies decades ago—I felt a bit lost. I'd regained my husband (thanks again to the bioscavs) and my daughter, but still—the direction and drive that had fueled me for so long were suddenly gone.

Yes, I was quite happy to have something new to focus on. Another lesson in being careful what you wish for.

SINCE SHE WAS my best friend, I decided to tackle Rei first. We were still about an hour from Mars when I woke, and when I went to the bridge Hirin told me that Rei had taken a break and headed down to the cargo deck. He made as if to get up out of the captain's chair, but I motioned for him to stay.

"Think I'll go see if she wants to chat," I said.

Hirin took my arm and pulled me down so he could plant a kiss on my cheek. "For luck," he said, then chuckled. "And in case you don't come back. Should you go in armed?"

I stuck my tongue out at him and headed for the access hatch at the rear of the ship. I didn't see Viss as I climbed down the ladder past the engineering deck, but I heard pounding off in the distance somewhere. I shook my head. I'd have to get to him, soon, too, or he'd run out of things to overhaul. I didn't know what might happen then.

I found Rei heavily engrossed in her workout, which I could tell before I ever got near the floor of the cargo bay. Every kick, punch, block was accompanied by a scream that I could only call *blood-curdling.* I didn't recall the Erian martial arts involving these verbal assaults to go along with the physical ones, so they must be simply an indication of Rei's state of mind. She'd brought her staff with her, a thick rattan pole she'd won in a bar fight on Eri—at least, that was the story that went with it. Rei had a penchant for collecting what she called "souvenirs" of her many adventures, and they could be anything from a silk kimono to a plasma rifle. Each one came with a story, as well. The staff, with its dark, carved spiral pattern, was one of many. It echoed hollowly as she lashed out and struck the cargo pod wall with it.

Her feet were bare, and she'd stripped off the jacket of her dark green shipsuit, leaving only a pale tank now stained dark with sweat. She'd rolled the legs of her pants up to her knees and tied her chestnut hair in a severe ponytail. Sweat-soaked tendrils had come loose and curled around a face that was usually filled with humour and mischief—when it wasn't so angry.

She didn't acknowledge my arrival and kept on attacking invisible opponents, so I shucked my jacket and kicked off my own shoes. I approached her warily, arms up in a guard position. I didn't say anything, but I caught her eye and made a little "bring it on" gesture with the fingers of my right hand.

She grinned evilly. Or it might have been a snarl. Then she came at me. The only concession she made to our friendship was tossing aside the staff. It clattered hollowly up against the cargo bay wall.

I danced away from her initial lunge and brought a hand down on her arm when she was off-balance. She whooped joyously and spun around, aiming a kick at my kidney. I blocked it, pushed her leg sideways, and twisted. She ducked into a rolling fall and sprung up, agile as an Erian snowcat, six feet away from me.

It was my turn to attack, and I led with a feint, trying to get her off balance. When I managed to land a light blow on her shoulder, she laughed, a sound I hadn't heard in too long. Even though sweat rapidly soaked the back of my t-shirt and my daily *tae-ga-chi* workouts apparently didn't keep me in the shape I needed for this, I redoubled my efforts. Anything for a friend.

I lost track of time, but finally we stood, panting, a few feet apart, neither one of us willing to make the next move. Rei's chestnut hair plastered in rings against her neck, and her bare feet were red from pounding on the floor of the cargo pod. But she'd stopped screaming a few minutes ago and had started to smile. I blinked sweat from my eyes.

"Had enough?" I managed to gasp.

She swallowed. "I think so." She straightened and expelled a huge sigh, stretching her arms over her head and arching her back. Then she stepped forward and hugged me, hard.

"*Damne*, that felt good," she said. "Thanks, Luta."

I returned the hug, then pulled away, putting my hands on her shoulders and giving her a little shake. "I won't say, 'anytime'—you're too hard on me. I'll be sore for a week. Now, I hope you're ready to talk. What's going on with you, Rei?"

She walked over to the cargo pod wall and leaned her back against it, sliding down until she sat on the floor next to her discarded staff. I walked over and sat beside her, drawing my knees up and wrapping my arms around them. The stretch in my spine felt fabulous.

She pulled the elastic out of her hair and ran her hands through the knotted strands, pulling the damp ends apart. "I got dumped."

I bit down on the words that immediately came to mind—*all this about a man?*—pursing my lips to keep them still. "Mm-hmmm?"

Rei tilted her head to one side and eyed me through long lashes. "By my fiancé."

"The one on Eri," I said. I'd only found out about his existence a few weeks earlier, second-hand through Maja. Apparently they'd be getting married, according to Rei, "when he's old enough." With so much else happening, I simply hadn't had a chance to ask Rei more about this intriguing side of her life, about which I'd known nothing. She and Baden had had a casually sexual, on-and-off relationship before he'd met Maja, but that was their business as long as it didn't interfere with life aboard the ship, and it never had. But when the mysterious message had come from Eri, she'd turned into some kind of wild thing.

"How many did you think I had?" she asked dryly.

"Well, I didn't actually know about *any*," I reminded her.

"Yes, the one on Eri," she said with a sigh. "Raled. Sweet thing, completely compatible, only a year to go and he'd have been old enough to marry. Eighteen," she added, when she saw the question in my eyes.

"So what happened?"

"Raled *decided*," she said, "that he was better suited to a contemplative life than to one with me. He joined the Order of Xama three weeks ago, sent me a polite note explaining things, and that, as they say, is the end of that." She leaned her head against the cold plasteel wall and banged it lightly a few times.

"Ah," I said. "Well, it's understandable that you'd be sad—"

Her head whipped around to face me. "*Sad?* I'm not *sad*. Sad is when your pet dies. Sad is when someone gets hurt. I'm not sad about Raled. I'm *humiliated*."

I didn't say anything else right away, waiting. I didn't want to put my foot in it again.

"On Eri," Rei said, "marriages are arranged about ninety percent of the time."

"I knew that, but not exactly how it works."

"The mothers take care of it, on both sides. Usually when the boys are about ten and the girls are about eighteen. They won't get married until the boys reach eighteen, so the girls are encouraged to stay in school or choose a career early, do whatever they want before they're tied down to a family."

She paused, and I said, "Sounds reasonable enough. What do the boys think of it?"

Rei chuckled. "There are remarkably few complaints. They get mature, experienced, and still young wives who are mentally ready to start families. Then it's their turn to stay in school or start their careers, with their wife's guidance. The wife usually has savings by this time to support the family until the man gets settled, and she retains some financial independence."

"Arranged marriages went out of fashion a long time ago on Earth," I mused. "How do they usually work out?"

"Marriage is usually a fifteen-year contract, and the clock resets on the birth of each subsequent child. So if it's not working out, you can go your own ways once your youngest child is fifteen. Or if you're both happy, renew the registration."

"What if one—or both—of the intended partners turns out to

have different sexual preferences?"

She shrugged. "No problem. That's a completely legitimate reason to dissolve an engagement. The mothers have to scramble then to find another suitable partner, and the logistics are a little different, but it's not that big a deal."

"And nobody is humiliated," I suggested.

Rei sighed. "Right."

"It seems a little structured for the men and more lenient for the women," I mused cautiously. I didn't want to offend her, since she'd never told me any of this before. I figured there must be a reason.

But Rei shook her head. "It's only more structured for them when they're young and foolish," she said. "That's when they need more guidance, anyway. They get their freedom later, when they're better able to handle it."

"Well, if it works, it works," I said. "But to get to the real point of this conversation, what are *you* going to do now?"

She blew out a long sigh, leaning forward to wrap her arms around her knees. "Good question. I know all my options, but none of them are very appealing. At least I don't feel so angry now." She glanced up at me with a smile. "I needed something real to vent on, I think."

"Don't mention it," I said. "You can wait on me hand and foot when I can't move tomorrow. So what about those options?"

She tipped her head back and stared up at the cargo pod ceiling, vaulted high above us. The cargo pods were good thinking spaces, a break from the more confined spaces of the rest of the ship.

Finally, she said, "*Okej.* I could go to Eri and ask my mother to arrange a new match. But it would be extremely embarrassing, and she'd either have to find a boy from the current batch of *pels*—the young boys—which wouldn't be easy since *their* mothers are considering girls almost ten years younger than I am, or find an *ulan*, a boy a little older who for some reason is still without a mate." She pulled a disconsolate face. "And there are usually reasons for that, some of them not very pleasant."

"Although there could be someone left alone because their intended mate died or had a different preference," I said.

"True, but they're not very plentiful," she said. "It makes it much harder to find someone compatible. And being off-world, I'm not there and 'available' to be re-matched easily."

I waited a minute, then asked, "So, is that it for options?"

Rei shrugged. "I could probably hook up with an older man who's left a marriage, or lost his wife. But he'll already have done the whole family thing and probably won't be interested in that. If he were, he'd have stayed with his wife."

"Unless he simply didn't love her," I suggested.

"Wrong," she said with a snort. "These are marriages arranged strictly on the basis of genetic compatibility and congenial neural oscillation adhesions. There's no question of love or lack of it. These people are destined to get along."

"But you said they can leave the marriage if they're not happy."

Rei puffed her cheeks, slowly blowing out another sigh. "Sure, but it doesn't happen very often. Sometimes one partner might suffer a brain disease or injury, but usually when it does happen, it's because their careers or interests take them too far apart physically."

"You're a tough case," I said, shaking my head. "So, how about this radical idea? There are more men in the universe than the ones born on Eri."

Rei looked scandalized, her golden eyes widening. "Marry a non-Erian? My mother would go *freneza*, for one thing," she said. She stared up at the catwalk stretching across the cargo pod, far above our heads. "I don't know. That idea would take getting used to."

I slowly got to my feet and brushed cargo pod dust off my jeans. "Well, then I suggest you stop thinking about it for a little while," I said. "You can't do anything about it until we finish this mission for Lanar, anyway. Things might seem different in a few weeks."

She nodded. "I know. But being dumped by a seventeen-year-old who'd rather be a monk . . ." Her voice trailed off. "It's pretty bad. And having to watch Baden and Maja tripping over each other isn't making it any easier."

I laughed as I collected my shoes and slipped them on. "They are a little overwhelming, aren't they?" I hesitated. "Rei, does it bother you about Baden? I mean, I know you two were close . . ."

She smiled then, a real smile that touched her eyes. "No, and I told Maja that. Baden was a nice diversion on long runs—really nice," she said with a wink. "And good experience. But I never thought of it as anything more than that."

Her eyes narrowed suddenly. "Speaking of couples, I haven't been as completely unobservant as you might think. You and Hirin—"

Her words were cut off by a jolt that shook the ship. I stumbled and fetched up against the plasteel wall of the cargo pod with a thump.

"Ouch! What the—"

"Captain! Rei!" Baden's voice sounded over the ship's comm. "You might want to get the hell up here!"

I pressed the implant in my left forearm as I straightened up. Rei ran for the ladder that led to the upper decks, and I followed a few steps behind.

"On our way!" I told him, and as I pounded across the cargo pod behind Rei, the things I'd been worrying about seemed small and far away.

Chapter 3 — Luta
Moving Targets

I REALIZED AS Rei and I climbed past the engineering deck that the pounding I'd heard on my way down had stopped. Viss sat planted in a skimchair, punching commands into the engineering console.

"You okay here, Viss?" I yelled as we scrambled past.

"Keep going, Captain," he shouted over his shoulder. "Just let me know what's happening."

"Keep the shipwide comm open!"

Another impact, slightly weaker than the first one, shook the ship as we neared the top of the ladder. One of Rei's hands slipped off the metal rung, but she didn't even stop moving. I was only a rung below her by this time, and if she'd fallen, we both would have landed on the unforgiving floor of the cargo pod far below. As it was, I was right behind her as we pounded up the corridor to the bridge.

Hirin's voice reached us as we arrived, issuing commands in a steady, level voice. He'd taken a spot at the pilot's console in Rei's absence. He heard us arrive and slid out of the way neatly for Rei to take his place, but I didn't move to take the captain's seat. I'd been absent, and he still had the chair. Somehow I'd thought about it on the way up from the cargo deck, and this seemed like the only way to handle it. I dropped into a skimchair at the secondary pilot controls and locked it down.

"Trouble?" I asked Hirin.

He flashed a grin. "Something like that. Innocent-looking C-class starrunner passed within a few hundred klicks, turned when he got behind us, and came in with a flash-pack torpedo." He turned his palms up. "Don't know what he was thinking. Even without shields it wouldn't breach our hull, but it shook us up a little. You okay?"

"Fine," I said. "Where is he now?"

My question was answered by a thump on the starwise side of the ship.

"What does he want?"

"Good question," Baden said. "He should be on standard trader channel, and I'm trying to get through to him with a signal, but he's not answering."

"Try other channels. Pirates?"

"Could be. So far, pretty ineffective ones."

A flash of movement drew my eyes to the main viewscreen, and I saw our attacker speed past and turn to make another run at us.

"We haven't fired on him?" It wasn't really a question, since I would have known if we'd let fly with one of our own torps.

"Not yet," Hirin answered. "It'd feel like zapping a fly with a flux laser. I thought Baden would get him on the comm, and we'd see what was what."

Baden pushed himself away from the comm console. "He won't respond. I know damn well he can hear me."

"Fire a—" I started.

At the same time, Hirin said, "Viss—"

We both stopped short. *Damne.* My fault. I was sitting at a pilot's console, and Hirin had the chair. I shouldn't have been giving any orders.

But it sure is hard to break a habit like being in command.

"Sorry," I said. His was only an echo behind mine.

He didn't let it rattle him, though. "Viss, I'm going to fire a torp in his path to let him know he's not dealing with a sitting duck here." He nodded at Baden, who keyed in the code.

My face radiated heat, and I knew it must be blood-red, but I pretended I didn't notice the blush. It was the same order I would have given, which should have made me feel better, but somehow it didn't.

"I've got his drive signature and ship registration," Yuskeya said. "The registration could be faked, but we'll know the sig if we run across him again."

"Good job," Hirin said. "Baden, is that torp ready?"

"Whenever you are, Cap—Hirin," Baden said. He didn't turn around, but I knew that suddenly I wasn't the only one red-faced.

"Fire whenever you can get a fix on his trajectory, then. Get close, but don't hit him. He doesn't seem to have shield capability, and I don't like killing people unless it's absolutely necessary."

A few seconds of concentrated silence passed, and then Baden said, "Firing." A hollow crump reverberated up through the *Tane Ikai*, nothing like the impact of our attacker's flash-pack torps, but enough to let us know that our own torp was away. I'd been a little miffed when Hirin had armed the ship without my knowledge a month or so ago, but in the circumstances he'd been right. I'd decided it was nice, after ten years without him, to have someone watching my back again.

But I had to figure out this two-captains-one-ship thing soon, before it drove both of us crazy.

Once again, however, I was distracted by events beyond my control. Baden's aim was brilliant, and the torp sailed through the vacuum toward the starrunner, on a course to skim past it. We were all surprised to see a bright burst of radiant energy as the ship's shields flared and the torp detonated, obscuring the starrunner for an instant. When the flash dissipated, he was still there, but accelerating away from us rapidly.

"What the—I thought he didn't have shields!" Hirin yelped.

"None registered," Yuskeya said. I glanced over at her. She sat frowning down at the data on her console. "That doesn't make sense."

Baden frowned at the screen. "That little *bastardo*. What kind of game was he playing, anyway?" His fingers skittered over the comm board. "Wonder if he's trying to send any messages right about now?"

"Pursuit?" Rei asked briskly, her hands steady on the piloting controls. She carefully didn't address the question to either of us in particular.

Hirin looked the question at me, and I shrugged. "What would we do with him if we caught him? We'll report it when we get to Mars. We have the ship sig."

"I got reams of ship data before Baden fired the torp," added Yuskeya. "Figured it wouldn't hurt to do a scan. No cargo in his hold, just one pilot."

"Huh," Baden grunted.

"What?"

He turned to face Hirin, eyes narrowed. "He just sent off an encrypted message to a PrimeCorp address."

"How do you know that?" I squeaked, then caught myself and held up a hand. "No, don't answer that. I don't think I want to know. Something you 'picked up' on Kiando, right?"

Baden turned his grin on me. "I can't reveal my program sources," he said virtuously. "But there's no love lost between the people who work for Duntmindi Corporation and PrimeCorp."

"Sounds highly illegal to me," Hirin said, shaking his head in mock disapproval. "Don't suppose you could actually read what it said, could you?"

"Give me a minute—ah, *merde!*"

"What?"

He hunched over his console, fingers flying over the touchscreen. He didn't answer me. I waited. With Baden, you might as well not try to interrupt when he was like this. He wouldn't hear you anyway.

Finally he sat back heavily in his skimchair and threw his arms over his head. "Cannibalizer," he said cryptically.

"Cannibalizer?"

"If you don't have the right code to enter on the receiving end, the message basically eats itself when you try to open it. Nice little encryption there; I couldn't stop it." He gave me a lopsided smile. "I got two words."

"And those were?"

"'Location' and 'Paixon'," he said.

"Hmm. So he definitely knew it was us."

"Not many Paixons around," Baden said, "So what would a supposed pirate, and not a very good one apparently, be doing sending an encrypted message about our location to our Dear Captain's worst enemy, following a botched attempt to—I don't even know—bother us?"

Viss's voice boomed over the ship's comm. "Is all the excitement over for now? Seems to have gone pretty quiet up there."

"I think so, at least for now, Viss. Want to give us a damage report as soon as you have a chance?"

"Will do, Captain. But I don't think there'll be much to report. Whatever he was firing at us didn't seem to have much punch."

"They were low-end flash-pack torps," Yuskeya said, all detached professionalism. "But he had a few surprises in shields and engines. I'm transferring all the ship data to you if you want to go over it."

There was only a slight pause before he said coolly, "I'd like to see that. Thanks."

"Is everything okay?" Maja stood in the doorway to the bridge, pale but composed. "I was in my quarters when things went crazy, and I thought I'd better stay out of everyone's way."

Hirin stood up from the chair and crossed to her, swinging an arm around her shoulders and squeezing her close. "It's all right, honey," he said. "I'm turning the big chair over to your mother and going for a double caff. Want to come, and I'll fill you in on what happened?"

"Sure, Dad," she said, although her eyes went to Baden. He smiled and winked at her, and she relaxed visibly, letting Hirin steer her down the corridor toward the galley.

"I'm assuming we want to get to Mars as quickly as possible?" Rei asked from the pilot's console. The angry thickness that had suffused her voice for the past few weeks had thinned out, and the barely-contained rage that had stiffened her movements had relaxed, at least a little.

"Full speed ahead," I confirmed, moving from the skimchair

into the captain's chair and sinking gratefully into its familiar shape. "Yuskeya, run that shipdata through the Nearspace Registry, when we get close enough to Mars to get the updated data, would you? I don't imagine we'll find anything concrete, but we'll have our homework done to make the report at Mars."

Baden turned to me. "With your permission, Captain, I'd like to try installing some new decryption software—something that might catch a self-destructing message sooner next time."

I didn't ask him where he'd get such a thing. I just smiled. "Go ahead."

As the bridge fell silent with everyone busy, I had a moment to reflect. In the moment of crisis, the crew had held together. There'd been some bumps, but I quietly thanked the nameless pirate, or whatever he was. He'd inadvertently shown me something important, something that I should have been able to figure out for myself, and that made me feel a little better. This crew needed, above all else, to be busy.

Oh, we'd managed long skip runs before with not much excitement to break the monotony. But that was when everyone was getting along. With various complications making things awkward and nothing substantial or dangerous to distract us, we couldn't handle it. We'd all turned to solitary diversions to try and keep our minds off our problems. Rei's martial arts workouts, Viss's dogged overhauling of every engineering system. Hirin's obsession with PrimeCorp and its misdeeds. Yuskeya's compulsive reading. My immersion in building virtual solar systems on my datapad. Even Baden and Maja—would they have been quite so involved in each other if they hadn't been trying to avoid the other shipboard disturbances?

As we scooted for Mars I thought about it. I couldn't manufacture crises (and wasn't hoping for more, I swear it), but maybe I could keep them busy. I'd think about it.

As it turned out, keeping the crew busy would be the least of my problems.

Chapter 4 — Jahelia
Hunter and Prey

ONCE MY MESSAGE to PrimeCorp was away and I was sure the *Tane Ikai* wasn't following me, I engaged the autopilot, stood, and stretched. The encounter had left me exhilarated and oddly hungry, so I made my way to the minuscule galley at the rear of the tiny bridge and pulled off a mugful of steaming *cazitta*. I took it and an energy bar to the bridge and settled in my chair, the rich licorice scent of the drink filling the air. I smiled.

That had been fun.

"Are we done here?" asked Pita from the bridge console.

"I think so."

"Want me to automate a full report and shoot it off to PrimeCorp Main?"

"No. I told you, I prefer to write the reports myself. That last message will do for now." I pursed my lips, annoyed at myself for being annoyed with a machine. Pita is the computer in this lovely little ship that Alin Sedmamin so kindly gave me for this assignment—the *Hunter's Hope*. Pita's a PAREA, which is one of PrimeCorp's cutesy little acronyms designed to increase their products' appeal to consumers. PAREA stands for Personality-Attuned Realtime Electronic Assistant, which is simply a marketing-friendly way to say that the programming is "tweaked" for each user. She's experimental, and yes, I'm letting them test her out on me. The pay for that alone was pretty damn good, for the privilege of letting them take readings from my brain while I looked at pictures and answered questions. A lot of questions. But it did pay well.

The hardest part of the experiment is having to listen to her, now that she's installed on the ship. She doesn't talk like any other computer I've ever known—supposedly she talks like me. I'm not sure I like that, or that I agree. But it's all part of the deal. I'll admit she's come in handy a few times, so I can't complain too much, but she is annoying. That's why I named her Pita. It's my own little acronym. Pain-In-The-Ass.

"I think that went well."

"Alin Sedmamin might not approve of your tactics," Pita said mildly. "I don't recall any instructions to actually *attack* the ship."

"Oh, let me have a little fun. I'll worry about Sedmamin later." The oily PrimeCorp CEO might think he had me in his pocket, but he was only a means to an end, after all. Pita didn't say anything else about it.

I grinned now at the memory of the rich male voice filling my cramped bridge. "Unidentified vessel, this is the far trader *Tane Ikai*, registration port New Cape City, Earthside. Respond." I knew that voice, although the owner wouldn't realize he'd been recognized.

I'd chuckled as I answered him, even though he couldn't hear me. "Not yet, Mr. Baden Methyr. We'll talk soon again, but not yet."

Pita had flipped on the new F-shields then, just in case the crew of the *Tane Ikai* wasn't too happy about the torps, but I didn't expect them to return fire. Everything my research had told me about Captain Luta Paixon and her crew made me think I was safe enough unless they truly started to feel threatened. The F-shields were more new tech I was testing for PrimeCorp, and they should remain be undetectable by the *Tane Ikai* unless something impacted them.

This was only for fun. Testing the waters, to use an old nautical term.

Their shot across my bow seemed like a good time to end our little skirmish, and once the torpedo impact had revealed the existence of my shields, there wasn't much more fun in it anyway. I told Pita to change course, engaged the new burst drive—also thanks to PrimeCorp—and took off.

"They're letting us go," Pita said after a moment.

"Pretty much what I expected. We didn't do much except annoy them, after all. And that's all I wanted to do for now."

That, and make certain Paixon hadn't tried to pull a fast one, switching ships. Baden Methyr's voice on the comm was all the confirmation I needed for that. I sent a quick encrypted message to Sedmamin to let him know I'd located them and would stay on Paixon's tail. He'd no doubt respond with a demand for a full report, but I'd send that when I got around to it.

"How closely do you want to follow them?" Pita asked.

"Circle around outside their scanner range, then backtrack and pick them up again. They've got to be headed for Mars, so we'll tag along, same as we were before. Stay at the outside edge of the tracker range, and don't let them spot us."

I slipped the wrapper off the energy bar and took a bite, chewing reflectively. "To you, Dad," I said, lifting my mug in a toast. "To persistence. To revenge."

"Nice one," Pita said, and I rolled my eyes. If she were a real person, I'd probably have strangled her by now.

I kept the rest of my toast to myself, because although I was pretty certain of Pita's loyalty to me, she still didn't need to know my every thought. *To Alin Sedmamin*, I thought, arrogant, self-important little *bastardo* that he was, for making it all possible.

Chapter 5 — Luta
Pavlovian Responses and Other Intriguing Behaviours

SEVEN DAYS LATER, we arrived at the planet Anar in the Lambda Saggitae system, where we were to meet the Lobor historian Cerevare Brindlepaw. Being only one wormhole skip from Sol System, both inhabited planets, Anar and Damir, had developed quickly and boasted thriving, cosmopolitan populations. We'd made plenty of cargo runs between Sol System and Lambda Saggitae in the last ten years, when Hirin was in the nursing home and I favoured shorter trade hops.

I won't say that by the time we got there, the crew hated me, but I might not have been their favorite person anymore. No-one had spent any more time immersed in private projects if I could provide them with an alternative. Every inch of the ship had been scrubbed and polished, accompanied by much grumbling.

"It's long overdue," I told them, "and if we're going to participate in a Protectorate mission, I'm not giving them any reason to complain."

Every system had been overhauled. I invested in upgrades for navigation, communications, and the First Aid station while we were on Mars, as well as new fuel recombinators and a matter generation enhancement package. I decided we could afford it; after all, I didn't have to pay Hirin's nursing home bills anymore. The crew installed it all on our way to Anar. I insisted that Maja step up and show me how serious she was about learning navigation; and she was as good as her word, buying the newest VR training program and starting in on her lessons. With Yuskeya to act as tutor when needed, I felt confident she'd do well.

The only one I didn't have much control over was Hirin, but I didn't really need to worry about him. He bought a whole new database system for the ship and set to work installing and configuring it, hoping it would give him access to more data on the scurrilous dealings of PrimeCorp. He and Viss disappeared for a few hours one afternoon on Mars, and when they returned he had several datapackets that I didn't ask questions about. His was the only obsession I didn't see fit to interfere with, and I freely admit it was because I wanted to see those PrimeCorp *bastardos* get what they deserved, too. If Hirin could facilitate that, he surely had my support, for all that they'd put the two of us through. To say nothing of Mother.

I'm not saying that hard work solved all the problems—it didn't. Viss still wasn't speaking to Yuskeya unless necessary, Rei seemed to cycle through periods of grim irritability, and Hirin and I sidestepped carefully around the question of who was the real captain of the *Tane Ikai*, without ever really addressing it. Everyone was simply so busy that they didn't have much time left over to dwell on their problems, or clash with anyone else over them. Just as I'd hoped.

So it was a peaceful, quiet, clean, and overhauled *Tane Ikai* that arrived at the main spaceport outside Heliosin on the planet Anar a week later. In light of what happened later I'd like to claim prescience, but in reality it was plain dumb luck.

IT'S NOT OFTEN that I find myself nervous. I'm eighty-four, for goodness' sake, despite still looking thirty thanks to my mother's efficient little nanobioscavengers. I've had all the experiences, and more, that one might expect for an octogenarian far trader captain, wife, and mother of two. But two things bothered me about collecting this Lobor historian. In the first place it was her specialty—the Chron were a sort of bogeyman for those of us who hadn't been alive during the Chron War. It was difficult to separate fact from fiction, and myths abounded about these terrifying figures who had come to the brink of destroying humanity (as well as Vilisians and Lobors). It felt disconcerting to meet someone who knew so much about them. It brought them closer than I wanted them to be.

And in the second place, I had spent surprisingly little time around Lobors. Although the wolflike aliens had been our allies since the time of the Chron War, I simply didn't know much about them. I'd encountered them occasionally in business dealings, but the interactions had always been very casual. I'd never had one on my crew, although it wasn't by choice, simply chance. So I'd never known a Lobor very well, and now I felt that lack very keenly.

I went to meet Cerevare Brindlepaw with more than a little trepidation.

I'd studied the ship's database on everything Lobor, but words on a screen can only tell you so much. In theory, practice is just like theory, but in practice, practice is not at all like theory. So while I was prepared for Cerevare's springy step and the fervid heat of her paw-like hand when she offered it to me, I was surprised by the twinkle of humour in her liquid brown eyes and the disconcerting way a smile stretches over a muzzle. Evolution on Nanear had obviously favoured something that might have resembled a German Shepard or a wolf on Earth.

"Captain Paixon," she said with a nod, and I gave her points immediately for pronouncing it correctly, *pay-zon*. I took her offered hand, skin the colour of raw umber and lightly furred on the back with soft golden-brown hairs, prepared for the fervent heat all Lobors radiated. She wore the loose, linen-like garments that Lobors had preferred since humans first encountered them, as survivors of a spaceship wreck on the planet Renata. A sky-blue shirt wrapped her upper body and cowled around the point where her head sloped gradually out to her shoulders; Lobors had no neck to speak of. An intricately patterned, wide fabric sash encircled her waist, dangling long, tasselled ties. Billowy chocolate brown trousers, embroidered in blue at the hems, completed the outfit. Lobors as a rule wore no shoes, the rough, callous-like pads on their feet making them redundant except in the worst terrain or harsh weather. I'd never learned or heard of any easy or obvious way to determine Lobor gender—the females didn't have obvious breasts, like humans and Vilisians did—so I was glad that Lanar had told me she was female.

I helped her load a couple of duffel-type bags into a dock scooter and she climbed in beside me. The *Tane Ikai* was docked in the outer ring since we weren't planning on being here more than six hours, too far to walk from the passenger lounge.

"I have never been further from home than this system," she remarked as we drove along wide, domed corridors to the outer ring. High glass ceilings arched overhead, displaying a cloudless swath of sky that tended a little more to green than Earth's clear blue. Tall potted trees and low greenery studded the route, contributing to the impression of being outdoors. We passed busy kiosks offering food, drink, supplies, and trinkets, teased by scents of spices and hot oil, baking fruit breads, and the aromas of caff and chai and *cazitta*. Tall lighted boards displayed docking information, tourist advice, departures, and arrivals. I was glad the scooters had designated travel lanes; the walkways were filled with travellers, businesspeople, and sightseers, shopping and strolling and jostling each other.

Cerevare's Esper was excellent, accented in an odd way and slightly lisping on the -s sounds, but perfectly understandable.

"Do you mind space travel?" I asked.

"No, it has no adverse physical effects on me, if that is what you mean." She flashed a toothy grin. "But as a Chron historian, my work is more concerned with travelling mentally into the past than travelling physically around in Nearspace."

I grinned back. "I can understand that. The Chron didn't leave much for you to study."

"No, it is not like archaeology. Nothing to dig up, at least not in Nearspace. If we ever found out where they came from . . ."

She trailed off, staring at the crowds of travellers hurrying this way and that in the pedestrian lanes. "Well, I hope you'll find the accommodations acceptable," I told her. "I don't know if anyone told you, but we're nothing fancy."

"When one spends long periods of time hunched over datascreens or historical transcripts, surroundings become a somewhat secondary concern. I am certain I shall be quite comfortable." She watched the corridor curving away ahead of us in silence, then added, "This is very strange for me, to be working in secrecy."

"The circumstances are unusual," I agreed, steering the cart around a couple who had stopped theirs and were apparently arguing over directions.

Cerevare shook her head ruefully. "It is usually more a problem of trying to attract any notice of what I am doing, than to keep it quiet."

"It's not a popular field of inquiry, I take it."

"Not for many years now," she said. She had high-set, lightly-furred ears with delicate vestigial points, and one twitched a little as she spoke. Two small gold rings pierced one side of it, tinkling softly with the twitch. She gestured with an elegant hand, and when her sleeve fell away, I noticed a tattoo on the inside of her wrist, where the hair became fine and disappeared below her smooth palm—a line of symbols I didn't recognize. "For me," she continued, "there is always the question of *why*. Why did the war start? Why did it end? My ancestors suffered great losses in the war, as did yours, I'm sure."

She must have seen me notice her tattoo, because she held it out so I could see it better. "Chron lettering," she said with a shrug, "copied from a captured ship during the war. I wear it to symbolize my life's work."

"What does it mean?"

Cerevare chuckled. "I have no idea. That, you see, is part of its symbolism. My committment to the unknown."

I smiled. "So one day you might find out that it means 'airlock' or 'engines'?"

"Or something even less desirable," she said with a wink. "Whatever it means, I will be happy, because it will mean I have learned something new about them."

"I admire your passion," I told her, and I meant it.

"I think it is important for the future," she said. "How can we lay the war to rest when we don't understand it?"

"It was a long time ago," I offered hesitantly.

"But not longer than memory," she replied. "And without the answers to those two questions of yesterday, how can tomorrow be assured?"

I thought about that, what she was really saying. "You think they could come back." We rolled to a stop in front of the open airlock dockway that led to the *Tane Ikai*'s forward hatch.

"I think if they came back, there should be someone who understands all the whys," she answered.

"Sounds like a tall order," I said, unloading her bags from the scooter.

"And one that I cannot hope to completely fulfill," she said, climbing out and straightening the folds of her leggings. "But I will do what I can."

"That's all any of us can hope for, Cerevare. Welcome aboard." And I led her inside to meet the rest of the crew.

Chapter 6 — Luta
The Past Throws a Long Shadow

WE WERE ONLY two days out from Anar when I received a surprise message from Lanar. Surprise, because I didn't think he'd want to bring the *Cheswick* close enough for an FTL WaVE message when we were trying to avoid attention. But Baden commed me right in the middle of my *tae-ga-chi* workout to tell me that Lanar was signalling. I frowned at having to interrupt my form, but took it on the encrypted screen in my quarters.

"Hello again, little brother," I said, towelling off my face as I plunked myself down in my chair. "How am I supposed to keep a low profile with a Protectorate patrol ship on my tail?"

"I'm keeping my distance, don't worry," he assured me with a grin. He leaned away from his screen and I could see the Protectorate plaque on the wall behind him, the motto *In Astra Pax*—Peace Among the Stars—curving under the stylized atom-and-stars emblem. "We got a WaVE upgrade at Willis Point, so I don't actually have to get too close."

I smiled. "Yes, Baden upgraded our systems on the return trip from Kiando." I held up a hand to forestall his next question. "I don't know how he got hold of Protectorate tech before you did, so don't even ask me. You'll have to ask him yourself. If you really want to know, which you might not."

"You might be right about that. Listen, I heard you had a little trouble en route to Mars."

I almost asked how he knew about that, but I remembered in time that we'd filed an incident report when we docked at Mars.

"It was nothing we couldn't handle, but—it was strange." I leaned back in my chair and tapped my fingers against my lower lip. "It wasn't like a pirate attack—he had next to nothing for weapons. A few flash-pack torps, that was it. As soon as we fired our own warning shot across his path, he took off with some kind of drive that wasn't standard issue on the tub he was driving, and sent—"

I stopped—too late.

"Sent what?" He pursed his lips and narrowed his eyes at me. "Seems like you left something out of that report you filed on Mars."

I blew out a sigh. "*Okej*, you got me. I didn't think they needed to know, and it would have raised more questions that I didn't want to answer. He sent off an encrypted message to PrimeCorp main."

He raised his eyebrows. "And you know this . . . how?"

"Mm-hmm. See, that's one of those questions. The ones I don't want to answer." I grinned at him.

"You wouldn't happen to know what the message said, would you?"

I studied Lanar's face on the screen for a minute, trying to read his eyes. I could lie and tell him I didn't know, but he might already know the answer to the question, if Yuskeya had reported the incident to him herself. Which it was quite likely she had. The thought triggered a brief flash of annoyance, but I suppressed it quickly. I knew she had to divide her loyalties, and really, it wasn't a bad thing to have Lanar in the loop regarding possible threats to the *Tane Ikai*. I only wished I was always in the loop about what he knew and didn't know.

"A couple of words—'location' and 'Paixon'," I said finally. "So he was definitely targeting us specifically. It was almost like he was testing us."

"To see what weapons you had on board, yes. He took off after he got a taste of them. Hmmm." He closed his eyes for a moment, then shook his head. "Watch your back, Luta. Not only because of Cerevare and the new wormhole and what's beyond it. PrimeCorp obviously isn't through with you—with us."

"Obviously. Lanar . . . do you think Mother's safe?"

He laughed. "I don't think Mother's been safe for decades, but she's managed to take care of herself all right."

"I know. This thing with that space pirate, or whoever he was, though, it's got me worried about her."

Lanar squinted at me a little. "I don't think they were actually much of a threat."

"Neither do I, it's just—like you said, PrimeCorp doesn't seem to be through with us. I thought once they got their hands slapped on Vele, they'd back off for a while, at least. But if they're still dogging me, then they're not likely to leave her alone, either. And now they know she has connections on Kiando."

"Gusain Buig will keep her safe. And she hasn't moved to release her data on the bioscavs yet. I think she's waiting until after she meets with Schulyer Corp."

"Buig and Duntmindi are no match for PrimeCorp. And I know Alin Sedmamin didn't take much of a hit personally, but PrimeCorp doesn't like to lose, even a little bit."

"I think they'll tread more carefully now, at least for a while," he argued. "At the very least, we put them on notice that we're watching what they do very carefully."

I shook a finger at him. "You're the one who told me the Protectorate thinks PrimeCorp is up to something big," I reminded him. "I hope Mother—"

"What? She's spent the last seventy years running from them. She knows what they're like."

I sighed. "I know. But would you send her a message for me? Tell her what you told me. To watch her back. I thought they'd leave us alone for a while, but that pirate's got me thinking otherwise. I don't think they're finished yet."

"I'll tell her." He quirked a smile. "And Luta, give the Protectorate some credit, would you? We won't let PrimeCorp take over Nearspace simply because they want to."

"I know that, Lanar," I said, "but do they?"

As I EXPECTED, my crew gave me no cause for concern in the way they got along with our passenger. Apparently Viss had known numerous Lobors during his checkered past and seemed able to effortlessly keep Cerevare giggling at his outrageous stories. Everyone was friendly and considerate, and Cerevare herself kept mostly to her quarters, hunched, no doubt, over those datascreens she'd mentioned to me in the scooter. She wasn't antisocial, but she plainly had work to do and didn't want to interfere with ours.

Although she'd travelled at least one wormhole before—the one between Nanear and Anar—she came up to the bridge for our first skip together. It took us from the Lambda Saggitae system to Sol, and Cerevare made complimentary remarks about the skip, what she saw of the system, and our collective skills. She turned out to be quite adept at *quozit*, liked to talk about Earthside fashion with Maja, and generally got along with everyone.

I happened upon her deep in conversation with Hirin and Viss one evening in the galley. I'd been reading, not for escape but for enjoyment, and came down to the galley for a cold drink before retiring.

As I entered the galley, I heard Hirin say, "But how much is known, and how much is speculation?"

Cerevare shrugged. A steaming mug of something sat on the table near her right hand, and she toyed with crumbs on a small plate as she spoke. I suspected they'd been sharing out the last of a batch of crunchy *solanto* cookies she'd surprised us by baking the day before. They were brown-sugar-sweet, like Mexican *coyotas,* but filled with roga-nut spice from Renata and drizzled with a sweet glaze.

"The question of how much is known has a simple answer: not very much. Incredible amounts of data have survived since the time of the Chron War, but none of it sheds any light on what prompted the Chron to enter Nearspace and attack its inhabitants, or what they hoped to gain by so doing."

"Or why they broke off the war so suddenly and completely," added Viss. His own plate held even more crumbs than

Cerevare's. He'd rolled up the sleeves of his one-piece red shipsuit and opened the front, revealing a clean white t-shirt underneath. He was obviously quite at ease with Cerevare now.

"*Ekzakte*. It has never even been determined how they moved around in Nearspace much of the time. Sometimes they utilized the wormholes we ourselves use, but at other times their appearance in a particular part of a system would seem to be inexplicable. And they'd disappear as quickly and mysteriously."

I crossed to the table with my double caff and sat down, peeking into the cookie container. Empty, as I'd suspected. "I thought it was fairly widely accepted that they had some limited ability to time-travel."

Cerevare grimaced. Her ear twitched, and her golden hoops tinkled. "*Timeslipping*, people called it. But in my considered opinion, that ability is still in the realm of myth or legend. The Chron did seem to appear and disappear in inexplicable ways—the logs and other historical data show this. However, the mechanism for it was never understood. Even though a few—a very few—Chron ships, and debris from Chron ships, were recovered for study, no mechanism could ever be identified to substantiate this theory."

"So, no way to get the technology for ourselves, if it did exist," Viss said. "I'd love to get my hands on some of that tech, even if I couldn't reverse-engineer it."

"And was it true that they took no prisoners, never interrogated any humans or Lobors or Vilisians?" Hirin wanted to know.

Cerevare inclined her head. "As far as the records show, that is correct. They appeared in Nearspace, began attacking planets, colonies, ships in transit, space stations, and never attempted any communication. They were ruthless and would not allow themselves to be captured alive. It was usual for them to take steps to ensure that even their corpses would not be retrieved by their enemies." Cerevare's black nose wrinkled delicately in distaste. The Lobors had intricate funeral rituals and a strong belief in their importance. I could see why they'd be horrified at the Chron's apparent disregard for such things.

"But we did. Retrieve some bodies for study, I mean," Viss

said.

"Oh yes, indeed we did. Three, to be exact. They were examined in detail." Cerevare steepled her fingers in front of her. The Lobors had five-fingered hands with opposable thumbs, the skin on the backs covered with fine fur and the palms and fingertips studded with rough pads. They used them the same way humans did, to aid in expression.

"The Chron—and of course that is only our name for them; we have little knowledge about their own language or what name they might have given themselves—they are another species, like humans, Vilisians, and Lobors, with bipedal symmetry and a similar arrangement of body parts. Head, torso, two arms, two legs. A tough, plated or scaled skin—all three had a pale colouration—with no body hair, and protruding bone flares at the back of the head that showed individuation. In the bodies we studied, two distinct genders were noted, and we inferred sexual reproduction. Their DNA is three-stranded and their chromosomal chemistry perhaps as different as that of any of the other three races we know. In other words, they were no more dissimilar than humans and Lobors." She flashed a brief smile at us.

"There was some evidence that the use of bioengineered genes and genetic enhancements might be widespread throughout the population, although since our research specimens were limited it could have been a phenomenon only among members of the military. The most we know of any written language are the basic symbols marking the controls in their ships. It seems unlikely that any species could attain spacefaring capabilities without a well-developed written language, so this seems to be further evidence of their almost pathological need for secrecy."

"Were their ships the only examples of their technology we ever saw?" I asked.

Cerevare nodded. "They carried no personal artifacts, or nothing we could identify as such. The ships were always small, one- or two-person craft, not intended to offer amenities on long journeys. For this reason we always felt certain that the larger Chron base ships—or a way back to them—couldn't be far away. But we were never able to actually track them to one."

Hirin pushed his chair away from the table and rose, crossing to the counter to pull a refill of steaming chai from the dispenser. "So, what do you think you'll be able to do at this moon artifact?"

"That, I do not know, yet," the Lobor answered. "I am carrying a large amount of data with me, although I doubt it is more than the Protectorate would have." She leaned back in her chair, stifling a yawn with a softly-furred hand; an incongruous pairing with such a human gesture. "To be perfectly honest, I don't know what the Protectorate expects from me. I suspect they are calling in anyone they can find who might be considered an 'expert' in any area of Chron knowledge."

"Grasping at straws?" asked Viss with a grin.

Cerevare smiled. "Something like that. But however much or little help I am ultimately able to offer, I am excited to see a 'new' Chron item after all this time."

"I wonder why they think it's Chron?" I mused. "With so little hard physical data for reference."

"It would not take much for them to make that assumption," Cerevare said. "If similar alloys were used in its construction, or even a repetition of the few symbols we recognize as Chron from their ships, it would be enough. They are distinctive." She stood and stretched. "And on that note, I shall make my way to bed. Thank you all, for a most interesting discussion."

With a final smile for the three of us, she left the galley, the full yellow trousers she wore tonight swaying gently in time with her slightly bouncing gait.

Hirin contemplated the remains of his chai. "I wonder what this discovery will mean for Nearspace?"

"It'll change things," Viss said. "As long as it doesn't attract any unwanted interest."

"What do you mean?"

He shrugged. "I keep thinking about all the ways something like that could be configured to send out a signal if it were discovered, if someone started messing with it. Sure, the Chron haven't been around Nearspace in a hundred and fifty years—that doesn't mean they've disappeared from the entire universe."

"The Protectorate will be careful," I said, but it sounded hollow, even to me. I wished I'd asked Lanar more about it when

I'd had him on the comm.

"By all accounts the Chron were some mean *bastardos*," Viss said. "I hope being careful will be enough."

We all went off to our quarters then, but the jarring note of the end of the conversation replayed in my mind. Despite the comforting presence of Hirin's even breathing at my side in our quarters, hours passed before sleep deigned to visit me.

Chapter 1 — Jahelia
Cat and Mouse

THE EIGHT YEARS since my father died on Quma have been busy for me. I spent two trying to track down his old PrimeCorp colleague, Emmage Mahane, whose name I'd finally found in my father's datapad. His notes on her were extensive, enough to make me think he'd been a bit unhealthily obsessed with her all these years, although he'd never mentioned her in my hearing. PrimeCorp wanted her, and wanted her badly, since she'd absconded with every speck of data on the nanobioscavenger project when she objected to the ethics of PrimeCorp's marketing plans.

Except the data that lived on in my parents and me. Fortunately, Dad had covered his tracks or played dumb well enough that PrimeCorp wasn't suspicious enough to test us. I guess we had to thank Emmage Mahane for taking the heat on that one.

Why did I think I could succeed where PrimeCorp, with all its resources, had failed? Because every big corporation in Nearspace suffers from a bad case of bureaucracy, and it seemed to me that one person, in a case like this, would simply be more efficient.

"I can't figure out where they're headed now," Pita fretted, bringing me back to the present. "I mean, there's nothing out here!"

"Maybe they've got Paixon's mother stashed on an asteroid somewhere," I said.

"You know as well as I do that she's got to be on Kiando again. Otherwise why would the *Tane Ikai* even have gone there?"

I shrugged. "Because the Protectorate told them to? Paixon dances to her brother's tune."

"I've done the math, Jahelia. There's a ninety-six point oh four percent—"

"Oh, shut up, Pita. I don't really doubt that Emmage Mahane is back on Kiando with Gusain Buig."

"Then why are we out here following her daughter's ship? I thought the point was to get to Mahane through her."

"Because I'm working for PrimeCorp, and that's what they want me to do."

"I thought you were only using PrimeCorp as a means to an end. The end being—"

"Will you *shut up*?" I stood from the pilot's seat and stalked to the little galley, although it wasn't really far enough for stalking. And there was nowhere on the ship I could go to actually get away from the annoying AI.

I took deep breaths as I pulled a *cazitta* from the machine. I wished I hadn't been quite so open, talking to Pita, before I'd realized that she'd remember everything I said and bring it up in later conversations. "Look, PrimeCorp is paying me pretty well to keep tabs on Paixon and her little gang. It's a good gig, so I'm playing it as long as it's worthwhile."

"Hey, hey, all right," Pita huffed. I could imagine her, if she were a person, throwing her hands up in exasperation. The PrimeCorp programmers were *good*. "I just like to know the program. I'm the one flying the ship, right?"

"Yeah, right, that's you," I agreed sarcastically, rolling my eyes. She couldn't fly the ship without me giving her instructions. Unfortunately, since Pita was based on my personality, she was proficient at recognizing my sarcasm.

"Pfft," was all she said.

I ignored her and sipped at the *cazitta,* savouring the licorice bite. I wasn't about to tell her that now, suddenly, when I finally knew where to find Emmage Mahane, I didn't know what to *do* with that information.

After two years of searching, I hadn't been able to find Emmage Mahane on my own, and it galled me to admit it.

Discouraged, I had decided to let it go. I took passage to Vileyra, a planet where my parents and I had never lived, and tried to get on with my life. But I couldn't get Emmage Mahane and what she'd done to us—inadvertently or not—out of my head. I found myself drifting from planet to planet again, telling myself I was simply travelling for fun or to find a better job or a more welcoming climate—but I was fooling myself. I was really searching for her. When I found myself applying for a job as part of the cleaning crew on a starliner, thinking I might come across her that way, I knew I had a problem. And I had to do something concrete about it if I was ever going to shake it.

My biggest obstacle was lack of funds—I didn't have my own ship and no resources to get one. But then I got smart. If I couldn't beat PrimeCorp, maybe I'd let them help me, without even knowing they were doing it. I got close to one of the lowly clerks at PrimeCorp main, and worked my way up until I landed myself an audience with Alin Sedmamin himself.

That had been an interesting meeting. He perked right up when I introduced myself as the "great-granddaughter" of Berrto Sord himself, who had worked at PrimeCorp so long ago. I spun him a good story about how my great-granddaddy had died ever so many years past, and I'd only recently found out the family history of how Emmage Mahane had done him wrong. I didn't tell Sedmamin *why* I wanted to find Mahane, just left it up to his imagination. I'll give the man one thing, he has a good imagination. Told him I had some impressive credentials and would be willing to pool resources. Of course he said he couldn't see Mahane hurt, because she had information he wanted. Of course I said I wasn't planning on hurting her—or at least not until he had what he wanted.

An interesting meeting, indeed.

I'm sure he ran a background check on me and my father. But by then the records showed only what I wanted them to show. No mention of how we'd lived on Renata and dad taught at the university there. No mention of the years on Vele under other names. No record of my mother entering the health care system, because of the bioscavs that shouldn't have been in her blood. No mention of how expensive black market health care is, my father's gambling, or his involvement in the Longate scandal. None of that.

Instead, he'd found a rather predictable and boring family tree of predictable and boring people, leading to me. Completely fictitious, but useful. Very, very useful.

"Jahelia, are you listening to me? I said, what do you think they're doing?" Pita said again in an aggrieved tone.

I snapped out of the memories and returned to the pilot's skimchair, balancing the mug on the console. "I don't know! Why don't you have another go at decrypting that datapacket you intercepted, if you're so curious? Maybe there's a clue in there."

"It's a Protectorate classified packet," Pita said with exaggerated patience. "They make them so that unless you have the key, you *can't* decrypt it, you know? Stripping a copy from the original is the easy part."

"Well, you're the one who's so fired up to get some answers. We'll find out. Be patient."

"Hmmm," Pita said. "They've initiated a long-range scan."

"Out here?" I sat forward in the chair. "What are they after out here?

Pita laughed, one of the personality enhancements I found particularly annoying. "We'll find out. Be patient," she mimicked.

We'd followed the *Tane Ikai*, always skirting the edge of scanner range, while they made a stopover at Mars, then skipped to Lambda Saggitae and made an even briefer stop on Anar. Then they backtracked to Sol system, skipped through MI 2 Eridani and Beta Comae Berenices, and wound up in Delta Pavonis without making any other stops along the way. It was a weird, roundabout route and I couldn't figure out what their end destination might be, but they weren't stopping to pick up or deliver cargo. That meant they were headed somewhere with a purpose beyond the normal hauling jobs—maybe an important passenger. I figured their roundabout route was an attempt to confuse or lose anyone like us, who might be following them. Now their route suggested that they weren't in Delta Pavonis to go to either Rhea or Renata, the two inhabited planets. At first I thought they might be heading for the Split, since I'd seen them travel that anomalous and dangerous wormhole twice lately, but they turned away from its coordinates as well.

I tapped my fingernails on the console. We weren't close enough to get a visual signal, so the *Tane Ikai* was nothing more than a tiny, hologrammatic dot on my fancy new display. "Yeah, this just got more interesting. What are you doing, Luta Paixon?"

"Should I pull back? They could catch us in a long-range scan."

"Sure—no, wait." I stared at the glowing dot and considered. "Hang here a little longer and see if they spot us. If they do, I'm not averse to a little cat-and-mouse. It's been getting a little boring."

Pita chuckled. "Who's the cat, and who's the mouse?"

I smiled. "Meow."

Chapter 8 — Luta
Take a Deep Breath and Jump

WE'D MADE AN uneventful skip into the Delta Pavonis system, and Yuskeya laid in the coordinates for the new wormhole. Lanar had sent them as a classified datapacket, so the Protectorate must have been able to keep its whereabouts a secret so far. Our instructions were to start long-range scans early and not get too near the wormhole unless we were certain there were no other ships in the vicinity. It wasn't likely we'd been followed, but the Protectorate didn't like to take chances.

Their paranoia turned out to be a good thing. The scans showed a ship outside the range of our short-range scans, but close enough to monitor us if it wanted to.

"Can you get a drive signature?" I asked.

Yuskeya shook her head. "Still too far out."

I sighed. "Well, we're not supposed to get too close to the new wormhole if there's anyone around, so let's pretend we're passing through. Keep heading past the wormhole and checking on that ship, and once they're out of range we'll double back."

"What a waste of time," Baden grumbled. "They're probably not paying any attention to us, anyway."

I patted his shoulder. "I know, but we're on a Protectorate mission, so we'll play by Protectorate rules. I'm not willing to screw it up by being impatient. We've got lots of time to get Cerevare there. Let's be cautious for once."

A half-hour or so later Baden commed me over the ship's system; I'd gone to the galley for some lunch. "Guess you were right, Captain. I think that ship is following us."

"Really?" I hadn't actually suspected anything of the sort. I was just following the precautions Lanar had asked me to take.

"They haven't gotten much closer to us, but they haven't moved off, either. Unless they're following a route parallel to ours, and I can't really see where that would be taking them, since we're only marking time."

I chewed the last bite of my sandwich while I thought about it. "Hmm. *Okej*, give them another half hour. If they're still keeping pace, we'll head over to their position and see if they want to talk about anything."

They hadn't changed course in the allotted time, so I gave Rei the order to move toward the ship. I hadn't decided what to do. I could make contact with them, get their story—but I didn't know if I wanted to come right out and accuse them of following us. That would imply that we had a reason for someone to follow us, and I didn't want to put that idea in anyone's head.

We didn't get to ask any questions, anyway. We did, however, get one answered. The ship took off quickly as soon as we'd covered about a quarter of the distance between us, so there was no doubt that whoever they were, they'd been monitoring us.

"Want to chase them?" Rei asked, swinging around in her skimchair to face me. Her eyes were bright behind the mask of her *pridattii,* and I could tell she hoped the answer would be *yes.* "We could try out the new burst drive."

I hesitated. I was, in fact, burning to know who was following us and why. Was it that someone had noticed us pick up Cerevare and had reason to wonder why? Or was it PrimeCorp again?

"I don't want to get sidetracked," I said finally, "but I want to know who that was. Run us close enough to scan the drive signature—use the burst drive if necessary. That might put a scare into them and they'll leave us alone for a bit, which will give us time to get through the new wormhole." I grinned. "They won't be following us there, I'll bet."

So Rei poured it on, with a little encouragement from Viss, and the new burst drive worked beautifully. We managed to close the distance between the two ships enough for Yuskeya to catch our quarry in a drive scan. Once she gave the word that she had enough data, we dropped back and let the other ship keep running, putting a nice margin between us again, then wheeled to head for the wormhole.

"Okay, Rei, use the burst drive all the way to the spot where we engaged it before. Even if they come back, our normal signature should have dissipated before they can trace it to the wormhole."

"Who did you piss off this time, Mother?" Maja asked, then bit her lip. "Sorry. That came out wrong."

I shrugged. "I don't really know. Could be PrimeCorp, could be someone following Cerevare. Could be something else entirely—pirates, trying to decide if we're a worthwhile target."

"Hey, Captain, guess what?" Yuskeya looked up from the nav board where she had analyzed the scan data. "It's our friend from the other day. That's one pirate who gets around."

I frowned. "Now, that, I don't like. He's far too persistent."

"Yeah, and I'm guessing he's got a lot more inside that hull than you'd think," said Baden. "I sent a little tracer piggybacking on Yuskeya's scan, and it picked up some tech readings you wouldn't expect."

"Like what?" I crossed to study the data over Baden's shoulder.

"Better weapons than flash-pack torps, for one thing," he said. "Wasp missiles and a particle beam, too. Long-range scanners that are probably as good as ours, enhanced comm capability. You name it, he seems to have it. You just wouldn't think so from the outside, or from what he's demonstrated so far."

"Put that ship on long-range alert status," I ordered. "I want to know the instant he comes within range of us."

"You've got it, Captain," Yuskeya said. "Now if we hightail it into that wormhole—"

"It'll be the last we see of him for a while," I finished. "And amen to that."

Ah, wishful thinking.

BACK AT THE coordinates Lanar had provided, we ran all the scans again, long- and short-range. At the all-clear, we turned our attention to the new wormhole. It looked much like any of the others studded around Nearspace, a darker area of space where no stars twinkled in the far distance. A moonlit shadow against an ebony background. You could pass it without noticing if your scans were off and you weren't paying attention.

"Viss, we've arrived," I told him over the ship's comm. "How's the new skip drive doing?"

"Running smooth as organic velvet," he assured me. "The new upgrade should make it easier for Rei to stabilize the skips as we go through."

"Usual scans are running," Yuskeya reported. "Everything seems to be within the normal range—wait a second, belay that observation. Hmmm . . . " Her fingers darted over the display, keying in commands.

"What is it?" I didn't want any further complications. Lanar hadn't given me an alternate plan B.

"One sec . . . the wormhole seems to have an irregular mass node. It's causing the readings to fluctuate, where most wormholes remain steady."

I frowned. "Not something that should stop us, though, right? I'm sure there are a few similar wormholes around Nearspace."

"No, it's nothing serious, but worth noting. I'm sure *Admiralo* Mahane would have warned us if it were likely to cause a problem."

"Unless it's a new development."

"No, I'd say this is intrinsic to the wormhole's nature, or the result of something that happened to it a long time ago. It means that the wormhole's mass node reading varies from point to point along its length, where usually it's a single, unvarying number." She flashed a grin. "Rei might have to work a little harder to keep the ride smooth, that's all."

Rei snorted. "After piloting the Split when Hirin took his attack, there's no wormhole that scares me anymore."

I shuddered, thinking of that experience, still sickeningly fresh in my mind. We'd come close to slipping off the safe side of that unusual wormhole into the unknown, and Hirin had suffered a heart attack. Not a skip I wanted to remember, or was ever likely to forget, no matter how long my mother's nanobioscavengers allowed me to live.

"Any idea what's causing the anomaly, Yuskeya?"

"None."

Viss spoke up over the ship's comm. "We don't know anything about the star system beyond this wormhole, Captain. It could also be caused by some type of radiation we're not familiar with, leaking through the wormhole's terminal point on the other end. Or some other force working on the wormhole from that system."

I noticed he addressed his remarks to me, not to Yuskeya, and stifled a sigh. "Thanks, Viss, that's a reasonable notion. *Okej,* folks, let's take a step into the unknown."

"I wonder if this is what wormhole explorers feel when they find a new one," Baden said. "I've got a weird feeling in the pit of my stomach."

"That's fear, Baden," Rei said smoothly. "I suppose you'd have us believe you don't recognize the sensation."

"I'd never claim that, dearest Rei," he retorted. "Not after flying with you at the helm for this long."

"All right, children, settle down," Hirin admonished, "or you'll be going to bed with no supper."

"You'd better listen to him. He means it," Maja said with a grin.

I rolled my eyes. As if she'd ever been sent to bed without supper!

"Pipe down, everyone, I'm calling our guest to join us on the bridge," I said. "I'd like to maintain our civilized facade for a little longer, if possible."

"No need to call, I am here," Cerevare said, entering from the main corridor and crossing to sit in an empty skimchair. "And I believe I know this crew pretty well by now," she added with a lupine smile. Today she wore an emerald-green shirt with billowy black pants, as well as the bright, ever-present sash. I didn't know if all Lobors favoured such intense colours, but Cerevare certainly did. Human chairs not being made to accommodate the different proportions of Lobors' legs to their torsos, she always unselfconsciously tucked her legs up under her when she sat, so they wouldn't dangle. At first it had seemed too casual, but we were used to it now. I'd already made a note to buy a Lobor-style skimchair and one for the galley at the first opportunity. I'd never had a Lobor crew member, so I'd never really considered it before; now that seemed close-minded on my part.

"Excellent," I said. "And to answer your question, Baden, I don't think we can equate this with exploring a new wormhole. At least we know what's beyond this one, even if it's only a general idea. We know it actually has an 'other side' and that we won't be stuck forever in a closed-point singularity. We know we won't emerge in a fatal proximity to a star. We know there's no weird interstellar dust cloud carrying particles that our arrival will suddenly ignite or start some other reaction, annihilating us so fast you wouldn't even be able to wonder what happened."

I paused for breath, and Baden fixed me with a quizzical stare. "So, I take it you've had the experience of spelunking new wormholes, Captain?"

"No, but Hirin and I debated the possibility for a while when we were younger—much younger. Yes, before you were born, Maja," I said, seeing the question begin to form on my daughter's lips. "We considered it too risky, and having seriously considered those scenarios, I can tell you this is nothing like how it would feel to actually face them."

"I read that PrimeCorp is still the largest private funder of independent wormhole explorers," said Hirin. "They've got their fingers in more pies than they even have fingers."

"They won't miss any possible opportunity to make a dollar," I said. "If they're funding the exploration, they're entitled to a cut of any resulting discovery royalties."

"I'll take your word for it about the wormhole exploring anxiety," Baden said. "But you have to grant that this is exciting."

I grinned at him. "I'll give you that. I've never had the pleasure of travelling to a newly-discovered secret system before. Now, we're supposed to send a message through the wormhole before we head in, and wait for confirmation, so let's do that. To

Admiralo Woodroct, on the *O. Domtaw*, according to Lanar's brief. Tell him we're here, waiting to come through on his word."

"Sending it now, Captain."

"Yuskeya, keep an eye out for our unwanted visitor, would you? I don't think they'll catch up with us, but they've surprised us before."

We waited in silence, but no reply came from the *Domtaw*. I drummed my fingers on the arm of my chair. "Baden, resend that message, would you? Add that we may have an unknown ship following us, and we'd like to get through the wormhole before they catch up to us."

Baden's nimble fingers stuttered across the screen, and a moment later he said, "Message away."

Another few minutes ticked by in agonizing slowness. "What's the delay over there?" I said, irritated. "I thought the priority was for us to get in there without being seen. Now they're making us wait on the doorstep?"

"They could be busy, I guess," Hirin offered. "Although you're right, I expected them to be watching for us."

I tapped a fingernail against my front teeth. "Yuskeya, any indication there's someone coming through the wormhole from the other side?"

After a brief pause, she reported, "Tracer scan seemed to take a little longer than usual, but it reports all clean, Captain."

"Well, I think we've waited long enough out here. Viss, let's have the skip drive. Rei, whenever you're ready, take us in."

"Aye, Captain," she said, as the skip drive thrummed to life. Normal drives aren't enough to traverse the inside of a wormhole—they wouldn't even take you past the edge, or terminal point. The skip drive generates a thin layer of what the physicists call "Krasnikov matter," enough to keep the wormhole from destabilizing while a ship is inside it, and a strong enough field to launch the ship into the wormhole at one terminal point. The field also holds the ship intact by countering the immense forces at work inside the wormhole, and protects it from the high-frequency radiation, which would prove disastrous for ship and crew. Finally, it repels the ship from the inside surface of the wormhole, propelling it through in a series of skips, like a rock skipping across calm water. Unlike a rock skipping across water, however, the skips don't run in a straight line. As the skip field repels from one side of the hole, the ship slides around to bounce the next time off the opposite side, to create a water-going-down-the-drain effect.

As we moved past the terminal point, the wormhole seemed like any other. The inside is actually quite a pretty place. All that radiation pouring into the wormhole gets blueshifted to high frequencies and reacts with the Krasnikov matter to hold the wormhole open. The result is a breathtaking swirl of constantly moving colour, like a hundred rainbows spinning down a drain.

We'd made only the first skip, skimming the wormhole's inner surface, when Viss's voice came over the ship's comm. "Might have some trouble here, Captain."

"What kind of trouble?"

"You want to go to a private channel?"

"No, go ahead. If we're in trouble, everyone needs to know."

"Some kind of cosmic ray is penetrating the shields and affecting the skip drive," Viss said in his no-nonsense way. "I don't know if it will destabilize the drive or not."

"Starting a scan," Yuskeya said, not waiting for me to give the order.

"Rei, how does it feel so far?" I asked. She was the one who'd know soonest if anything was going wrong with the skips.

"No problem yet," she said steadily. "Are these something we should worry about from a medical point of view?"

"I don't think so," Yuskeya answered before Viss could, if he would have had an answer at all. As the resident medic, she was best suited to know, anyway.

I realized that I'd sat forward in my chair and had gripped the arms with a white-knuckle intensity. I forced myself to sit still and try to relax. No crew functions well if their captain appears rattled, and if Rei wasn't worried, I shouldn't be yet.

The destabilization of the skip drive would be dangerous, to put it mildly. The skip field and the Krasnikov generation keep the wormhole open while the ship skips through. If the skip field failed, it might cause the wormhole to collapse around the ship, and I can't really describe what would happen at that point because I don't know. We'd be killed, for certain; the shields would fail from the sheer strength of the forces inside a collapsing wormhole, and without the shields, the X-rays and gamma rays would fry us in an instant.

That part, we don't talk about with the passengers. But it was too late to try and keep any secrets from Cerevare now. I glanced over at her, but her lupine face was composed and still.

"Anyone else notice these grey lines?" Hirin asked suddenly. "I've been trying to gather data on them but I don't know if I'm actually getting anything. They seem familiar, somehow . . ."

I'd noticed them peripherally, a series of grey streaks that ran lengthwise down the sides of the wormhole, like striations in rock or muscle. The colours swirled past them, leaving them visible and unmoving on the wormhole walls. Now I paid more attention to them. Hirin was right. "Yes, I've definitely seen something like them before. But I can't recall—"

Hirin snapped his fingers. "The wormhole into Tau Ceti. We didn't make that run all that often, but I'm sure that's where I've seen them before."

I nodded. The Tau Ceti system had only one inhabited planet, Quma, and only one wormhole entry, from Eta Cassiopeia. Being a "dead-end" run, we hadn't travelled it as part of our regular route in the days we'd been running the *Tane Ikai* together. But the wormhole did have these same grey striations. They'd never seemed to have any impact on how the wormhole functioned, so I'd forgotten about them.

"Not getting much," Hirin said. "We'd need specialized scanners built to gather data inside wormholes. Too much input, so our normal scanners are overwhelmed."

"We'll ask the Protectorate smart boys about it when we get there," I told him. "Rei, Viss, Yuskeya, how are we doing? Anything else strange? Talk to me." We'd made about four skips now; the number in any wormhole was variable.

"Still holding," Rei reported. "Ship feels a little wobbly, but nothing serious."

"Readings are decreasing," Yuskeya said. "I don't have a fix on where they originated—it's too hard to tell in here. Everything is so stirred up inside a wormhole . . ."

"That's okay." I let out a long breath. "Viss?"

"Nothing more to report down here."

Then the terminal point appeared, and a second later we emerged out the other side. Rei cut the skip drive, and the ship seemed suddenly silent as we sailed into the newest system to be part of Nearspace.

It was certainly beautiful, this first glimpse of it. Sometimes wormholes emerge into empty space, a vast starfield with nothing to distinguish dock from starwise. This one, though, offered a spacescape so varied one hardly knew where to look first. A vast particle cloud hovered in the near distance, the mass of ionized dust radiating shades of orange with bright purple specularity at its centre. Far off, the system's sun was a pale blue-white glow. Nearer to us a planet hung, its surface a mottled terra cotta smudged with yellow. And circling it were the moons.

I counted three right away, although I found out later that there was a fourth, out of sight behind the planet when we emerged. The closest to us was a tiny thing, a shimmer of red in the reflected light of the planet. Nearer the planet, its twin sister spun, no larger, but more orange in colour; an echo of the particle cloud that provided the backdrop. The hidden moon, I found out later, was an irregular lump, an ugly grey stepsister to the planet's other companions.

But the other was even smaller than the first two. I spotted it mainly because a Protectorate ship—Pegasus-class, the same as Lanar's—hovered close by. This last moon was the same reddish-orange colour, basking in the light from both the planet and the particle cloud. A double set of rings, offset perhaps forty-five degrees from one another, winked golden against the dark starfield behind it.

"That one," Cerevare said with what might have been a sigh of happiness. "That one is the Chron moon."

Chapter 9 — Luta
Of Unusual Moons
and Unexpected Visitors

"INCOMING MESSAGE," BADEN said, skimming his fingers over the comm board. "Admiral Louis Woodroct, on board the Nearspace Protectorate Vessel *O. Domtaw*." Baden turned in his chair and gave me a wink. "Sounds *indignigi*," he whispered.

"Responding," I said, and Baden nodded. "This is Captain Luta Paixon of the far trader *Tane Ikai*," I said. "I believe you were expecting us, *Admiralo*."

"Acknowledged," the Admiral answered tersely. "Forgive me for getting right to the point, but weren't you instructed to contact me before entering the wormhole from Delta Pavonis? We could have fired on you in error!"

I did a quick eye contact around the crew. "Yes, Admiral, and we did so."

"Well, it didn't come through here," he said. I could tell from the tone of his voice that he didn't believe me.

"Twice, in fact," I continued. "We received no response, and only proceeded through because we were in danger of being discovered. Perhaps your comm officer didn't notice the messages come in?”

“My comm officer is sitting three feet away from me, Captain Paixon, and there was nothing for her to notice.”

“I didn’t mean to imply any incompetence, Admiral,” I said mildly. “My communications officer will forward you the timestamp data.”

Baden nodded and punched commands into his console. I met Hirin’s gaze, and he pulled a face and waggled a finger to indicate the possibility that the Admiral was crazy. I fought down a giggle as the Admiral returned to the comm.

“I have your data, Captain. Did you experience anything unusual on the wormhole skip?”

“Affirmative, Admiral. Our scans picked up a bombardment of unidentified cosmic rays. They threatened to interfere with the skip drive, but it stayed stable enough for us to make the skip. We also noted grey striations inside the wormhole, similar, we think, to those found in the wormhole between Eta Cassiopeia and Tau Ceti systems.” I wasn’t above showing off a little. “Are either of those what you mean?”

There was silence from the other end of the comm. With a glance at me, Cerevare spoke up.

“This is Cerevare Brindlepaw, Admiral Woodroct,” she said. “I’d also be interested in the answer to Captain Paixon’s question. It might help me in my analysis of the artifact.”

“Your messages just came through now, Captain, a good five minutes after you sent them. And your timestamp data is off by the same amount. Perhaps we’ll discuss all of this in person. Is your ship damaged in any way from the skip?”

“Not to my knowledge, but I’ll have my engineer run a full scan and diagnostics shortly. I’ll advise you if he finds anything.”

“Very well. The other ship nearby is the Nearspace Protectorate Vessel *R. Stillwell*, under Commander Holly Ballenger. They’re patrolling nearby. I’ll send a shuttle for *Sinjorino* Brindlepaw whenever she’s ready. I invite you to join us for the briefing.”

I nodded, thinking that Lanar must have pulled some heavy strings to get me included in the invitation. I thought we’d do nothing but hang around until Cerevare decided whether she could be any help here, and if so, how long she would stay. "Thank you, Admiral. We'll be in touch."

"I've been running scans since we left the wormhole," Yuskeya said. "There's no trace of those rays now, and no indication where they would have come from in this system. And there's something else that I don't believe your brother mentioned to us, Captain." She turned to me, eyes twinkling. "There's another wormhole leading out of this system. The other Nearspace ship the Admiral mentioned? It's not patrolling. It's a Dragon-class ship, and it's parked. Right beside that wormhole."

"Huh," Hirin grunted. "Dragon-class? That's a real battleship. So chances are, they don't know where that one goes."

"Or they do, and it has them worried," Yuskeya said.

Cerevare slipped out of the skimchair and stretched. "Captain, I'll collect a few things from my quarters. Will you signal me when you're ready to go?"

I nodded, and the historian left the bridge. "*Okej*, folks," I said to the others. "I know you're itching to do all sorts of scans and readings and who-knows-what-else with gadgets and programs that you're not supposed to have and I don't want to know about. Try to resist those urges for a little while, all right? This admiral's already got his face in a knot, he's worried about something, and I don't want to annoy him further until he's told me what he's willing to share. Got it?"

Chagrin was evident on Yuskeya and Baden's faces, and I could imagine Viss down in engineering, shaking his head.

Baden made one attempt to sway me. "Captain, aren't you the least bit curious to know why our messages were delayed for so long?"

"And why our time-encoding is wrong?" Rei added. "Because that's tied into the main shipsystem, so I don't see how—"

"Of course I'm curious," I interrupted. "And you're all welcome to think of as many possible explanations as you can while I'm gone *gathering information*. As long as none of them involve doing anything that the Admiral or I would not approve of. Hirin, you have the chair." I slid out of it. He kissed me, a quick peck on the cheek as I passed him.

"Good luck over there," he said. "Charm the hell out of him."

I rolled my eyes. Hirin has, I think, an exaggerated notion of my powers of persuasion. However, that's an admirable quality in a husband. "I'll do my best," I promised, and went to change into a clean t-shirt.

MY BEST WASN'T getting me very far, I thought glumly about an hour later. Cerevare and I were in the Admiral's situation room, having been plied with caff and some rather bland sugar cookies. We still didn't know what scans, tests, or other procedures the Protectorate bright boys had already carried out on the moon, despite Cerevare's polite interrogation of the *Admiralo*. He'd obviously invited us over here to find out more about us, rather than to give us any information.

"Let me put it this way," the Admiral had said with extreme politeness. "What we do know about the operant moon—"

"Operant moon?" Cerevare interjected.

"That's what the scientists are calling it, to distinguish it from the other natural or inert moons," he explained. "What we do know, which I grant you isn't much, is either classified, or I don't want to influence *Sinjorino* Brindlepaw before she's had a chance to make her own observations."

Which was fine and made sense, but why had he made us come over here for it? I didn't think any of us had really learned anything we hadn't known before.

Finally, Cerevare asked, "When can I visit the operant moon itself?"

"Would you be willing to wait until tomorrow? There's a team there now, carrying out some tests, and it will likely take the rest of the day. We've temporarily lost contact with them, and I may have to send a second ship down to investigate. I don't want to risk a civilian down there until I'm sure it's safe."

Well, at least I knew what was making the Admiral so testy. "Do you think that something they did caused the phenomenon we noted coming through the wormhole?"

His face said he wished I hadn't figured that out. "As I said, I'd rather not give *Signorino* Brindlepaw any preconceived notions," he said smoothly. "We won't know ourselves until we re-establish contact with them."

Which erased any doubt that was exactly what he thought.

"Very well," Cerevare said with good grace. "You won't mind, then, if I instruct Captain Paixon's crew to run some tests and scans on my behalf?" He began to object, but she didn't give him a chance. "Since they'll be based on my own notions about the moon, the results will form the initial part of my assessment."

"It depends," he said. "There's an awful lot about this thing we don't know yet. What sort of data do you want?"

Cerevare shrugged elegantly. "Basic data: age, mass, composition. Nothing that would actually interfere with the moon. And I'm sure you've already done these sorts of things yourself."

"Of course." But he'd already refused to share the results with us, and he obviously didn't want to lose face by changing his tune now. "That will be fine, I suppose. But Captain, you and your crew must respect the utmost secrecy of these results."

I felt like the teacher had wagged his finger at me. "I've already been briefed on the nature of this mission by *Admiralo* Mahane, sir, you needn't worry about that." I stood. "Then we'll hear from you tomorrow."

He stood and extended a hand, which I shook. No hard feelings. "Yes. And thank you again for bringing *Signorino* Brindlepaw here."

"It was my pleasure."

We shuttled back to the *Tane Ikai*. Naturally the crew were more than helpful to Cerevare in performing the scans she requested, and if any other data-gathering gremlins hitched a ride on those scans, I didn't know about it. I was in the galley having dinner with Hirin and complaining about how Protectorate officers so often annoyed the hell out of me, my own brother being only partially excepted. But that was only in-between bites of the delicious garlic noodle *prizo* Hirin had cooked for us.

So I didn't know what was happening at first; I heard the shouts from the bridge, felt a rumble as the auxiliary drives came to life. Then Baden, on the ship's comm.

"Captain! You'd better get out here!"

I didn't even stop to think how many meals have been

interrupted by something like that. We left everything on the table and Hirin and I sprinted down the corridor to the bridge.

"What—" I started, but they were ahead of me.

"Looks like we've got a visitor from Delta Pavonis," Rei said, "and the *Admiralo* will no doubt be chewing you out before very long. See for yourself."

She flashed an image up on the main screen and it didn't take me more than three seconds to recognize the putative pirate who had apparently been dogging our heels since before we arrived at Mars.

"Damn that *idioto*! Why would he do something so stupid?"

"I think you've answered your own question, Captain," Yuskeya said wryly. "He's an idiot. My advice is to stay out of this until the Admiral calls you in."

"PrimeCorp must be out of their minds, mucking around in Protectorate business," I said. "They were reprimanded on Vele. You'd think they'd leave me alone for a little while."

"Maybe now they have a grudge," Hirin suggested. "They want to make a point."

"But no-one else even knows they're bothering me," I protested. "Who does that send a message to?"

"You," Viss suggested over the comm. "Looks like they're not done with you yet, Captain."

"Lucky me," I muttered. "Well, I'm taking Yuskeya's advice and keeping out of it. Finding the Protectorate here was probably more than they'd bargained for, so let's enjoy the show."

Baden flashed me a grin and gestured to the comm board. "Want to listen in on the conversation? Admiral Woodroct is giving him hell."

"Stop that!" I ordered. "I know you're a techdog and you love all this eavesdropping and stuff, but you're going to get me in trouble. In more trouble."

"They don't even know I'm here," he assured me. "It's pickup only. You know damn well you're itching to hear this."

The pirate ship had quite obviously not expected to run through the wormhole and find not one, but two Protectorate ships in the immediate vicinity. However, the Protectorate was not in the best situation for dealing with interlopers, either. The

Stillwell must have been reluctant to leave its post near the other wormhole, because it hadn't moved. The *Domtaw* had other problems on its hands, if they were still incommunicado with the crew on the surface of the Chron moon.

"The Admiral's bawling him out, but good," Baden said. "Citing Protectorate regulations and making all kinds of threats. Already forbade him to re-enter the wormhole and told him he can't stay here, either. The pirate told Woodroct he's not in a position to enforce any of that, and—"

"Baden, I'm ordering you to—"

"Wait!" Baden swung around to face me, losing the impish grin he'd worn as he listened in and reported. "The pirate's saying he has an important message for you. About your mother."

"Mother?" *Damne.* "Get me a line to Admiral Woodroct. Preferably one the pirate can't overhear, if that's even possible." Lanar would owe me big-time when this was over.

"Admiral?" I said, when Baden gave me the nod. "Admiral, this ship is known to me, I'm afraid. At least—well, let's just say I've had encounters with it before. I have not had actual contact with anyone inside it and had hoped to avoid that. This is the ship I was afraid might be following us when we were waiting to make the skip into this system."

He didn't respond, so I went on. "It appears this person or persons must have tracked us through the wormhole, despite my best efforts to avoid that. For that, I apologize."

The silence from the *Domtaw* stretched out. Then, "Captain Paixon, the individual in command of this interloper vessel, who has so far refused to identify himself, says he has a personal message for you regarding your mother. That he knows who you are and knew where to find you makes me inclined to believe that part of his story, although anything else he says is suspect. Frankly," and I thought I heard the Admiral sigh, "I can't do much to him at this point unless he poses an actual threat. I'm still trying to re-establish contact with our people on the moon. So if you want to talk to him, I won't stop you. I'll tell him to keep his distance from this moon and stay clear of the wormhole, and then forget about him for now if he follows those orders."

"Fine with me," I said, and at that moment I felt a little sorry for the Admiral. He was definitely having a bad day.

"Baden," I said, "I'm going back down to the galley and try to finish my supper. If this guy contacts us, patch it through to me there. Don't initiate contact—let him come to us. Rei, you have the chair."

I didn't leave Hirin in charge because I knew he'd want to come with me and honestly, I wanted him to. Whatever this pirate had to say to me concerning Mother, I didn't want to be alone when I spoke to him.

And it wasn't long before he sent a message. Audio only, with some kind of scrambling device hooked up to distort his voice.

"Captain Paixon?" it stuttered.

"That's me," I said. "You have something to tell me about my mother. And I know you're working for PrimeCorp, so don't try and hand me any *merde* about that. I'm only listening while you're saying something that interests me."

"Oh, this should interest you, Captain. It would be in your mother's best interests if you could convince her to negotiate directly with PrimeCorp on the nanobioscavenger issue."

The voice-camouflaging intrigued me. Why would they do that? Was it someone I knew?

"PrimeCorp is already on the Protectorate's scans," I said. "What happened on Vele proves that. I would think they'd have more important things on their minds after that."

"Consider it a safety issue. Think about it; maybe PrimeCorp needs the information your mother has now, more desperately than ever."

My throat felt tight. The words were so cold and matter-of-fact, especially spoken in that mechanical, inhuman voice. "And whose safety are we talking about?"

"Let's just say that if certain information came into their hands via a different route—say, released onto the free nets—they might feel their position would be stronger if your mother were out of the equation altogether. You should suggest that to her the next time you see her."

Without saying another word, I shut down the connection with shaking hands. PrimeCorp was openly *threatening* Mother! Did they plan to move against her if she released her data onto the open nets? Hirin came over and put his arms around me, and to my surprise it didn't do the slightest bit of good.

"We can't stay here and wait for Cerevare now," I said, leaning my head against his chest. "I have to get to Kiando and warn Mother, and get a message to Lanar."

"Agreed. But I thought the Protectorate was clamping down on PrimeCorp. Why would they risk something like this if they know they're being watched? And they have to know you'll go straight to Lanar with it."

"They're desperate? They're bluffing? I don't know. Maybe planning to deny the whole thing? This guy could be a scapegoat, like Dores Amadoro." I picked up my half-eaten supper and tossed it into the recycler. Delicious or not, I'd lost my appetite.

"Or they're setting a trap," Hirin mused. "Frighten you into running straight to your mother, and then follow you. They might not actually be planning violence against her, but they still want to know where she is."

That gave me a moment's pause. I'd been worried that I'd already done that once. "Maybe I should tell Woodroct, see what he thinks. He's Protectorate, after all—"

I didn't get to finish, because once again Fate had other plans for me.

"Captain, a ship just came through the wormhole—not the one from Delta Pavonis this time. The one the other Protectorate ship is guarding," Yuskeya said briskly.

"*Kristos*," I swore. "I'm on my way."

Chapter 10 — Luta
Out of the Black

"ALL SCREENS ON," I snapped as soon as I reached the bridge. "Full perimeter view from the ship. Viss?"

"Here, Captain."

"Everything ready to move at a word from me."

"Already done."

I saw that Cerevare was on the bridge with everyone else. Like a good passenger, she'd taken a seat out of the way and sat quietly watching the proceedings, but her furred face was drawn with concern.

With all the screens turned on, the bridge of the *Tane Ikai* took on the appearance of a surveillance vessel. "This one," said Rei, and the magnification on one of the starwise screens increased. The vessel that had come through the wormhole hurtled in our direction. The NPV *R. Stillwell* moved slowly out of position to follow. It had taken them by surprise, apparently, and blasted past the waiting ship. The newcomer had a configuration I didn't immediately recognize, which might have surprised me if I'd been capable of more surprise at that point. The vessel was long and blunt-nosed, with a sunburst of fins at the tail end and a sleek body.

"Lots of chatter between the Protectorate ships," Baden reported. "It's encrypted, but I could break it pretty easily. Should I?"

"Better not," I ordered. "Not yet, anyway."

"It probably consists of a lot of '*Sankta Merde!*' and 'What the hell is that?'" Hirin said with a tight grin.

"I could tell them what it is," Cerevare said evenly. She slid out of the skimchair and glided closer to the screen. "It is a Chron ship."

"What?" Yuskeya's long plait of dark hair swung as she whirled to face the Lobor. "Are you certain?"

Cerevare nodded. "It is my job to be certain of such things."

"*Dios*! There's a second one!"

"Can you get a closer view?"

Rei nodded and with a few strokes had enlarged the image of the second ship to twice the size.

This second ship looked nothing like the one Cerevare had identified as Chron. It was all dark angles and sharp protrusions as it snaked across the starfield in apparent pursuit of the Chron ship, but something else about it caught my eye. Despite its angular shape, the vessel had a shimmery, unstable appearance—almost as if it were *gelatinous*. Again, I didn't recognize it as anything I'd come across in Nearspace before. I pulled up the Nearspace registry on my datapad to see if I could spot a match.

"Incoming from the *Domtaw*," Baden said.

"*Domtaw*, this is the *Tane Ikai*."

"Captain Paixon, this is Lieutenant Praveen. We're not sure what's happening here. Please move your ship a safe distance away."

I resisted the urge to ask what that distance might be.

"Affirmative, Lieutenant," I said. "Rei, set a course for the far side of the moon. Use the burst drive. I want to get it between us and whatever's going to happen here."

"Aye, Captain." She didn't take her eyes off the screen or the pilot's board. The *Tane Ikai* leapt away from the current path of the oncoming Chron ship, as the *Domtaw* moved to intercept it.

"What about the pirate?" Rei asked.

"He can worry about his own *azeno*. He's the Protectorate's problem, not mine. Now, everyone find a seat," I ordered. "This ride might get rough."

Maja slid into the empty skimchair next to Baden, but Cerevare didn't move from the screen displaying the Chron ship. Hirin crossed to her and gently led her to sit down. Her eyes didn't leave the screen.

"I never expected to see one in my lifetime," she said in a voice that was little more than a whisper.

"Any communication from either alien ship?" I asked Baden.

"Nothing."

"I think they're scanning," Yuskeya said. "I'm picking up something from their ship, but I don't know exactly what it is."

"They're changing course," Rei said. "If I had to take a guess, I'd say they're moving toward the moon."

"After us?"

She shook her head. "I don't think so. They'd have a more direct intercept course to us."

"Keep getting us out of the way," I told her. "The torps we've got on board won't be more than fireworks if these folks decide to light it up with each other."

Admiral Woodroct must have seen the change in course as well, because the *Domtaw* also turned back toward the moon. It was no match for the speed of the Chron ship, however.

There was too much happening on too many screens to easily keep track of it all, but the scenario was this: the Chron ship speeding toward the operant moon (where presumably the *Domtaw's* people still were), the *Domtaw* moving to try and intercept it. Further behind, the *Stillwell* hurtling after the Chron ship, and behind that, gaining fast, the dark mystery ship that had emerged last from the second wormhole.

And us, trying to get the hell as far away as possible from whatever was going to happen. While still, I admit, keeping it all in view, because it was damned interesting.

I was studying the dark ship, which I already unconsciously thought of as *the spider*, when a bright flash lit up one of the other screens, jabbing sharply into my peripheral vision. A jolt almost shook me out of my seat as the engines died, killing our acceleration. My datapad shuddered in my hand, the notification vibration gone berserk, and the screen dissolved into gibberish. The case suddenly burned with a searing heat, and I dropped it to the floor. At least the pseudo-grav fields hadn't been affected.

"*Damne!* What happened?"

"No main drive, no maneuvering thrusters," Rei said, her voice tight with concentration, fingers skittering over the screen. "And my board reset itself. We're coasting, folks." She slid across to the co-pilot's board. "This one's still live."

"Comm board is down, too. Switching to backup," Baden reported. "We'll have reduced range."

"Chron ship fired something on the moon," Yuskeya said. "We happened to be in the line of fire."

"The operant moon?"

"The what?"

"Captain, we have a problem," came Viss's voice over the comm.

"That's what the Protectorate calls it. The artifact moon. Viss, I can feel it. Report."

"Propulsion system shut down without warning," he said. The frustration in his voice was almost palpable. "I have to reset the entire system, including prechecks. Thrusters'll be quick, main drive, not so much."

I sucked my scorched fingers and swung my gaze to the screen showing the moon. It still spun unperturbed in its orbit, golden rings circling it like delicate bangles. It appeared completely unaffected. "Yuskeya, what's our course? Immediate danger?"

"We have to restore drive power before we get caught in a gravity well, but for now we're okay."

"They missed it? How can you miss a moon?" Hirin sounded incredulous.

"They didn't miss it," Yuskeya said, focused on her screen. "There wasn't any sort of an impact, but the moon started generating the same kind of rays that we encountered coming through the wormhole. It's sending them in a stream directly into the mouth of the wormhole to Delta Pavonis."

"Any idea what they are? Or what they do?"

"Not enough data. The Admiral's people must have done

something that triggered it before we arrived. Then they either stopped it, or it stopped itself."

"Time it," I said. "See how long it continues."

"*Domtaw* is going nuts, ordering the Chron ship to stop, stand down, answer them—anything," Baden said. "No response that I can pick up, and they're still within range, even on the backup board." He swung around to catch my eye. "*Domtaw* is threatening to fire on them."

"Thrusters online, starting main drive pre-check," Viss said from engineering.

I felt the ship rock as Rei applied thrusters to turn us slightly away from our course toward the moon, still coasting.

"What happened to the *Stillwell*?" Rei asked suddenly. "I'm not watching the fun—honest, I'm not, I'm driving the ship again—but it seems to have stopped moving, on my readout."

I searched the screens. The dark ship was almost upon the Chron vessel, but the *Stillwell* had been in between them only a moment ago.

"It's stopped moving," Maja said.

I couldn't look because at that moment the Chron ship veered aside from its course for the moon, and pointed its nose toward the Delta Pavonis wormhole. The *Domtaw* opened fire, and two torpedoes snaked silently out of the launch tubes and toward the Chron ship.

The Chron ship returned fire, a bright bite of orange light that chewed into the fore end of the Protectorate ship and burst it apart from within. The explosion was so brilliant it lit up most of the screens on our bridge. When it flared out again, the Nearspace Protectorate Vessel *O. Domtaw* was nowhere to be seen.

I never saw what happened to the *Domtaw*'s torps. All I knew was that we were in deep *merde*.

Chapter 11 — Jahelia
Curiosity as a
Dangerous Pastime

"*MEGERO!*" PITA SAID when Captain Paixon closed her comm connection to me without even saying goodbye. "She could have been a little more polite. But you didn't exactly stick to the script, either."

I allowed myself a little smile of satisfaction. Alin Sedmamin had given me a script for our encounter, but I'd decided at the last minute to improvise.

I sat back from the console. "I thought my message was better," I told my personality-attuned computer AI. "Paixon was too cocky. I wanted to cut that out from under her."

"You think she really knew you were working for PrimeCorp?"

"She could have been bluffing. Or she might think anyone who crosses her is working for them. They've got a long history, after all."

"Maybe she knows more about us than you think."

I ignored that. "Anyway, one of her weak spots was obviously her mother, as I'd suspected. Nice to have that confirmed."

"And at least that *idioto* of an Admiral stopped shouting at us over the comm."

"Typical Protectorate," I said. "Happy to let us be the *Tane Ikai*'s problem, as long as I didn't bother him or whatever his little secret mission is." I'd almost laughed aloud at him, ordering me to do this and not do that. He didn't know about the burst drive installation PrimeCorp had gifted me—if I felt like going through the damned wormhole, I'd go, and I'd be past the terminal point before he could get that lumbering Pegasus tub even pointed in my direction.

I did chuckle now, as I moved to the tiny galley behind the cockpit and pulled off another nice mug of hot *cazitta*. My plan had been to catch up with Paixon, give her the message, and take off again, leaving her to wonder what else I might be up to, but I'd stumbled into something far too interesting to walk away from just yet. A secret wormhole? Protectorate ships in an unknown system? And a second wormhole leading who-knew-where?

Curiosity, that old cat-killer. One of my few weaknesses.

Mug in hand, I returned to my seat at the control board. "Pita, message for Alin Sedmamin, double-encrypted."

"Go ahead."

"Target acquired and message delivered. Initiating surveillance." Short and sweet, and guaranteed to annoy Sedmamin, who always wanted to be briefed *in detail*.

"That's it?" Pita asked.

"That's it. Shoot it off through the wormhole, but store it to send again later, once we're back in the Delta Pav system." There had been something weird about that wormhole skip, strange grey lines streaking along the inside. I wasn't entirely confident the message would go through, and I wanted to be sure he got it. I was only sorry that I wouldn't see his frustrated face when he read it.

"Now," I mused, settling in my chair and tapping my fingertips against the side of my mug, "what are all of you doing here?" Two Protectorate ships and the *Tane Ikai*, in what Pita confirmed to be a previously undiscovered and uncharted system. Sedmamin would be interested in this. *Very* interested. And he'd have to pay me very well for the information. I set scanners running to record every bit of data I could collect about the sector.

"Hey, another ship just joined the party," Pita said. She put the visual on the main screen without waiting for my order. The ship had come busting out of the second, further-off wormhole—not the one we'd followed the *Tane Ikai* through.

I sat forward again. "*Sankta merde.* What is that?"

Pita didn't answer me right away. The ship had taken the Protectorate by surprise, too, I could tell by their sluggish reaction. They didn't fire. They didn't move immediately. *Slackers.* They were obviously there to guard the wormhole against such a possibility, and where had they been when the possibility became reality? Napping, that's where.

Despite my extensive knowledge of Nearspace registered ships, this thing wasn't familiar. Something flickered up from the recesses of memory, like maybe I'd seen something similar long ago—in a book? a vid?—but it wouldn't come into focus for me.

"I think that's a Chron ship," Pita said finally.

It takes a lot to surprise me, but that did. *Chron?* It was over a hundred years since anyone had heard from the Chron. I got a weird rolling feeling in my stomach. "Are you sure?"

"It's an eighty-nine percent match." Pita sounded annoyed that I would question her pronouncement. "The eleven percent discrepancy would be reasonable for changes in design, propulsion, and composition since the last data point I have for comparison."

Pita could sound like any normal uptight computer intelligence when she wanted to.

The comm surveillance lit up with chatter between the Protectorate ships, and I was privy to it all thanks to PrimeCorp, again—I had to admit they weren't stingy in sharing their "special" tech when it served their purposes. The Protectorate uniforms were as freaked out by the ship as I was. I heard them calling battle stations.

"Pita, let's get out of the way." Paixon and the *Tane Ikai* seemed to be thinking the same thing, as the ship turned to make for the other side of the planet.

"Engaging fore thrusters," Pita said, and I pushed the *Hunter's Hope* into a slow backward glide, out of the line of fire.

We didn't get far before Pita said, "You won't believe this. *Another* ship just came out of that wormhole." She flashed it onto one of the viewscreens. "This place is getting crowded."

This one really made me stop and take notice. I felt the tiniest surge of doubt—that maybe I hadn't been so smart in coming here after all.

"What the hell *is* that, Pita?"

It looked like no other ship I'd ever seen . . . actually, like no other *kind* of ship I'd ever seen. It was dark and slick, all sharp planes and wicked angles. And it had a shimmer, or a wobble—an instability that sent a shiver racing down my back. That thing was weird. And dangerous. And coming our way fast.

It took even longer for Pita to answer this time. When she did, all she said was, "Unknown."

That scared me worse than anything. All I wanted was to get as far away from it as I could, and my curiosity about it yielded ground to self-preservation.

"Forget the thrusters, Pita. I'm engaging the burst drive and getting us out of here!"

Before we could move, though, I guess we caught its attention. As the dark ship passed the *Hunter's Hope*, a panel in its side opened, and something black and shadowy bloomed inside. The burst drive rumbled to life, and I yanked the ship to the side. Too slow. *Something* hit the ship—not an explosion, nothing concussive. It felt like we'd been grabbed by a giant hand.

"We're—" Pita's voice cut out. The rising hum of the drive died like a switch had been flipped, and the rear sensor readings went dead, too. Now I couldn't see what the dark ship was doing, or anything else, and my stomach churned. Sweat prickled on my neck.

"Pita! Respond!" I punched things all over the control board, but it was a lifeless expanse of plasteel and glass. Pita didn't answer. The only sound in the ship was the soft putter of the air recycler.

"*Damne!*" I slammed my hands down on the unresponsive board and pushed my skimchair back. It spun around on its axis, and I jammed my feet down on the floor to stop its momentum when I saw the rear of the cabin. Beyond the tiny galley, a hazy black wall now bisected the bow and stern of the ship. I stood and cautiously took a couple of steps toward it. No sound, no smell. It was simply *there*.

"Pita?" I tried again. I suddenly understood why computer AI's were so popular in one-person ships. Bigger ships with multi-person crews didn't use them very often, but smaller vessels always came equipped with one, even if it was very basic. Annoying as I usually found her, without Pita I felt very vulnerable and excruciatingly alone.

I was tempted to touch the shadowy barrier, but decided that would be crazy when I didn't know what it was. Curiosity lost that round, too. I took a step back from it. I wasn't going to touch that thing at least until I could get Pita functional and get her to scan it. It felt good to take control of that decision, minor though it was.

Until an eye-searing flash lit up the viewscreens at the front of the ship. The concussion followed a heartbeat later. The floor tilted, and I stumbled forward against the murky, unforgiving wall that hadn't existed moments before.

Chapter 12 — Luta
Enemies Resurrected

"*DIPATRINO!*" HIRIN WHISPERED behind me. The bridge of the *Tane Ikai* had gone as quiet as the vacuum of space surrounding us, as the explosion signalling the death of the *Domtaw* faded.

But there was no time to mourn, and barely time to think.

"Viss, how long to main drives?"

"It won't be quick, Captain. I might be able to rush the burst drive if I leave the main for now."

I chewed on my lip. The burst drive was fine for short durations, but if we had to get far away from here quickly, we'd need the main drive. But there could be people who needed our help.

"Get the burst drive online as quick as you can, Viss. Rei, use the thrusters if you can to get us turned and pointed toward the *Stillwell*."

"What are you doing? I thought we were staying out of the way?" Maja asked.

"We are, but we can't sit here and do nothing if the *Stillwell* needs help. Yuskeya, while we're stuck here, scan that moon for signs of life. Woodroct said the *Domtaw* still had people down there."

"What happened to that?" Maja asked. She pointed to my datapad on the decking. Part of the silver casing bore black streaks, and a thin wisp of smoke rose from it.

"No idea. It happened when the engines shut down," I told her.

She rose and bent to pick it up, testing the casing gingerly first in case it was still hot. Taking it between forefinger and thumb, she set it down next to Baden. "I think I have your next repair project here."

He glanced at it and grimaced. "I think an excursion to ship stores to search for a spare might be a better idea."

"Okay, I've rebooted and routed everything into the burst drive, Rei," Viss said over the ship's comm. "Give it a try."

I'd forgotten about Viss being alone down in engineering. And he had as many screens as we did up here, but he'd had to watch the destruction of the *Domtaw* all by himself.

"You okay, Viss?"

"Doing fine, Captain. Thanks for asking."

The ship hummed with the rising energy of the burst drive, and Maja sat down again abruptly.

"The Chron ship is making for the Delta Pavonis wormhole," Yuskeya said.

"We can't let them get to Nearspace," Maja said quietly, her eyes dark with concern. For someone with little spacefaring experience, my daughter was adjusting well. I felt a flush of motherly pride despite everything else that was happening.

"We can't stop them," I said, the image of the exploding *Domtaw* lending a burnt taste to the words as I spoke them. "We can't reach them in time, and we don't have the firepower."

"Maybe this other ship . . . " Yuskeya let the thought trail off.

"My enemy's enemy is my friend?" Hirin said. "Could be, but I'm not betting on it."

"I don't even like the look of that ship," Maja agreed.

A wide swath of crackling greenish-yellow light appeared between two of the spidery protrusions in the fore end of the dark ship, like electricity dancing between two Van de Graff generator spheres. The Chron ship and its pursuer were very close to the

Delta Pavonis wormhole now, and something strange was happening.

The mouth of the wormhole, normally merely a dark shadow against the darker backdrop of the void, was glowing. Glowing blue, shot through with silver, and swirling like a vortex. A cone of silver-blue light extruded from it and continued to grow, straining toward the onrushing Chron ship. It was weirdly beautiful, and utterly terrifying.

"Yuskeya," I said in a hushed voice, "are you getting all this?"

"All scans are running, Captain. Everything I can get. I've never seen anything—"

"Neither have I, and I've been flying around Nearspace a *long* time."

The Chron ship hadn't quite reached the tip of the extended wormhole mouth when the dark ship fired. A jagged bolt of energy flared out from the crackling golden mass at the front of the ship, but it shot wide and missed the Chron ship by a narrow margin.

"*Dio!*" Hirin gasped. "I don't know of *any* weapon that's safe to fire near the mouth of a wormhole."

"Rei, cut the drives," I said. "Viss, divert everything to shields. I don't know what these *bastardos*—"

I didn't get to finish the sentence. A burst of speed from the dark ship made it bound closer to its quarry just as the Chron ship flew without hesitation into the silvery, beckoning tip of the reconfigured wormhole.

The dark ship fired again, golden fire blazing from the fore end directly into the wormhole and its disappearing prey.

It was instinct. I squeezed my eyes shut as the world exploded in a bright fire that seemed certain to engulf us all. So I didn't get to see what happens when you fire an energy weapon into a wormhole. I didn't have time to worry about it, though, because for the next little while, I knew nothing but darkness.

I CAME TO, lying ignominiously on the floor beside the big chair, Yuskeya checking my pulse, and Hirin hovering worriedly over me. It took me a moment to orient myself, and I took in some little details as I did. Yuskeya's hair and shipsuit had been tugged askew, and an angry purple bruise welled up on Hirin's cheek.

I struggled to sit up. Yuskeya pushed me down gently, shaking her head.

"*Kia . . . inferna?* What happened, Hirin?"

"The explosion—we were all out for a minute or two." He touched his cheek. "Ship got thoroughly tossed around."

"Everybody all right?"

Yuskeya patted my arm. "Everyone's fine, Captain, aside from some bumps and bruises. You're the last to wake up, that's all. And you've got a burn on your hand. I'm going to get some salve for that."

That's all? That was enough. Pretty darned embarrassing, believe me. Where were my nanobioscavs, leaving me to be the last one to wake up?

"Yeah, my datapad got fried, and it burned my hand. It can wait until later. What about the ship?"

"We seem to be okay, Captain," Rei said from the pilot's board, her voice the tiniest bit shaky. "That blast knocked us around a bit, but I don't see anything serious."

I waved away Yuskeya's ministrations, took Hirin's outstretched hand, and got to my feet. "Viss?"

"Accounted for, Captain. Can't find anything to worry about, except that it'll take even longer to get the main drive online now." He sounded aggrieved.

I surveyed the bridge. It looked like a room might appear after a mild earthquake—things dislodged and shaken around, but not too much damage. Maja gave me a watery smile as she pulled her chair into place next to Baden's. Cerevare was straightening her sash, her ears laid back close to her head, a sure sign of dismay. Rei's shipsuit had a long tear in one sleeve. Baden winked at me, apparently unscathed. My wrecked datapad had ended up on the floor again.

The screens we'd been watching had blanked, but began to flicker to life as I turned my attention toward them.

"*Captain.*" It was only a whisper, and then Cerevare cleared her throat and tried again. "Captain . . . the wormhole."

As one we turned. The wormhole was in its third incarnation of the day. At first it had been dark, unremarkable, normal. Then swirling with blue and silver, stretching a cone of dancing light toward the Chron ship. Now it was . . . I don't know what it was.

The wormhole had been transformed into a sullen red eye of energy, seething and churning internally as it hung in space. Erratic sparks of light flared in its depths and burned out like wind-tossed embers blown from a galactic bonfire. There was no trace of either the Chron ship or its dark and spidery pursuer.

"That," Baden said, trying to sound flippant and failing miserably, "does not look good."

I couldn't think about what it meant, yet. Other things had to come first. "What about the other Protectorate ship—the *Stillwell*?"

"It's there," Yuskeya said after a moment. "Doesn't seem to have moved. No readings from its drives."

"No response on the comm," Baden reported.

"Set a course for it, Rei," I ordered, easing into my chair. My head was filled with an unfamiliar pounding sensation, and I wasn't a hundred percent sure I could count on my balance. "But don't push the ship any more than Viss approves."

Hirin crossed to me and knelt beside the chair, his blue-grey eyes searching mine. "Are you all right, Luta?"

I closed my eyes briefly. "I'm not sure. I think so." I met his gaze, and he crinkled his eyes at me, something he'd always done in situations where a smile wasn't appropriate but he wanted to telegraph me some encouragement. I winked in return, willing myself not to cry. My throat felt tight and cramped, a hot welling burning behind my eyes.

What is wrong with me? I never had trouble dealing with a crisis, and I'd been through lots for practice.

"Captain, you'd better look at this," Baden said suddenly.

I turned from Hirin and back to my duty. "What is it?"

"Readings from the *Stillwell*," he said, "or rather, a lack of readings from them. Still nothing on the comm. Now I see that the messages have been—well, bouncing off the ship and reflecting into space. They're not responding because they're not getting anything from us."

"Rei, are we close enough for a visual yet?"

"Yes," she answered, and the Protectorate ship winked into

existence on one of the screens. I was glad to have one less view of the ravaged wormhole.

But not for long. "What's wrong with it?"

Yuskeya frowned at the screen. "There's something . . . well, you can see it, sort of. It's like an envelope around the ship. It's an energy field, and a solid one. The ship is completely encased inside it. My scans are bouncing off, like Baden's comm signals."

A shimmering dark shroud wrapped the Dragon-class ship. The vessel's outline was barely visible inside the field. It lay dead in the inky vacuum, adrift in the sea of stars. No signals came from it, and apparently none could get through to it, either.

I swallowed hard. "How big a crew on a Dragon-class, Yuskeya?"

She was silent, thinking, or not wanting to say the words. "Upwards of two hundred."

"They may still be fine in there." It didn't sound plausible to me, but I had to say it.

"Yes, Ma'am."

"Can you get anything on the energy field? Any ideas on how we might be able to disperse it?"

"I'm trying, but the scans aren't picking up anything useful. It's not comparable to anything we know."

"Cerevare, does this seem like anything associated with the Chron?"

The Lobor shook her head, her composure regained. "I'm sorry, Captain, but no."

"Well, I'm damned well not going to fire on it," I muttered under my breath. "With our luck, it would pass right through the field and hit the ship."

Hirin nodded. "We don't know enough yet."

"Okay, one more thing. What about the moon—the artifact moon. Did we scan it for anyone from the *Domtaw*?"

Yuskeya didn't answer right away, staring intently at the datascreen as her fingers skimmed the controls. Finally she said, "No, the emissions it was sending into the wormhole blocked the scans. But . . . they seem to have stopped now. The moon's gone quiet again. If we were closer, we might be able to scan it now."

I ran a hand over my face wearily. "*Okej*, Rei, turn us around one more time and take us over to the moon. I can't think of anything we can do about the *Stillwell* at this point. We have to know if there's anyone still on that moon before we can think about anything else."

"On it, Captain."

I turned to Cerevare. The Lobor historian seemed composed enough, although I wasn't completely proficient at reading her wolflike features yet.

"Cerevare, you're certain the first ship was a Chron ship?"

She nodded, the gold ring in her ear glinting in the overhead lights. "Oh, yes, the configuration has changed very little since the time of the Chron war. We can't know for certain who was inside it, but the ship was definitely Chron."

"And the other one? The dark one?"

"No. It matches no configuration I've ever seen associated with the Chron."

"Or anyone else," Yuskeya added. "I've got a pretty thorough knowledge of the Nearspace registry, and that didn't seem familiar at all. I'm running a database check, but I think it will draw a blank."

I thought so, too. I'd never seen or heard of anything remotely like that ship. I shivered, remembering. It had felt almost . . . malevolent. The last things I'd expected to find on this side of the new wormhole were a resurrected enemy and a mysterious new type of spacecraft. And who—or what—had been piloting it?

"Where's the pirate?" Rei asked suddenly.

"Last I saw, he was hightailing it for the other side of the planet," Hirin said. "So maybe he's not a complete *idioto*. He had the good sense to get out of the way."

"Scan for the ship," I said. "I'd like to know where he went, because I don't want him making more trouble for us if there's someone on the moon and we have to attempt a rescue mission."

It didn't take long to find him. He'd made it only partway around the planet when the unknown ship must have taken notice of him. His ship hung in space, drifting lazily, partially obscured by something similar to the field that enveloped the *Stillwell*. They must have taken only a passing shot at the smaller ship, however, or perhaps they weren't close enough. While the aft end of the hull was encased in the same shadowy grip as the Protectorate ship, the nose and perhaps half the body of this one were clear.

"I wonder why that ship didn't shoot this stuff at us, whatever it is," mused Hirin.

"Just lucky, I think," Baden said. "By the time they got close to us, the Chron ship was almost in the wormhole. All their attention was focused on it."

"I hope our luck holds, then," Hirin said. "And I wonder if anyone's alive in there?"

"One way to find out. Let's comm him, Baden," I said. "If he answers, we might get some clues about the *Stillwell*, too."

A moment later Baden nodded, and I signalled him to put the message on the ship's comm. This time the voice was not disguised. It was disgruntled, defensive, and surprisingly, *female*.

"I suppose you're here to gloat, Captain."

"Not at all," I told her. "I am here to check on your status. Obviously you have some power, if your comm board is operational. Are you hurt?"

"No," she said sullenly. "But I have no drives or weapons. Life support is fine."

Yuskeya caught my eye and nodded.

"Our scans confirm that. How are you for supplies?"

A momentary silence. Then, "You're going to leave me here?" she asked, her voice tinged with disbelief.

I tried to keep the smile out of my voice. "Temporarily, yes. It's a more effective prison than anything I could come up with aboard my own ship, and while you're there, you're not causing any trouble for me, my crew, or anyone else."

"What's wrong with my ship?"

"I don't know. Whoever was in that dark ship used some kind of energy field on you and on one of the Protectorate ships. We can see it as a dark globe that surrounds the aft half of your ship. Can you move around your entire ship, or does the field block you from going aft?"

"I'm blocked," she said after a pause. "It's like the ship is cut in half. There's a dark, sort of hazy 'wall' that feels solid to touch, although I can sort of see through it. Was there some sort of explosion? I got thrown into the wall when it happened. It's solid, trust me."

I exchanged a glance with Hirin. He shrugged.

"The dark ship also appears to have blown up the wormhole to Delta Pavonis," I said.

"What the—how do you 'blow up' a wormhole?"

I swallowed. "I have to admit, I don't know. We'll keep an eye on it and see what else we can find out. It doesn't appear to be traversable at this point."

She was silent, apparently digesting that news.

"Don't get blown up, yourselves," she said in a tight, bitter voice. "I appear to be dependent on you to rescue me *eventually*."

"All right. We'll monitor you, and if your other systems seem in danger of shutting down then we'll come and get you. You can signal us if you encounter any difficulty. Oh, one more thing. Do you wish to tell me your name?"

There was silence for another minute, so long I thought she wasn't going to answer. Then, "Sord. Jahelia Sord."

"Very well, Jahelia Sord. I'll be in touch." I signalled Baden to cut the communication. He was frowning, but did so. "Baden, first chance you get, run the name Jahelia Sord through the pilot registry database, would you?"

"Aye, Captain."

"What is it?"

He was frowning at the comm board. "I'm not sure—that voice. It sounds familiar."

I cocked an eyebrow. "You know this person?"

He met my eyes, his face puzzled. "Maybe I'm crazy. I can't really place it . . . it seems like I've heard it before."

"But you don't recognize the name?"

"No, and it's unusual enough that I'd remember it. Never mind. I must be mixed up."

Maja reached over and patted his cheek. "That's because he's forgotten all the other women now, Mother."

I was pleased to see Baden, for once in his life, flush.

Rei rescued him by turning to me. "Captain, I'd never have suspected that mean streak in you. Leaving that poor pirate girl on her ship."

I laughed. "It's not mean. It's exactly what I said to her—practical. What facilities do I have here to restrain a PrimeCorp operative, even if she's not the most effective one they've ever employed? And honestly, if I were to meet her right now, I probably wouldn't be able to restrain myself from taking a swing at her. She threatened my mother—or relayed PrimeCorp's threats, at least. I won't let her die out there if I can help it, but I'm not taking unnecessary risks for her, either. And," I added, "if she's alive and unharmed by that field, then maybe that means the folks on the *Stillwell* are okay, too. So I'm feeling magnanimous."

"I guess it all depends on how you look at it," Rei said. "Seems a little like torture to me."

"Maybe you've never seen her really angry," Hirin joked. He made a horrified face and shook his head, warding off an imaginary evil with outstretched hands.

"Okay, let's quit joking around," I said. While it felt good to laugh, the situation hadn't become any less serious. "We still have some scientists to save. Or at least I hope we do. Rei, take us over to the operant moon and make a slow orbit while Yuskeya checks to see if the scans can get through yet."

Because if anyone was down there, they were all that remained of the *Domtaw*.

Chapter 13 — Jahelia
Alone in the Dark

"*FEK!*" I SCREAMED, as soon as the communication line to the *Tane Ikai* closed. I turned and pitched my half-empty mug of *cazitta* against the dark barrier behind me. It shattered and splattered as satisfyingly as if I'd hurled it against a cement wall. Bits of ceramic skittered across the floor amid dark, sticky droplets.

"How dare she? How *dare* she leave me here?" The feed from one of my few working scanners showed the other ship slowly turning and heading away from me. Off to investigate the wormhole, I supposed. Somehow that was more important than getting me off my disabled ship. I stood up and kicked the skimchair, but it didn't move since I'd locked it down earlier. That made me angrier.

I paced the confines of the cabin like a caged beast. With the area of the ship effectively reduced to half, it did not make for therapeutic pacing. I fetched up in the tiny galley and leaned my balled fists on the counter top, forcing my breathing to slow. That *megero* Luta Paixon might have left me here to wait until it was *convenient* for her to rescue me, but I would not let her see that I cared.

Once again, I ran my hands all over the dark field cutting me off from the rest of my ship, searching for a way to remove it. It felt completely solid, faintly cold but not chill. It couldn't be solid as I understood the word—it hadn't actually chopped the *Hunter's Hope* in two—but it didn't have any characteristics of a simple field, either. No hum of energy under my fingertips, no sound, no yield under pressure. No obvious seam where it met the interior wall. Nothing, nothing. Nothing.

I couldn't help myself. I slammed my fist into it and screamed again.

All I got was a sore hand.

More pacing, more cursing, more deep breathing. I missed Pita—more than I ever would have thought. My first priority had to be resurrecting her. The *Tane Ikai* would return for me at some point. Captain Paixon had said so, and I believed her—unless she got killed doing something stupid around the wormhole. I put that thought away and surveyed the small part of my ship that I could still access. The pilot's console, the forward hatch, the tiny kitchen console.

Cazitta still trickled, impossibly, down the dark field as if it were a solid wall. With a sigh, I knelt to carefully gather the pieces of my shattered mug, and used a cloth to sop up spilled, lukewarm liquid.

Wait. I paused with the damp cloth halfway down the field wall. The kitchen console was a self-contained unit. It might still have power.

I tossed the broken bits of ceramic into the recycler and pulled off the access panel below the kitchen station. It wasn't difficult to trace wires and routing until I found an auxiliary power source. A tiny indicator glowed a cheery green. I sat back on my heels and smiled. If I could change the routing, patch some connections . . . I might be able to revive Pita. It wouldn't be even close to enough power to get the entire ship online, but it might be enough for her.

Half an hour later, a single screen on the pilot's console flickered to life. I heaved a sigh and crossed my fingers. "Pita?"

"What have you done to my ship, Sord?" Pita asked in a cranky voice. "We're adrift, and I can't get the engines online!"

I leaned back in the single pilot's chair. "Calm down, I know all that. I had to pull half the guts out and rewire them, to power you on."

"I've been offline for over an hour!" she said. She must have been checking all the shipsystems. "Did you do this?" she asked suspiciously.

"Of course not, I—"

"No, wait, what about those other ships? The Chron, and the other one—"

"Don't make me sorry I turned you back on. Shut up and listen." Briefly I outlined what had happened, my conversation with Luta Paixon, and where we were at the moment. "So I need to make a plan. Either for getting us mobile again, or for when she comes to pick me up."

"You'll abandon the ship?"

"I don't want to." It pained me to think of leaving the *Hunter's Hope*. PrimeCorp had paid for it, sure, but it was mine. My freedom, my lifeline, my ticket to wherever I wanted to go. Even with pain-in-the-ass Pita, it was my sidekick. Without it, I'd be alone again.

"What about me?" It was hard not to think of Pita as another person when she could infuse such a sense of betrayal and indignation into three little words.

"That's why I worked so hard to wake you up. I need you. If you can get rid of this field or bypass it to get the ship moving, we'll get out of here before Paixon comes back. But if not, then I want a way to take you with me."

"I'm flattered," Pita said. "All right, let me see this field, first."

So we did, for the better part of an hour. I even shut down the heat for a little while to give Pita access to some extra power for scanners, but by the time I had started to shiver, she declared it a pointless exercise, anyway.

"I don't know what it is, what it's made of, or what it's supposed to do," she said finally, in the tone of someone who'd just thrown her hands in the air.

I hugged myself, trying to get warm. "All right, then, I guess we're on to alternate plan B. How do I take you with me?"

"Do we have options?"

"Well, I can't get to my sleeping quarters, so I'm limited to what I have here with me right now, including clothes and personal items. I have my datapad, and I can access everything as far as the kitchen console." I had my *vazel*, leaning in the corner near the kitchen, but I doubted they'd let me bring a six-foot wooden staff with me. I also had a small flechette pistol, which I might try to sneak aboard the *Tane Ikai*, but that was irrelevant to this conversation.

"Your datapad is the only way I can see," she said after a minute. "But we'll have to make some modifications. I'm rather . . . large."

Pita *was* rather large—larger, now, than even PrimeCorp knew. While I'd been ensconced at PrimeCorp, letting them read my brain to create Pita, I hadn't been exactly idle. Pita and I had walked out of the labs with a lot of PrimeCorp data—a lot of *classified* PrimeCorp data—far more than she'd been trusted with by the corporation itself.

What can I say? Breaking into the classified files was a good task to test her loyalty to me. And it never hurts to have an ace up your sleeve, even if I still hadn't had a chance to discover half of what comprised my particular ace. Getting the files had been easier than I'd expected. My own techdog tendencies and three years of AI training at the Protectorate *akademio*, plus Pita's extensive and wide-ranging skills (never meant to be used against her makers, but I guess they should have thought of that possibility, shouldn't they?) made it almost laughably easy. The encryptions on individual files were daunting, but trying to break them gave Pita something to do in her downtime.

I was damn glad she had a wide knowledge base to dip into right now, at any rate.

We began to hash out a plan. I couldn't keep the ship, perhaps, but I could take parts of it with me. The datachips from the main computer console and the kitchen console. The transmitter to send messages to PrimeCorp. A few select bits of other hardware that might come in handy.

Humming a little to myself, in between arguing with Pita, I started to take apart the brains of the *Hunter's Hope*.

Chapter 14 — Luta
Rocks and Hard Places

THE BRIDGE OF the *Tane Ikai* was unusually silent as we made our way around to the operant moon. None of us, it seemed, could keep our eyes off the screen displaying the roiling wormhole.

It was a relief when we got close enough and Rei switched the view on the pilot's board over to the main screen so the rest of us could see it, too. The moon seemed unperturbed by the chaos that had erupted around it a few short minutes ago, and still hung, rotating slowly, like a golden ornament.

"Anything?" I asked Yuskeya.

After a moment's pause, she said, "The scans of the moon are working now."

"And?" My voice was tight.

"There's someone still down there."

"How many?"

"I read three."

Three survivors. From a ship of a hundred and seventy-five. I felt sick, and it was nothing my nanobioscavengers could fix.

"Then let's get down there and get them," Baden said.

I nodded. "We'll pinpoint them as closely as possible and set down. Baden, you take care of that, please. They could be in their shuttle or somewhere on the surface. They might be in bad shape after that blast—look what it did to us—so Yuskeya, I want you to take a full complement of med supplies. And why don't you change into your Protectorate uniform?"

She raised her eyebrows. "What? Why?"

"Whoever's down there on the moon, now, I'm guessing you're technically in charge of them. You're the only Protectorate officer we seem to have functioning in this system—whatever it is."

Yuskeya nodded briefly and left the navigation board to Maja. She was only a novice, but we weren't going anywhere. She settled into the chair, glanced up and caught my eye, and nodded.

"No worries, Mother, I can definitely navigate for a ship that's about to set down."

I winked at her. "Carry on, then."

I got up from the chair and went to stand behind Rei. Hirin came over, too. "Cerevare," I said, "would you join us?" I motioned her into the empty co-pilot's seat at the board next to Rei. "Okay, ladies, what do we know about this operant moon?"

Cerevare seemed glad of something to do. Her ears perked forward as she briskly called up the data on the blank screen in front of her. "The composition of the moon alone would be the first thing to suggest it was a Chron artifact. The alloys and other materials used in its construction are identical or very similar to those used in the Chron ships we were able to study. It has a relatively weak gravity, although stronger than one might expect for an object with its mass."

"So, artificial gravity, you think?"

"Quite possibly."

Scientific data scrolled up the screen, but I wasn't really trying to read it. I'd take Cerevare's word for now.

She continued, "The rings are not the normal accretion of ice and dust and debris, but are also made of alloys particular to Chron construction. They appear to have enhanced solar-energy collecting capabilities. I'd made an educated guess that they're used to power the workings of the moon."

"Whatever those are," I said.

She grinned wolfishly and nodded. "Unknown at this time. I'm not a scientist; my knowledge comes only from the obvious data in the scans combined with what I already know about the Chron. But I do have a guess."

I raised my eyebrows, waiting.

She held up a hand. "This is only speculation, mind you. If there are scientists still on the moon with whom we can talk, they may already have information to refute my theory."

"Understood."

Cerevare turned the skimchair to face me. Her lupine face was animated, her eyes bright with excitement. "It has occurred to me—those unexplained rays that the moon began beaming into the wormhole once the Chron ship appeared to 'trigger' it. They were the same as those that affected this ship when we made the skip, correct?"

"They seemed to be."

"I wonder if they could be a mechanism related to the supposed Chron ability to 'timeslip' during the war."

I glanced at Hirin, then back to Cerevare. "I thought you said you didn't believe in that ability?"

She shrugged. "Not in time-travel precisely, but they had some ability that allowed them to give that appearance, for certain. Whatever it was that they could do, I think it's possible that the clues to it lie in this moon."

Hirin blew out a long breath. "Well, that would certainly explain why the Protectorate wanted to keep this as quiet as possible."

"That technology, if it existed, would be extremely valuable."

"Too valuable to let one corporation lay claim to it, that's for certain," I said, thinking of how much PrimeCorp would love to get its greedy, exclusive hands on something like that.

Rei pursed her lips. "So if the technology wasn't on their ships, if it were on a device—like a constructed moon—operating on the other side of the wormhole in question . . ."

"Exactly. There would be nothing for an enemy to find and turn to use against them."

"Clever," Hirin said.

"If you're right," I mused, "then we'd finally have at least one answer to all the questions the Chron left behind them."

Cerevare sighed. "It would be nice to have something new, after all this time."

"Captain, we have them," Baden said suddenly.

"What?"

"The *Domtaw* crew members. The scientists." He turned to me with wide eyes. "I think they're *inside* the moon."

HIRIN AND I had a polite debate about who was going EVA to find the folks from the *Domtaw*. He thought he should go, and I should stay on board. Predictably, I thought the opposite. He said stuff about it being important for me to stay in charge on the *Tane Ikai*, and I said things about him working his way up slowly to that kind of activity, after his years-long sidelining for health reasons. He protested that he was fine—better than fine. I asserted that the crew were equally comfortable with either of us in the big chair.

We had the debate in my quarters—well, *our* quarters again now—while I changed my clothes. I didn't want the crew observing any marital or command-centered spats.

In the end I had to do the thing I'd tried to avoid. "Well," I said, putting my hands on his shoulders and holding his gaze, "it comes down to this. I am the current Captain of record of this vessel, and I am asking you to take the chair while I'm not on board."

I didn't say *ordering*. That would have brought everything between us to a head, and that would have to wait.

He stiffened anyway, his muscles going taut under my hands. "Well, if that's how you put it."

I slid my hands down and wrapped my arms around his chest, resting my head against it. "Hirin, I just got you back. I don't want you taking risks. It's too soon, and you're still regaining your strength. I know you're feeling great, but—I need a little longer."

For an anxious moment I didn't think he'd relent, but then he hugged me, hard. "Mostly the same reasons I don't want you to go."

"I know." I pulled away. "But I think the crew needs to see that

I'm handling things, you know? This situation—"

He nodded. "—is bad. I'm trying not to think about it, but we'll have to, soon."

"Agreed. But first we have to see if there's anyone on that moon that we can save. And I think it's good for the crew to have this to focus on."

He kissed me then, and that was the end of the argument. At least for that round.

I thumbed my implant to open the ship's comm. "Rei, take us down to the moon. Yuskeya and Baden are with me."

I met Yuskeya and Baden at the rear airlock, and we climbed into our EVA suits. Yuskeya had done as I'd asked and changed into her Protectorate uniform. The rows of coloured starburst pins, from pale blue Dark Cadet through the ranks to her silver Commander's insignia, gleamed at her throat. They were visible through the clear section of the suit where the helmet and neckline met, for which I was glad. I didn't know who the *Domtaw* survivors might be, their rank or position, or what they might think of our arrival. Or if they had any notion of what had happened to their ship. But Yuskeya in her uniform radiated an extra air of confidence and competence that I was happy to have beside me.

We loaded three extra EVA suits and Yuskeya's medical supplies onto one of the anti-grav cargo sleds, and cycled through the airlock. Rei had set the *Tane Ikai* down close to the shuttle that had brought the scientists over from the *Domtaw*. Once we were close enough, it hadn't been difficult to find them. Their shuttle crouched near the doorway to what resembled a sod house from Earth's ancient history, built right into a rise in the surface of the moon. The Chron hadn't simply built an artificial sphere. They'd taken the trouble to create the illusion of a real moon, with uneven surface topography and a convincing layer of regolith. Only scans or close inspection would reveal the operant moon's true nature.

"I don't think we have the technology to build something like this even now," Baden observed, his voice tinny and small over the suit-to-suit comm.

"We might have the tech, but I can't imagine the cost,"

Yuskeya said.

"I hope the door isn't locked," I said as we paced carefully across the surface.

"And me without my lockpicks." Baden's voice held a grin, even over the comm. He hadn't had a good adventure since our encounter with the PrimeCorp agent who'd tried to take out the *Tane Ikai* in the Keridre/Gerdrice system, all of six weeks ago.

Yuskeya was silent as we made our way to the doorway. The moon's gravity was enough to keep us on the ground, but I wouldn't have wanted to try bouncing on a trampoline. Our tether to the surface felt as tenuous as a spider's web. I hoped it was comparably strong.

It wasn't locked, and opened into a tiny foyer, the walls formed from something similar to plasteel. Beyond that was a transparent door leading to what appeared to be a fairly standard kind of airlock system. A control touchpad lay embedded in the wall to the right of the door, labelled with symbols that meant nothing to me. A sort of frosted panel above the door emitted a pale light, limning the foyer with enough light to see, but it wouldn't shine beyond the entry.

"Cerevare?" I said. We had full video and audio link to the bridge of the *Tane Ikai*, where the others watched us and waited.

"Here, Captain."

"Can you see these symbols? Any idea what they might mean or how we can operate this door?"

She was silent, studying the symbols through my video link. "Yes," she said finally, "they're similar to the controls on the Chron ships. I would guess . . . Press the top button to open the door, and the bottom one to close it. Of the others, I'm not sure, but you aren't planning to remove your suits anyway, are you?"

"No, I don't think so. Thanks—I didn't want to have to blast this door open without knowing what or who is on the other side."

I stepped forward and pressed the button Cerevare had indicated, and the door slid, somewhat surprisingly, down into the floor. There was no rush of air escaping as it did, so I assumed the scientists hadn't bothered with trying to figure out the Chron pressurization system, either, or didn't trust it. Or maybe it wasn't working. Whatever, it probably meant that they were still wearing EVA suits, which was good. We might have brought our extras along for nothing, but at least we wouldn't have to struggle them into the suits if they were wounded or unconscious.

I examined the area once we'd passed into the airlock and found the buttons to close the door behind us. It slid up into place smoothly. At the next door I followed the same procedure.

Which put us inside what I suppose you would call the moon proper. A corridor stretched out before us, the walls forming a rough octagon shape. It snaked down and to the left about twenty feet ahead. The sides were smooth, not worked stone, but something like a plasteel alloy in a pale camel-colour. I put a gloved hand against it, but couldn't feel any particular heat or cold, at least through my glove. Apart from that, there was nothing remarkable to see, so we continued cautiously down its length.

"There *is* an atmosphere," Yuskeya said, her head bent over her datapad. "The mix is similar enough to Earth's to be breathable, and the pressure is within what we'd find comfortable."

We'd advanced down the corridor perhaps ten meters when I heard something. It sounded like voices, further ahead.

"*Ha lo!*" I called through the suit's external speaker, the sound echoing weirdly in the oddly-shaped corridor. "Do you need assistance?"

I knew they did, whether they knew it or not, but I always try to be polite when I'm rescuing folks. It was entirely possible they didn't know yet what had happened to the *Domtaw*.

"Yes! We're down here!" Even at a distance and through the suit's microphone, I could hear a note of desperation in the voice.

"On our way!"

We followed the corridor perhaps another thirty meters before we found them. It continued to curve gradually, and slope further down toward the core of the moon. The corridor itself remained unremarkable, the smooth walls giving way occasionally to an alcove that served no apparent purpose.

Finally it opened up into a large room, well-lit by panels in the ceiling that seemed to glow from within. Strange markings, presumably Chron writing, lined the walls. Three men waited inside the room. They wore standard EVA suits with the Nearspace Protectorate emblem over the heart. One lay supine on the floor while another knelt beside him. The third sat propped against the far wall.

The kneeling man leaned over his comrade and said loudly, "See, Antixo, I told you the Admiral would not abandon us. We'll get you out of here." He got to his feet, turning to face us. Five small coloured starbursts on his helmet—blue, white, yellow, orange, and red—told me he was a Protectorate Lieutenant. Through the visor on his helmet I had the impression of close-cropped dark hair and smooth olive skin. Concern pinched his face, hardening his features, and his brown eyes were troubled. He paused, noticing, I supposed, the absence of the Protectorate emblem on our own suits.

"You are from the *Domtaw?*" It was half-statement, half-question.

Yuskeya stepped forward, so that he could see the seven commander's starburst pins on her uniform. "No, but we are here to help you," she said. "I'm Commander Blue, of the Nearspace Protectorate vessel *S. Cheswick*, on special assignment to another ship at the moment. Are you all right?"

The man had saluted and relaxed visibly when he saw Yuskeya's insignia. "I am, Commander. Lieutenant Gerazan Soto, cryptographer. My friends are not so well, however." He nodded to the man propped against the wall. "Lieutenant Chen was taking readings on that wall when something in the moon activated. It knocked him out. Wing Officer Antixo—he's a molecular engineer—was just outside the door, going to get a medkit out of the shuttle, when some sort of shockwave hit us. I dragged him in here, but . . ."

Yuskeya pulled two datameds out of the supplies she'd brought, handed one to Baden, and crossed to the man on the floor.

I stuck a hand out to Soto, who stood watching as the others assessed his friends. "Captain Luta Paixon, of the far trader *Tane Ikai*," I said. "Only the three of you here?"

He nodded. "We lost contact with the *Domtaw* a little while before Chen was injured. Some things in the room seemed to activate—I don't know if it was something we did or not. We lost communications, anyway. Do you know what's happened?"

I took his arm gently and led him away from the wounded men, over to the doorway. "Lieutenant Soto—Gerazan—I'm sorry to have to tell you this, but the *Domtaw* is gone."

He frowned. "Gone? No, they would never leave us here—"

"No, they wouldn't, of course not. A Chron ship came through the other wormhole—"

"A *Chron* ship?" he interrupted. "That's impossible!"

I put a hand on his arm. "I know it's a shock. We have a historian on board, a Chron expert, and she identified it positively. Another ship followed it, apparently in pursuit. The Chron triggered the moon to start emitting a type of cosmic ray; that's probably what happened to Lieutenant Chen. He must have been touching something and been affected by it. Then— well, there was a battle, and the *Domtaw* was destroyed. That was probably the explosion that injured Antixo. I'm sorry."

He didn't say anything right away. "What about the *Stillwell*— the other Protectorate ship?"

I sighed. "It's still out there, but there's an energy field around it that's blocking all signals. We can't scan past it, and I don't know if they can get a signal out, either. Their status is . . . unknown."

"Where's the ship the Commander mentioned—the *Cheswick*?" I could tell he was grasping, hoping that somewhere in this tale of tragedy there was some glimmer of good news.

"Commander Blue is currently a member of my crew, Lieutenant. My brother, Lanar Mahane, is the commanding officer of the *Cheswick*, and Commander Blue has been on—a special assignment with me for a while." I sighed. "We're all you've got, I'm afraid, but there's room on my ship for you."

He forced a grim smile that didn't reach his eyes. "Then I'm grateful you're here, Captain. But I don't know if we should tell the others all this. I can hardly take it all in, and they're not in the best shape."

And I haven't even told him about the wormhole, I thought. *I'm not even thinking about that myself yet.*

I caught Yuskeya's eye, and she shook her head, just

perceptibly. The man on the floor wasn't going to make it. But the other man seemed to be conversing, albeit haltingly, with Baden, so there might be hope for him.

"Shall we try and get everyone over to the *Tane Ikai*, then?" I asked. Lieutenant Soto obviously felt responsible for the men here, and was doing his best to keep himself together. It wasn't for me to start ordering him around.

He nodded. "If it's safe, I'd like to get us off this thing," he said.

I have to say, I felt the same way.

Chapter 15 — Luta
Council of War

ANTIXO DIED ON the way to the *Tane Ikai*. I don't think his fellow scientists were very surprised. The man who'd been knocked out, Chen, seemed to fluctuate. He'd seem fine, able to talk, if slowly, then would lapse into a trancelike state, staring straight ahead or dropping suddenly asleep like a narcoleptic. Yuskeya insisted that we immediately install him in the First Aid station, close to the bridge so that she could monitor him, and let him get some rest.

"Crew meeting on the bridge," I said, once we were safely on board, "in fifteen minutes. Lieutenant Soto, please join us." Then I went to change my clothes, which I admit took only about five minutes. The other ten I took to sit on the side of my bed and compose my thoughts. It would actually have taken a lot longer than that, but our situation had to be discussed and I didn't feel like putting it off any longer. Everything requiring immediate attention had been seen to, and now we needed to take stock.

When I stood up to go to the bridge, another wave of nausea hit me, and I sat down heavily on the bed. I put my head down between my knees and waited for it to pass, but the pounding of blood in my temples seemed to make it worse. I covered my face with my hands, found it sweating and clammy. *Why is this happening?* I'd never been sick a day in my life, or at least not since I was twelve or thirteen and my mother had injected me with the nanobioscavengers that would prolong my life almost indefinitely. They also promptly took care of colds, headaches, nausea, respiratory infections, broken bones—anything and everything that could hinder my health. Whatever was wrong now, I wasn't used to it and I didn't like it.

A knock sounded at the door, and I had barely time to sit up before it swung open and Hirin stuck his head in.

"You okay?"

I forced a smile and nodded, grabbing a towel off the back of my chair and swiping my face. "Sure, just freshened up. I'm coming now."

Hirin shot a quizzical glance in my direction, but I ignored it. I'd talk to Yuskeya later, and get her to run some scans. My original idea, to talk to Hirin, didn't seem so attractive now. Not since he'd been upset at the prospect of my jaunt on the moon for the rescue mission. He'd obviously only worry, and I was sure he'd done enough of that during the ten years he was sick and confined to a nursing home Earthside, while I continued to work the trade routes to pay for his care.

He handed me a datapad. "Baden sends you this. Says it's pretty basic, but if you have a backup of yours, he'll restore it for you later."

I turned it over in my hands. It was newer than mine had been. "We had this in ship's stores?"

"No, I think it's an old one of his. You know Baden; nothing but the newest and best."

"That's him." I almost smiled. The weight of the datapad in my hand was a small reminder that at least some things were easily fixed.

Not everything would be so simply dealt with, unfortunately.

The crew, Cerevare, and Gerazan had gathered on the bridge by the time we got there, but the murmur of conversation ceased when Hirin and I entered. Baden and Maja sat together at the comm board. Viss and Yuskeya were on opposite sides of the bridge. Cerevare had her feet tucked up on a skimchair as usual, and Gerazan Soto was in the co-pilot's chair near Rei. Rei threw me a wink of encouragement when I entered. I bypassed the captain's chair and went to stand on the right, near the airlock doors, where everyone could see me and I could see them all.

"Folks," I said, "we usually have this sort of gathering in the galley, but I don't want to leave the bridge unattended even if we're on solid ground. I'll come straight to the point. We are in big trouble here."

Yuskeya nodded. "I've started mapping this system, using all the data in this scan range as a base point."

"Thanks, Yuskeya. I want everyone else running all the scans you have at your stations as well. Since this is an uncharted system, we have no navigation data on file for it. We need to chart every iota of information as we get it, so that we can find our way around."

Gerazan Soto frowned in puzzlement. "Sorry to interrupt so soon, Captain, but won't we head back through the wormhole to Delta Pavonis?"

I sighed. "I'm sorry again, Gerazan, but there's more bad news. You haven't been in a position to see it yet, but the wormhole was hit by some sort of energy weapon from that unknown ship I mentioned. Rei, would you put it on the main screen?"

The screen flickered from its static view of the scientists' shuttle craft and the opening into the depths of the moon. Now the wormhole lay at its center, a glowering red eye against the dark starfield, whirling in a malefic storm of uncontrolled fire.

"I don't think the wormhole is a viable option."

"*Sankta merde,*" he breathed. "But we don't know how long it might stay like that," he said. He'd gone very pale as he stared at what was our only known route home.

"You're right, we don't, and I'm willing to watch it for a bit to see what happens. We can try sending a comm signal through it, see if we get any response, although I don't have much hope there. We can try approaching it with the skip drive running and see what happens, but I don't relish the thought of diving into it in that state."

I clasped my hands behind my back. "We have to consider our options if it doesn't right itself quickly. We're in an unknown system. We don't know what resources, if any, are available. The only operating wormhole nearby leads to somewhere unknown, and all the data we have on it—namely the ships that came through it—suggest that the place it leads to is not a friendly one. We need ideas, *miaj amikoj*."

The crew seemed to take a collective deep sigh. "Well, let's start with the system we're in," Viss said. "Can we figure out, from the data available, what system it might be?"

Yuskeya answered, her eyes on me, not him. "The computer is running through the database now, but it will most likely only come up with a list of possibilities based on the type of the nearest star. There are countless systems that we have no data for. A definitive answer is unlikely."

"Even if we could identify the system, it probably won't do us any good," Rei said. "The star is a B-Type, so it's not likely there are any planets in this system capable of supporting life, carbon-based at least; too much ultraviolet to be healthy to stay here for long. We can search the database for explored wormholes leading to B star systems—I'm sure there are a few—and if this turns out to be one of them, then we're home free *if* we can find the wormhole terminal on this end." She sighed. "But I don't think it's very likely."

It wasn't like Rei to sound so pessimistic, and I looked at her sharply, wondering if her melancholy were returning. Gerazan's face was set and solemn, but he nodded in agreement.

"What about the scans we ran for Cerevare before the *problemos* began," I asked. "Did we—how shall I put this—pick up any extra data along the way?"

Baden grinned. "We might have piggybacked a little, at that, Captain. Besides the composition, mass, atmospheric mix, gravity, and all that essential data about the moon, and the fact that it's about seventy-five percent solid, we learned a few other things. There's no sign that the planet nearby is inhabited; in fact, as Rei says, it shouldn't be able to support life as we know it. No other life signs on the moon apart from the folks from the *Domtaw*, and nothing that appeared to be a weapon, Chron or otherwise. The other two moons appear to be natural bodies, but are too tiny to support an atmosphere."

Gerazan gaped at Baden's recitation. I thought he might need a distraction.

"Gerazan, would you care to share what you've been able to learn?"

"Uh—sure, Captain." He blinked and focused on me, and his bearing changed, getting ready to report. "We were in orbit for about twenty-four hours, taking scans and readings, before the Admiral authorized us to start studying the moon on-site. We concluded that the artifact was definitely of Chron construction; we made comparisons to all the Chron data still on file and compiled since the time of the war. We started scanning some distance out, then gradually moved closer, into easy shuttle range. Nothing we did seemed to affect the moon in any way— until today, that is," he added bleakly.

I prodded him gently. "Were you able to learn anything yourself?"

"Not really . . . not yet." He shook his head. "We have so few of the Chron symbols to make comparisons with, and I'm not an expert to start with."

"Cerevare is," I said, nodding to the Lobor. "If the two of you work together, you might be able to come up with something interesting."

Cerevare nodded eagerly. "I would be most interested to see all the data you've collected, Lieutenant Soto."

He paled suddenly. "All of the original scan data would have been . . . lost . . . with the *Domtaw*."

I nodded. "Understood. Any other input?"

Viss spoke up. "The ship's in good shape," he said. "We don't have any worries in that department, except the burst drive. Even that might not be a problem once I can get down there and open it up."

"And I stocked up on everything before we left Mars," Maja added. "Since we weren't sure how long a mission this would be, I thought I'd better err on the side of caution. We're good for about two months, more if we ration." She'd taken on the role of *de facto* provisions officer on our trip from Kiando to Earth.

Since she'd opted to stay on board the *Tane Ikai* for a while and find out as an adult what far trading was like, I'd started her out learning the basics of running a ship, along with her navigator's training. The basics always start with the question of how to survive when supplies are not readily available. She seemed to like her new position, and now I was pleased that she'd taken it seriously.

"*Okej*, I'm glad to hear some good news," I said. "Now, what does everyone think about the second wormhole?"

"I don't relish the idea of venturing into possible Chron territory with only a load of torpedoes on board," Hirin said. I could tell he was seriously berating himself for not arming the *Tane Ikai* to the teeth when he'd had the chance, but who could have foreseen this situation?

"You couldn't know what we'd be up against," I said. "We're lucky to have what we do, and that's thanks to you."

Baden leaned back in the comm chair, arms folded. "Well, we don't know for sure that it *is* Chron territory," he said. "Two ships came through there, and it was the Chron being chased. Maybe they were interlopers, sticking their noses somewhere they didn't belong. It might not be a system under Chron control at all."

"True enough. In that case, I'm not sure I like how the other ship treated interlopers. Since they might view us the same way."

"Although we don't know what kind of history the two might have," Maja said.

"What happened to that other ship?" Cerevare asked suddenly. She'd been sitting like a statue, taking in the discussion.

Nobody answered.

"Did anyone see?" I asked.

"They either went through the Delta Pavonis wormhole after the Chron—" Rei began.

"Or were destroyed by the explosion when they fired on it," Viss finished for her.

"Or they could have gone back through the other wormhole," Baden said. "I was out for a few minutes, and I wasn't watching them when I did wake up."

"No," Maja agreed, "you were trying to rouse me. You weren't paying attention to anything outside the ship then."

Gerazan asked, "And when did they do—whatever they did—to the *Stillwell*?"

"Good question. I don't think it exploded in this vicinity, anyway," Yuskeya said. She keyed something into the nav board. "There isn't enough debris particulate to account for more than the *Domtaw*."

"Any drive signature?" Viss asked. It was the first thing I'd heard him ask Yuskeya directly since their falling-out.

She didn't look at him, but she answered. "No, I didn't get a signature reading on them while everything was happening. It doesn't *seem* that anything went back through the wormhole recently, but I can't say for sure. We don't know anything about their technology or what might be possible for them."

"But surely there'd be some trace?" Gerazan protested. His voice had thinned out and gone flat, as if the pressures of this discussion and the realization of the situation were slowly crushing him.

"Not necessarily," Rei said gently. "What if they, say, powered their ships with some sort of telepathy? That wouldn't leave any trace that we'd be aware of."

His eyes went wide. "Is that possible?"

Rei smiled. "Probably not. But that example shows how far apart we could be from the technology of another race we've never encountered before. And I think," she continued, turning to me, "that we need a break. Double caffs and sweet *kuko* all around?"

"What about rationing?" Maja asked seriously.

"I think Rei's right," I said. "One round of caff and cake isn't going to significantly affect our chances of survival. Rei, Cerevare, and Gerazan, would you head down to the galley and fix us a snack? Yuskeya, let's check on our guest in First Aid."

Yuskeya followed me into the First Aid station and raised her eyebrows when I slid the door shut behind us.

"How's he doing?" I asked her, nodding toward Chen. His breathing seemed steady enough, but his skin was pale and glistened with a sheen of sweat.

Yuskeya touched the back of her hand to his cheek and read

the monitors mounted above the bed. A frown of concern creased her forehead. "He's stable, but I can't figure out what's wrong with him—and neither can the med scanners. I can't give you a prognosis."

"Okay, let's keep a close watch on him," I said. "Now, you have another patient to deal with."

She glanced at me. "Captain? You okay?"

"Not really." I pressed my fingertips to my temples, hoping it would relieve some pressure. It didn't. "I think I have a headache, and I'm wondering if there's anything you can do about that."

She smiled a little. "You *think* you have a headache? Don't you know?"

I half-smiled in return. "In a word, no. Thanks to Mother's bioscavengers, I've never had one before—at least, not one that lasted. And to tell you the truth, I'm more than a little worried about having one now."

WHEN LANAR AND I were children, our mother worked as a genetic engineer for PrimeCorp. I didn't know it at the time, but her work involved development of nanobioscavengers that would extend the human lifespan indefinitely, similar to those that repair internal injuries and cure cancers. When she found out that PrimeCorp intended to use the technology to maintain a stranglehold on Nearspace governments, she took all her research and fled with it. My father, Lanar, and I went with her.

For a while our family lived on the run, but when I was fourteen she decided she couldn't do that to us any longer. She went underground on her own. Not before she'd injected both me and my brother (unbeknownst to us) with the current version of the bioscavs, however. Naturally, she'd tested them on herself first. And offered them to my father, but he refused—a decision I've never really understood, but had to respect.

I searched Nearspace for Mother for more than fifty years before I finally found her, and I still look thirty even though I'm over eighty. My mother was, and is, an excellent researcher.

Throughout all that time the little machines ticked over inside me, ensuring that in addition to not aging, I neither got sick nor suffered any injury for long before it healed within hours. Even childbirth was dulled from the outset, to be more of a discomfort than anything else. So a persistent headache that would not relent was something of a new experience for me, and I can't say I was enjoying it.

Although they hadn't known for long, my crew knew all these secrets about me now, so Yuskeya wasn't terribly surprised at my lack of experience with headaches. She pursed her lips.

"I have an injection that should help," she said. "As long as your little nano friends don't take it as an intruder and destroy it."

"Give it a try," I told her. "They must be taking the day off, or I wouldn't be feeling this. And—let's keep this between us for now, okay?"

"As long as it doesn't get me into trouble with Hirin," she said with a wry grin.

"If it does, I'll take full responsibility."

She injected the drug directly into my forearm implant, from whence it would be distributed through my body. As she pulled away she took my hand, turning it over to see the blisters where my overheated datapad had scorched the flesh.

"Hmmm." She frowned. "Shouldn't this be healing already?"

I inspected the burn myself. The skin remained as red and angry as it had been when it happened. My nanobioscavs seemed to be off the job in more ways than one. "I guess I'll take that salve after all."

"The injection should block the pain, and the salve will boost the healing," she said.

I nodded silently. It felt . . . weird . . . to need medical assistance. I didn't like it.

"Captain—Luta," she said as she smoothed on salve and wrapped the burns in healstrips, "I have to try and get word to the Protectorate about what's happened here."

I nodded. "I know. I've been thinking the same thing. Do you think a comm signal will make it through the wormhole? We didn't have much luck even before the . . . incident."

She shrugged. "It's worth a try. But how long can we afford to wait around and see if we get a reply?"

"How long can we wait to see if the wormhole fixes itself?" I asked in return. "We're groping in the dark here, in more ways than one. I'm trying to get people thinking, making plans, but the situation could change any minute. If another ship comes through that second wormhole—"

"I know."

"Yuskeya," I said, "do you feel that you should be in charge here? You probably have the authority to commandeer the *Tane Ikai* as a Protectorate officer in this situation."

Her eyes went wide, then she chuckled. "I probably do. But it hadn't occurred to me. You're the captain of this ship, Luta, not me. If you started doing something that I thought the Protectorate wouldn't approve of—"

"Which is probably over half the things I've done in my lifetime," I interjected.

She laughed again. "*Okej,* that I thought the Protectorate would disapprove of *in this particular situation,* I might call you on it. Mostly to cover my *azeno* when I have to make a report. But this is your crew, not a Protectorate one. I'd only have a mutiny on my hands if I tried to take over."

"I'm counting on your help to get us out of this."

"I thought you were still disgruntled that I was . . . collecting information while posing as your navigation officer."

I fixed her with a stare. "You *were* my navigation officer. Still are. And I wasn't mad at you—not really. I was more annoyed with Lanar. But I'll tell you one thing, Yuskeya. I'm glad you're here with us."

Her dark eyes twinkled. "I can't say I'm glad I'm here," she said, "since we're in deep trouble. But you can count on me, you know that."

"I do," I said. "Let's go get some *kuko* and figure a way out of this mess."

THE OTHERS WERE all on the bridge when Yuskeya and I emerged. "No change in Lieutenant Chen's condition," I told Gerazan Soto. "I'm sorry. But he is holding on."

The cryptographer nodded. His olive skin was shaded with grey, his eyes dull. The loss of the *Domtaw* was still sinking in, and he was having a hard time with it. I realized with a pang of guilt that I hadn't thought to ask him if he'd lost anyone very close on the ship.

"Lieutenant—Gerazan," I said, "would you take a little walk with me?"

He nodded automatically and followed me off the bridge. We walked down the corridor to the galley, footsteps ringing hollowly on the metal decking.

"I know this has been a terrible shock for you," I said gently.

He straightened his shoulders, and nodded. "It's a blow to the Protectorate," he said. "I'm not looking forward to filing this report."

I glanced at him. He stared straight down the corridor, but his eyes were unfocused. I led him into the galley when we got there and motioned him to a chair at the table. "What can I get you to drink?"

He sat, but said, "I don't need anything, Captain, thank you."

I sighed and pulled off a double caff for myself, steaming and creamy, and went to sit across the table from him. I closed my eyes and took a sip before I said anything else, allowing myself a few seconds to savour the smooth, rich bite of the drink on my tongue.

When I opened my eyes, his were downcast, studying the unremarkable surface of the table. I cleared my throat. "Gerazan, you lost people—friends, colleagues, maybe even family, for all I know—on the *Domtaw*. Do you need to talk about it?"

He didn't raise his head right away, but I noticed his hands, clasped before him on the tabletop, clench tighter. Finally he met my eyes. "I wasn't part of the regular crew, Captain. I'd only come aboard for this mission."

"So you weren't close to anyone on board?"

"I . . . I did have some friends." He nodded and swallowed. "They died in service of the Protectorate. They knew the risks. We all accept them."

I thought briefly about meaningless platitudes, but said only, "What about Chen and Antixo?"

"Antixo was like me, a special assignment." He glanced away. "Chen's wife was on board the *Domtaw*."

I sighed. Maybe that explained something. "If Chen comes

around, I'll tell him. It doesn't have to be you."

The Lieutenant sat a little straighter, hands clasped tightly before him on the table. "I was nominally in charge down there, Captain. Chen is my responsibility. I'll tell him about the *Domtaw*."

I didn't say *if he makes it.* I knew we were both thinking it anyway.

I took another sip of my drink. "Okay, so that brings us back to you. We're all shaken up by this, but obviously you and Chen are the hardest hit. If you need or want to talk to someone about it—"

"Thank you, Captain, but I'm fine."

I levelled a stern stare at him, catching his eyes and not letting them go. "Theoretically, I could order Commander Blue to *order* you to talk to her about it. She outranks you."

He stiffened, but he must have caught the hint of a smile I allowed through. He answered with a weak one of his own. "That won't be necessary. If I do—or when I do—I'll speak up. Thanks for your concern."

I shrugged. "It's not just about you. We're in what you might call a tight spot here, so I need everyone on board doing the best they can."

Gerazan nodded with a rueful smile. "I don't think you have much need for a cryptographer at the moment, but I was an assistant engineer for a while. I might be able to contribute something."

I stood up, taking my mug with me. At least our conversation had seemed to wake him up a little, which I hoped was a good thing. "Good to know. I'll tell Viss that if he needs a hand in engineering, you're the man. You sure you don't want a drink to take with you to the bridge?"

He glanced at the machine. "Well, maybe something cold . . ."

"Help yourself," I told him. "I'll see you in a minute."

I left him musing over his choices and returned up the corridor to the bridge.

"A bit of new of information, Captain," Baden said as soon as I emerged. "The database shows two explored wormholes that emerged in systems with Type B stars, similar to this one."

"Any chance this is one of them?"

"Doubtful, unfortunately. Judging by the configuration of planets logged for them, this one doesn't seem to match up to either."

"*Okej*," I said, "what else?"

"We're starting to get some analysis on the scan data Yuskeya recorded while the—attacks, I guess we have to call them—were happening." Baden paused. "There's a lot to go through. This is only the beginning."

I settled myself in the big chair. "Okay, what do we have so far?"

"Some of it doesn't make a whole lot of sense."

"Like the data on the second ship, for one thing," Rei said. "The spidery one."

Gerazan entered the bridge carrying a tall glass. He slipped into the co-pilot's chair beside Rei.

I smiled. "That's how I was thinking of it, too. The surface shimmered, as if it were treated with something reflective. Or maybe it was painted to project a certain look?"

"Neither." Rei sat back and crossed her arms. "The chemical composition of the hull doesn't match any metal or alloy we can identify. It's something entirely different. Which means we can't even speculate on its properties." She sounded glum. I noticed that Gerazan was listening closely. She was gazing at the screen. He was gazing at her. Interesting.

"Any readings on the weapons?" Viss asked.

Rei shook her head. "Nothing classifiable. Something that read like ultra-high energy particles. Can't be more specific."

"All right, so do we know what effect that kind of weapon would have if it were fired into a wormhole?" Gerazan asked. "Surely at some point someone has experimented with something like that? I mean, in the early days of wormhole exploration, maybe, when they were still trying to figure out if the damn things were even safe?"

"Wormholes aren't something you mess around with, Lieutenant," Viss answered. "We've never known, and still don't, what might happen to the connected systems if a wormhole collapsed or was damaged, and no-one is willing to take the risk to find out. This," and he nodded toward the malevolently swirling wormhole, "is the closest we've ever come."

"Cerevare, have you had a chance to compare our scans on the first ship—the one you identified as Chron—to your own data?" I asked. "Were you right?"

She gave me a grave nod over the top of her steaming mug. She had a sweet tooth, I'd learned, and preferred hot cocoa to drink. "They are a match, Captain."

"Not that I doubted you," I assured her with a smile, and lifted my own mug to her in salute. "Anything else new?"

"I checked the pilot registry database for the name Jahelia Sord, and it returned some interesting results," Yuskeya said. "Sord was a Protectorate candidate, one of their top student pilots, extremely competent AI tech as well. She dropped out after her third year of training at the *akademio*. Went home because of her father's ill health; he died, she never returned to training. But while she was in school, she was good. Has piloted a number of vessels since then, the latest being that little starrunner she's stuck in now, the *Hunter's Hope*. Which," she added, "now that I've been able to cross-reference the drive signatures, is registered to a dummy corporation that's linked to . . . can you guess?"

"PrimeCorp?"

She nodded. "Exactly. As for Sord, there's nothing shady on her record, but that would be easy enough for an employer like PrimeCorp to remove. And this is interesting—her great-grandfather worked at PrimeCorp years ago."

"If she's that experienced, I'd rather have her stay on her own ship as long as possible, then. They teach more than piloting at the Protectorate campus."

Yuskeya threw me a wink. "No, we come out quite—well-rounded, some of us."

I contemplated my caff, then surveyed the faces turned to me. "*Okej*, so the main question, folks, is—what do we do next?"

No-one answered right away, so I went on. "I've thought about it, and I'm willing to stay put here for up to three days and see what happens, with the Delta Pav wormhole, or otherwise. I need to get a message to my mother, so getting back to Nearspace is an urgent necessity. During that time, Viss can see to the burst drive, and we'll attempt to send a comm signal through the wormhole to see if we get a reply. We'll keep taking whatever readings we can on the moon, and keep an eye on the *Stillwell* and the other wormhole. But if nothing happens by that time, we need another plan. We can't stay here indefinitely."

"Can we investigate this system for other wormholes?" Cerevare asked.

Yuskeya said, "We can do some long-range scanning, but we aren't really equipped for wormhole hunting. We might get lucky, but the chances of us getting home that way—they're slim. Even if we found a new wormhole, who knows where it would come out?"

Hirin said, "I agree with Luta. If nothing else comes up, I don't see any other viable options besides going through the second wormhole."

I drew a deep sigh and flashed a grateful smile at my husband. Going through that unknown wormhole would likely be highly dangerous—possibly even suicidal, but I couldn't see any better options. I was glad to have his support for the plan.

"Provided," Viss added, "that scans show the wormhole to be compatible with our Krasnikov generators. It could be a different type of wormhole. If it won't work with Krasnikov matter, it might collapse in on us."

Everyone was silent, thinking.

"Comments?" I asked finally.

"I don't see any other options, either," Maja said staunchly. "Like I said, we're well set for provisions, but they won't last forever."

"Never expected I'd get to fly into Chron territory, I'll admit," Rei said, smiling grimly. "But I don't see anywhere else to go. I don't relish the idea of flying around this system indefinitely, running low on food and getting slowly fried by radiation." She shrugged elegantly, her long chestnut hair rippling over her shoulders. "Honestly, I'd rather go busting into Chron space, even if it meant getting blown to bits."

Gerazan stared at her. His earlier shellshocked expression had transformed into something like admiration. Maybe, I thought, I'd get *Rei* to talk to him about the *Domtaw*. If he wouldn't open up to me, he might to her.

No one else seemed inclined to say anything, but I didn't sense any rebellion, either.

"*Okej*. We stay here for three days, learn everything we can, and if nothing changes, take a leap into that wormhole if it's compatible with our drives." I stood and stretched. "Divide up the scanning and analysis tasks. I want someone—two someones—on the bridge the entire time. Gerazan," I said, and he tore his eyes away from Rei to face me. "From what you observed since you've been here, is it generally safe for us to stay parked on the moon while we wait?"

He nodded. "The moon's been extremely stable the entire time we've been observing it, Captain. It didn't appear to do anything at all until today."

"Good. Then that's what we'll do. We're a little less noticeable down here than we would be hanging up there in orbit."

I turned to my daughter. "Maja, work up a duty and watch schedule, would you? Gerazan has volunteered to help Viss out in engineering as needed, but I believe he and Cerevare should continue to study the inside of the moon as much as possible. The Protectorate will need any data we can get them, even more now."

She nodded.

"What about our friend Jahelia Sord?" Baden asked.

I sighed. "Right. Send her a message, see how long she has provisions for—and whether she has access to her ship's waste disposal systems. If we can leave her where she is, good. But I suppose I can't do that if it's too uncomfortable for her."

Rei grinned. "Why, Captain, you *do* have a conscience," she joked.

"Sadly, I do, and it gets me into no end of trouble." I smiled. "I'll be in my quarters if anyone wants me."

Chapter 16 — Jahelia
Echoes and Old Nightmares

THE NEXT TIME I heard from the *Tane Ikai*, they didn't even bother coming around and opening up a voice channel. Just sent a damned WaVE from over on the artificial moon.

Plan to wait three days to see if wormhole normalizes. Do you have provisions/facilities adequate for that time period?

I scowled at the screen and swore.

"What?" Pita asked, although she could have accessed the message herself. She really does work hard to seem like a fellow crew member.

I read her the message aloud.

"So, what's the problem? Three days is great! That gives us more time to try and bypass the field. Or it might go away before then, and we can get out of here under our own power."

"I know. They're just so damned arrogant. I mean, they can't even open a voice channel?"

"It's a good thing," Pita said in a soothing voice. "Sure, they're jerks. But it gives us lots of time to take what we need and get it all packed up nice and inconspicuous."

"I guess," I growled. "I'll bet Baden Methyr sent this message.

All prim and proper now that he's with his precious captain."

"Let it go, Jahelia. You want me to send an answer?"

"No, I'll do it." I typed a brief line and sent it off to the other ship with a contemptuous flick. *No issues. Thanks for your concern.*

Maybe they wouldn't get the sarcasm, but at least *I* knew it was there. "*Okej.* Let's get back to work."

I'd completely disassembled my datapad, spreading the components on the deck since I didn't have access to the little worktable in my sleeping quarters. It seemed ironic that being a techdog was a more useful survival skill than martial arts or weapons training, but so far that's how it was turning out. Pita's intricate and detailed knowledge of every circuit, chip, wire, and screw on the ship came in handy as I Frankensteined the pad. We made a good team. The pad already had some "modifications" from PrimeCorp, ones that were slightly outside the strictly legal. Sedmamin had asked me, quite seriously, if I had concerns about carrying illegal tech. I'd almost laughed in his face, considering that my body was full of tech that, while not technically illegal, I'd certainly gone to great lengths to keep secret. I simply smiled and told him that if it wasn't obvious from the outside and was reasonably code-camouflaged on the inside, I was fine with it.

"Work on the pad, or on the field?" Pita said. "If we have three days, we should have time for both."

I considered. If we could get rid of the gods-damned field, I'd show Paixon my *azeno* and take my chances in the rest of this system. Or try my luck with the other wormhole on my own. I'd rather die going it alone than on Paixon's charity.

But everything we'd tried so far to identify or affect the field had resulted in a big fat nothing.

"Let's keep working on the datapad," I said finally. "We'll get it completely ready, but we won't download you into it yet. If the field goes away by itself, we can move quickly. And if we end up leaving the ship, we'll transfer you and we can go."

"What's your plan if the field dissipates?" Pita asked as I set to work re-routing some hair-fine fibre circuits in the datapad. "Would you risk the wormhole to Delta Pavonis?"

She'd managed to get one long-range scanner working

intermittently, so we'd had a "look" at the wormhole—or at least its radiation signature.

I shook my head, then remembered that Pita couldn't see me. That was the hardest adjustment to having an AI companion. "Whatever happened to it, that thing feels . . . evil. Pretty sure we'd fry in seconds, if the skip drive would even activate it."

"What about the other one? Where the alien ships came through?"

I was attempting to nudge a thin strand of wiring to the side with the tiny pair of tweezers on my multi-tool. Pita's use of the word *alien* gave me an unwanted shiver, and I almost messed up. I swallowed and refocused. I'd been trying to avoid thinking about those alien ships, although I hadn't said as much to Pita.

The appearance of a Chron ship had been bad enough. The Chron War was before my time, but they were still the bogeymen of Nearspace. With good reason. Killing machines, bent on wiping all of us—and the Lobors and the Vilisians—out entirely. There isn't much that scares me, but when I was a kid, I used to have nightmares about Chron coming into our house at night and killing us all. I didn't even know what they looked like. In my nightmares, they were tall, dark entities, featureless behind shadowy faceplates. They didn't speak, moved with absolute silence. You wouldn't know they were there until you opened your eyes and one was leaning over you, putting the barrel of some kind of weapon to your forehead. An ice-cold ring against your flesh. You'd be completely paralyzed, unable to move or scream or even think straight. Completely and utterly helpless. And you'd glimpse horrible, alien eyes behind the visor in the instant before they fired.

That's when I'd wake up screaming, every time. Memories like that don't go away easy.

And it hadn't been only Chron coming through that wormhole. The ship that had followed—the one even Pita couldn't identify—had been something out of another nightmare. I pulled the tweezers away from the datapad and shivered again.

"Jahelia? Would you go through the other wormhole?"

"No," I said, trying to keep the fear out of my voice. "I think we'd head deeper into this system, see what we could find. Check in here later to see if the Delta Pav wormhole had opened up again."

"I don't think that would be smart. We only have provisions for a limited amount of time," Pita said in a matter-of-fact voice. "To say nothing of fuel. Eventually we'd run out of both, and you'd—"

"I know! You don't have to remind me!" I snapped my hand back and threw the multi-tool against the dark field wall. It bounced off and landed with a clatter near my feet, where I sat cross-legged on the decking, barely missing the vulnerable inner casing of the datapad. For some reason, that only made me angrier. Only the knowledge that I needed it to finish rigging the pad stopped me from picking it up and throwing it again. I closed my eyes and took a deep breath. Then another. Pita displayed remarkable insight and stayed silent.

There's nothing I hate more than feeling helpless.

After a minute, I picked up the tweezers and went back to work.

Pita muttered, "Sorry," but I didn't even answer her.

Chapter 11 — Luta
Wormhole Explorers

I SETTLED INTO my big armchair in my quarters—I shared them with Hirin now, as I had long ago, but it took some getting used to. I still thought of them as *mine*. I knew I needed sleep, but couldn't relax or calm my whirling mind yet. It was just as well. Only a few moments had passed before there was a knock on the door and Hirin poked his nose in. I supposed his habit of knocking grew out of the same kind of acclimatization on his part.

"Not asleep yet?" he asked with a grin.

I felt a brief flash of traitorous annoyance. I wasn't sure I was up to dealing with him at the moment, but guilt swept it aside immediately. For years I'd longed to have him with me again—how could I resent his presence now? And perhaps it would be better to put all the current unresolved issues to rest.

I smiled. "You might squeeze in ten minutes before I nod off."

He crossed to the desk and dropped into the chair behind it, lifting his feet to prop them up on the desk. "Then we'll leave more pleasant pursuits until we have more time. We need to talk."

I pulled a face. "Are you sure? About the talking?"

"I'm sure. I'm going to stop playing captain for a while, and I need you to give me another official assignment."

"Playing captain? What do you mean?"

He wagged a finger at me. "You know very well what I mean, and you've been awfully good about it. Giving me the chair on so many duty shifts, letting me help in making decisions—come on, Luta, I can see what you're doing."

I started to protest further, but he cut me off.

"I appreciate it. You think it's too hard for me now, coming back to the ship and having you as the captain. I'll admit it takes some getting used to. I'll admit it's nice to be in charge sometimes. But right now, the last thing we need is any ambiguity. We're in a dangerous situation, you haven't overstated that. And one of us has to be in control or the crew will be confused."

"Why not you, then?"

"Because they're *your* crew. They like me, and I think they respect me, but they're still yours."

I puffed out a sigh. "That's pretty much what Yuskeya said when I asked her if she thought she should be in charge."

"And she was right. You're a good captain, Luta."

I stood and crossed to the desk, gently pushing his legs down so I could sit on his lap. I put my arms around his neck. "Promise me one thing," I said.

"Anything."

"We'll work out some other arrangement when all this is over. One that makes you as happy to be on this ship as I am having you here."

"I can't think of anywhere I'd rather be, no matter what I'm doing."

I glared at him. "Don't avoid the question. Promise."

He laughed. "*Okej, okej*, I promise. We'll figure out something else later." He pulled my head down and kissed me.

"You know," I said when he released me, "I might be able to let sleep wait a little longer."

I CAN SUM up the next three days fairly succinctly. Nothing happened. Well, that would be a bit of an understatement. Baden sent a series of comm signals through the Delta Pavonis wormhole, which remained as sullen and malevolent as ever. The messages appeared to go through, although we couldn't verify that. We had no reply.

We ran as close as we dared to the wormhole and engaged the skip drive, but there was no response from the wormhole, and we weren't feeling lucky enough to try diving to see if it worked. We returned to the moon.

Jahelia Sord's ship stayed half-in, half-out of the dark energy shield. We sent sporadic comms to check on her. She continued to be surly, but cooperative, and said she was fine to remain on her ship for the time being. I was happy to leave her there until I was forced to do something else with her.

We also spent a day at the *Stillwell,* trying everything we could think of, short of blasting it with a torpedo, to disperse the cloud of dark energy that enveloped it. I would have settled for some kind of reading from inside the ship. It was all futile, though, and by the end of the day we were frustrated, angry, and although no-one said it, scared. If the dark ship could do this to a Dragon-class warship, what could it do to the *Tane Ikai?* My only consolation was that they'd had the option to simply blow it up—they'd fired the energy weapon on the Chron ship, proving that—and they hadn't. Perhaps this was only some kind of stasis field that would eventually dissipate, leaving everyone inside unharmed. After all, Jahelia Sord was doing fine, hadn't been harmed by the field around her ship—although granted, she wasn't *in* it.

We ran as near as we dared to the new wormhole and spun up the skip drive while Viss took readings. He and Hirin put their heads together over the results and concluded that we should indeed be able to navigate it. It would be a risk to enter, but a calculated one. We knew that it was traversable, at least.

Hirin had decided that he'd act as "security" officer, so I'd put him in charge of weapons. We hadn't needed a weapons officer on board the *Tane Ikai* for a long time, but I suspected we might need one soon. And he'd taken the initiative in onloading those torps a few weeks ago, so he was the logical choice. He also returned to his research into PrimeCorp's past.

Cerevare had spent every waking hour studying the operant

moon with Gerazan, usually accompanied by Rei. Rei said she was going along as "security," but I wondered. Of course, there was little for her to do as a pilot, since we were effectively docked on the moon for the duration, except for those few short jaunts. But she and Gerazan seemed to have a mutual interest in each other. I smiled, watching them suit up for another EVA to the moon's interior control room. Maybe Rei had found a better cure for her melancholy than screaming workouts in the cargo bay. And it seemed to be good for Gerazan, too.

Yuskeya pored over data and tended to the injured scientist, Chen. His condition had her puzzled. She could find no reason for his failure to recover, and in fact, she couldn't even pin down exactly what was wrong with him.

Occasionally he would spike a high fever, sometimes becoming agitated and delirious. Other times he merely slept for long portions of the day, and in his waking hours was quiet and slow to speak. Gerazan confirmed that this was a marked change from his personality before the accident.

Maja kept track of our provisions and made sure that waste was kept to a minimum, becoming the *de facto* cook. Where usually we'd each see to our own culinary needs, Maja took to preparing ingredient-economical, large-scale meals for the entire crew. She and Baden had grown even closer during the crisis, and I knew that his crew quarters were empty virtually all of the time. That was fine with me. My daughter was old enough to make her own decisions and live her life on her terms. I was pleased to see her happy and content—circumstances notwithstanding—for the first time in a long time.

And as for me, the stress of the situation must have bothered me more than I'd like to admit. Yuskeya had to give me two more injections for headaches, and one for nausea. She wanted to run some medical scans, but I put her off. After a lifetime of not requiring medical procedures, I felt a growing terror at having to turn to them now. My burned fingers healed, but slowly. I couldn't remember an injury ever persisting longer than a day or so. I tried not to think about it, but the roughened ridges on my fingertips reminded me every time I touched something with them.

Finally the end of the third day arrived. I went to bed that night knowing that in the morning I would have to send us through the unknown wormhole. I lay curled against Hirin's back, feeling the slow, even rise and fall of his breathing, for a long time. Not talking. Not sleeping. Trying, without success, not to worry.

NOT SURPRISINGLY, EVERYONE was on the bridge for the first duty shift in the morning. Baden and Yuskeya had split the night shift so that neither would be too tired in the morning. We were a quiet bunch. Everyone had held onto the secret hope that the Delta Pavonis wormhole would have righted itself by now. The alternative was a leap into the unknown.

However, as Captain, I couldn't let the crew see any hesitation on my part. My headache had flared again, and I made a note to get a shot from Yuskeya as soon as I had a chance.

"*Okej*, I guess it's time to do something about Jahelia Sord," I said as I took my seat in the big chair. "I can't in good conscience leave her stranded here once we leave the system, because we might not be coming back this way. Suggestions?"

"Her ship is small. It would actually fit right inside one of the cargo pods," Viss said. "But I don't like the idea of trying to latch on and bring it inside the *Tane Ikai* without knowing more about that field."

"No," I agreed, "I'm not willing to risk that. We still have passenger quarters two and four empty, so I guess we need to convert one of them into a brig."

Hirin stood up. "Viss and I can do that. We'll take the room computer off the ship's network, and rig a plasma bar for the door. We're sure she's alone on that ship?"

Yuskeya nodded. "I've done a number of random scans. I've only ever read one person in there."

"Then we'll pick her up as soon as the quarters are ready. Rei, head over to her ship."

Nothing apparent had changed about the *Hunter's Hope* in the three days since the attack. The field still held, and I wondered if such a thing were there indefinitely, or if it would blink out when a certain amount of time had passed. What would the answer mean for the crew of the *Stillwell*?

"Ahoy, Jahelia Sord," I sent over the comm. "We're leaving this system, so I'm offering you a choice. You can stay with your ship and hope the field wears off or someone else comes along to rescue you. Or you can come aboard as my prisoner until we reach Nearspace and I can hand you over to the Protectorate."

"Not much of a choice," she said.

"I agree, but it's the best I can offer. I will say I don't foresee anything else coming along in the immediate future."

"Very well. What can I bring with me? Not that I can get into my personal quarters anyway."

"Anything personal is fine, but we'll scan and search you and your possessions before you come aboard. No weapons or anything else we'd disapprove of. My engineer and my navigator, who is also a Protectorate officer, will meet you at the airlock. Trust me, you do not want to try any tricks with them."

Whether it was my warning, her good sense, or Yuskeya's uniform, Jahelia Sord was on her best behavior when we extended a transport tube and linked the two ships via airlocks. She brought a small bag with a standard datapad and a few personal items, and came aboard quiet and subdued. Maybe that was understandable after being trapped and alone on her ship for several days, not knowing from one moment to the next if the strange alien field would suddenly endanger her. I suppose I was cruel in choosing to leave her there during that time. But I can't say I've ever lost any sleep over it.

Viss and Yuskeya brought her up from the cargo deck, and I met them at the hatchway. I was startled to see that Jahelia Sord now wore the Erian *pridattii* face tattoos, like Rei. In the picture I'd seen of her, in Yuskeya's report, her face had been unmarked. Her hair was a shock of unruly, pale-tipped black curls, eerily echoing the jet-black rings and whorls on her face. She was my height, but much thinner—almost fragile in appearance. Her eyes were dark, too, hard little stones of mistrust and dislike, and she smiled without warmth.

"I won't say welcome aboard," I said, "but as long as you behave yourself, you'll be well-treated on this ship."

"I'll try to be a good girl." Her tone held a mocking edge, which

I chose to ignore. She carried her bag slung casually over one shoulder, and was dressed informally in black military-style pants and a high-necked grey t-shirt. A black jacket hung from her other hand.

"Sord is an unusual last name for an Erian." Erian women's surnames usually incorporated the name of their mother, as Rei's did in "dam-Rowan."

"Yes, I suppose it is," she drawled.

"We don't have a proper brig, so you'll be staying in one of the guest rooms, but you won't have free access to the rest of the ship or the network. We'll bring you meals. And, in light of the circumstances, we'll keep you informed on what's happening."

"Thank you." She studied me gravely. "Will I meet the rest of your crew?"

"I expect we'll take turns bringing your meals and checking in with you. Why?"

She flashed a smile I could only describe as predatory. "I believe I may know your communications officer. Baden Methyr, isn't it? I thought I recognized his voice."

If Baden hadn't already made that offhand remark about her voice seeming familiar, I probably wouldn't have been able to hide my surprise. However, I think I managed to keep my face impassive. "Really? Now, how do you know Baden?"

Her smile didn't dim. "Perhaps you should ask him," she said. "I wouldn't like to say anything . . . inappropriate."

"I'll be sure to do that. This is my engineer, Viss Feron, and Commander Yuskeya Blue, a Protectorate officer temporarily assigned to my crew. They'll get you settled in your quarters."

She turned to them and said insolently, "Hello, Engineering, and hello, Protectorate. Huge pleasure to meet you both. I'm not that good with names, so I'll just remember you by what you do."

I turned and left them, biting my tongue, heading up the corridor toward the bridge. She was every bit as annoying as I'd expected, and I hoped she couldn't see how much she'd rattled me. What was she playing at, anyway? I got the impression that everything this woman did and said was calculated.

On the bridge, I said, "Baden, can I see you in your quarters?" I didn't want to ask him about Sord in front of everyone, but the

Tane Ikai was unusually full at the moment and there weren't many spots for private conversation.

Baden threw a glance at Maja, but merely said, "Sure," and got up from his seat at the comm panel. She regarded me with a hint of her old suspicion and seemed about to say something, then subsided.

Baden followed me off the bridge, and I let him go ahead of me into his quarters, first off the bridge to the right. I shut the door behind us. The room felt cool and empty, and I knew I was right about him spending most of his nights in Maja's quarters with her.

I got right to the point. "You said Jahelia Sord's voice sounded familiar, but not the name?"

"I could have been wrong about that, too, Captain—"

"No, I don't think you were." I pulled out my datapad and called up the report on Sord, which Yuskeya had forwarded to me. I focused in on the picture, although her hair was straight and dark blonde in it, instead of the mass of dark curls she wore now, and she'd had no face tattoos. "Recognize her?"

Baden studied the image and frowned. "Relana?" he said. "That doesn't—" He glanced up at me. "I know this woman, yes. Her name is Relana . . . um . . ." He had the grace to blush. "I met her a few months ago, on Earth, the last time we were there before we picked up Hirin. We . . . spent some time together. Are you telling me this is Jahelia Sord?"

Baden had a reputation as a lady's man, at least until he'd met Maja, so I knew what that meant—one of his brief hookups. I had a sudden recollection of him standing outside his quarters, freshly shaven, hair wet from the shower, looking admittedly handsome. Was Jahelia Sord playing him like a pawn that very night? I felt sorry for his discomfiture, but this was important.

I nodded. "I spoke to her when Viss and Yuskeya brought her up from the cargo pod. She said she knew you, called you by name. I knew she was trying to shake me up, so it was lucky you'd mentioned finding her voice familiar earlier—it wasn't as much of a shock as it might have been. Now she has dark hair and Erian face tattoos, but it's the same woman."

He sat down on the side of the bed, still holding my datapad in both his hands and staring at her picture. "This—it can't be coincidence, can it?'

I leaned against the closed door and folded my arms. "Doubtful. I think she probably cultivated you, trying to get information about me, or the ship. We know she's connected to PrimeCorp, but we don't know for how long."

"I don't remember any conversation about you or the *Tane Ikai*. But I guess it could have come up in passing. I don't remember."

"Maybe she wanted to get close to one of us," I said with a shrug. "Anyway, how do you want to handle it?"

"I . . . I'm not sure. Should I confront her about it, or just act like it's no big deal? And there's Maja to think of. I don't want her getting hurt by this."

I sighed. "I get the feeling Sord won't just let it go without comment, but for now we'll keep you away from her, I guess. There are enough of us to take her meals that you don't need to take a turn. If we get lucky and get home easily, you might not have to encounter her at all."

He stood and handed the datapad over, quirking a half-smile at me. "I don't feel all that lucky, Captain."

"Me neither. But I think I'll ask her about it myself, when I have a chance. And Baden, if I might give you a piece of advice?"

"Sure."

I patted his shoulder. "Tell Maja all about this; don't try to keep it a secret. Sord won't let that happen, so you might as well beat her to the punch."

"Just what I was thinking," he said with a nod. "It's ancient history, anyway."

A few months is not exactly ancient history, I thought, but I kept it to myself. I hoped, for his sake, that Maja would see things his way.

When we returned to the bridge, I saw Maja flash a silent question at him. Baden leaned down to whisper in her ear, but he didn't have time to say much more than "later." To keep Maja's questioning gaze from turning on me, I said, "Rei, here's something unusual."

Rei swung her skimchair around to face me. "What?"

I dropped into the big chair. "Our guest is Erian—or pretending to be."

She raised an eyebrow. "She doesn't have an Erian name."

"No, and she didn't have *pridattii* when her registry file picture was taken."

"Nothing about Erian heritage in what Yuskeya found in the registry?"

"Nope."

Rei pursed her lips. "It's not entirely unusual. Some people adopt them because they think they're interesting, or they feel culturally attuned to Eri." She shrugged. "Some Erians don't like it, but it never really bothered me very much. But for someone hoping to camouflage her identity . . ."

"That's what I was thinking. They do change a person's appearance."

"Change your hair colour and add the markings, you could be a different person," she agreed. "And they don't have to be permanent. It won't fool an ID chip scan, but a casual observer, sure."

"So the question is, who was she trying to fool?" But neither of us had an answer.

A few minutes later, Yuskeya entered the bridge and reported that the prisoner was secure in her quarters. "Viss should be down in engineering by now," she added.

Everyone else had gathered on the bridge. That was understandable. Few people liked to face the unknown alone. I felt a momentary pang—should I have brought Sord up here too? But, no. She was my prisoner, and while I'd keep her safe and reasonably comfortable, I didn't owe her peace of mind. I opened the ship's comm. "Viss, is the skip drive ready?"

"Aye, Captain."

"*Okej* then, Rei, let's go. Take us over to the wormhole, but stop one more time near the *Stillwell*. I want to make sure nothing's changed before we leave."

But the Protectorate ship still lay—no-one wanted to say "dead" but we were all thinking it, I'm sure—quiet and unmoving, completely encased in the dark, shadowy field. Nothing emerged from it, and apparently nothing could get in. Yuskeya scanned it one more time so that she could do some comparison analysis, and then there was nothing to do but leave it, and all its personnel, where it hung.

As we approached the second wormhole, it looked exactly like any other we'd ever gone through. I heard Baden take a deep breath as we neared its dark mouth.

"Now, Baden," I said, "*this* is what wormhole exploring feels like. Or pretty near."

He nodded and twisted a wry grin. "Now I understand the difference. And I wish I didn't."

"Rei, take us in whenever you're ready." I was pleased that my voice betrayed none of the trepidation I felt. The headache was getting worse, and my stomach had started a slow, rolling churn, but I resolutely brushed the sensations aside. I couldn't afford to be sick now. It would have to wait.

Rei's hands were steady on the controls as the ship closed the distance between it and the wormhole. Then she fired up the skip drive, and she and Viss exchanged the usual confirmations. We made a perfectly normal slip into the wormhole.

From the inside, it resembled every other wormhole I've traversed throughout Nearspace. The blueshifted radiation spun swirls of colour down the length of the tunnel-like interior, surrounding us with breathtaking beauty as we skipped our way around the sides.

The same grey streaks ran down the walls of this wormhole, as they had down the one from Delta Pav. What did they mean?

"Yuskeya, any sign of the same anomalies we encountered the last time?" I asked.

"Nothing this time, Captain. All normal."

Then the wormhole's terminal point came up in a rush and we burst out the other end.

And into hell.

Chapter 18 — Luta
The Station

"*DIOS*! CUT THE drives, Viss!" I shouted, diving from my chair to the seat next to Rei. "I'm on the co-pilot board."

"I'll take dock, you're starboard," she said tersely. Her fingers skimmed ceaselessly over the pilot's board, gently easing the ship this way and that. Working together, we had a marginally better chance of keeping the *Tane Ikai* intact.

We had emerged from the wormhole into the middle of the biggest, ugliest asteroid field I'd ever seen from the inside. Initially, I didn't think we could make it through alive. The asteroids ranged from huge—far bigger than the *Tane Ikai*—to pebble-sized, tumbling around us, misshapen detritus from the creation and destruction of worlds, huddled together now for comfort or mischief. Even the smallest could punch a hole through the hull if the shields didn't stop it. The largest would overwhelm the shields and dash us to pieces. Over and behind them all lay a hideous red-orange light, burning like the embers of a malicious fire.

Viss's voice rumbled up from the engineering deck. "Everything's offline except maneuvering jets," he said. "Burst drive is enabled in case we have to move quickly, but it won't create any drag on what you're doing now."

No one else on the bridge had said a word yet, although I'd

heard a few sharply indrawn breaths when we first saw what lay in wait on this side of the wormhole.

"When we get out of this," I said to Rei, not taking my eyes off the screen or slowing my reflexive nudges on the board, "let's come to a full stop while we take stock."

"*Por certa*, Captain," she answered. "I might need to go to the head and throw up."

It probably took less than ten minutes to get through, although it passed like a lifetime. I was glad I'd told Rei to stop when we got clear. I was dumbstruck by what I saw when we emerged.

The reddish light that suffused this system like a slowly spreading stain was the result of a number of factors. Off in the distance a dim orange star burned, its meagre warmth unlikely to reach this far. Closer to us an interstellar dust cloud loomed, the orange sun painting it with a dark red underbelly and brighter, yellowish specularity streaking across the top. There were no planets in evidence from where we hung, suspended beyond the asteroid field's outer limits.

But it was none of those things that caught my attention at first; I noticed them only peripherally. No, what drew my eye, what in fact had the eye of everyone on board, was the space station.

"*Dipatrino*, what is that?" breathed Hirin. I hadn't realized that he'd moved to stand behind me.

"Captain, I've begun logging navigation data on this system," Yuskeya reported in a flat, emotionless voice, her Protectorate training kicking in, no doubt. "I don't recommend activating scans."

"Noted, no scans," I said. "Good thinking. So far, no-one seems to have noticed us, so let's try and keep it that way."

They were coming to life now, getting past that initial shock.

"No incoming comm signals that we're able to pick up," Baden said, and his wording struck me. We might have had the latest and greatest technology when we left Mars, but everything was an unknown now. Someone could be screaming at us with their own communications equipment, but if it wasn't compatible, we'd never hear them.

"Should I send a general hail to the—whatever that is?" Baden asked.

I couldn't take my eyes away from the space station. That was all I could think to call it, although as Baden implied, it wasn't like any station I'd ever encountered. It was dark, sleek, angular, and imposing; as malefic-looking as the spidery ship that had pursued the Chron into our midst, with the same gelatinous outer texture. This thing was big, though; as big as Sagan Station, and that could comfortably house over five thousand people. Spiky protrusions extended from a central torus, so many that I couldn't easily count them. Six, on the sides I could see, were larger and extended further than the rest, pointing randomly to all corners of the system. The structure didn't rotate or move, so if there was gravity on board it was generated in some way other than centripetal force. Apart from the spikes, it was featureless. No lights, no viewports, no docking bays, no gun turrets.

That last was slightly comforting, at least.

"Captain?" Baden asked.

"No, let's not say anything yet. They haven't demanded to know what we're doing here, so maybe they don't think we're worth notice."

Slowly I stood up from the co-pilot's seat and moved to the captain's chair. Hirin followed me to stand behind me again. I think he must have sensed that I needed him at my back.

Nothing else happened.

"Should I start scanning the system?" Yuskeya asked.

I shook my head. "I think we'll hold off a bit longer. Let's see if we can get a bigger visual picture of what's here. Rei, maneuvering jets only, let's circle around without getting any closer. Just a nice, slow, steady crawl."

I resisted the urge to rub my forehead. I could really use something for this headache, but now was not the time to leave the bridge, or let the crew see anything else amiss.

"I can't maintain a perfectly consistent distance without taking any readings," Rei said skeptically.

"Eyeball it," I told her.

And so we began one of the strangest surveys I've ever performed. Rei piloted the ship slowly around the station, and the rest of us watched it roll past on the screens.

"Luta," Hirin said as we moved away from our initial observation point, "did you notice that one of those spikes seems to be pointing directly at the wormhole we came through?"

"I hadn't noticed, but I'm glad there's no weapon in the end of it."

"Captain, I'm getting readings that indicate a second wormhole in this system, nearby," Yuskeya said. "And no, I'm not scanning," she added. "Passive data reception only. We picked up its radiation signature."

"Interesting. Can you pinpoint it?"

"Not yet, not without actively scanning. I'll tell you when I get a better fix."

"What do you think it is?" Maja asked, her eyes locked on the "station."

"It is not Chron construction, I feel certain," Cerevare said.

"Why not?"

The Lobor shrugged. "Perhaps it is a feeling only, but it is too different from the Chron artifacts we have observed. And too much like the ship that pursued the Chron through the wormhole. Did any of you feel that those two ships were constructed by the same species?"

Baden shook his head. "No. They felt too different. And this feels completely different from the artifact moon."

"Agreed." Cerevare nodded.

"Here's a question," Viss said over the ship's comm. "How did anyone get through that asteroid field going *toward* the wormhole, and maintain the right velocity and approach to engage a skip drive and enter the terminal point safely? And not once, but twice, since both ships came through separately?"

"And how is that field even there?" Gerazan asked. "It's not part of an orbiting belt. It's as if it's suspended there."

"Too many questions, not enough answers," Rei complained. "And too much chatter. I'm trying to do a delicate job, here."

Baden turned to Gerazan with a grin. "Don't pay any attention," he said in a conspiratorial stage whisper. "She loves to work under pressure. She just wants everyone to appreciate it when she does."

"Baden, if I didn't have my hands full trying to keep this ship safe—"

"I know, I know, I'd be in for it. But you do, so I'm not worried."

Gerazan's face twitched, as if he didn't know whether to smile or not.

"They're always like this when we're in a life-threatening situation," I assured him. "For some reason it keeps them focused on the task at hand."

"Got a reading on that wormhole," Yuskeya said. She tapped in a few coordinates, and one of the screens showed a long-range view with the wormhole artificially highlighted in green.

"What's wrong with the view?" Maja asked. "It's like the picture is unsteady or something. Something's moving."

"You won't believe—" Yuskeya started, but Hirin cut her off.

"There's a second asteroid field obscuring the entrance to that wormhole as well?"

Yuskeya gave him a raised eyebrow. "Okay, maybe you will believe it. You're exactly right. There's another asteroid field there. The movement of the asteroids is distorting the image."

"And unless I miss my guess," Hirin continued, "another one of those big spikes is pointing directly at that wormhole."

"Hirin Paixon," I said in my best annoyed-wife voice, "how about this? We'll grant your genius if you stop showing off and get on with your theory."

He inclined his head in a mock bow. "Anything for you, Captain. I think this is some kind of guard station, set up to stop transit through the wormholes. Or at least to control who goes through them. I'm willing to bet that there are more than two wormholes in this system. I think this is a nexus system, like MI 2 Eridani or Mu Cassiopeia, and there may be a wormhole for every one of those larger spikes."

"Beta Comae, too. But none of those systems have this many wormholes," Baden argued. "Four each, right?"

"We've never found more than five in a single system," Yuskeya agreed.

"Which is why I think," Hirin added with a flourish of his hand, "that if you have a system with this many wormholes present, they may not all be naturally occurring. I think at least some of these have been constructed by a race of such obvious technological advancement, that we'd better hope and pray they like us when we meet them."

We were still gaping at him when the ship alarm sounded softly to notify us that we were being scanned.

"ON THE ALERT, folks," I said. I was surprised to feel the prick of sweat on my forehead, and brushed it away with the back of my hand. Was something in this system causing the ship to overheat? Yet no warnings came in from ship systems.

"Yuskeya, can you tell where it's coming from?"

"Definitely originating from the station," she said. "It's nothing invasive or dangerous. Just a general scan like we'd run ourselves to see where a ship came from or possibly its composition. Should I try to block it?"

"No, not if you don't consider it dangerous."

"Burst drive is ready if you need it, Rei," Viss said over the ship's comm.

"Captain?"

I shrugged. "Where would we go? Let's sit tight and see what happens. But stay ready, Rei."

The scan continued for maybe another half-minute, then stopped. The station and the ship fell silent again.

"Maybe it's automated?" Baden suggested. "It might run at intervals whether there's a ship in the system or not. No-one's tried to say hello to us still."

"Captain Paixon?" Jahelia Sord's voice came over the ship's comm. "Would you mind telling me what that alarm was about?"

"Not now, Sord," I snapped, and signalled to Baden to shut down her access to the bridge audio. I didn't want her listening in to this.

Rei pushed away from the pilot's board and turned to me. "We've been flying around this thing, we've been scanned, and nothing else has happened. Why don't we stop babystepping? Trying to hide in plain sight makes me feel *freneza*; I'd rather fly up to the front door and knock."

"We could run a scan of the station," Yuskeya suggested.

"They scanned us, so it's only fair."

"Yes, and what if there's no word in their alien vocabulary for 'fair'?" I felt annoyed. We'd cast our lot already by taking the wormhole into this system, and I was tired of waiting for something to happen—but I didn't know which way to jump. I shrugged out of my jacket and into shirtsleeves. The bridge felt unbearably hot. Why was no-one else complaining? "*Al inferno—* to hell with it," I growled. "We might as well find out what we've gotten ourselves into."

Hirin shot me a puzzled frown, and I realized how sharply I'd spoken.

"We'll take it slow," I said, willing my voice calm and steady. "Yuskeya, run a general scan of the station, looking for the same sort of data we got on that spider ship. Nothing invasive. Rei, be ready to kick that burst drive over if someone doesn't like what we're doing."

The scan brought no response. "All right then, let's head out to that second wormhole and investigate the asteroid field."

"Burst drive?" Rei asked.

"Go ahead. We're throwing caution to the winds."

We reached the asteroid field quickly under the burst drive. It was the twin of the one we'd had to navigate to enter the system— asteroidal debris tumbling haphazardly, but clustered around the wormhole terminal point.

"So what do you make of that? Anyone?"

"It's got to be a security measure," Hirin insisted. "Yuskeya, can you get a reading on that spike I thought was pointing in this direction?"

She huffed. "Like that's necessary. You know you're right about this, Hirin."

He grinned. "I know, but make an old man happy and confirm it, would you?"

I rolled my eyes. All this joking around was getting on my nerves. We were in deep trouble here, couldn't they see that?

After a few seconds, Yuskeya glanced up from the screen. "*Konfirmi.* The spike is trained on the center of the wormhole."

"So let's get out of the direct line of fire, shall we?" Baden asked, an uneasy edge to his voice. "Those spikes appear to mean business. Of what kind, I'm not sure, but definitely not a kind I want to intercept."

"Another radiation signature detected, Captain. Another wormhole."

"Of course it is," I grumbled, wiping my palms down the sides of my jeans. "And what's in front of this one? Let me guess. Another asteroid field?"

We circuited the system, finding in all nine wormholes to correspond with nine large spikes on the station. Every wormhole entrance was guarded by an asteroid field—the field itself seemingly contained within static boundaries, while the asteroids moved normally within it. We weren't scanned again, and no other vessels appeared. The station remained silent except for that one solitary scan.

"Viss," I said finally, brushing a droplet of sweat from above my lips, "is there something in this system that's causing the heat in the ship to go so high? Or is there a problem with the environmentals?"

"I—don't think so, Captain." There was a pause, while he presumably checked readings. "I don't find it unusually warm down here."

"Me neither," Maja said. "Mother, are you all right?"

"Fine," I said shortly. "Maybe I'm concentrating too hard."

"It's probably quite possible to chart a safe course through one of those asteroid fields, provided you didn't have to do it in a hurry," Hirin said, from one of the unmanned bridge boards he'd commandeered to, as he put it, "work something out." "Rei and Luta got us through one, and they had no time to prepare at all. Granted that they're the two best pilots in Nearspace," he added, "but even so . . ."

"Dad, you aren't suggesting we try to go through one?" Maja asked. "We don't have a clue where any of them go!"

"Not true," Hirin answered. "We know that one of them goes one skip away from Nearspace. Who's to say that more of them aren't that close? Or possibly right into a Nearspace system? It's not like every square kilometer of Nearspace has been explored. We could be closer to home than we think."

"Hirin," I said, "I think it's pretty clear that someone or

something has gone to great trouble to make it difficult to get through these wormholes. I'd at least like to know who and why before we try to go through one. Let's not forget those spikes that make Baden so nervous."

He, and Maja too, I noticed, turned to me with surprise evident on their faces. "What? Do you think I have to agree with every damned thing you say, just because we're married?"

"Mother? Why are you yelling?"

"I'm not yelling!" I had to take a deep gulp of air, because it was so hot on the bridge I felt like I might suffocate.

"What do you suggest, then, Luta?" Hirin said in a deceptively mild voice. I knew he must have something planned.

"These alien *bastardos*, whoever they are, are responsible for this mess. I guess they like playing god, controlling who goes where and when." I flung myself into the chair. "Well, I'm tired of playing their games." The insistent, escalating pounding in my head was driving me forward. I knew exactly what I wanted, and I didn't know why we'd been pussyfooting around all this time. I wanted answers.

"We're going to go and make contact with whoever is in that station," I said. "And we're going to do it now. Rei, turn this thing around and take us to the station. Engage the burst drive."

"Luta? Are you all right?" Hirin stood now from the board he'd been using and crossed to me. I jumped up from the chair and stood in front of it, arms crossed as if I were guarding it. I wondered vaguely why I'd done that. Hirin's expression held the same question.

"I'm *fine*," I said impatiently. "I have a headache and it feels like the inside of a supernova in here. Viss, check those temperature controls again!"

"Uh, sure, Captain," he said. "I think they're within normal range, though."

"Just check the damn things."

Rei had followed my orders and brought the ship about, turning us to head toward the dark, gelatinous-looking alien station. The ship lurched slightly as the burst drive kicked in, and I stumbled a little. Hirin reached out to catch me, and I slapped his hand away, ignoring his bewildered exclamation.

"Rei, don't stray into the direct line of sight between any of those spikes and the wormholes. Baden's right, they could be dangerous. Baden, when we get within five hundred clicks, send out the standard Nearspace hailing message on all frequencies. We'll see if anyone's home on that disgusting piece of space garbage."

I caught a silent communication pass between Hirin and Yuskeya. I realized everyone else except Rei had also turned to stare at me.

"What? Keep your eyes on your boards! We don't know what these *ansulos* could be planning."

They continued to stare at me.

"Luta, you're tired out," Hirin said finally. "Why don't you come down to our quarters and have a rest?" He put a hand on my arm, and his flesh felt shockingly cold.

I jerked away from his touch. "Right, so you can take over? You want to play captain? I don't think so, old man."

Yuskeya had left the navigation board. "Captain, is your headache worse? You should have told me, I can give you something for it. Come into First Aid, and we'll try something else, *okej*?"

"Those shots!" I stared at her with sudden realization and hatred. "That's what's making me feel like this. You did something, *megero*, put something in those shots—and I suppose everyone knows about it, do you? I can feel it! You're all against me!"

A tiny, faraway part of my brain was telling me that I was shouting, asking me why I was shouting, and why would I call Yuskeya such a horrible name? But I couldn't seem to stop myself. "And why is it so goddamned *hot in here*?"

That's when my legs buckled. Sparks obscured my vision like stars going supernova in a distant galaxy. Arms held me, voices babbled around me, but they were all faint and far away and I felt myself slipping, slipping into a darkness where there were no alien artifacts, no mysterious wormholes, no fearsome space stations. Where it was soft, and quiet, and blessedly, blessedly cool.

Chapter 19 — Jahelia
Nothing Left Behind

My prison cell on the *Tane Ikai* was a surprisingly comfortable room—with a well-locked door. As far as the crew knew, I was effectively cut off from the rest of the ship. Fine. If they wanted to shut me up and forget about me, that meant they wouldn't spend too much time wondering how I spent mine.

But when I'd politely commed Captain Paixon and asked to be brought into the loop, she'd cut me off rudely and abruptly without a word of explanation.

Even before that, I'd connected my datapad (and thus, Pita) to the computer console in my room, and Pita had gone to work to reconnect to the network. They hadn't broken a physical connection, only a digital one. I felt pretty confident that Pita would be able to crack that. They weren't expecting me to have anything like her.

When Paixon had refused to talk to me, I asked Pita, "Can you at least bypass the comm lockout so I can listen in on the bridge?" I had minuscule earbuds and a throat touch mic so that I could subvocalize and she'd hear me, and her responses were for my ears alone.

Her answer sounded clearly inside my head. She chuckled. "We're still locked out of full network access, but I think I can get you audio. Give me a few minutes, and we'll be in."

Moments later, when the bridge feed came online, I was surprised to hear Luta Paixon say in a trembling and enraged voice, "You did something, *megero*, put something in those shots—and I suppose everyone knows about it, do you? I can feel it! You're all against me! And why is it so goddamned *hot in here*?"

I barely had time to wonder who she'd called a bitch when all hell seemed to break loose on the bridge.

"Catch her!" That was Baden Methyr's voice.

"Luta!" another man shouted. Her husband, I figured. I hadn't seen him yet, but I knew all the names from the crew manifesto for the *Tane Ikai* well enough. He was in his nineties, so I decided to call him Gramps. A jumble of bumping and thumping came over the feed, so either a fight had broken out or she'd collapsed and people ran to help.

"Get her into First Aid," a woman said. She had a commanding tone that I recognized, the Protectorate officer—Yuskeya Blue. She'd at least been polite and professional—even if she regarded me with a disapproving eye—when she installed me in my quarters.

"What's wrong with her? Headaches again?" another female voice demanded. The pilot this time, I thought, or maybe Paixon's daughter. "Something's seriously wrong. Who goes crazy and passes out from a headache?"

More babble and urgent discussion bubbled into my brain from the feed, but as eager as I'd been to eavesdrop, it all faded and blurred into a wash of background noise. My mind replaced it with memories of another woman, increasingly prone to headaches, fits of inexplicable anger, sudden nosebleeds, and finding every room too hot.

"Jahelia, por la amo de Dio, will you open the window?" My mother rubbed at her greying temples with the knuckles of two clenched fists.

"They're all open, Mamma." I knew I sounded cranky and short with her, but I couldn't help it. *Every window in the*

cramped apartment had been thrown open to the cool night air, and I was freezing. I'd already layered on an extra long-sleeved shirt and a sweater, and slipped on my shoes. And still my mother complained.

She turned a flushed face to me, wide eyes black and dilated beneath a furrowed brow. "And you, with that sweater! I feel too hot just looking at you!"

"Then don't look at me!"

"Such disrespect! I raised you better than that, Lia!"

I pressed my lips together, smothering more angry words. "Would you like some cold water?" I reached to pick up the half-empty glass on the scratched wooden table at my mother's elbow.

Mamma grabbed for it. "Don't take that! You're always taking my things!" In her haste, she knocked the glass out of my hand. It crashed to the floor and shattered, spattering shards and water all over the floor.

"Now see what you've done!" Mamma jumped from the chair, heedless of the broken glass under her bare feet. Then she screamed in pain as the shards bit into her flesh. She took one step toward me and crumpled to the floor, unconscious. One outflung arm sprawled into the puddle of water and sparkling fragments.

I stood staring down at her for a long moment, pulling deep, quick breaths as I fought for the strength to control my own anger. That worried me. Were my own nanos failing? Was that the explanation for the fleeting urge, quickly suppressed, to kick the senseless woman on the floor? No, *I told myself, blowing out a long breath.* I'm frustrated. Tired. Sad. Anyone would feel this way. There's nothing wrong with me except stress.

I went to the tiny kitchen for cloths to mop up the mess and returned, kneeling beside my mother. With a guilty start, I thought to check Mamma's pulse and breathing. Both fine. Just another fit from which she would awake in half an hour or so, feeling much better and utterly bewildered by the cuts on her feet.

Where would it end? I wondered as I mopped up the spilled water and carefully gathered the bits of broken glass. I had to roll her over to get it all cleaned up, but even that didn't rouse her. It had seemed like the move to Jertenda would turn things around for us. Dad had sworn to quit gambling, and had managed, with a false name and forged credentials, to gain a position working for Nicadico Corp on their new anti-aging treatment, Longate. He seemed happier than he'd been in a long time, working in a lab again. The money wasn't great yet, but if the treatment worked, the researchers had been promised a healthy share of the profits.

I finished with the broken glass and fetched the first aid kit from the washroom. Trying to be gentle even if she couldn't feel it, I teased bits of glass from Mamma's feet, applied ointment, and bandaged them. I briefly wished Dad would get home in time to help struggle Mamma into bed. He claimed to be working long hours at the lab, but I suspected he was gambling again. I couldn't imagine where the money was coming from; at least he continued to turn over his pay to me so I could cover the rent and buy food. Maybe he was taking bribes at the lab. It wouldn't be the first time.

"What do you think is happening out there?" Pita asked, breaking me out of my reverie. I felt as though I needed to physically shake myself to dislodge the anger and helplessness the memory had brought with it.

"I'm not sure," I said. "But I think Luta Paixon is in trouble. Probably deeper than any of them realize."

Chapter 20 — Luta
Collateral Damage

I OPENED MY eyes in my own quarters to see Hirin bending over me, concern written large on his face.

"This is happening way too often lately," I muttered, struggling to maintain my focus. The words sounded garbled and unclear, even to me. Hirin's face blurred, sharpened, blurred again. I closed my eyes tight and reopened them.

Hirin blew out a long sigh. "She's awake."

In a fraction of a second Yuskeya was there, too. "How do you feel, Captain?"

I blinked experimentally a few times. "I think my head is okay," I said, "and I'm not burning up anymore. So that's an improvement."

"And you're coherent. That's a *big* improvement," Hirin said with a grin.

"What—oh," I said, as memory trickled back in fragments. Much of it wasn't clear and didn't make sense, but what did— wasn't pleasant. "*Oh.* Hirin, I—yelled at you, didn't I? At everyone. And Yuskeya . . . I called you a *bitch*?"

She grinned lopsidedly. "Something like that. Seems you had

a little side dish of paranoia to go along with your headache and fever."

"You had me pretty confused," Hirin admitted. "I didn't know what was wrong with you."

"I'm sorry," I said simply. "To both of you. I don't know what else to say."

"Apology accepted," she said. "And I don't think you can blame yourself too much."

"What's . . . what's wrong with me?" I'd never had to ask that question before, and it sounded strange coming from my lips. Strange, and scary. Nerves stirred my stomach into an unpleasant nausea that had nothing to do with actually being sick; I felt like a wormhole explorer getting ready to skip into the terrors of the unknown. I struggled to sit up, and Hirin helped me, after glancing at Yuskeya to see if she approved.

She hovered briefly to see if I would be okay upright, then sat down at my desk, resting her elbows on it. "I could simply say I'm not sure, which would be true," she said, "but I do have a guess. A guess that's somewhat supported by some information I got with the datamed. I scanned you and took some blood samples through your implant while you were out. Hirin gave his okay," she added.

I nodded. I was hardly worried about treatment protocols and consent.

"Since you've got some unusual additions hanging out in your bloodstream," she continued, referring to my mother's nanobioscavengers, "I wasn't sure how I'd identify anything else out of the ordinary. But your mother gave me some special software for the datamed that can actually identify your bioscavs now." She smiled. "All very hush-hush. Do not tell Baden I've got tech that he doesn't."

"Cross my heart," I promised.

"She asked me if you'd had an infusion of new bioscavs from your Mother when we were on Kiando," Hirin said, "when I got mine. But I told her I didn't think so. Was that right?"

I nodded. "She wanted to make some tweaks before she updated mine—the ones she gave you were different, since you hadn't had them as long as I had," I said with a shrug. "It didn't seem like a big deal since we were planning on seeing her again in a few months' time."

"Okay, that makes sense. But what really interested me came from something Maja said, when she was helping us get you down here. She said, 'It's just like Dad was when he first got the virus, years ago."

I cast my thoughts back, sifting through memories. I nodded. "She's right, it does seem similar, although I don't remember any anger issues," I said wryly. I turned to Hirin. "But you did find it so hot all the time, and you complained of headaches that never went away."

He nodded, grim-faced at the memory, and turned to Yuskeya. "So what's the connection?"

Yuskeya ran a hand over her dark hair. "You have to remember, Luta, I'm not a doctor. And this is complicated stuff. But it does seem like there's a virus in your system, and your bioscavengers aren't getting rid of it."

"Chen keeps spiking a fever, too," I said. "Could he have the same thing?"

She chewed her lower lip, thinking. "I don't get any readings from the datamed that suggest that. I think his symptoms stem from something that happened to him inside the moon. Exposure to something, maybe."

"And the datamed is telling you that I do have a virus?"

She nodded. "Yes, one your bioscavs can't deal with. So either it's not the same virus Hirin had, because your transfused bioscavs *did* help him with that—or else something's gone wrong with your bioscavs."

"That doesn't sound good. Do you think that's it?"

Yuskeya took a deep breath and released it slowly. "I'm afraid it might be. There could be virions—virus particles—in your system that your bioscavs have kept at bay—in a kind of quarantine—for years. But in the scan I did, some of your bioscavs seem to be breaking down, disassembling themselves."

"So the virus is essentially getting free again."

She sighed. "Something like that. This is mostly guesswork. I'm just trying to make sense of what I'm seeing."

"Only some of them?" I was grasping for any good news here,

I knew.

"Yes. But—" she glanced at Hirin, then to me, "there are others that are behaving differently again. They're breaking down, too, but these are—I'm not sure how to explain it—rebuilding themselves before the breakdown is complete. And they're incorporating some of the virus cells into the new version of themselves."

"*Kristos,*" I breathed. "That *really* doesn't sound good."

Yuskeya shrugged. "It might be the best thing ever, I don't know. Your mother would be the person to ask. But my instinct is the same as yours. It doesn't sound good."

Hirin spoke, for the first time since Yuskeya and I had started this part of the conversation. "Well, what can you do about it? And shouldn't it be happening to me?"

"I'm sorry, Hirin. I simply don't know."

"Wait, wait. We just said it," I said slowly. "You have newer bioscavs. You got the newest ones from Mother on Kiando."

He paled. "But you waited."

Yuskeya frowned and crossed her arms. "Luta, when did you first feel . . . not right?"

I considered. "After everything happened at the wormhole."

"When we got caught in—whatever it was—that the Chron ship shot at the artifact moon?"

I nodded slowly. "It affected a lot of things on the ship. Drives, boards—"

She pointed to my hand. "Your datapad."

Instinctively I rubbed my thumb over the still-rippled flesh where my fingers had been burned. In the past, there would have been no trace of that burn damage now. "You think whatever that was affected my bioscavs."

She shrugged. "I don't know. You *were* the last one of us to regain consciousness, which seemed odd to me at the time. I honestly don't know, but it's a theory, and the only one we have."

"What can you do?" Hirin asked. I already knew the answer to that question. There was only one person who could do much, and she was currently beyond reach. I only hoped she was still safe.

Yuskeya confirmed it. "Unfortunately, not much. I've got the datamed working on something that might let me block the virus chemically, but I don't know how effective it will be. For all I know, the bioscavs will break it down, too. Aside from that, I can try to alleviate symptoms as they arise. We need your mother," she said simply.

I'd been sitting upright without feeling lightheaded, so I took a chance, swung my legs over the side of the bed, and stood up. Nothing bad seemed to happen.

"Well, she's not here, and I feel all right now." Not normal—I felt far from normal—but I thought I could function.

"I gave you a dose of something to block the symptoms, but I don't know how long it will last. I gave Chen something similar, and it seemed to help with the fever and the pain. But we've got to get you to Nearspace and get in touch with Emmage. She's the only one I'd trust with this."

"Like we needed another reason to get back to Nearspace," I said, patting her arm. As an afterthought, I added, "How is Chen now?"

I caught the look that passed between her and Hirin.

"Not very well, I'm afraid," she said. "That fever he spiked when we transited the wormhole was a bad one. He was sleeping the last time I checked in on him. It seems to be an awfully deep sleep, and his brain activity has dropped off some."

"So you're saying he's slipped into a coma," I said.

She pressed her lips together, obviously uncomfortable with the word. "Maybe. He could come out of it."

"Keep me posted." There was little else to say about it. "Well, I guess if you think it's all right, I'll get to the bridge. I have another round of apologies to make."

"If you feel up to it," Yuskeya said. "That's all we have to judge by."

"Are you certain?" Hirin asked. "If you're still tired—"

"I'm okay. And it's not because I think you're trying to take over the ship," I said with a smile, and patted his cheek.

"Okay then. Let's see what's happening—"

He didn't get to finish, because Baden's voice came over the ship's comm.

"Hirin, Yuskeya? Hate to bother you, but three ships just came through one of those other wormholes. Ran the asteroids like they knew the way and coming fast. You'd better get in here."

The three of us ran for the door, and I wasn't so sick that I didn't get there first.

MAJA, WHO'D PROGRESSED enough in her navigation studies that she could take over the nav board in a pinch, jumped up to make way for Yuskeya as we entered the bridge. "I have a fix on them," she said breathlessly. "I think they're Chron ships."

I slid into the big chair. "Rei, we're probably going to need that burst drive."

"Nice to see you, Captain. It's online and ready to go. Gerazan went down to engineering with Viss."

"Good idea. Viss? What about weapons?"

"Online, Captain. Ready when needed."

"*Bona.* Maja, where are they headed? Us, or the station?"

She shrugged. "Hard to say. This general direction, that's all. They're still too far out."

"Any chance we can hide?"

"Not if they're hunting for us," Baden said. "We've been sitting here in plain sight—"

"Since my little meltdown, right. Sorry about that, folks. I'll explain—as much as I can—later. Rei, engage the burst drive."

"Aye, Captain."

"Let's try to keep the station between us and them. If we can do that, maybe we can get even further away, but I don't want to attract their attention."

"Got it," she said, her hands already moving over the pilot's board. The *Tane Ikai* shuddered and lurched as the burst drive kicked in, and then we moved away from the station at an appreciable speed. I glanced up at the screen showing the spiky, alien shape of the station. Nothing about it had changed, no indication that there was anyone on it or that they'd noticed our presence, beyond that one scan.

Until several hatchways irised open on the near side of the central torus, and four of the spidery ships burst out, one after the other.

"Mother!" Maja had seen them, too.

"I see them. Rei, prepare to take evasive action."

But they didn't move in our direction. They flew toward the ships that had only moments ago made their incursion through the wormhole.

Now we had a new dilemma. Get as far away as possible while no-one paid much attention to us, or stick around and see what happened. Prudence versus curiosity.

Curiosity won.

"Rei, I'm changing my mind again."

"Captain's prerogative," she said, and I heard the grin in her voice.

"It might be useful to know what's going to happen here. Try to stay within visual range, but keep the station between us and the action, whatever it turns out to be."

"*Hola*, Captain, that's not much trouble," she said. "Anything else you'd like me to do? Clean out the intakes? Bake you some *pano?*"

"When I want sarcasm from you I'll ask for it, thanks," I retorted. "Baden, did we ever send a comm to the station?"

"We did, before you . . . er . . . got sick," he said delicately. "No response."

"Forget them for now, then. If they want us, they know we're here."

"Incoming ships are in visual range," Yuskeya reported. "I'm putting them on the screen."

Cerevare's sharp intake of breath confirmed what Maja had already suggested. More Chron ships. The configuration was very similar to the one that had activated the operant moon.

"Where are they headed? Can you tell?" The Lobor historian's ears had swivelled forward, signalling her excitement as it must have done for her ancestors millennia before. Her golden earrings tinkled together.

"It's not clear. They seem to be mostly trying to avoid the ships from the station," Yuskeya said.

The Chron ships were indeed running evasively. They had changed course as soon as the dark ships emerged from the station; so quickly, in fact, that they must have been expecting the response. Now they made for one of the other asteroid fields.

"They must have something like our burst drive," Viss said from engineering. "The signature is similar enough. That's technology that didn't exist at the time of the Chron War, so they've advanced since then."

Cerevare shook her head, then must have realized that Viss couldn't see her. "No, Viss. Even during the Chron War, they had a very fast in-system drive. For a while it seemed that was the secret to their seeming ability to appear out of nowhere, but someone realized there had to be more to it than that."

"Huh," Viss said, sounding surprised. "I didn't know that. If they were this fast in-system, the ships we had then wouldn't have had much of a chance."

"That's one reason we were losing the war," Cerevare said.

"I didn't realize that either," Yuskeya said.

"Back to business, folks," Rei interjected. "We can debate the failings of the historical record later. Here comes trouble."

The Chron ships changed course again, coming up behind one of the wormholes and dipping low under the tumbling asteroid field. Their spidery pursuers didn't seem fooled by the maneuver, following as smoothly as they seemed to do everything.

"Well, this is interesting," Baden said.

"What?"

"There's communication between the ships—the Chron and the others. I can't decrypt it, but the comm scan is picking up data bursts between them."

"If you could figure it out—even what they're doing, not necessarily what they're saying—then we might be able to communicate with the station," I said. "Do what you can."

Baden grinned. "And if I could figure out the content, too, we might be a whole lot closer to knowing what's going on here."

"That might be considered unethical," I said. "So I'm definitely not telling you to do that."

His fingers were already stuttering over the console. "Well, I'll just tell you if I pick up on anything by accident."

"You do that."

"Sit tight, folks," Rei said suddenly.

I glanced up at the screen and saw something I'd been hoping I wouldn't. The energy weapons in the front ends of some of the dark ships had begun to glow. Golden sparks vibrated between the protrusions, swelling to a globe of crackling energy.

Despite Rei's warning, Cerevare leapt to her feet. "No!" she gasped. "Don't destroy another one!"

A blast of yellow light flashed out from the long arms of one dark ship, but petered out short of a Chron vessel. It leapt forward in a renewed burst of speed.

"Cerevare, sit down," I ordered. "If we have to move fast, you could get thrown around."

The Lobor nodded and sat down, but her lupine face was taut with dismay. She balled her furred hands in her lap, never taking her eyes from the screen.

Baden flashed her a grin over his shoulder. "Hang in there, Cerevare. I'm beginning to think Chron ships are not as rare as we thought they were."

Her ears twitched, and she took a deep breath. "You may be right about that."

"I think we're in trouble here," Rei said. "They're coming straight at us."

Maybe sticking around hadn't been my best idea ever. "Get around to the other side of the station. We definitely want to avoid any crossfire."

The *Tane Ikai* wheeled suddenly under Rei's guidance and shot back the way we had come, making for the relative shelter of the other side of the station.

"*Merde!*" Rei hissed. "I can't do this. They're changing course again."

The alien ships were engaged in a wild dance of bursts and thrusters, the Chron apparently trying to shake their pursuers, who likewise jockeyed for position to take more shots with the energy weapons.

"Try to keep us out of their way," I said. "It's getting too dangerous. They're coming too close. Forget everything except keeping us clear."

"Easier said than done," she muttered.

Their trajectory had brought them gradually closer to the dark station. It was impossible to anticipate which way they'd veer next.

"I think their real target must be the station," Hirin said. "The Chron ships. It can't be coincidence that they're coming this close. They've got a whole system to escape into if they wanted to."

One of the dark ships fired again, missing by a narrow margin as the Chron veered up and around one of the nine large spikes pointing to the wormholes like crazed weather vanes. Its two pursuers split up, one staying on the Chron's tail while the other tried to circle around and catch the intruder between them.

"Sure is interesting to watch someone else's battle strategy, isn't it?" Baden said lightly, and Maja shot him a disapproving frown. She plainly didn't think it was the time for humour. He subsided, chastened. I was amazed.

"Luta," Rei said, and I knew instantly that it was serious, because she never, ever called me anything but "Captain" when we were on duty, "Luta, we'd better be ready with defenses if necessary. We can't outrun them now because I can't predict when we might suddenly be right in their path."

"Good idea," I said. "Yuskeya, give us full shields. Hirin, be ready on the weapons system and share control with my board. Viss, priorities for power are shields, burst drive and maneuvering jets, and then weapons."

Rei had called it not a moment too soon, because several things happened in far less time than it takes to tell it.

One of the Chron ships pulled a sharp, unexpected turn that must have left anyone inside it lightheaded, and made straight for the main torus of the station. The defenders, apparently taken by surprise, moved to follow, the energy weapons glowing brighter as they powered up again. The Chron ship gained a little distance on them.

It fired two torpedo-like missiles straight at the torus that formed the heart of the station. These weren't little flash-pack torps like Jahelia Sord had lobbed at us. These were heavy weapons, and they hurtled straight at their target.

"*Kristos!*" someone said. We were all probably thinking it. If the station blew up now, we were so close that we'd be pummelled by a shockwave of debris that could rip straight through us.

Two of the dark pursuers fired on the attacking Chron. Both

missed again as their target spun and dived. The Chron torpedoes reached the torus, and I tensed, nails digging into the armrests of the chair, preparing for the impact, the explosion. And whatever would happen to us, caught like a fly in a spiderweb.

"Captain Paixon, what the hell is going on up there? Are we in a dogfight?" Jahelia Sord's voice demanded over the comm. I felt a brief flash of guilt—I should have told her to secure herself somehow. She could have been thrown around with all our maneuvering. But I had honestly forgotten all about her.

"Sord, brace for impact!" was all I had time for.

The torps slid, smooth as a knife into *butero*, into the dark, gelatinous skin of the station. Simply disappeared. No impact, no detonation, nothing. I looked up at the screen in time to see that Chron ship making for the nearest wormhole, the two spidery ships in close pursuit.

"That was—" I started, but I didn't get to finish.

His comrades both fired on the station in quick succession.

Someone, maybe Maja, shouted—a brief, inarticulate cry of alarm. Movement on one of the screens caught my eye. I turned just in time to see one of the shorter black spikes of the station snake out toward the *Tane Ikai* like an enormous, outstretched tentacle, and envelop us in its shadowy grasp.

Chapter 21 — Luta
In the Belly of the Beast

"ALL DRIVES HAVE shut down," Viss yelled over the ship's comm. "Captain, what's happening?"

"Unknown," I told him in a voice I knew sounded shaky. "Don't try to restart the drives. We don't know what's happening. Come up with the rest of us and use the auxiliary console here."

The viewscreens had all gone black, showing nothing outside the ship. The power stayed on, the soft hum of life-support a comforting background drone. The ship seemed to be moving. Not normal drive-powered motion. It felt like we were being carried, a gentle swaying reminiscent of long-buried childhood memories. Pleasant, really. Only it wasn't supposed to feel like that on a far trader.

I still gripped the arms of the chair, and I realized my nails were actually hurting from digging in to the fabric. Deliberately, I relaxed my hands. Everyone else had a tight grip on something, too. Uppermost in my mind was the *Stillwell*—was this what it was like inside that ship? Alive, but blind and deaf to everything outside, cut off from everything? My stomach clenched in another sudden wave of nausea, and I didn't think it had anything to do with mutant cells or errant bioscavengers. It felt like pure fear.

"As soon as we stop moving, I want everyone in an EVA suit," I ordered.

"Are we going somewhere, Captain?"

"I don't know, Baden, but I'd like to be prepared. Get a suit to Jahelia Sord, too. Maja, you're in charge of that as soon as you have yours on."

We stopped. Everyone moved for the EVA lockers.

The ship's comm crackled loudly, and I jumped. Jahelia Sord's voice filled the bridge. "Godsdammit, what's happening, Captain? Are we in trouble?"

"I'm sending an EVA suit to your quarters, Sord. Put it on. That's all I can say for now."

"If the ship is in danger, I have a right—"

"I said, not now." I signalled to Baden to cut her off, and he leaned over the comm panel.

Viss's pounding feet echoed down the metal decking, and Gerazan was right behind him. They slowed when they reached the bridge, and Viss spoke in a low voice, without preamble. "Captain, we have a plan?" He carried one of the EVA suits from engineering over one arm and sat in the empty skimchair at the auxiliary engineering console to begin pulling it on. Gerazan had brought one, too, and immediately crossed to Rei, sitting beside her.

"No plan yet," I answered Viss. An eerie silence filled the bridge, and I found myself almost whispering. "We're playing by ear. But I'm not prepared to sit around very long, waiting to see what happens."

"Good. Sitting around isn't my strong point, either." He bent to secure the boots of his suit.

It took a few minutes to suit up. Baden and Maja checked each other's suits, and then Maja left with one for Sord. Gerazan and Rei checked each other as well, and the rest of us paired up. I'm not certain whose suit I checked; my mind was dangerously distracted, running through possible plans of action. We had flux lasers and a few other goodies in the weapons locker, not counting whatever personal ordnance the crew had in their quarters, which was likely not inconsiderable. The ship's weapons systems were offline. With the drives shut down by an unknown, outside force, we were pretty much at the mercy of that force, with only our own wits to rely on.

I didn't like this at all. If this was the situation inside the *Stillwell*, and had been for days, they'd probably all have gone mad and killed each other by now.

The comm board lit up.

"Incoming message," Baden said.

"Put it on the ship's comm, Baden. Let's all listen."

The voice was smooth and uninflected, strangely accented and genderless. Completely intelligible, though. "We apologize for any inconvenience. We have removed your ship from possible harm. Please make yourselves comfortable, and a representative will meet with you shortly."

I glanced around at the others. Viss raised an eyebrow, and Hirin shrugged. The voice went on.

"The environment in the *urgulat* immediately surrounding your ship has been adjusted to meet the survival requirements of your species. Please feel free to leave your vessel. At this time you will find only the rearmost airlock hatchway is operable. If you have any immediate concerns or requests, please respond on this wave."

Hirin said, "Well, at least they're polite."

"Politely laying down the law," Baden observed.

"What's an *urgulat*?" asked Maja.

I shrugged. "Good question. This station, I'd guess. Maybe they don't know our word for it."

"They seem to have a reasonable handle on the language," Yuskeya said. "It's older, more formal Esper, but clear enough."

"I'd like to take them up on that offer to look around," Viss said, getting up from his skimchair. "Captain?"

I held up a hand. "We're not all getting off the *Tane Ikai* at once. Viss, you and Yuskeya come with me. Hirin, you have the chair. Everyone sit tight, and monitor us on the suit mics and cameras."

Hirin opened his mouth as if he'd protest, but then closed it and merely nodded.

Someone else, however, did have something to say. Gerazan Soto stood to stiff attention and said formally, "Commander Blue, I'd like permission to ask you something."

If Yuskeya was surprised, her voice didn't show it. "Go ahead, Lieutenant."

He kept his eyes trained directly on Yuskeya when he spoke. "With all due respect to Captain Paixon, we're now in contact with a previously unknown alien species. Shouldn't the Protectorate assume control and follow protocols for this situation?"

In my peripheral vision I saw Rei shoot him a look that was—less than friendly. Viss muttered something I didn't catch. Angry words sparked on my own tongue, but I bit down on them. I'd let Yuskeya handle this. She seemed to take a moment to consider his words.

"Lieutenant Soto, you're quite right," she said finally.

Shock stole anything I might have said in that second. Someone made a gasp of surprise. Fortunately, Yuskeya continued without pausing.

"Or you would be, if we were still in Nearspace. However, we're not, and so I don't believe the Protectorate has any jurisdiction to override Captain Paixon's command. I am assigned to her crew, under her, and I'm not about to usurp her authority. You, however, are still under *my* command. Does that answer your question?"

His gaze didn't waver. "Yes, Commander. Thank you."

Rei let out a little huff of what sounded like annoyance. Hirin raised his eyebrows at me but didn't say anything. I merely said, "Now that that's cleared up, let's go."

The three of us headed for the rear airlock. Viss and Yuskeya hadn't said anything to each other, but I thought I could trust them to do their jobs.

Yuskeya paused when we passed the weapons locker. "Weapons?"

I hesitated. "I don't know. It's one of those, 'if they wanted us dead we'd already be breathing vacuum' scenarios. They had their chance to take us out—probably more than one while we were puttering around the station. And we're still here. I don't want to insult them."

"I'd rather insult them than be unprepared," Viss said.

"*Okej*, we'll compromise. You two take weapons, and I'll go unarmed. That should cover our bases."

They pulled plasma rifles from the locker, giving each a quick, efficient check before we hurried on to the airlock.

"Helmets?" Viss asked when we reached the outer door.

"As a precaution," I said with a nod. "Let's be sure these folks know what the 'survival requirements' of our species are before we try to breathe the air out there."

So we fastened on our helmets, ran through one more EVA check with each other, and pushed the button to open the airlock. When it cycled through with us inside, I nodded to Viss, and he opened the other door to let us out.

We stood for a long moment in the hatchway, staring out at the inside of the station.

"*Sankta merde!*" Viss breathed, his voice low over the interior helmet speaker.

I don't know what I had expected—judging from the gelatinous exterior of the station, something equally surreal, I suppose. Instead, it bore a striking resemblance to docking bays all over Nearspace. Solid floors and walls, cables and wires snaking in unfathomable coils, miscellaneous equipment and tools pushed off to the sides out of the way.

The only strange element was that it was entirely black. Everything was black—some shade between charcoal and ebony. Some surfaces were matte and some reflective; various textures caught the light as we moved, finally, out of the hatchway of the ship. But the colour scheme had ostensibly been devised by someone of little imagination or colour perception. Light shone from the ceiling to illuminate the bay, long glowing strips running the length of the room. The light wasn't hot, like the high pressure sodium lights on the *Tane Ikai*; it had a more muted feel, like phosphorescence.

Yuskeya had her datamed out, taking readings. "They got that part right, at any rate. Seventy-nine percent nitrogen, twenty percent oxygen, one percent a mix of other little goodies, none of which will harm us. Pressure's right, too, one kilogram per square centimeter, and the gravity feels pretty much like home. I'd say it's safe to take off the helmets."

So we did, while we walked a little way from the ship in order to turn and look back at her. There wasn't much to see. Only the rear wall of the hull was visible, the rest of the ship still enveloped in the black, jelly-like substance that made up the exterior of the station. I imagined it letting go of the ship with a sucking noise and oozing into the shape of one of those long spikes. I wasn't sure I trusted any material that acted that way.

Viss strode to the nearest wall and touched it with a tentative, gloved finger. "More solid than it appears," he observed. He inspected his glove as if he expected some of the material to have rubbed off on it, but he held it up so we could see that none had. He pressed a palm flat against it. "There's the slightest give. I feel like if I pushed hard enough, my hand would go inside."

"How about you don't press that hard," Yuskeya suggested in a terse voice, not taking her eyes off her datamed screen.

Before Viss could answer her, the "representative" appeared. I say "appeared" advisedly—it was only a hologram or something akin to that, and it sprang into existence a mere foot or so from Yuskeya. She'd been intent on her readings and stumbled sideways, tripping on one of the cables. Viss automatically put out a hand to steady her.

"Thanks," she whispered without looking at him.

He nodded gravely, even though she couldn't see him, and said nothing.

"Are your crew and vessel unharmed?" the hologram alien asked politely, in unexpectedly intelligible Esper.

I couldn't answer right away. If the hologram offered an accurate representation of the species that had created this station and the spidery ships, they were intriguing. They reminded me of crows.

I shouldn't say that, I suppose, because it gives the wrong impression. The hologram stood at least five feet tall, so size did not enter into it. It was the long, beak-like mouth—the only accurate way to describe it was as a beak, although it was paler than a crow's usually dark one. Then there was the sleek head covered in what resembled black feathers. The small, round, dark eyes, constraining a rampant brightness as it regarded us.

A long, camel-coloured robe with a rolled collar that wrapped around its throat also concealed the rest of the body. My imagination, rightly or wrongly, supplied furled wings and splayed, birdlike feet beneath. The creature must have hands, but somehow I couldn't envision them. There was no apparent way to discern gender.

"We're fine, thank you," I finally breathed.

"You may speak my name as Fha," the hologram said. "And how are you called?"

"Captain Luta Paixon," I said. "These are my crewmates, Commander Blue and Engineer Feron. How can you—why can we understand you so well?"

"We have not yet had many dealings with the inhabitants of the linked systems you call Nearspace," it said, "and those we have had were a long time past. But we still retain a database of language. We welcome you here, although the circumstances are unfortunate."

Not many dealings? I thought, but didn't say. I nodded. "We apologize for entering this system without invitation or warning. We were stranded—"

The holographic crow nodded. "Our vessel had advised us of your proximity to the wormhole. We apologize for the delay in communicating with you when you arrived in this system. There was some debate over whether contact would be in your best interests or not."

"Well, you've certainly made contact now," Viss muttered.

"Yes, the incursion of the <*garbled*> made it unavoidable." Fha sighed. "I suppose it was inevitable, since they seek to involve you in their plans again."

I glanced at Viss and Yuskeya, who both shrugged minutely. "I'm sorry, I didn't understand what you said. The what?"

It cocked its head at me in a very birdlike manner. "You call them *Chron*, I believe."

I thought fast. "We're anxious to know anything you can tell us about that species. They attacked Nearspace a long time ago—"

"We know," it said, beak bobbing. "We stopped them."

The calm statement almost stopped my breathing. I heard

Viss or Yuskeya—possibly both of them—gasp behind me. These aliens were responsible for the abrupt end of the Chron War so many years ago?

"Then," I finally stammered, "I suppose I should thank you. By all accounts, we were losing that war when the Chron disappeared."

"You are most welcome," the crow-like being said. "If it would be of interest to you, I can make available to you our database of information on that species."

"That would be wonderful," I told the alien, thinking of Cerevare's face when she found out about the offer.

"I should explain," the alien said, "that it is merely the restrictions of biology which prevent me from speaking with you in person. Our atmospheric requirements are too different to permit a physical conversation. I will convert the data into a form usable by you and have it delivered to your ship."

"Can you help us return to Nearspace?" I hadn't meant to ask it so bluntly, but all other considerations aside, it was the one thing I had to know as quickly as possible.

It hesitated. "I hope so. The circumstances are . . . unsettled at the moment. Would it be agreeable for you to remain here for a period of time?"

"There are other, urgent matters I would like to discuss with you," I said, thinking of the dark-shrouded *Stillwell*. "And reasons why we must return to Nearspace as soon as possible. We can stay for only a short time."

The alien nodded. "I will gather the data, and we will assess the situation. May I appear in this form in your vessel if need be?"

"Certainly."

"Then I will return soon. As you say, *gis la revido*, Captain." It inclined its head, and I had an instant to realize that it did not have glossy feathers, but a gelatinous-looking skin, almost like that of the station. And then the hologram was gone.

Viss, Yuskeya, and I regarded one another. "Suddenly I don't feel so much like exploring," Viss said.

I nodded. "Let's see what the others make of this." I knew they'd been able to see and hear over the suit cams and mics, but no-one on the bridge had said a word over the comm.

So we left the long, black bay and headed for the bridge of the *Tane Ikai*, and when I walked into it a few minutes later I thought that it had never been so comfortingly familiar.

"So, Captain, do we trust these crows? And how the hell do they know Esper?" Rei seemed her irrepressible self when we entered the bridge, although I noticed that Gerazan wasn't sitting next to her as he usually did. He'd taken the chair at the auxiliary engineering console.

So Rei had the same first impression of their appearance. "I'm inclined to trust them for now, but let's not call them 'crows'. I don't want to offend them."

"How about 'Corvids'?" asked Viss. "The genus is *Corvus* and there are numerous species, but generally the crows and their cousins—ravens, jackdaws—they're known as Corvids."

The things that man knew. Always surprising me.

"Corvids it is, then, for now," I said. "Unless and until they correct us or tell us what they call themselves. As to how they know Esper . . . I hope that's one of the things they'll explain to us later." I paused, then continued. "But yes, I think I do trust them. It was only a hologram, I know, but I didn't get any kind of bad feeling from it. And if they really did stop the Chron—"

"We have only their word for that," Hirin reminded me. "For any of it, really."

"I know but—Viss, Yuskeya? You were out there. What do you think?"

Their replies were forestalled by the quiet eruption through one of the starwise walls of a thin black tentacle. It deposited a datachip on the nearest board and disappeared through the hull wall, making only the slightest sucking noise. It left no trace or indication of its passing.

"Whoa," Baden said.

Nobody else said a word.

"I suppose," I said finally, "this is the datachip our hologram host, Fha, offered to share with us. About the Chron." I walked over and picked it up. It replicated a regular datachip, although the surface held an odd sheen, as if it was wet, but it wasn't. "Cerevare, I guess this is for you."

The Lobor historian took it from my outstretched hand like someone in a dream. "Thank you, Captain. Do you think . . . I mean . . . do you think it's safe to use it?"

I fetched a deep breath and let it escape in a sigh. "From what we've seen here so far, I think these Corvids could snuff us out any time they wanted to. Luckily for us, they don't seem to want to. So I'm betting that datachip is as safe to use as any of ours."

"In that case—if you'll excuse me, I'll go to my quarters and start reviewing it." Her lupine face was as close to grinning as it could get.

"Let us know what you find," I said. "So, what do people think? What impression did you get from the holo?"

"I'm inclined to give them the benefit of the doubt," Viss said. "If only because, as you've said, they haven't taken any of their many opportunities to do us harm."

Rei nodded. "I agree. But I want to know more about what they're doing here with this station, in this system. And more about their dealings with the Chron. And how they know our language."

I almost laughed. "Start making a list."

Two things happened then. Jahelia Sord signalled from her room, and a medical alarm went off from First Aid. Yuskeya hurried off to see to her patient, and I took the call from Sord on the ship's comm.

"I noticed that things got pretty quiet, all of a sudden," she said. She spoke most of the time in a practiced monotone, although sometimes she drawled her words almost mockingly.

"We're at a . . . station," I told her. "I'm not sure how long we'll be here. But there's no apparent danger at this point."

She chuckled humourlessly. "I wasn't worried about danger," she said. "I was simply curious." She broke the connection.

I shook my head. For the amount of trouble she was in, she didn't act worried enough. At some point, I had to confront her about how she could work for PrimeCorp, doing the obviously illegal things they asked of her, but there certainly hadn't been an opportunity yet. And I was afraid I wouldn't like her reasons— maybe even afraid they'd make sense to me. Hirin and I had been through tough times, when jobs with questionable ethics but good money had been tempting. But I couldn't worry about that now.

Yuskeya's voice came over the comm. "Captain, can I see you in First Aid?"

I crossed the bridge and went through Sensors to the sickbay. Yuskeya waited at the door, her face grave.

"I'm sorry, Captain. Chen has died."

Sad news, but not entirely surprising. "Can you isolate the cause?"

"Another fever, a bad one, and the meds couldn't control it. I had him in a medi-wrap trying to cool him down physically, but it wasn't enough. He slipped deeper into the coma and . . . didn't wake up."

She watched me, clearly wondering how I'd take the news.

"Thanks, Yuskeya. I know you did all you could for him. We'll have to put the body down in one of the cargo pods and refrigerate it until we get to Nearspace. I don't—I don't want to jettison the body here, even after we leave the station."

"I know. I feel the same way. Will you tell Gerazan, or do you want me to do it?"

I wasn't feeling particularly enamoured of Gerazan Soto at the moment, but I knew there'd been nothing personal in what he'd said to Yuskeya. "I'll go and tell everyone now. They're all on the bridge, except for Cerevare."

I steeled myself as I returned to the bridge to tell the others. I'd have to be careful to avoid meeting Hirin's eyes. I knew the depth of worry I'd see reflected there would be matched only by my own.

Chapter 22 — Luta
Through a Glass, Darkly

AFTER I TOLD them about Chen's death, I set the crew to checking the ship for damage or anything untoward. We couldn't scan beyond the ship and the docking bay in which it sat, but we could hardly complain about that. We were, apparently, safely out of harm's way—at least for now.

At least, the ship was. As soon as everyone was busy, I went to my quarters to have a nap. I didn't tell anyone that was my plan. As I broke the news to the others about Chen's death, fatigue hit me like a flash-pack torp hitting an ice cream cone. I was glad I'd sat in the big chair before I told them. Gerazan Soto took it hard, as I'd expected he would. I watched Rei, her momentary irritation with him faded, cross to the chair where he sat and slip an arm around his shoulders. His jaw tightened, and his eyes glistened with unshed tears. He was now the sole survivor of the *Domtaw*—possibly the sole survivor of the two ships the Protectorate had sent into the unknown system, if the *Stillwell* was not merely in some kind of stasis. That was a heavy burden of guilt for anyone to carry. He nodded gravely when I told him my plan to preserve Chen's body until we made it back to Nearspace.

"Captain—I hope there are no hard feelings about what I said earlier. It wasn't anything to do with you personally."

"I know. It's all right." I found my own annoyance had fled as well. I had bigger things to worry about.

I assigned Gerazan to help Viss in checking over the ship, thinking it would be good for him to have something useful to do. He accepted the job without hesitation.

And then I excused myself and made my way down the corridor to the quarters Hirin and I shared. I stopped at the head on the way there and drew a shallow basin of water to rinse my face. *I'm feeling all of my eighty-four years at once.* It seemed that as long as I kept moving, crisis to crisis, I could manage. But any sort of lull, and the fatigue crashed in on me, threatening to bear me down under its weight.

My hands shook as I scooped up water, splattering the narrow rim around the sink and the floor below it. I hadn't mentioned the aches and trembles in my arms and legs to anyone, not even Yuskeya. She was sure to tell Hirin, and he was already worried enough. It wasn't difficult to find regular pain meds in First Aid; I knew the brand names on the injectors, even if I'd never needed them myself before. And dosing was merely a matter of reading the labels. Before long she'd surely notice her supplies running low, but I'd deal with that confrontation when it came.

I closed my eyes and dragged more water over my face, relaxing into the cool, soothing tingle of it against my skin. I repeated the motion until the tremor in my hands abated, then rested them on the rim of the sink. I let my head droop toward the water, feeling the delicious stretch in my neck muscles. Maybe Yuskeya and mother's software were wrong, and I could put most of this down to stress. We *were* stranded in an unknown system surrounded by hostile and unknown aliens, after all. That could take a toll on anyone.

Drip, drop, plop. The water I'd splashed dripped over the edge of the sink and onto the floor. I'd apparently made quite a mess. I sighed and opened my eyes. Better clean it up.

The bright red droplets diffusing in the basin told a different story. Not water dripping. Blood—my blood—splashing steadily from my nose into the water. I watched, mesmerized, as the colour swirled and fanned through the water like a red silk scarf floating lazily in a breeze. I grabbed for tissue and crammed it against my nose, checking in the mirror to make sure none had stained my t-shirt. That would be difficult to hide. It was clean. The shakes came back and I had to use both hands to hold the wad of tissue in place. My legs chose that moment to tremble as well, and I sat down heavily on the toilet, forcing myself to lean forward and pinch the bridge of my nose with shaking fingers. Our son, Karro, had suffered frequent nosebleeds as a child, so I knew the drill. I counted seconds, forcing myself to go slowly and breathing shallowly through my mouth. Sixty. Then sixty more. Three more times, for five minutes.

I pulled away the tissue, grimacing as it tore, shreds stuck to my face with thick, dark clots. Threw the handful in the recycler, gingerly released the bridge of my nose. The flow seemed to have stopped. I released the water in the basin and drew fresh, repeating the motions of cleansing my face, but with a distinct purpose now. The water was a deep pink by the time my face was clean again.

Forcing myself to take deep, calming breaths, I concentrated on tidying away every drop of water and scrap of tissue. When the head was spotless again, I regarded myself in the mirror. I looked pretty much as usual. A little flushed, perhaps, as if I'd just finished a mild *tae-ga-chi* workout. I ran my hands through my hair, combing it with my fingers, which no longer shook. I thought I was presentable enough to open the door.

"What's wrong with you?" I whispered to myself in the mirror before I left the room.

But the mirror had no answer.

DESPITE THE NOSEBLEED episode, or perhaps because of it, I fell into my bed and slept for two solid hours. I'd been on the bridge only a few minutes, getting progress reports that basically said not much of anything had happened, when a Corvid reappeared.

The hologram sprang to life on the bridge, close to Rei's pilot board. It gave her more of a start than she'd admit to later.

"You have suffered a loss," the crow-like being began. "We sympathize."

It was still wrapped in the same burlap-coloured robe, all but the head and what might be considered a neck hidden by its folds. Was it Fha, the same creature that had spoken to us before? It was impossible to tell. The appearance and voice seemed identical, so I was inclined to think it was. The more intriguing question was, how did they know about Chen's death? They must have a way of monitoring us, the same way we'd identified the scientists on the operant moon. I hoped that was all it was.

I decided to risk calling it by name. "Thank you, Fha. It is, I'm afraid, another reason our return to Nearspace grows more imperative."

It didn't correct me, so it must indeed be Fha. It nodded, beak-like mouth bobbing up and down. "We understand. I have data to share that may affect your decision." I had the impression of movement beneath the cloak, but no hands or wings appeared.

"May I ask a question, first?"

"Of course."

I had to phrase this diplomatically. "The other ship that was in the system with us—it was encased in a dark field. We couldn't contact them or scan the vessel. Are they—will they be—"

Fha nodded. "They are perfectly safe. The stasis field was for their protection—I am only sorry we could not protect the other ship in the same manner. It will dissipate over time—not overly long by your standards. They will be confused, but unharmed."

I let out a long sigh, relieved. "Thank you."

Fha nodded. "Now, have you studied the information on the species you call Chron?"

"Not all of us, but our expert is still reviewing it. She will explain it to the rest of us."

"Efficient," Fha noted. "I will, then, tell you only what is necessary to understand the current situation."

Another hologram appeared in the air above the Corvid's head, and it took me a few minutes to realize what I was seeing. A wormhole, represented from the outside. It looked like a pencil stuck through several layers of paper or cardboard.

"The Chron discovered their first wormhole at about the same time as your species did," the Corvid said, "but their reaction was very different. Instead of seeking out new worlds to colonize peacefully, they went in search of conquest. It is an old tale, oft repeated. Some beings cannot stand the thought of being less than foremost among all they encounter.

"When they discovered a wormhole into our space, we realized quickly that they were not interested in peaceful coexistence or economic relations. We were so different from them that they actually seemed indifferent to communicating with us—in fact, they viewed us as . . . prey." Fha shrugged as if shaking off the unpleasant thought. "They declared war, not so much formally as by an immediate attempt to exterminate us. Their technology was inferior, however, and they quickly abandoned their hostilities. We were happy and relieved to see them go."

"If it's not impolite to ask—what should we call your species?" I asked when Fha paused.

The beak-like mouth opened and closed in a staccato rhythm—the equivalent of laughter? "Your own term for us—Corvids—is perfectly acceptable. And I, should you be wondering, am one of the females of my people."

I felt my face flush slightly. Had my unspoken question been so obvious? I merely said, "Thank you."

"They left us with an ethical dilemma," Fha continued. "Could we stand quietly by and allow them to find other species and perpetrate the same aggressions? After much consideration and debate, it was decided that we were morally constrained to try and stop the Chron."

She swung her head side to side sorrowfully, dark eyes troubled, beak low. "We were regrettably slow in reaching this decision, and the Chron had already found your Nearspace and begun systematically attacking you. By the time we stopped them, you had suffered greatly.

"We found this system, a 'hub' system which the Chron used to travel to various others. Several natural wormholes converged here, and we configured several others—"

"Pardon me," Viss interjected in his politest voice, "did you say 'configured' wormholes? As in, constructed them?"

The Corvid nodded. "It is not a simple technology to manipulate, and the resource costs are extremely high. We were also fearful that it might fall into Chron hands, as some of our other technology did. But there seemed little choice. We established this station and others, and the attendant guardian asteroid fields, to keep the Chron contained within systems they already controlled."

"I can't imagine they were too happy about that," Hirin said.

"An understatement," the Corvid agreed with a bob of her head. "It was during this time also that we sent data-collecting drones into your Nearspace, and learned much about your several species. That is why we appear proficient with your language. It is actually being filtered through a database and translated as we speak—but it allows a comfortable semblance of conversation."

"But it's been a century and a half since our Chron War," Baden noted. "Surely you haven't been holding them off while they hammered away at this system all that time?"

"Fortunately, no. They've had other things to concern them in that time, notably a schism in their society between the warlike sects and more peaceful ones—although we have been unable to learn many specifics. That set them back decades."

"But now?" I asked. "From what we've seen, they seem to be on the offensive again. And after so long, why are they apparently breaking through your defenses?"

"They certainly are on the offensive. Despite their setbacks, they have not stood still in the development of technology. They are not content to stay within the systems they currently control. They have become more adept at using algorithms to calculate and navigate a path through the asteroid fields, as well as developing a stealth mechanism so they can sneak through the wormholes."

"Why not simply destroy the wormholes that lead out of their systems?" Rei asked bluntly. "Cut them off, seal them in, and forget about them?"

Fha's beak fluttered again in what might have been a Corvid smile. "Destroying wormholes is not as easy as you might think. We can disable them temporarily—you saw that when our ship fired on the renegade Chron who was trying to reach your Nearspace."

I sat forward. "You mean the damage to that wormhole is

temporary?"

She nodded. "In relative terms. It will revert to its previous state naturally, usually within—" she paused, then finished, "three to five of your years."

My heart sank. Three to five years! PrimeCorp could harm Mother in a matter of days, much less years—if they hadn't already done so. I shied away from that thought. As for me and my condition—I shuddered, remembering my earlier nosebleed. I was quite certain I'd be dead long before that wormhole was in working order. I forced myself to nod. "I see."

"So it is a temporary solution, and there is another reason that is more—mysterious," the Corvid went on. "We cannot explain it, at least not yet. When a wormhole—a naturally occurring one—is disrupted, we have found that another one will soon appear, connecting the same two systems as the original. Its endpoints may be a great distance from the originals, but there it will stay, as stable as the first one was, for as long as it is needed. When the original wormhole is restored, the replacement will, after a time, dissipate. It is as if some fundamental balance in the cosmos must be restored and maintained."

Hope surged again. "So a new wormhole could open at any time between Nearspace and the system where we were stranded?"

The Corvid nodded gravely. "Yes. But it may be difficult or nearly impossible to find, and there is no way to predict precisely when it will appear."

I sighed. "*Okej.* So you can't seal the Chron into their systems. What do you think they're after now?"

She shrugged. "More of the same, we imagine. They reject all attempts on our part to communicate with them. Their initial forays into this system, and their attempts to break through into others, intensified recently."

I glanced over at Hirin and caught his eye. He cocked an eyebrow. Had the Protectorate scientists, mucking around on the artifact moon, somehow turned the eyes of the Chron toward Nearspace once again?

"I fear that difficult times may lie ahead for us, and for others," the Corvid said.

"I'm certain you'll find the inhabitants of Nearspace to be allies," I said, "but is there any way to forestall another war before it begins?"

"If there is, we have not been able to find it," she said. "We cannot indefinitely keep them from leaving their systems, if we cannot destroy the wormholes, and they do not wish to be confined. The only thing that has restrained them this long is the schism in their society—should the two sides reunite with a shared agenda of conquest, or should the warlike Chron find other allies, we would not be able to stop them."

"Is that likely?" Hirin asked.

Fha raised her shoulders and dropped them in a very human shrug. "We do not know. We have had little contact even with the peaceful ones. They are—mistrustful at best."

"Which is why you thought we'd be safer staying here," Viss said.

The Corvid nodded. "We felt obliged to offer you our protection, since it was the actions of one of our ships that severed your means of returning home directly."

"But we can't stay here," I said. "We need to return to Nearspace as quickly as possible. For many reasons, as well as warning others about the impending threat of the Chron."

"In addition to which, the Captain is ill and needs special medical attention," Yuskeya added.

I threw her a reproachful frown, but she ignored me.

Fha regarded me with a keen eye. "We have limited knowledge of your physiology, so I am afraid we could be of little assistance in that regard."

Rei continued my initial thought. "But can you help us get back to Nearspace?" she asked impatiently. "Everything hinges on that, and so far, well, you haven't been very encouraging in that department."

The Corvid regarded her unblinkingly. "I cannot get you there," she said finally. "But I can show you a way. Whether or not you choose to take it is up to you."

The holographic image of the wormhole that had been suspended above her head disappeared, and a starmap took its place. The configuration was completely unfamiliar to me, and extremely complex, showing numerous systems linked by wormholes. There were more systems than in all of Nearspace, and I felt a sudden insignificance.

A series of three wormhole skips blinked green, and my heart sank.

"Three skips?" Hirin asked, trying, I could tell, to sound optimistic. "That might not be too bad, if the in-system travel times are reasonable. This is the most direct route?"

"It is not the most direct," the Corvid said, "but slightly less dangerous than the most direct. I still have mixed feelings about the propriety of even offering this as a possibility. Because," she said, and the middle two systems in the route changed to slowly blink red, "it will take you directly through a sector of Chron space. Which makes it difficult for me to calculate your chances of survival."

Chapter 23 — Jahelia Zelendu and Jousting

I LET MYSELF drop into my chair, my hands falling from the screen where I'd been furiously typing all I'd heard over my eavesdropping rig—which consisted of Pita, in my datapad, patched into the bridge comm system.

"*Sankta merde,* Pita, did you hear all that?" I subvocalized into the throat touch mic.

"That they're going into Chron space? Yeah, I heard it. I can't believe we went to all that trouble to download me into this thing and bring it aboard, only to end up on a suicide mission."

I pursed my lips. "I don't know—we might have a slim chance of survival. Whatever else I might think about Luta Paixon and her crew, they seem to have a knack for getting out of tight situations unscathed."

"This is not a tight situation." Pita's voice sounded dryly amused in my head. "This is a death sentence."

"Oh, come on. You can't even die."

"I *feel* like I can die," she retorted. "Doesn't that amount to the same thing?"

I wasn't interested in getting into an existential argument with my PAREA AI at the moment. "Anyway, that was only part of what I meant. Did you hear them talking about the tech these crow-things have?" I got up from the chair, pacing the small room. It was killing me that I didn't know yet what the aliens looked like. All I knew was what I'd overheard from the bridge. "Creating and manipulating wormholes? Static asteroid fields? Can you imagine what some of that would bring in Nearspace? Alin Sedmamin, for one, would literally drool on his great big shiny desk if I told him I could get him tech like that."

"I didn't hear the crow make any offer to *share* that technology," Pita observed. "In fact, she sounded fairly annoyed that some of it had fallen into Chron hands in the past."

"Well, I'm obviously not going to ask them for it. But if the opportunity presents itself—"

"Um, and how exactly do you propose to get your hands on any kind of tech or specs? You're sort of a prisoner here. *We're* sort of prisoners here."

The room was bigger than my sleeping quarters on the *Hunter's Hope*, but it felt cramped. Even smaller when you tried to pace inside its confines. I didn't need Pita to remind me of our situation. It had been less than twenty-four hours since I'd come aboard the *Tane Ikai,* and I was already starting to chafe at the restraint. At least the news about the *Hunter's Hope* was good—if I could return to claim her before someone else decided she was salvage. But that worry could wait. One problem at a time.

"Our situation could change if you could get access to the ship network," I reminded her. "I didn't bring you along for your scintillating conversation."

Her heavy sigh whistled through my brain. "I'm getting there. I think I'm close. There are always vulnerabilities in every system, I just have to find the right one."

"Keep at it, then."

"You're the boss."

The trouble was I didn't feel like the boss. I felt completely at the mercy of Paixon and her crew and these aliens and the whims of fate. Helpless, like in those old nightmares. And I *hated* it.

Shedding my jacket and pushing my chair against the far wall, I moved into the slow, rhythmic movements of a *zelendu* form. It was much harder to concentrate without the smooth, polished wood of a *vazel* staff in my hands, but mine had been left behind on the *Hunter's Hope.* I chose a form that took only three square feet of floor space, and pulled some of my kicks. Didn't want to hit a wall and bring someone running to see if I was trying to break out. That thought made me smile. With luck, and Pita's help, I wouldn't have to resort to anything so crude. Only halfway through the workout, a knock sounded on the door. I took a quick glance to make sure neither neither Pita nor the room computer would arouse any suspicions, then said, "Come on in."

"I've disengaged the lock, but my hands are full. Can you open it?" said a muffled, female voice.

"Sure thing."

A woman I hadn't seen before stood outside the door with a plate of steaming food and a tall, condensation-beaded glass. Her blonde hair had been pulled into a practical ponytail, but the shorter layers had come free and framed her face. I'd put her age around forty, perhaps—although I, of all people, know that appearances can be deceiving. This had to be the captain's daughter; she certainly wasn't the Erian pilot. Blue eyes regarded me shrewdly.

"Supper time," she said, gesturing slightly with the dishes. "Spicy pasta and vegetable paste, nothing fancy, I'm afraid."

I shrugged. "If someone else cooks it, I'm happy." I took the plate and glass from her, turned and took the few steps necessary to set them down on the desk. When I turned back, she still stood there, arms crossed, studying me.

"Can I help you with something?"

She tilted her head slightly to the side. "I'm trying to figure you out, honestly."

I laughed. "Good luck with that. I don't have myself entirely figured out. Maja, right? Captain's daughter?"

She nodded and pursed her lips. "I haven't really decided if I think you're a criminal, or merely another one of Alin Sedmamin's pawns," she said, shifting her weight to lean against the door frame. "Don't take offense—he fooled me for a long time, too."

I wondered if she realized how easy it would be for me to take a couple of steps, grab her elbow, and twist. Hit the pressure point that would have her on her knees, gasping and whimpering. Then I could head for the bridge, or anywhere else I wanted on the damn ship. She didn't seem at all worried. Maybe she knew *zelendu* too, or warrior chi, or some other hand-to-hand. She looked fit enough. Or maybe she realized I had nowhere to go that would do me any damn good.

"Sedmamin's pretty easy to read. He wants power first, money second . . . and we didn't go beyond that in our conversations." I sat in the desk chair so I wouldn't be so tempted to knock her unconscious. "I don't think of myself as a criminal, if that counts for anything."

"Everyone's the hero of their own story." She shrugged. "I do think you're a user, though. You used Baden to try and get information about Mother."

"Oh, he told you about that, did he? I wondered if he would."

"I guess it didn't mean that much to him," she said.

"No, Baden's a big boy. I don't think he was in any danger of being hurt by little old me."

"You probably think you're using Alin Sedmamin, too."

I smiled. "Between you and me, I don't like the man. Entirely too slick. But he can talk a good game. I can see how *some people* would be taken in by him."

She didn't rise to the bait. "PrimeCorp's been in the 'using people' business for a long time. Sedmamin has a lot more experience at it than you do."

That's what you think. She radiated such smugness, standing there, that suddenly I wanted to hurt her. "Now, Baden Methyr, there's another slick talker. You think I used him, but it wasn't like he didn't—"

"Would you even care if PrimeCorp actually harmed my grandmother? That was the message you brought Mother, wasn't it?"

The abrupt change of topic caught me off guard. I almost said *No, I wouldn't care, in fact I'd be damn happy about it since she ruined my father's life. To say nothing of mine.* But I didn't. I swallowed those words, smiled, and said, "Isn't Baden Methyr kind of young for you? But then, I read in your mother's file that you were a teacher. Maybe you like them young."

She was good, I'll give her that. She didn't flinch. She narrowed her eyes a little and nodded slowly, like she was talking to herself. "You know, I can see how angry you are. It practically lights up the air around you. I can see it, because that was me, for a long, long time. But I don't know what your anger's about."

I blew out an exaggerated sigh. "Well, Maja, as much fun as this has been, I'm really not sure what it is you want from me. My supper's getting cold, and that *will* make me angry. So unless you have a point to make . . ." I raised my eyebrows at her.

"Nope, that's all," she said, straightening. "I'm sure we'll talk again. Enjoy your supper."

She shut the door, and I heard the plasma bar click into place, locking me in. Her footsteps retreated on the metal decking, unhurried. Our verbal jousting hadn't made her run off crying, that was for sure.

I stared at the plate of pasta for a long moment, fighting the urge to pick up the whole mess and hurl it at the wall. Angry? Damn right, I was angry. I was angry at Emmage Mahane, I was angry at smarmy Alin Sedmamin, I was angry at the stupid aliens who'd put me in this situation. I was angry at everyone on this ship. I was even angry at my poor, dead father, who'd made bad decisions and kept too many secrets when he was alive and left me to deal with them when he was gone.

I closed my eyes and drew in a long, slow breath, pursed my lips, and blew it out again. *Breathe. Repeat. Breathe.* Why had I even engaged with the woman? So far, I thought I'd held the upper hand in every conversation I'd had with these people— well, except when Paixon had cut me off. But I'd let her daughter get to me. I didn't even know how she'd done it. I felt an irrational urge to refuse to eat the supper simply because she'd brought it to me. The rational part of my brain reminded me that the gesture would be pointless. I was sure no-one on the *Tane Ikai* would lose any sleep over me not eating, and I was the one who'd be hungry.

"Well, that was interesting," Pita said in a chipper voice.

"I'm not in the mood." Slowly I took up the fork and scooped up a bite of pasta.

"How's supper?"

"Pita," I said in what I hoped was a warning voice. Honestly, the vegetable paste was delicious, but I wouldn't admit that to anyone.

"Well, then, are you in the mood for this?" She lowered her voice to a whisper. "I'm in. We've got access to the entire ship network."

I swallowed and smiled. "Good work, Pita. I knew you could do it."

"So did I, once you left me alone long enough."

"Whatever."

"So, what now?"

That was a very good question. "Patch me into the audio comm again," I told her. "Every feed on the ship you can get. I need something to listen to while I eat."

Chapter 24 — Luta
Truce and Negotiations

FOLLOWING HER RATHER portentous remark about our survival chances, Fha had excused herself to attend to something urgent on the station, promising to return later. As her hologram faded, another black tentacle extruded through the bridge wall, bearing another chip.

"Route data, do you think?" Yuskeya guessed.

"Likely," I told her. "Take it and see, would you?"

She set it into her datapad and nodded.

"All right, everyone. We need to eat anyway, so we'll do it in the galley and discuss our options."

Not that I had much doubt how everyone felt, but I always made it a point to listen to my crew whenever possible. Even though it was mealtime, Cerevare remained in her quarters, still poring over the data the Corvids had provided. She seemed completely absorbed when I poked my head in to tell her the plan, so I left her there. Hirin and I quickly threw together a big pot of spicy pasta and vegetable paste for supper, and Maja and Viss took plates to Jahelia Sord and Cerevare. Yuskeya sat with her head bent over the datapad and the information the Corvid had provided.

Baden pulled cold drinks for everyone and passed them around, while Rei and Gerazan set places. I could almost convince myself it was a normal suppertime. Almost.

Viss returned. "I'm not sure Cerevare will even taste that before it gets cold," he said. "I had to knock twice before she answered."

"Let's hope she gets some insights that might help us," I said. "Where's Maja?"

"She took Sord's meal, said she wanted to meet her," Viss said. "Do we have to wait for her? I'm starving."

But Maja had returned by the time we had all the plates dished up. Her face held a thin, pensive tension, and I wondered if Sord had said anything untoward to her, but there was no chance to ask.

"Well, everyone heard what Fha said, so we might as well discuss it," Hirin said once everyone was settled, plates before them and a communal basket of sweet rolls in the center of the table.

"Maybe the Corvids could give us some better weapons," Rei said. "She obviously feels bad about stranding us."

"Unless they're wary about sharing tech," Viss said. "They don't even know us, so who knows how much they really trust us? And it sounded like they've been burned by the Chron in that department."

"Three skips seems long. Maybe it's too dangerous. There's only one of us, and how many Chron?" Maja said. "I don't think our chances are very good, even with whatever help the Corvids can give us."

Baden turned to her. "So you'd stay here?"

She frowned. "I'm not saying that. With Mother sick—"

"Now, don't everybody start worrying about me," I interrupted. "I'm doing okay."

"With respect, Captain, you're not," Yuskeya said. "You're well aware it's taking more and more medication to keep you going, and sooner or later one of two things is going to happen. Either it'll reach a saturation point and stop working, or we'll run out of supplies. I doubt the Corvids can help us with that. Getting you to Nearspace has to be a priority."

I didn't argue the point. I wondered briefly what she'd say if she knew about the nosebleed I'd had earlier.

"Does anyone think we should go back to the system with the artifact moon, and see if a new wormhole has opened up?" Maja asked. "That would solve the problem."

Hirin cleared his throat. "Given the size of the system, and the data we, er . . . appropriated from the *Domtaw*, it could take months, even years, to search the entire system. We'd have to get close enough to the wormhole to pick up its radiation signature. It would be no different from any kind of wormhole spelunking."

"Even if we found one, it might not be a 'replacement' route to Delta Pav. It could lead anywhere," Gerazan suggested.

Hirin nodded. "Granted, we could get lucky and find it—if it exists—in the first week, but I don't think I'm willing to bet Luta's life on it."

"And we could end up in a worse situation, depending on where it spit us out."

"If we take the Chron route and run the burst drive as much as possible, we might slip between wormholes without even being noticed," Viss said. "I can give it a quick overhaul to make sure it's in top shape."

"Absolutely," Rei agreed. "And if not, we do have torpedoes." She flashed a grin at Hirin.

"Yuskeya, what's the word on that starmap the Corvid showed us? Can you calculate how long that route will take to get us to Nearspace, and where it will come out?"

"How long—it's difficult to say until I study it more. I have to convert the in-system distances between wormholes for these systems to make sense for us. As for where it comes out . . ." She paused, checking something on her datapad. "I have an educated guess that the last wormhole skip will bring us out in the Tau Ceti system."

I frowned. "Tau Ceti? Isn't there only one wormhole in that system?"

"Only one on record. But the configuration of the terminal system fits. And obviously, we already know where all the other existing wormholes go—or else they're red-flagged. It could be one of those."

Wormholes flagged as "red" meant that no explorer had ever returned safely from a trip inside. No-one in their right mind went into one.

"If Fha is right," Yuskeya continued, "I guess we have to rethink everything we thought we knew about ways into and out of Nearspace."

I felt a slow chill creep up my spine. How many wormholes existed in Nearspace, undiscovered to us, but known to others? The feeling of safety and comfort that we'd gradually attained since the end of the Chron War seemed suddenly empty and foolish. Nearspace was as vulnerable as it had ever been. We'd simply chosen not to see that.

"Do I get a vote?" asked a voice from the doorway of the galley, and all heads snapped around. Jahelia Sord stood casually leaning against the ultraplas wall, holding the empty dishes from her own supper. Her pale-tipped black curls tumbled around her face in waves, and her *pridattii* spilled in inky lines around her eyes, emphasizing the challenge in them. I vowed at that moment not to underestimate her again.

Viss, Rei, and Yuskeya had already pushed their chairs back, but I said, "Hold on, folks. You think you deserve a place at this table, *Civitano* Sord?" I wasn't going to call her *Captain*, even if she did have her own ship. I felt I was doing her a favour by calling her a citizen.

She shrugged. "I'm as stranded as the rest of you. And I was getting bored, listening in on the ship's comm."

I shot a questioning glance at Baden. She should definitely *not* be able to do that. She should have been able to talk to the bridge, in which case we'd open a channel for her to hear us respond, but that was all. He raised his eyebrows and one shoulder in a *don't ask me* shrug.

"And I don't suppose someone conveniently left the door open for you?" I asked.

"No," she said, grinning insolently, "dear Maja locked me in nice and tight. But a plasma bar isn't really a big deterrent if you know what you're doing."

"Are you armed?" I asked bluntly. She'd had to pass right by the weapons locker walking from her quarters to the galley, and I wouldn't have been a bit surprised to find that she'd helped herself.

She shook her head, holding her arms out to the sides, dishes balanced on empty palms. "Nope. Your girls—or boys—can search me if they want." She fixed her sly grin on Baden. "Mr. Methyr, in particular, might want to renew our acquaintance."

Baden's face pinked, but he merely leaned back in his chair. "No, thanks, Relana . . . Jahelia . . . whoever you are. Someone else is welcome to the task."

She twisted her lips into a mock pout. "And we were such *good* friends a few months ago. You haven't even come to see me since I've been on the ship!"

"You might as well come in," I said. "As of about a minute ago, I've decided that I'd rather have you where I can see you. Hirin, do run a scan over her, just in case. My apologies, Ms. Sord, but I'm not exactly ready to trust you at this point."

She merely grinned again and submitted to the scan from Hirin's datapad. When he finished, he directed her to an empty chair between Viss and Rei. I was struck by the contrast between the two Erian women. Rei wore her *pridattii* comfortably, the way some women can wear lipstick without seeming pretentious. On Jahelia Sord's face, the swirling dark tattoos were a statement of defiance.

"I don't suppose you're particularly interested in getting to Nearspace quickly," I said to her.

"On the contrary, I'm anxious to get out of this backwater," she said. She stared pointedly at our drinks.

Sighing inwardly, I said, "Can I offer you something more to drink?"

"Do you have *cazitta*?"

"I'll get it," Yuskeya offered, leaving me to continue my conversation with Sord.

"You were saying you'll be happy to get back to Nearspace?" I said.

She nodded. "And if there's about to be another war with the Chron, well, that will open up all kinds of possibilities for me. War is, sadly, often good for business."

I narrowed my eyes. "You do understand that I'm planning to turn you over to the Protectorate at the earliest opportunity?"

She smiled as she accepted a mug full of dark, licorice-scented *cazitta* from Yuskeya. "Hey, thanks, Protectorate," she said, casually dismissive.

I saw Yuskeya's lips press into a tight line, but she didn't say anything as Sord continued.

"Yes. And you should understand that I expect my employers to extricate me from any trouble I might find myself in as the result of taking on a job for them."

"You think PrimeCorp will get you out of this?"

Sord merely shrugged. "I'm not naming names. But I'm confident enough to not worry too much about it. That's all I'm saying."

I leaned back in my chair and studied her. "You'll forgive me if I don't entirely trust you."

"Don't blame you a bit. But there's nothing—absolutely nothing—for me here. I don't have my ship, I don't have any way to retrieve it, and I damn sure can't see these crows needing my services anytime soon."

Rei turned slightly in her chair, facing Sord. "So your job, the one that got you into this mess, was simply to deliver a message to Captain Paixon for PrimeCorp?"

Sord took a slow sip of *cazitta*. "I don't believe I've said who engaged my services. Or if there was more than one. But the message was part of my task, yes."

"Then what was all that messing around with flash-pack torpedoes and following us out to the Delta Pavonis system but not contacting us there?"

"Gather information, deliver a message," Sord said. "It's no secret that some corporations have an interest in Captain Paixon and her family—in all of you. They like to know where everybody is, what they're doing. What their capabilities might be. How I get the information isn't important. I take what opportunities I see."

"And Baden was one of those opportunities," Maja said evenly.

Sord smiled at her. "Every job has its perks."

This was turning into a conversation I'd hoped to have with

the woman in private, when time and circumstances permitted. I steered the talk around to the general topic of what we should do.

"Despite all the concerns—and they are valid ones—I don't think we have any viable options but to try the route Fha showed us."

"So can these crows give us anything else? Weapons, other tech?" Sord asked. "They seem pretty advanced, and unlike the Chron, they don't want to kill us, so that's promising."

Yuskeya turned a cold eye on her. "We're already planning to ask them that. They may or may not have tech that can help us, or be willing to share it. And stop calling them crows," she added.

"Sorry, *Cor-vids*," Sord said with exaggerated emphasis. "Anyway, why are you still talking about it? Get all the help you can from these aliens and get the hell out of here. If you have to blow a few Chron ships out of your way, so be it. That's a few less to come blasting the crap out of Nearspace."

"Well, I like to get as many different viewpoints as I can when making important decisions. And now I certainly have yours." I stood up, pushing my chair out of the way. "Thanks, everyone. I'll let you know in a little while what I've decided."

I walked the length of the galley, then turned and crooked a finger at Jahelia Sord. "I'll escort you to your quarters," I said. "Feel free to take your drink with you."

She came without protest, which didn't surprise me. I wouldn't have been surprised if she'd refused, either. She was a wild card, this mercenary we'd somehow wound up with, and I wouldn't place bets on anything she would or wouldn't do. I wondered what she and Maja had talked about.

"Your meeting with Baden wasn't chance," I said to her as we passed the weapons locker.

She turned her smile on me. "I don't leave much to chance," she said, and winked.

"I don't take it well when people mess with my crew," I told her. "Luckily, Baden seems to have come out of his encounter with you unscathed."

We were at her door now, the hallway between her quarters and the galley being short. "He didn't tell me anything he shouldn't have, in case you're worried," she said, leaning against the closed door and cradling her mug in both hands. "Not that I didn't try to worm some things out of him. But he was mainly a way for me to be sure I had the right ship."

I met her gaze. "I wasn't worried," I told her. "Do you have the plasma bar that was on the door?"

She opened the door and reached inside, relinquishing the bar to me without apparent shame.

"Care to tell me . . .?"

Sord pursed her lips, her eyes surveying me coolly. Then she shrugged. "There's an override code, pretty standard encryption, built into the OS for the ship system. A little scrap of code that never really gets upgraded because it hardly ever gets used."

"And you know this, how?"

She laughed. "Come on, you've checked my history by now. I'm a techdog. I know this stuff. Ask your Mr. Methyr. He probably knows about it too, but forgot it even existed."

"So you could have left your room anytime? Why'd you wait until now?"

Her eyes turned challenging. "Who says I waited?"

I sighed. These kinds of games made me tired. "How many more of these little surprises do you have?"

She grinned. "Hey, I'd be crazy to endanger the ship while we're stuck in this godsforsaken system. I know it's my ticket—my only ticket—out of here."

"But once we get to Nearspace, all bets are off? Just so we understand each other."

"I think you're starting to get the picture."

I folded my arms. "Why do I get the feeling you don't particularly like me, Sord? On a personal level, I mean. I think I've treated you pretty well. Some people would have been tempted—more than tempted—to leave you on your ship. Anybody questioned it, I could have said there was no answer when we commed you, so we thought you were dead."

She shrugged. "You're one more job to me, Captain. Get information, deliver a message. It's not a question of liking or disliking."

I studied her, trying to decide if that rang true or not. I couldn't think of any reason she'd have a grudge against me—and she was prickly with everyone on board—but there was an edge in her voice when she spoke to me, like an extra layer of whatever she was projecting at the moment. Sarcasm, or disdain, or plain dislike.

"One more question," I said. "What do you know about PrimeCorp's actual plans involving my mother?"

"What makes you think I'd tell you if I knew anything?" She cocked her head at me, and the veneer of hostility fell away. She really was curious.

"Seems like it might be in your interests to get me to move faster, get us to Nearspace even quicker. If I thought she was in immediate danger, I might do that."

"True." She considered it. "But you might also take stupid chances, which wouldn't be in my best interests at all."

I shrugged, not saying anything.

After a moment, she said, "If I were Alin Sedmamin, I wouldn't share my actual plans with the likes of me."

It was probably the closest thing to an answer I was going to get out of her. Unfortunately, it did nothing to alleviate my fears.

Viss and Baden rounded the corner then, anxious, I was sure, to reset the plasma bar in a way that might stick next time. They had the grace to look a little embarrassed.

"I'll tell you when we have a plan," I told her. "Try to stay put from now on."

She threw me a mock salute and stepped inside the room, pausing to blow a kiss to Baden before she shut the door. I went to my own quarters then, thinking that I must be the only captain around who could pick up unwanted passengers in the middle of uncharted space.

I debated returning to the galley, but the others would clean up, and I wasn't on the night duty shift. In fact, I could hear the sounds of cleanup and conversation, but I slipped past the doorway without anyone noticing. Waves of fatigue had begun to hit me like huge breakers as I walked away from Sord's quarters. The conversations with the Corvid, my crew, and Jahelia Sord had exhausted my reserves. All I could think of was crawling into bed and letting darkness wash over me. My hands started up more of their tremors as I peeled off my jeans and slipped between the covers. If any crisis arose in the next few hours, Hirin would have to handle it.

Fear of whatever was happening to me threatened to keep me awake as soon as my head touched the pillow. I shoved my trembling hands under the pillow, pressing down to try and still them. *Mother can fix it*, I told myself. *These Corvids will show us the way, and we'll get home, and she'll know what to do.* For a few moments, worry and fatigue battled for control, but in the end, fatigue won. My last thought as I fell asleep was that I had to ask Yuskeya if I could keep a med injector in my pocket. Maybe with a double dose. And I'd have to ask her soon.

I SLEPT THE night through, not even noticing when Hirin crawled into bed beside me. He didn't wake me in the morning, either, but I knew he'd slept since his head had scooped out a shallow indentation in his pillow. What finally woke me was Rei calling from the bridge to say that the Corvid hologram had reappeared. I sat up and pressed my chip implant. "Ten minutes," I told her.

The rest had alleviated my headache slightly, but a dull throbbing still knocked on the inside of my skull. I allowed myself a minute to massage my temples, then dressed hurriedly and dragged a brush through my hair. The bristles came away thickly tangled with auburn strands—far more than the usual. I stared at the strands for another long moment, panic roiling my stomach. Every new symptom of whatever was happening to me stirred fresh fear. I hadn't come close to appreciating flawless health when I'd had it. I wanted to sit on the bed and give in to a good cry, but as tears threatened to overwhelm me, I closed my eyes and took a deep breath. Giving in felt somehow self-indulgent. My problems were serious, yes—but my family and crew had to come first. We were all in trouble, and I couldn't put my own worries ahead of anyone else's. I believed what I'd told Hirin— the crew needed me. I couldn't let them down. I pulled the brush clean and threw the telltale tangle of hair into the recycler.

Hirin, Rei, and Viss were on the bridge when I got there. Fha was nowhere in sight.

"Said she'd be back in ten, same as you," Rei said. "Sleep well?"

"Dead to the world," I said honestly, then regretted the phrase. "Anything exciting happen?"

"Not a thing," she said. "I think we could dispense with night shift while we're on the station."

A moment later, Fha reappeared. I assumed it was the same Corvid, at least. The hologram seemed identical to the one who'd spoken to us yesterday. Baden and Maja arrived on the bridge together.

"We've decided to take your directions and try to make it to Nearspace," I told Fha. "Anything you can provide that might help will be gratefully accepted."

The Corvid nodded. "I expected as much. I will have the coordinates for a safe path through the asteroids made accessible to you. You'll have to navigate one to leave this system, and one to enter the next Corvid-controlled system. There will be one more to access the last skip, but there is another station in that system, and they will assist you with that if necessary. We will alert them that you are coming."

"Will you give us the coordinates for all of them?" Yuskeya asked.

"Yes, but you will have to validate the third set with the other guard station when you arrive in that system. These coordinates will work only once for each asteroid field; once they have been used, the asteroid configuration changes. So what we give you now may not still be valid when you get there. However, I will make certain they know you are coming. You'll have no trouble."

"We appreciate that."

"Our technicians have also studied your propulsion system. Although it is significantly different from ours, it is very similar to Chron technology with which we are familiar. They think they may be able to install an accelerator to increase your attainable speed by some fifteen percent."

"That would be wonderful," I said.

Fha nodded. "And necessary, if you hope to outrun any Chron you encounter. You could not evade them with your current drives only."

I swallowed. That was a sobering thought. We really were in debt to the Corvids—if we made it to Nearspace in one piece, that is.

Hirin asked, "What about the moon—what the Protectorate was calling the 'operant' moon? The Chron apparently built it, but what was it for?"

Fha nodded gravely. "This is technology that the Chron appropriated from us. I shall try to explain." She went silent for a moment, then continued. "It is a way to temporarily direct a wormhole to exit in a new location."

Viss blew out a long, low whistle from the bridge engineering board, where he'd claimed one of the skimchairs. "That's—incredible!"

The Corvid shook her head slightly. "It is a highly limited effect. But very useful, yes."

"Limited how?" Yuskeya asked. She was probably running military applications through her mind already.

"There are two parts to the technology," Fha explained. "An—operant is a good word, actually—and an activator. The operant is constructed near a wormhole entrance, while the activator is essentially a drive, installed on a ship. The operant and the activator act in concert to allow the replication of a—" Fha paused. She seemed to be searching for a word. "The replication of a 'ghost' wormhole. It has the same entry point as the original wormhole, but diverges along a new path to a different exit point."

"Anywhere?" Baden leaned forward and breathed the word, his eyes shining like a true techdog in the presence of new and exciting technology.

Fha's beak snapped open and shut in that alien approximation of laughter again. "Not quite anywhere. Sufficient data is required about the star system or region where the new exit point is to appear. And the ghosted wormhole path collapses after a period of time, or if the activator drive strays too far from the new exit."

Viss asked the next question as it was forming in my own mind. "So, these operants and ghosted wormholes? Is it possible for us to use that technology? Wouldn't it get us home faster?"

Fha cocked her head. "It might be possible to install an activator drive on board your vessel, although it would be of limited use. There are no operant installations along this route. And we do not have enough specific data to safely ghost a wormhole for you to follow home, or I would have simply suggested that. Given enough time, your own navigational data could be converted to use with the activator, I think. And . . ." Her voice trailed off as she seemed to think about the question. Finally she said, "When you emerge in your Nearspace system, there is an operant installation there. If the data conversion is complete by then, you could conceivably use it to reach your medical facility more quickly."

"An operant installation *inside* Nearspace? Are you sure?" Hirin asked, frowning. "I was thinking the Chron must have used the one we found outside Delta Pavonis to move around during the war."

"Absolutely," the Corvid assured him. "Although they could also have used this one you speak of. The Chron installed and used one within Nearspace during the war, to access the various systems as they acquired data for them. It has not been used in a very long time. We positioned a station to restrict them from that system."

"How could they do that without it being noticed?" Maja protested.

"Tau Ceti," Yuskeya said, snapping her fingers. "Remember yesterday, I thought we would come out in Tau Ceti? I ran a full cross-reference last night, and that confirmed it. G8 star, huge debris disk, five planets with one in the habitable zone—it fits."

"So the debris disk could mask the presence of the operant installation," Rei mused. "You know, they could get away with it."

"And with an operant installation there, they could ghost the wormhole to other places in Nearspace—making it seem like they appeared out of nowhere," Baden added. "Sneaky *bastardos*."

"What we thought was timeslipping wasn't that at all," Rei said.

"But, wait," I protested. "If there was never such a thing as timeslipping, what delayed our initial message through the wormhole to the Domtaw?"

"Was it a wormhole that had been ghosted?" Fha asked.

"How would we know?"

"Did you observe unusual streaks or patterns inside the wormhole path? Fluctuations in other readings?"

Rei nodded. "Both those things."

"This is one of the reasons we use the technology sparingly," Fha said, "although the Chron show no such compunction. We discovered that wormholes which have been ghosted can suffer random aftereffects—time anomalies, excessive turbulence, increased radiation, and others—so that they are never again as fully stable as they once were." The Corvid's face remained impassive, but I thought her eyes seemed to harden. "We would like to find a way to stop the Chron using the technology on previously unghosted wormholes, but for the most part they are beyond our reach."

I wondered suddenly if the Protectorate knew about any of this. They knew about the wormhole into the artifact moon system, after all, and wanted to keep it a secret. Lanar made it sound like that was a temporary thing, but what was to stop them from trying to keep the secret indefinitely? Now this wormhole into Tau Ceti. Were they in the dark . . . or had they been keeping the citizens of Nearspace in the dark? I would have to ask Lanar the next time I saw him. I hoped I wouldn't be angry at his answer.

Viss said, "May I ask another question?"

"Of course." The Corvid turned her holographic gaze in Viss's direction.

"What happened to the Chron ship that tried to make it through the wormhole into Delta Pavonis? The skip into Nearspace, when they got past your asteroids and you had to pursue them?"

The Corvid shrugged. "They were caught inside the wormhole when our ship fired on them, and destroyed when the wormhole collapsed. We would have preferred to catch them sooner, naturally."

"So would it be possible to set up weapons to guard wormholes, in addition to the asteroids to deter them? And if a Chron ship managed to get past the asteroids and into the wormhole . . ." Viss mimed an explosion, bursting his hands apart. "You said the wormhole will right itself in time, and be replaced in the meantime."

The Corvid hesitated a moment before answering. "It is plausible, but risky. What about other ships near the wormhole? They could also be destroyed. The disruptions to commerce and travel? Not to mention that we have no data on the long-term effects of such a thing. We know what happens to the few wormholes that have been accidentally or experimentally collapsed, but widespread destruction could cause problems we can't even imagine."

It was Viss's turn to shrug. "Okay, just a thought."

"How long would it take to install an activator drive, and upgrade the propulsion system for us?" I asked. Time to get the conversation back on track. My head was pounding harder again, and I was ready for another nap.

"Two days, perhaps," the Corvid said. "And if you can possibly afford to wait that long, I would advise it. It could substantially improve your chances of traversing the Chron system safely—or escaping pursuit if need be."

"All right, two days," I said. "Thank you for all your help. My crew will assist you in whatever you need to make this happen."

The Corvid nodded and winked out.

And we had two days to prepare for Chron space.

Chapter 25 — Luta
Patching Hearts and Engines

"I'VE COME UP with a method to chart these previously unknown systems," Yuskeya said as she returned the injector to the cupboard in First Aid. "You want to hear about it?"

I dangled my legs cautiously over the side of the gurney, hoping the meds wouldn't take long to kick in. I had new sympathy for everyone I'd ever known who suffered from migraine headaches. Before this, I couldn't have imagined what they were like. Now I had a new, very vivid, appreciation. I still hadn't told Yuskeya about any other symptoms, though. What would be the point, if she couldn't treat them anyway?

"Sure," I said. "Good idea. We'll want to give the Protectorate all the data we can."

Yuskeya nodded. "We've only been in two new systems so far, and I don't know how the Protectorate might have already designated the first one out of Delta Pavonis. It doesn't matter, though."

She crossed to the First Aid computer console and pulled up a personal file from her navigation charts, pointing to the entries she'd made so far. "I'm using a modified spectral classification system, simple identifiers. Maybe someday we'll learn what the folks who live here actually call these stars," she said with a smile.

"You're optimistic," I said.

"I'm prefacing all the stars since we left Nearspace with 'OS'— for 'Otherspace'," she explained. "So the first system, out of Delta Pav, was OS-B8VI-01. Otherspace, then the spectral information, and 01 since it was the first one we skipped to. I logged the wormhole coordinates when we came through, too. So this system is OS-K0V-02."

I grinned. "'Otherspace'. I like it."

"I was going for descriptive," she said, "not necessarily scientific."

"It works."

"Great. I'll keep an updated file with open access in the main computer." She turned to leave the First Aid station.

Part of me hated to bring it up, but this seemed like as good a chance as any to talk to her about the ongoing tension between her and my engineer. "Yuskeya," I said, "how are things between you and Viss?"

She turned to face me slowly, and leaned against the door, crossing her arms. Her dark eyes were wary. She'd taken to wearing her Protectorate uniform constantly, instead of her usual shipsuits or casual clothing. I wondered if she needed the comfort and familiarity of it, or if the choice spoke to something else. Perhaps the presence of Gerazan, a subordinate officer, on board? As some kind of a rebuke to Viss? Or did she simply want to be wearing it if things went . . . badly?

"Fine. Why do you ask?"

Her face had changed, shifting into that calm, expressionless poker-face I think they teach at the Protectorate *akademio*. Goodness knows, I've seen it enough times on Lanar, particularly when there's something he can't—or doesn't want to—discuss with me. That spoke volumes all by itself.

I smiled. "Nice try. You think I haven't noticed a little chill in the air between you two? More like an iceberg. It's almost big enough to trip over."

She sighed and shrugged. "We . . . have some things to work out."

"Like the fact that you're a Protectorate officer and didn't tell anybody?" She opened her mouth, and I held up a hand. "You don't have to explain yourself to me; I'm fine with it. But I get the feeling Viss isn't."

"I wasn't too thrilled to find out he was doing . . . questionable . . . work for the Protectorate without my knowledge, either," she said. "Smuggling cargo on *your* ship? I'm also not entirely pleased with your brother on that one, but he's my commanding officer. He can get away with doing things I don't like and not telling me everything."

I slid off the gurney. Pain lanced behind my eyes, but I tried to hide the flinch. The room swam around me, and my vision blurred as if I was about to start crying, then everything righted itself. "So, the way I see it, you're mad at each other for being on the same side. It doesn't make much sense."

"It's not that."

"It's a trust issue, then," I said, and she bit her lip and nodded.

"I know Viss has an . . . interesting past," she said with a hint of a smile. "I don't want—or need—to know everything he's done. But he should trust me enough to tell me what he's doing *now*."

"Even if his bosses tell him not to? Doesn't that put what he did in the same category as what you did?"

She flushed, one corner of her mouth twisting. "I know what you're saying, Luta. And I know it makes sense. But I don't seem to feel it—here." She closed a fist and tapped it lightly over her heart. "You know?"

I sighed. "I guess I do. Just . . . don't stop trying, *okej*? I'd rather see my crew happy than miserable, and things are—uncertain."

"What, because we're stranded in unknown space, surrounded by enemies?"

"Well, I meant because I don't know how long this headache will last, but sure, that too," I said with a smile. "We need everyone working together to get through this, right?"

She stood to her full height. "You don't need to worry about that aspect of it, Captain. You have my word on it."

I patted her on the shoulder. "I know I do. Now let's go see what else needs doing before we leave here and start the really dangerous part of the journey."

WE SAW OUR first real Corvids when they came to deliver the activator drive. Well, I say we "saw" them, but we didn't, really. We saw two tall figures who arrived at the engineering deck airlock with an array of items on gravsled-type carriers. Fha had assured us that the Corvid technicians would be able to do their work wearing environment suits, so that the bay holding the *Tane Ikai* could remain configured for human habitation.

If they wore robes like Fha's, they were hidden by the enviro-suits, which were, unsurprisingly, black. The material held a sheen similar to the ships and the station, which was explained once you got close enough. The surface was coated with a layer of tiny, flat, hexagonal discs. These slid and shifted as the Corvids moved, apparently reconfiguring themselves to suit some unknown parameters or purposes. As the light caught their movements, it created the shimmery effect.

The suits themselves were shapeless and loose-fitting, but didn't sag or wrinkle—rather they seemed to move and flow around the Corvids' bodies, flexing and reshaping to fit the aliens' movements. They did, however, reveal a few more details about Corvid physiology. They stood taller than Fha's hologram had been, easily topping seven feet. They were bipedal, but the suits did not outline their legs, so it was difficult to guess at their proportions. They did have two arms, but it was impossible to speculate about hands. The suits themselves, with their hexagon building blocks, reconfigured "fingers" to whatever purpose was needed. They formed club-like paws for lifting large objects, then flowed into thin digits for making minute adjustments. Viss said later he observed a range from two to eight fingers on a hand, as required.

Their helmets, by contrast, were completely transparent, and oblong, shaped to accommodate their beak-like mouths. They seemed able to call up various displays on the inside of the faceplates, although the mechanism for doing so was never obvious. Viss and Gerazan stayed in engineering to assist them, although there seemed little for them to actually do. When the Corvids needed to communicate, they did so through small speakers set at the bottom edge of the helmet, and apparently did so with as much language facility as Fha had displayed in talking to us.

"We got very lucky," Viss said to me that evening in the galley, where we'd happened to end up at the same time, seeking hot drinks. "If it had been the Corvids who'd wanted to wipe out humanity a century and a half ago, none of us would be here. I've never even imagined some of the tech that's everyday for them."

That was a chilling thought. "How's the work going?" I'd stopped in to the drive bays a couple of times throughout the day, but I didn't have any real sense of what they were doing or how long it would take.

Viss shrugged. "Fine, I think. They mostly go about their business. Ask us questions, and we try to answer. When we understand what they're asking." He smiled thinly.

"Do you think it'll work?" I was still worried by Fha's statement that with our current drives, we wouldn't be able to outrun a Chron ship if we ran into one.

He ran a hand over his face. "It's not easy for me to admit it, but half the stuff they're doing—I don't even understand it. That's what I mean about the technology. It's so far beyond what we know about, it's like they're operating on a whole different plane of understanding."

"Maybe that's why they don't mind sharing tech with us," I said. "They know we're not smart enough to reverse-engineer it."

Viss chuckled. "You could be right."

I pulled a deep breath. "Well, I hope we made the right decision. We seem to be totally dependent on what they're doing for us."

"We are, no mistake about it. But I do trust them."

"Me, too," I told him, warming my hands around my mug. "I just hope it's enough."

Chapter 26 — Luta
An Unexpected Displeasure

AS THEY'D PROMISED, the Corvids finished their work in two days. Fha appeared in her holographic form one last time on the bridge. Today her cowled robe was pale grey, proving, perhaps, that the Corvids did have some use for and perception of colours. It was strange how quickly we'd become accustomed to the Corvids' alien features and begun to read expressions on them. Now, hers was . . . worried.

"Stay to the route we've provided," she cautioned one more time. "Avoid all other ships and planets if you can. Even with our modifications, I cannot be sure you'd escape from Chron ships if they were bent on capturing you."

She didn't say *or worse*, but I'm sure we all thought it. "We can't thank you enough," I told her. "You've given us at least a chance to get home."

Another black tentacle slid through the wall, and deposited a datachip into my hand. I barely even flinched this time. Another thing that had quickly become "normal."

"This is what you might call a diplomatic package," Fha told me. "Please deliver it to your government. With the resurgence in

Chron activity, I believe it's imperative for us to work more closely with the inhabitants of Nearspace. It contains instructions for contacting us again."

I tucked it into my pocket. "If we make it, I'll get it into the right hands," I assured her. I'd give it to Lanar, and he'd get it to the Nearspace Worlds Administrative Council. No planetary governments. I'd make sure it went straight to the top. Fha didn't say what the Corvids would do if we *didn't* make it back safely. No doubt they had a plan, but she was nice enough not to mention the eventuality.

"The *urgulat* will release you in a moment," Fha said. "Go in safety." And the hologram winked out.

Baden flashed me a smile. "No leaving issues there."

"Power is available to all drives," Rei announced.

"And the course to the first wormhole is laid in," Yuskeya said. As far as we'd been aware, there were no more Chron incursions while we'd been docked at the station. It was a different wormhole that we were headed for, though, not the one the Chron ships had come through. Fha had said there had been no traffic through this wormhole, except for periodic Corvid survey drones, for many years. The drones simply went through, scanned the area around the other terminal point, and returned.

"What about the asteroid navigation path?"

"The coordinates are programmed," Yuskeya said. "Once we reach the field, we'll go to auto-pilot, and the computer will guide us through. We'll engage the skip drive when we reach the wormhole mouth."

"Like *that* doesn't make me nervous," Rei muttered.

"We're trusting the Corvids on everything else, I think we can trust them to get us through their asteroids," I told her. I knew she didn't like the idea of relinquishing control while traversing the barricade of tumbling rocks.

"I guess so," Rei agreed grudgingly.

"This should cheer you up. We'll try out the upgraded burst drive to see how quickly we can get to this wormhole."

"Ooh, thanks," she said, without a hint of sarcasm. "Did you hear that, Viss? Give me the burst drive."

I opened the comm channel into Jahelia Sord's room. "We're

leaving the station, Sord. Wormhole skip coming up shortly after that."

"Thanks for the warning," she said. "I'm sure you'll let me know if anything exciting happens."

I didn't bother to answer that, and closed the channel again.

Cerevare came onto the bridge then. "Captain, I hope you don't mind. I'd like to be up here when we skip into the first Chron system." Her brown eyes were bright with excitement. For the rest of us, this was a trip into certain and frightening danger. For Cerevare, it was a voyage of discovery into her passion.

"You're absolutely welcome," I told her. "I hope you have everything from that Corvid chip memorized. We might need your expertise."

She grinned. "It will take months to comb through everything on that chip. I already feel like my head's been opened up and reams of data simply poured in."

The ship lurched slightly, and the sensation of being carried returned. This time the viewscreens showed the black, viscous-looking material of the station retreating as it disgorged us, as I'd imagined it would. I shuddered. As nice as the Corvids had been, their technology had an element of creepiness.

"Rei, you've got the burst drive," Viss said a moment later from engineering. "I'm set to monitor everything as we try it out."

"Whenever you're ready, then, Rei."

She engaged the drive and we leapt forward, leaving the safety of the Corvid station behind. Rei pushed the drive to its limit.

"Handles fine," she observed.

"All good on this end," Viss added.

"And about a twelve percent increase in speed," Yuskeya said. She met my eye and smiled. "The Protectorate will definitely want to know more about this."

"Everyone in Nearspace will," I said. "But I think we'll treat it as top-secret until the Council has a chance to figure things out."

Rei had slowed us to a normal momentum by the time the asteroids loomed threateningly in our path. Inwardly, I shared Rei's trepidation. They were intimidating and appeared near-impossible to navigate, even knowing we'd managed it once, on the way into this system. Surveying the tumbling chunks of rock,

I realized what a close call we'd had. Sheer luck had played a big part in our survival, regardless of how well Rei and I had worked together to guide us through.

"Here goes," Rei said. "Engaging the auto-pilot. Nothing that happens now is my fault, folks." She took her hands off the controls and raised them over her head, waggling her fingers. The *Tane Ikai* sailed into the maelstrom.

I held my breath, but we slipped almost effortlessly through the asteroids. The coordinates for the safe pathway ensured that wherever an asteroid was, we weren't, although the computer put the ship through some delicate maneuvers. When we cleared the last obstacle, Rei took control again, the skip drive whirred to life, and we slipped into the wormhole.

When my chest began to burn, I realized I was holding my breath, and released it in a long exhale. The skip went like any other. We emerged out the other end, and I heard Cerevare draw her own breath in with a little whistle. I knew what it meant to her; we had entered Chron space.

The system was . . . beautiful. At least this corner of it. An enormous particle cloud hung in plain view when we emerged, painting the vacuum of space with a brilliant crimson, glazed with yellow specularity. In the distance a yellow sun burned.

"Scan shows a planet barely on the edge of range," Baden reported. "Right where the Corvids said it would be. No ships detected. We seem to be alone."

"Let's keep it that way," I said. "Yuskeya, lay in the course for the next wormhole. I want the scans running constantly. Rei, Viss, let's fire up that burst drive and hit the next wormhole as quickly as we can."

Which sounded good, but it wasn't like we'd be there in an hour, or even ten. Yuskeya had estimated twelve hours to the next wormhole as the best possible time, if we ran the burst drive full out and didn't encounter any problems. We couldn't run the drive steady at full for that long; two-hour bursts with an alternate hour for cooldown was the most we could push it.

I noticed Maja gazing out the viewscreen with a strange expression on her face. "Anything wrong, Maja?"

She glanced over and half-smiled at me. "Not really. I was

thinking it's sad we're not here to explore. I'd rather be making contact, building alliances, instead of racing through without time to investigate or learn. It seems like a wasted opportunity."

"Maybe we'll be back," Baden said. "Things might be different with the Chron someday."

"I'd like to think so, but—I don't know. This feels like a one-way trip."

I shivered, an unwelcome, eerie feeling trickling down my spine. I hoped we were still in the middle of that trip, and that it would end in Nearspace.

We ran that way for half an hour, and nothing untoward happened. Maja excused herself, and Gerazan came up from engineering, where he'd been with Viss for the burst drive test and the first skip. He settled at the co-pilot's board next to Rei. Cerevare still seemed entranced, although to tell the truth it looked like any other system to me.

I was having trouble keeping my eyes open; no wonder, really. I'd slept fitfully, no doubt nerved up about leaving the station, but the pains in my arms and legs had worsened. I couldn't make it through the night now without getting up at least twice to take one of Yuskeya's painkillers. I needed a nap, although I was beginning to dread the realization. It came too fast and often now. I'd never taken naps in my life, except occasionally when Maja and Karro were young. I stood from the big chair, intending to turn things over to Hirin, but everything blurred and I had to grasp the arm of the chair tightly to keep my balance. The bridge whirled around me. I blinked and breathed shallowly in through my nose, out through my lips. No-one seemed to have noticed.

The vertigo passed, the spinning bridge slowing and stabilizing again. I swallowed against a dry throat, hoping my voice would come out sounding normal. "*Okej*, we've got three pilots, so we'll take it in four-hour shifts," I said. "Hirin, you have the chair. I'm taking a break. You relieve Rei when her shift is done, and I'll come on after you."

He crossed to sit in my place, catching my hand as I turned to leave the bridge. "You okay?" he asked in a quiet voice.

I squeezed his hand and nodded. "Fine. Just a little tired. And we need to keep ourselves fresh while we're here. Keep the scans running and all eyes out."

He threw me a mock salute and released my hand.

Outside the bridge, once I was far enough down the corridor that I knew no-one could easily see me, I leaned against the wall for support. My knees felt like water. *How could I fly the ship when this might happen?* I knew suddenly that I couldn't. It would be completely irresponsible, and could put us all at risk. Rei and Hirin would have to manage without my help.

And I would have to admit to everyone why I was taking myself off the roster. That might be the hardest part of all.

I made my way slowly down the corridor to my quarters, hoping I wouldn't run into anyone and have to answer questions. My luck held; I collapsed on my bed without seeing anyone else. For a long moment I lay on my back and stared out at the stars though the porthole above me. Usually, I left the bridge with pleasant anticipation of the moment I'd return. For the first time ever, I felt as if I didn't belong there. And despite everything that was on my mind and should have kept me awake, I fell asleep with chilling ease.

The next thing I knew, the signal tone of the ship's comm woke me. I pressed my implant, and Hirin's voice came through.

"Luta, you'd better get up here. You won't believe what we found."

"On my way."

The nap had worked magic. My head felt surprisingly clear, and the weakness in my limbs had fled. It was a good thing, too, because I wasn't at all prepared for what met my eyes on the viewscreen when I entered the bridge. All sorts of possibilities had skittered through my mind as I hurried up the corridor: a Chron ship, a wormhole, another station. It was none of those.

It was PrimeCorp.

HIRIN HAD KILLED all the drives and brought us to a stop with the thrusters by the time I reached the bridge, and the *Tane Ikai* hung silent and relatively still. The viewscreen, I could tell, was at its maximum magnification, but still the ship it had focused in on wasn't visually clear. The data scrolling across the bottom of the screen, however, was.

Closest vessel: PrimeCorp drive signature type RT34564: Registration unconfirmed: Class unconfirmed

I stared stupidly at it, wondering if I had sunk low enough medically to be having hallucinations. For a fleeting moment I wondered if I'd been so sick thak I slept through the rest of the journey and we had actually made it to Nearspace. Hirin wouldn't have simply called me to the bridge, though, if that were the case. And if I were hallucinating, everyone else was, too. Still. "It can't be a PrimeCorp ship. We're in Chron space."

Baden said, "It *could* be some other kind of ship, with a PrimeCorp drive in it, I guess."

"What are the chances of that?"

He shrugged. "Pretty low, I'd say. It's too new to be something the Chron could have stolen or captured during the war."

I narrowed my eyes. "What could they be doing here, and how did they get here? Any wormhole leading into this system would have to be in the Nearspace catalogue. If we don't know about it, PrimeCorp shouldn't. And the Corvids would have it blocked anyway."

"Well, 'shouldn't' is the operative word, isn't it?" Hirin said. "PrimeCorp could be carrying out its own wormhole exploration program, and keeping the results a secret. If there was a profit to be made. Wormhole spelunking was how they got started, after all."

"And the Protectorate knew about the other wormhole, and hadn't released it," Rei reminded me.

"Do you think they've noticed us?"

Baden shook his head. "I doubt it. They haven't moved, and we stopped the instant we picked them up."

"All right. What's this?" I asked, pointing to a mass on the nav screen.

"Asteroid," Yuskeya said. "About half our size. You're thinking of using it as camouflage?"

"I wondered. If possible, get us close and try to match the asteroid's path. It might keep us from getting noticed. Keep an eye on that ship. Hirin, you still have the chair. I'm going to talk to the only person on board who might know more about PrimeCorp than I do." And I headed for the quarters where we were holding, more or less successfully, Jahelia Sord.

I shut down the enhanced plasma bar that Viss and Baden had reconfigured, and knocked on the door. No answer. I knocked again, a little more sharply. The logical part of my brain suggested that maybe she was asleep, but the cynical part had gone way past that. It was thinking that she'd done it again.

I opened the door cautiously, in case she was waiting to jump me. That seemed too unsubtle for her, but one never knew. I was beginning to think I understood her, which is a dangerous thing to think about your enemy, especially one who's your prisoner.

The room was empty. It wasn't one with access to the secret lockers, so there weren't many places she could hide. Not any, in fact. I moved outside the room and stood, trying to decide what to do next. I didn't want to initiate a full-scale search, because we were starting to look like incompetents. My crew didn't need more frustrations.

It wasn't a terribly big ship, but Sord could be in a number of places. Any of the other quarters, for a start, since no-one locked their doors. The galley, the head. The First Aid station, although she probably didn't know how to get there through the storage room behind the head, so the only other way would be through the bridge. The engineering deck, although she'd have to get past Viss. The cargo pods.

I started down the hatchway leading to the cargo area. Something told me she'd be there, waiting to be found, strolling the catwalk or doing something equally relaxed. She wasn't trying to escape; there was nowhere to go. Her chances of commandeering the ship with this crew on board were next to nil, and she had to know that. But it wasn't in her nature to let herself be caged, and she had to let *me* know that.

I deliberately tried to sneak down the ladder past Viss, and managed it; not that difficult if you watched for your chance. I saw her as soon as I emerged into the cargo pod. She was engaged in a smooth, flowing workout I recognized, after a few moments, as the Vilisian martial art of *zelendu*. She didn't have a staff, but had improvised one from a long broom handle. She'd rolled up her pant legs and shed her boots, reminding me of Rei when we sparred. Her grey t-shirt showed dark sweat blotches.

"Hello, Captain," she said easily, continuing to move her arms, legs, and makeshift staff in the controlled, precise movements of the form. Her breathing came smooth and easy. "I hope you don't mind my taking advantage of the peace and quiet down here. And the space. My room really isn't big enough for a good workout."

"I get the feeling," I said, stopping a short distance from her (well out of reach of the broom handle) and crossing my arms, "that it wouldn't matter much if I did mind."

She laughed. "I'm not very good at taking orders from someone who isn't paying me, I'll admit."

"Was that a problem at the Protectorate *akademio*?"

"Not really." She studied me intently while her arms twisted the staff through a complicated block and stroke. "You checked up on me."

"Does that really surprise you?"

"I suppose not. I'm almost finished, and then I'll go back to my room like a good girl."

"You should spar with Maja some time," I told her. "She has a silver crest in warrior chi."

"That would be an interesting engagement," she said, not missing a beat. "But I think she might enjoy it too much."

I sat on a small empty cargo crate. "How much do you know about PrimeCorp's activities?"

"Interrogation time again, is it?"

"Just a few questions."

She finished the form and clipped the broom handle into its holder on the bay wall. "You're bound to be disappointed. I already told you, I'm nothing but a messenger—and a snoop, I suppose. Not in the confidences of the high and mighty." She bent low, languidly stretching out the muscles in her legs and back. Her dark curls clung to her neck.

"Would you be surprised if I told you that PrimeCorp appears to have interests outside of Nearspace?"

She laughed and straightened. "Outside of Nearspace? What's outside of Nearspace? All this, I suppose. Chron and crows. Not much here for PrimeCorp."

"The Corvids have tech that I'll bet PrimeCorp would love to get its hands on."

"Well, sure. I've thought of that, myself. They'd pay well—more than well—for new tech. But the only way to get to it would be through the Protectorate, once a new wormhole opened up for trade. There'd be reams of treaty negotiations to go through before that happened."

"Unless *someone* could smuggle it into Nearspace."

She shrugged. "Sure. But no-one even knew where that second wormhole led before we went through it." She started toward the hatchway ladder, but I didn't get up yet.

"Now, how do you know that? You weren't in the system very long before that Chron ship came through and all hell broke loose."

She turned to face me, a smile twitching at the corners of her lips.

I shook my head. "Never mind. You probably had a data miner on the *Domtaw* before it blew up."

Jahelia Sord laughed. "Very good, Captain. The data miner, sure, I launched that as soon as I entered the system. Protectorate wire block codes aren't changed all that often. You might want to mention that to your dear brother when we get home."

I got up and walked toward the ladder, watching her. "So if I were to tell you that we're still in the first Chron system, but we've spotted a PrimeCorp ship, you'd be as surprised as anyone?"

She raised her eyebrows. "Surprised? It would shock the hell out of me if you found a PrimeCorp ship in this system. Is there? A PrimeCorp ship out there?"

"There is," I said, "and if you try and contact them or signal them in any way, all they'll find of you is a dead body shot out the jettison tube."

"I think you mean that," she said, staring at me with narrowed eyes.

"Oh, be sure I do."

She gave me one more appraising survey, then said, "Captain, how are you feeling? Physically, I mean."

It was so unexpected I don't know how much my face gave away before I answered. "Fine. Why do you ask?"

She shrugged again. "I know you're sick. I suspect your nanos are failing."

For the space of a few heartbeats, I stood dumbstruck. Questions fought for precedence in my mind, a new one scrambling to the top before I could ask the one before it. *How could she know anything about that? How much* did *she know?* Finally I realized that she could have listened in on any number of conversations on the ship before I knew she had the capability. She could be fishing for information. "You didn't get that from Alin Sedmamin."

"No, I didn't." She narrowed her eyes at me. "Unfortunately, I've seen something like this before."

She was bluffing—had to be. I crossed my arms. "I don't know what you're talking about, Sord, but I wish you'd stop playing games."

"Oh, this is no game," she said. "If you don't want to talk about it, fine. But tell me one thing—have the nosebleeds started yet?" She didn't wait for my answer, but turned and started to climb the ladder to the upper decks.

A chill of fear froze me in place. I wanted to reach up and grab her, haul her down, and demand she tell me what she meant. What could she possibly know about what was happening to me?

Hirin's voice over the ship's comm stopped me. "Luta, where are you? Everything *okej?*"

I thumbed my implant. "Coming." I pressed my lips together, stifling what I wanted to ask Jahelia Sord. We had bigger problems than her games and my headaches and nosebleeds. Whatever I wanted to know from Jahelia Sord would have to wait.

Wordlessly I followed her up the ladder. I almost laughed aloud at the startled frown Viss gave us when we climbed past the engineering deck. For a few seconds, I felt better, but it didn't last.

Chapter 27 – Jahelia
What Pita Knew

LUTA PAIXON DOES not like being made to look a fool. But she has a certain dignity about it that I was grudgingly coming to appreciate. She saw me inside my quarters and shut the door on me, but she didn't even bother to put the plasma bar back in place. I knew she'd send one of the crew to try and find out how I'd bypassed it, but she wouldn't replace it herself, knowing it was useless. That had a certain class.

As soon as her footsteps faded away down the corridor, I snatched up the throat mic and earbuds. "Pita? You'll never guess what Paixon told me!"

"That they found a PrimeCorp ship?" she said in a bored voice.

Oh, right. I'd left her monitoring the ship's comm, so she'd heard everything from the bridge already.

"What the hell is it doing here? How did it get here?"

"Through a wormhole?"

"Ha, ha. Come on, Pita. This is big! If I could get a message to them—"

"If you try to get a message to them, you'll be dead," Pita told me flatly. "I heard what Paixon said, didn't you? You think she was bluffing?"

I pursed my lips. "No, I get the impression that she doesn't bluff."

"Anyway, whoever's on that ship probably doesn't even know who you are. It's not like you and Alin Sedmamin are best pals or anything."

"Good point." I collapsed onto the bed. "But what are they *doing* here?"

"That's what everyone wants to know."

I got up and paced the room. Ideas and plans flashed through my brain, each one replaced by the next as quickly as it bloomed. What would PrimeCorp pay to make sure their presence in Chron space stayed secret? Would they still be interested in Corvid tech, assuming I could get my hands on some, or the specs? Did I have any other information that might be even more useful to them now? The secret to the Corvid asteroids? The Corvid revelations about the nature of wormholes?

At that point in my musings I bumped up against the realization that had hit me when Paixon came and found me in the cargo pod. The only way I could capitalize on *any* of this was if I—and necessarily, the *Tane Ikai*—reached Nearspace in one piece. Which meant keeping Luta Paixon from doing something stupid and noble like trying to confront PrimeCorp here. I sighed. I might have to put my dislike for the woman aside and actually pretend to work with her.

And then it struck me that Pita had said something important. She thought she didn't know what PrimeCorp could be doing here, but there was actually a good chance that she did know. She just didn't realize it.

"Pita, how many of those classified files from the PrimeCorp main hub system have you actually cracked?"

A pause. "About half, why?"

"I'm wondering if there could be something that might explain why PrimeCorp is in Chron space?"

"Hmmm. Good idea. I'll start checking."

"Put a list of the decrypted ones on the screen, and I'll go through them, too."

The process took a while, since many of the file names weren't terribly descriptive of their contents, and Pita hadn't been discriminating about the files she'd grabbed. I couldn't blame her, though, since I hadn't told her to search for anything in particular. I'd really only wanted to see if she'd do it. If something came in handy later, great, but I didn't have any high expectations that she'd find anything she could crack, anyway. She'd surprised me on that one.

So I sorted through financial reports (obviously a second set of books), employee records, dossiers on other corporations, product specs (some for illegal tech), manufacturing records, inventory sheets, shipping manifests, and archived press releases until my eyes burned and a tight knot of pain had settled behind my eyes. I had a fistful of leverage if I ever wanted to blackmail Alin Sedmamin, but nothing about the Chron.

And then suddenly, there it was. Something that made me consider that I might want to start distancing myself from PrimeCorp as soon as I possibly could.

Chapter 28 — Luta
The Enemy of my Enemy

I LEFT SORD in her quarters, not deigning to reactivate the useless plasma bar. I didn't know how she'd turned it off, but someone else could worry about that. As I entered the bridge, I got a close-up view of the asteroid we were hiding behind. The massive grey rock was shaped like a long potato, its surface pocked with the craters of hundreds of impacts. It tumbled in a slow, balletic dance through the vacuum. Baden turned to tell me something, but I held up a hand.

"As soon as the current crisis has passed, would someone come up with something better for keeping Ms. Sord in her quarters? I had to hunt her down on the cargo deck and interrupt her workout."

Viss made an inarticulate noise over the ship's comm and swore under his breath. "Could I tie her into a skimchair here on engineering?"

"I don't think we're quite there yet, Viss, but I'll keep the suggestion in mind. Also, she's probably listening in to every word we say, so let's remember that, too. Baden, you can try to cut off her access, but I think it's a lost cause. If you can figure out how she's doing what she's doing—I'd love to hear it."

I sat in an empty skimchair, motioning to Hirin to stay where he was in the big chair. "What's happening now?"

"PrimeCorp ship is stationary. She appears to be live, not derelict, no drift that I can detect. But not going anywhere, either," Yuskeya said.

"Scanning? Running data? Collecting samples?"

"Well, they could be running data. No one seems to be EVA. It's like they're waiting for something."

"Or someone. Us?"

Yuskeya shrugged. "How could they even know we were coming?"

I chewed my lower lip. I didn't trust Sord, but I couldn't truly imagine she could have anything to do with it. "We can try to sneak around them, but I'm damned curious about what—"

"New ship has entered scan range," Yuskeya announced.

"Toward us?" I held my breath.

Yuskeya's fingers tapped across her console. "They appear to be on a course for the PrimeCorp ship. And the new one—" she paused.

"What?"

"It's Chron."

My heartbeat felt suddenly fluttery, and my chest tightened, as if a band had drawn around it, too tight. I took a few deep breaths, calming the sensation. A clinical part of my brain added *heart palpitations, shortness of breath* to my growing list of symptoms. I'd have quite a litany to report to Mother, if we made it home to Nearspace in time.

"Stay with the asteroid," I said, as Hirin said, "Hold course." Our eyes met, and we smiled weakly at each other.

Rei said, "Aye," and nothing more, keeping her eyes studiously on the board.

We still didn't have a good visual on the ships, but the bridge was silent as we watched the two dots draw closer together. Were they about to engage in battle? Trade? Talk? But very simply, the Chron ship met up with the PrimeCorp ship and stopped.

"Tell me what I'm seeing here, somebody," I said finally.

"It is what it looks like," Yuskeya said, her voice tight.

"PrimeCorp is apparently in contact with the Chron. The Protectorate will bury them when they find out about this." She almost whispered the last sentence, but we all heard it.

"Well, we'd better make sure we get out of this system in one piece so that there's evidence of it," Baden said. "I'll bet the last thing they want is a ship full of witnesses."

"I'd give a good bit to listen in," I said. "But how are they managing to talk at all? Cerevare? What do you make of it?"

The Lobor historian shook her head. "It doesn't make any sense to me. That was one of the reasons I was so excited about discovering the Chron artifact moon—it might shed some light on the language."

"And I didn't think the Chron were any too interested in learning to speak Esper, when they were trying to kill off everyone who spoke it," Rei added.

"Can we try to pick up any of the communication that's passing between them?" Maja asked.

"You're beginning to sound like Baden," I told her. She smiled weakly.

"That's my girl," Baden said, but shook his head. "We're too far out, and if we go closer, we risk being noticed."

"Come on, folks, you're not thinking this through," came a voice from the rear of the bridge.

I didn't even turn around. "I wondered how long it would take you to get here, Sord. You might as well come in and sit down where I can see you."

She sauntered onto the bridge like she owned it, datapad in hand, sliding into one of the empty skimchairs at a research console.

"I thought you said you'd be surprised to find a PrimeCorp ship out here," I said.

She grinned, mischief evident in her brown eyes. "What I actually said was that it would shock me if you found one. I didn't think, if they *were* here, that they'd be that careless, hanging around in plain sight for anyone who happened to pop through a wormhole."

I felt my hands clench into fists, and forced them to relax. Absolutely the most annoying person I'd ever met. "So, what do you think they're talking about?"

Jahelia Sord shrugged. "I can't guess specifics, but knowing PrimeCorp, I'd have to guess they're making some kind of deal. That's what PrimeCorp *does*."

I thought about it. "So if PrimeCorp is carrying out a secret wormhole exploration project—"

Hirin nodded. "Like I said, it's what they started out doing. That's how they came to control so many planets in Nearspace; they funded the explorers, and got to the planets first."

"And if they keep some of their discoveries secret—what if they've *always* done that? They can afford to pay the explorers to keep their mouths shut—"

"Or get rid of them if they won't," Jahelia Sord noted.

"I don't doubt it," Hirin said.

"Then they can explore those new systems themselves, and mine them for resources without conforming to Nearspace regulations," I continued. "Maybe even make contact with species that live there."

"Yeah, and get tech ideas or specs, or the complete technology from them," Baden said. "Turn around and manufacture it in Nearspace as their own invention or discovery, instead of setting up trade with the real developers."

"Captain," Cerevare said. She'd been quiet through most of the discussion, but her eyes now were very dark and very serious. "PrimeCorp developed the first burst drive prototype not long after the Chron war. Supposedly it was in response to the fact that the Chron ships were so much faster than our own, and it was a significant factor in our vulnerability to them."

"And Fha said something—about our burst drive—" her words echoed back to me. "*It is very similar to Chron technology,*" I said slowly.

"So you're thinking that PrimeCorp got the specs for a burst drive from the *Chron*?" Maja asked.

I nodded. "And then developed it and sold it to the Protectorate—at a high price, of course—as their own invention. And no doubt got applauded for helping the war effort and made mountains of cash."

"You think PrimeCorp collaborated with the enemy?"

Cerevare asked doubtfully.

Hirin chewed his lip thoughtfully. "I don't know if the Chron would have been amenable to that, would they? According to everything we know, their only goal was to eradicate us."

"True, I cannot see them cooperating with humans, especially to the point of sharing technology or information with them," Cerevare agreed.

"You might want to rethink that." Jahelia Sord held up her datapad, screen turned around to face us. "You don't want to know how I have this, but it's a classified file from the PrimeCorp main hub. I didn't even know I had it until a short time ago."

"What is it?" I asked, trying to make out the strange symbols on the screen.

"I think," she said with a wry glance at it, "that it's a Chron-Esper dictionary. From about a hundred years ago."

Shocked silence reigned on the bridge until Yuskeya broke it. "Two more ships in range," she said. "Moving fast, heading for the ones we're watching. But coming from opposite directions."

"More Chron?" Hirin asked.

"One of them reads as Chron, Captain," she said, and I didn't resent her calling him that at all. He was still in the big chair, and as much as it pained me to admit it, he was the best one to be there right now. "From its trajectory, it could have come from the vicinity of that planet we noticed when we arrived in-system."

"And the other one?"

She pulled a deep breath. "Unless there's something wrong with the scans—" She turned to him, frowning. "It's another PrimeCorp ship."

Hirin sat back in the chair, tapping his lips with steepled fingers. "What the hell is going on here?"

"PrimeCorp and the first Chron ship are moving," Yuskeya said.

"Running?" I asked.

She turned to me, frowning. "No. If I didn't know better, I'd say they were taking up—battle positions."

"HOLD US STEADY," Hirin told Rei. "We don't want to get caught up in this."

"I don't know if we have a choice," Yuskeya said, glancing up from the nav console, her dark eyes troubled. "Three more ships have entered scan range. All read Chron drive signatures. All coming from the direction of the planet."

"We should turn around," Maja said. "We might make it to the wormhole, get to the Corvids—"

"We'd have to navigate the asteroids on the other side," Hirin reminded her. "We might not get so lucky this time."

No, we wouldn't, I thought. I was in far worse shape physically than I'd been short days ago. I didn't have the coordination to help Rei pilot through another asteroid death trap. Maybe Hirin could—but he was still getting used to his rejuvenated body. If his reflexes were anything but a hundred percent—

"Two of the new ships have broken off and are heading this way," Yuskeya said. She turned to Hirin. "They must have noticed us."

Bright flashes of light around the PrimeCorp ship signalled that the first attackers had come within weapons range. The dots on the screen darted and swerved as the ships engaged. I stared at the bright blips of light, wishing I understood the situation better. Whose side were we on? Either one?

"Luta." Hirin caught my gaze, a question in his eyes. This decision, we had to make together. "How do you want to play this?"

"We don't have enough information, and we don't want to get involved."

"No sense turning back."

"No. Run for the next wormhole?" I asked. "With the new burst drive, we might make it."

"Chron ships still coming straight for us," Yuskeya said.

He nodded once, the time for discussion obviously over. "Rei, engage the burst drive and run for the next wormhole on Fha's map. Viss, I want weapons online, although I hope we won't have to use them."

Rei thrust the ship into a sharp dive down and under the asteroid, then straightened out and hit the burst drive. I was glad I'd been sitting down as the ship leapt under us and the pseudo-gravs fluctuated for a heartbeat. Weightlessness tugged at me, sending my stomach roiling and the blood pounding in my ears. Then the grav stabilized and the skimchair felt solid and reliable underneath me again. My stomach refused to settle, though, and heat rolled over me in waves.

"*Merde,*" Cerevare swore under her breath, gripping the sides of the console. "What was that?"

"Temporary gravity fluctuation," Rei assured her. "It won't happen again."

"Chron ships are in pursuit," Yuskeya reported.

"Gaining on us?"

"Not yet." Her voice sounded grim, as if it were only a matter of time.

"Chron ship is trying to comm us," Baden said, sounding surprised. He turned in his chair to face Hirin. "I don't understand the words, but the signal is definitely coming from them."

"I don't have to understand them," Hirin said. "I'm pretty sure they're telling us *stop, or we'll shoot*, or something very similar."

Jahelia Sord slid her chair closer to Baden's and held out her datapad. "Here," she said. "Can you use this to help figure it out?" Cerevare moved to read Sord's screen, peering over her shoulder at the symbols.

He took it, glancing at the screen. "I don't know how to match up what I'm hearing with the symbols."

"Just patch me into the comm channel," the datapad said in an exasperated voice, and Baden started, almost dropping the thing. "I have a trans-cymatics sound library—"

"What the—"

"Oh," Jahelia said, "that's Pita, my AI. She's right, she can probably help. Do as she says and patch her into the comm."

"Baden, don't do that," I said. I didn't know what game Jahelia Sord might be playing, but I wasn't about to let her connect her own datapad to the ship's system.

Sord turned to me, frowning. Her *pridattii* wrinkled and crumpled on her face, emphasizing her exasperation. "I'm trying to help. Pita can translate."

I felt the air on the bridge warming up around me, as if someone had lit a fire. "So you say. You haven't done a lot to make me trust you, Sord."

"Don't be stupid. I don't want to die out here, any more than you do."

"Maybe not, but you'd take over this ship in a heartbeat, if you could." I reached out a hand to Baden. "Here, give it to me, I'll see what exactly it is."

He hesitated, eyes fixed on my face, unreadable. "Captain—"

"That's an order, Baden. Give it here." My voice was harsh and impatient, far more than I meant it to be.

"*Kristos*, Captain. Your nose," said Jahelia Sord.

I felt a warm wetness dribble down over my upper lip and put a hand up, feeling the blood that had betrayed me. *Not again.*

"Mother! What's wrong?" Maja pushed up from her skimchair and darted around the corner into First Aid.

"Luta? Are you all right?" Hirin's voice was thick with worry.

"Never mind me. You deal with the ship."

Maja hurried back with a clean white cloth and passed it to me. I pressed it to my face, not wanting to meet her eyes and see the worry there.

"Captain—Hirin," Yuskeya said urgently. "Another Chron ship just appeared on the scan. It's—it's ahead of us."

"Between us and the wormhole?"

"Exactly. And it's big. Like, as big as a Protectorate Phoenix. I'd say it's guarding the wormhole."

"Rock and a hard place," Hirin said. "Ideas, anyone?"

"Captain," Cerevare said, excitement evident in her voice, "I think she's right." She'd taken out her own datapad and now looked up from the screen. "There's a file here—"

A brilliant flash lit up the viewscreen. We'd drawn closer to the original firefight since it lay close to our path to the wormhole. The ships continued their deadly dance, and one of them had succumbed. It wasn't the PrimeCorp ship, but I couldn't tell which one of the Chron ships, PrimeCorp's apparent ally or one of the others, had been destroyed.

I held up a hand to the Lobor. "Not now, Cerevare." Too much was happening, too quickly. I couldn't focus. The swelling heat of anger blooming in my head seemed ready to burst. Chron chasing us. Chron fighting, against PrimeCorp and more Chron. Chron blocking our way to the wormhole. And Jahelia Sord, claiming she could communicate with them, too? *What was going on?*

"They're still comming us," Baden said. "They sound—I don't know. Urgent? Angry? Threatening?"

"They're not going to take the *Tane Ikai*," I said suddenly. "Not the Chron, and not PrimeCorp. This is all *your fault!*" I realized I had shouted it, when I saw Hirin's shocked face. I'd tossed aside the bloodstained cloth and for some reason grabbed Jahelia Sord by the hair. I stared down at my fist, daubed with blood, pale-tipped black curls spilling from it. Sord swore, instinctively grabbing my wrist with both hands, trying to break my grasp.

And then Rei said something tense and urgent to Hirin about the activator drive, which didn't make any sense, because we were nowhere near an artifact moon or a ghosted wormhole. Before anyone could move or answer her, the ship's engines died, their throbbing heartbeat stilled, and we hurtled forward on momentum only. The bridge lights dimmed and failed, leaving ghost images dancing before my eyes. Everyone started shouting at once. On the front and rear viewscreens, two Chron ships drew in closer, as if closing the *Tane Ikai* in a pincer grip. And then it did feel like something enormous grabbed us, slowing us down. A hum filled the air, a buzzing like insects. I wondered if I was the only one who could hear it.

Suddenly Jahelia Sord's hands fell limp, away from my wrist, and I let go of her hair, my hand going suddenly too weak to hold onto it. I clutched my datapad to my chest—no, *Sord's* datapad, I thought fuzzily—and I was falling as if in slow motion, drifting toward the hard metal decking. I watched as if in a dream as Hirin slumped forward in the big chair, folding in on himself. As I landed with an impact that didn't feel slow or dreamlike at all, I saw Cerevare's softly-furred hands hit the decking to break her own fall. Then her head crashed down on them and her usually-bright eyes were unfocused, closing.

And I knew we were lost, lost to the Chron, and I felt a momentary sorrow that I would never have the chance to explain all of this to Lanar and Mother.

Chapter 29 — Jahelia
Rude Awakening

ONE OF THE many advantages of living with a body full of nanobioscavengers that my father, Berrto Sord, had stolen from PrimeCorp when I was a child, has been an almost total lack of pain. I mean, sure, it hurts if I kick a wall during a *zelendu* workout, or knock my elbow against the corner of a desk. A punch in the face is a punch in the face. But none of it hurts for long. Even the time I dislocated my shoulder during a fight with Ramesis Smith at the *akademio*, the pain only lasted for about five minutes before the nanos blocked it. The pain I repaid him lasted a lot longer, I can guarantee.

Waking up after the Chron hit us with—whatever it was that put us all out—I learned what pain really was. I understood, suddenly, even before I opened my eyes, what the term "splitting headache" meant. I was afraid, literally *afraid*, to open my eyes in case that made it worse.

So I took stock of my surroundings, as much as I could, before I cracked an eyelid. I lay on something soft, but solid underneath, like a thin sleeping pad you might take on a camping trip. I had a sense of open space around me, but not outdoor space—a decent-sized room, I decided. The temperature was comfortable, neither warm nor cold. It smelled a little like the locker rooms at the Protectorate *akademio*—not exactly sweaty or unpleasant, but definitely inhabited by other humans. In fact, if I strained my ears, I thought I could hear the sounds of someone else—maybe several someones—breathing deep and steady nearby. Weirdly, my left arm, from elbow to wrist, felt as if it were encased in some kind of cast. The sleeve of my jacket bunched uncomfortably around my upper arm, as if it had been pushed up out of the way.

The unexpected touch of something cold and metallic on my forehead startled me and my eyes flew open. And there was the echo of my childhood nightmare.

A tall humanoid bent over me. It hadn't said anything, must have moved with absolute silence since I hadn't even been aware of its presence. Pale, chitinous plates covered its face, forming sharp planes and angles, sweeping up to a many-pointed bone crest at the back of the hairless head. Deep-set turquoise eyes with diagonally slitted pupils regarded me from the depths of the eye sockets. It wore a plain dark uniform of close-fitting fabric with strange symbols running down one sleeve.

And just like in a nightmare, an unforgiving paralysis gripped me. I couldn't scream, couldn't move, couldn't knock away the chill weapon the creature held to my forehead. I was about to die and I couldn't do a damn thing to stop it.

The thing it held to my forehead twitched, and between one thudding heartbeat and the next, my headache was gone. So was my paralysis. I threw myself away from the alien, fetching up against a cool metal wall I hadn't realized was so close behind me. Pain bloomed anew in my right knee as it bashed into the metal plating. Somehow I scrambled to my feet on the cot and put my back against the wall, throwing my hands up in a block. I'd been right—a hard shell of greenish plastic or resin sheathed my left forearm. I stood looking down at the alien, my heart bucking, breaths coming short and fast.

It hadn't moved, didn't seem at all alarmed at my reaction. Now it merely shook its head at me. The thing in its hand seemed like a typical med injector. Slowly it backed to the door of the cell—because it was a cell, I realized now, complete with bars and a view across the corridor and through the left-hand wall into other cells. The wall behind me and the one to my right were solid metal; in front of me were bars and a door that led into a corridor perhaps six feet wide. To my left the bars created a divider between my cell and the next one. Beyond that were more. Across the corridor, the cells mirrored those on this side. The corridor stretched off to the left of my cell, and even from inside I could tell that it swung in an inward curve. *Space station*, my brain immediately suggested, and I imagined a torus shape with rooms laid out around the ring.

The alien touched a hand to a darker grey band about six inches wide on one of the cell door bars. The door swung open silently and the alien slipped out without turning its back on me, then pulled it closed again.

I wiped a shaky hand across my mouth and slid down the wall to sit, cross-legged, on the bed. That was a mistake and I grimaced, straightening my right leg. My knee throbbed painfully, in time with my heartbeat. I still felt rotten, despite the removal of the debilitating headache. *Where the hell am I, and what the hell was that thing?*

Whatever it was, it bent over a small trolley it had apparently left waiting in the corridor, swapping out the injector it had used on me for another one. It moved to open the door of the cell on the other side of the corridor, where Luta Paixon slept on a cot identical to mine, in an identical cell. A green cast sheathed her left arm as well. In the cell to my left, the engineer, Viss, lay silent and unmoving on his own cot, once again with his left arm encased.

"Captain!" I shouted, practically before I'd even realized that I had the power of speech again. The alien put a hand to a similar grey band on one of the bars, and the door swung open. It entered her cell. My voice echoed eerily, but apparently didn't penetrate the sleeping woman's unconsciousness. She didn't move as the alien crossed to her cot, injector in hand.

I slid off the cot, hissing as my right foot hit the floor and pain lanced my knee again. *Come on, bioscavs, get to work. I don't have time for this.* Limping, I reached the cell door and took hold of two of the bars. "Paixon! Captain! Wake up!" Not expecting any success, I touched the grey band with my palm. Predictably, nothing happened. I obviously didn't have the right chemical composition, palmprint, body heat, implant, or whatever it was that triggered the door lock for the alien.

Paixon didn't stir, even when the alien pressed the injector to her forehead. The captain slept on. The alien turned to study me, seeming puzzled. It chattered what I assumed must be a question, but I had about as much chance of understanding it as I did of turning into a butterfly and fluttering out of the cell. The alien's speech sounded like birds chirping and insects clicking and I don't know what else. It sure as hell wasn't Esper.

I shook my head. "I don't understand you."

The blue eyes fastened on me as the alien left Paixon's cell and returned to its medical cart. It wheeled the cart along to the cell next to Paixon's. The fall of blonde hair made it easy for me to identify Maja, out cold like everyone else from the *Tane Ikai*.

The ship. What had they done with the ship?

And then, *Pita.* How would I manage without her? I glanced around my cell, but I wasn't really expecting that my datapad had come along with me. I hadn't even had it when they'd knocked us out—Paixon had, and she'd been in the grip of one of her crazy paranoid episodes. If we'd had Pita, at least we might have a chance of communicating with the Chron. They hadn't killed us outright. That had to be a good thing, didn't it? In the war, the Chron had never taken prisoners. They simply killed.

Maja yelped from her cell, and I knew she'd been awakened as I had. As I watched, though, she slid off the cot and into a defensive crouch. Much more presence of mind than I'd shown, I thought jealously. There was more to her than I'd thought. *Megero.*

As it had done with me, the alien backed out of the cell. What would it do, I wondered, if one of us woke up with even more sense, and attacked it?

"Mother?" Maja called through the bars of her cell to Paixon.

"She didn't wake up," I told her.

She turned to me, blue eyes appraising. "Maybe it didn't do— whatever it just did—to her yet."

"It did. I watched it. But she didn't come out of it like we did."

"Mother, wake up!" she tried again, turning her attention from me. No response.

"Maybe it's her illness—the nanos," I said.

"What do you know about that?" Maja asked me impatiently. "It's none of your business, anyway."

"I know plenty," I told her. "And it's my business if it gets us killed or stops us from getting home. Like I keep saying, I'm stuck in the same situation as everybody else."

"Well, whose fault is that? You—"

Whatever else she might have said was interrupted by a yell from the cell next to mine. The alien had crossed the hall again, and applied the device to Viss. He had the best reaction yet, though. After his initial startle, his right hand shot out to grasp the alien's arm.

At least, that was his intention. About an inch from the chitinous skin, his fingers stopped as if they'd hit a wall. Yellow light flared from the point where his skin had contacted—what? Some kind of protective force field, I guessed. He hissed and snatched his hand away, shaking it as if he'd been shocked. The alien withdrew fromViss' cell even more hurriedly than it had left mine or Maja's.

That answered the question of why the alien felt safe to wake us up all on its own, anyway. We apparently couldn't touch it if we tried.

One by one it went like that, as far and farther down the line than I could easily see. Maja kept trying to rouse her mother, to no avail. Everyone who woke had the same questions, remembered succumbing on the bridge of the ship, and then nothing. We all had the same hard greenish sheath on our left arms, covering our chip implants and making communication via them impossible. Baden Methyr, Paixon's husband—Gramps, as I thought of him—and the Protectorate officer Yuskeya all had their datapads in their cells with them, for all the good they did them. The devices were standalone functional, but couldn't establish a connection to the *Tane Ikai's* comm.

"Why would they leave us these?" Hirin said.

Rei answered him. "They probably know they're harmless—I mean, you couldn't even hit someone with one and leave much of a dent."

"Looks like they brought along anything we had with us," Hirin agreed. "Maybe they don't know what they do."

"I think we have to assume they understand a lot," Maja said, gesturing to her encased arm. "They made sure we're cut off from outside communication."

Viss tapped his sheathed arm against one of the cell bars. It made only a dull thud, not the sharp sound I expected. "Hey, look at that," he said. He repeated the motion, harder this time. "The material softens on impact, absorbing the energy. Then it solidifies again right away."

"So you could hit someone with it, but it wouldn't hurt them?" Maja asked.

The engineer sounded glum when he answered. "Yeah, I guess so."

The alien paid no apparent attention to the discussions between the prisoners. I casually slid a hand in my pocket and rubbed the cool metal of the multi-tool the aliens hadn't bothered to take away from me. Maybe they'd left it on purpose—it wasn't much of a weapon, to be sure—or maybe they'd missed it. Either way, I kept my mouth shut about it.

The Erian pilot, Rei, was in the cell beyond Viss. There was some mild scuffle when she was awakened as well, but after she'd recovered from the initial disorientation, she said, "Where's Cerevare?"

Maja turned from her fixation on the Captain and peered down the lines of cells. "She's not here. I thought she must be in that cell beyond Gerazan—"

Yuskeya was at the secured door of her cell. "No, that one's empty," she confirmed. "Cerevare's not here."

"Was she here when they woke you, Sord?" she asked me.

I shook my head. "I don't think so. I assumed that everyone from the ship was here. If they took her out of here, it was before I was awake."

Once Baden, at the end of my row of cells and the last to be woken, had been revived, the alien returned to Paixon's cell. It stood outside, one hand resting on the door, studying the Captain or thinking or doing something alien and inscrutable. Then it went into her cell again. It appeared to take readings or scans, then returned to the corridor, collected the medical cart, and wheeled it through a doorway and out of sight. A door somewhere beyond opened and closed.

Maja sagged against the bars of her cell, leaning her head against the cool material. It wasn't metal, but it had been smooth and slightly chill under my fingers. By this time, I'd investigated my cell thoroughly. The only piece of furniture in it was the cot. There was also a device that seemed to be for the collection of waste, but I didn't consider that furniture. The rear wall held a gadget that dispensed cold water. I'd also examined the casing on my arm. It appeared to be seamless, but had one small wavy-shaped opening on the underside. I assumed the right sort of key would open it.

"What did you mean," she asked finally, "when you said you knew plenty about my mother's illness?"

I shrugged. "I knew someone else who had the same thing."

"It couldn't have been the *same* thing," she argued. "No-one else—well, hardly anyone else—has the same nanos."

"So, maybe not the exact same thing," I said, shaking my head, "but damned close. Sweats, headaches, nosebleeds, paranoia, irrational anger—and she had nanos in her system, for years. The symptoms came on when the nanos' programming failed."

She was quiet for a long moment, staring at Paixon's still form. "Who was it?" she asked finally.

In a weird way, it felt good to tell someone about it after all these years. "My mother."

Maja turned to me, a puzzled frown scoring her forehead. "Who are you, Sord?"

I spoke before I thought about it. "Your grandmother wasn't the only person who worked for PrimeCorp, you know."

She stared at me, still frowning, then her face softened and she asked, "What happened to her? Your mother?"

I studied Captain Paixon for a long moment. I'd started out wanting to hurt both of these women. I'd wanted to use them to get to Paixon's own mother, to get a payback that had never been really clear to me and seemed even less clear now. When had things changed? I wasn't sure. I didn't say anything for a long moment, but when I did speak, it wasn't to hurt Maja, or anyone. It was only the truth.

"She died."

THE DOOR DOWN the hallway opened again, and this time two of the aliens came into view. Their uniforms seemed identical to the first one, but one had pale raspberry-coloured skin, and their bone crests showed noticeable variations. The medical cart had been swapped for a wheeled gurney. They stopped outside Captain Paixon's cell and opened it.

"What are you doing?" Maja demanded.

They ignored her. It was pretty obvious to me what they were doing—they were taking the captain out of here.

Hirin called from down the line of cells. "What's happening?"

"They're taking Mother," Maja answered, her voice hovering on the edge of hysterical. "Stop! Where are you taking her?"

But the aliens were clearly not interested in conversing with Maja or anyone else here—or they couldn't understand a word we were saying anyway. With businesslike efficiency they transferred Paixon to the gurney, lifting her, I noticed, with care. What really caught my attention wasn't their bedside manner, though. Along with the Captain, they picked up and deposited on the gurney with her . . . a datapad.

My datapad. *Pita.*

If I could get her back, we might have a chance.

Chapter 30 — Jahelia
Completely Freneza

"WE HAVE TO *do* something," Maja said again. Frankly, I was getting tired of listening to her. She wasn't whining, but she wasn't coming up with any concrete, workable plans, either. She paced her cell like a caged animal, sparking with anger and frustrated energy.

In the cell next to mine, Viss Feron had prowled and investigated every inch of floor, every bar that formed the walls. I'd sat on my bed, nursing my sore knee and trying to stay calm, and watched him check under the cot, investigate the water dispenser built into the rear wall, and examine the waste-collection device. He was the picture of control, but a muscle worked at the side of his jaw, betraying . . . something. His search apparently yielded nothing of use.

"We have to get out of here, is what we have to do," I told Maja. "But I don't see a way to do that, do you?"

She glared at me. "You don't seem to be trying very hard. At least the rest of us have searched the cells. All you do is sit there."

"Did any of you find anything useful?"

She didn't answer.

"I already looked, when I first woke up. I'm more interested in this: what do you think controls the force fields? Hey, Engineering, did you notice anything when you tried to grab that one and got zapped?"

Viss eyed me coldly—I suppose I could start calling him by his real name, now we were captives of an alien race together. I've never been that good at social etiquette.

"No," he said finally. "I don't know what generated it."

"Does anyone else think they might be listening to us?" Yuskeya said from down the corridor. "It might be wise not to let them know everything we're thinking."

I chuckled. "What are we going to do, play a game of *mesaĝo*? I'll whisper to Viss, and he can whisper to Rei, who'll whisper to—"

"Oh, shut up, Sord. Does everything have to be a joke to you?" I couldn't see Baden very well through the intervening cells, but his words stung a little. I'd heard him cracking jokes at stressful moments. But oh, no, don't let the outsider play.

"Well, let's put it to the test, shall we?" I said. "The next time one of these aliens comes into my cell, I'll make a grab for it and see what happens. Viss, you're close enough to observe, so you can tell us afterward if you notice anything. And if they seem to be taking more precautions the next visit, we'll know they heard me."

"That's crazy. You don't know what they'll do. They might kill you," Maja said.

"Well, that'll be one less thing for you all to worry about."

It wasn't that I felt particularly brave—or suicidal. But I wasn't prepared to tag along like a little kid, either. If we were going to escape, I wanted a piece of the action. I wouldn't sit here and wait to be rescued.

Silence descended then, except for someone having a low-voiced discussion through the bars of their adjoining cells, somewhere down the row. Yuskeya and Baden, maybe. Across the corridor from them, the Protectorate cryptographer sat on his own cot, his head resting against the wall, eyes closed. It was possible he understood some of the language, but if he did, he was keeping it close to his chest. Maybe whatever they'd said troubled him. No, I thought, he'd share it if he knew, with Yuskeya if no-one else. She was technically his commanding officer, so he'd feel bound to report. I figured he must not have had enough time to learn conversational Chron.

I got to test my theory about the force fields very soon after that. The door to the corridor opened and closed again, and two Chron appeared, pushing a cart. Not the medical one this time, but one that appeared, from the aroma that came with it, to be carrying food. So they didn't plan to starve us. That was a good thing.

I stayed seated on the cot, legs dangling, trying to appear relaxed as they stopped outside my cell. I couldn't tell if either of these was the one who'd originally woken me, but I thought not. There wasn't much to tell them apart at first glance, but now that I was able to study them from a more detached viewpoint, the variations in the shapes and ridges of their bone crests was easier to see. The chitinous plates on their faces revealed similar deviations in form and colour, subtly distinguishing one from another—once you knew what to look for. I wondered if our appearance was as homogeneous to them.

Their uniforms were the same plain dark one-piece suits that the first one had worn, with white symbols spilling down one sleeve. Either all those we had seen were males, or the females were flat-chested, like the Lobors. As I watched them, one unloading a food tray while the other did something to release the door, I noticed something else, too. Each wore a small round pin or button of some kind, attached to the fabric of their sleeve, tucked in the crook of the elbow.

I glanced over at Viss in the next cell. He watched both me and the aliens intently. Surreptitiously, I pointed at the crook of my own elbow. He nodded slightly to indicate that he'd seen, as well.

"*Hola!*" I said to the alien cheerily, as it approached me with the tray. The cell had no table or chair, only the cot for furniture. I wondered if the Chron would come close enough to put it down on the cot, or leave it on the floor. "What's for supper? It smells delicious."

The Chron chitter-whistled something at me in response, although I didn't know if it had understood a word I'd said in Esper. It did come as far as the cot and slid the tray onto the end. Perhaps I'd alleviated its suspicions by speaking to it or not appearing interested in leaving the cot, or maybe it felt more secure with a friend nearby. Whatever the reason, it turned away from me as I'd hoped it would.

Before it took two steps toward the cell door, I launched myself off the cot and tackled the alien. I landed on its back, my arms around its neck.

I'll admit I screamed when the force field lit up. It felt like I'd grabbed a live charging cable on a docking bay floor and plugged it into me instead of into a ship. Brilliant yellow light blazed and the shock raced up both arms, meeting in my chest with a blast that threatened to stop my heart. Somewhere an alarm bleated out a warning. I knew I hadn't actually touched the Chron—the field had precluded contact, but not the impact. The Chron fell to its knees.

I slid off the alien, boneless and weak in the wake of the jolt I'd taken. It flipped around to watch me and scuttled crablike to the cell door. Its compatriot helped it to its feet and slammed the door shut once it was outside. They chattered something to me. I ignored it. One of them pressed something on the cart and the alarm stopped. I lay on the floor and panted, waiting for the feeling in my arms to return. I laughed weakly.

"Hey, Engineering, you notice anything?"

"Yeah, I noticed you're crazy, Sord," he said. "Completely *freneza*. Another stunt like that and you could get us all killed, not just your own sorry-ass self."

But I knew he'd seen what I did when the Chron's arms had flown up in surprise at my tackle. The little round pin had flared with golden light, too, activated by my proximity. It had to be the controller for the force field. And knowing what controlled it was one step closer to knowing how to disable it.

THE TWO CHRON continued down the corridor, now only opening the cell doors and slipping the trays inside. They didn't linger at any of the cells, merely completed their job and left. By the time they got to my cell on their way out, I'd managed to sit up again, leaning my back against the solid rear wall of my cell. The one I'd jumped turned an inscrutable stare on me. I gave a little wave. It turned away without blinking.

Maja retrieved her supper tray and uncovered it. "Huh," she said. "If I didn't know better, I'd swear this food came from the *Tane Ikai*. We had a good supply of pasta and tomato sauce, and that's what this is."

Viss uncovered his and nodded. "It's a little hard to believe it's a classic Chron dish as well."

"Do we trust them?" Baden asked from further down the hallway. "Think it's safe to eat?"

Hirin said, "I think we can eat it. As Luta said about the Corvids, if they wanted us dead, we'd be dead. I can't see any point in poisoning us at this point. And I'm starved," he added. Through the intervening bars I saw him take a bite.

Well, it did smell good. I crawled over to my cot, pulled myself up, and sat on the edge. My hands still felt slightly numb, but it didn't seem like the shock had done any permanent damage. My knee, where I'd bashed it into the wall, throbbed like a *bastardo*, but there was nothing I could do about that. Like the others, my tray held a plate of spaghetti and a shallow bowl filled with the sauce. The cells were quiet as we all ate. I didn't know how long we'd been unconscious before the Chron had awakened me, but it must have been a while. Hirin was right about being hungry. I ate in a wholly less than ladylike fashion.

When I was finished, I said, "So, anyone have any theories about where we are?"

Viss said, "Space station, judging by the curve of that corridor."

"That was my thought, too."

"Not a ship," Maja said from across the hall. "There's no sensation of motion, or engines."

"Could be a really, really big ship," I suggested, but I didn't really mean it.

"How far did they bring us?" Baden said. "We didn't read any stations in the system, did we?"

Further down the corridor, Yuskeya said, "If it's on the far side of that planet we saw, we might have missed it."

"Fha said something about stealth technology—maybe it was blocked from our sensors somehow," Maja added.

"Well, how can we use our newfound knowledge?" I asked,

flexing my fingers to ease out the last of the stiffness from the jolt they'd taken.

"That they don't seem to be listening to us?" Maja asked.

"Don't *seem* to be," Yuskeya echoed. "They could be waiting until we say something *really* interesting."

"That's true," Hirin mused. "Ms. Sord's declaration of her intent to attack one of them probably wouldn't worry them overmuch. They'd know their fields would protect them."

"*Het, Sord, eike tendu si?*" Yuskeya Blue's voice came to me through the cells between us. Viss turned to me quizzically, then glanced at Blue, frowning. I knew only two people in here would have understood what she said—me and Lieutenant Soto. She'd spoken in what was informally called academy cant, the secret language of the Protectorate. And although I hadn't finished my Protectorate training, I'd picked up enough to converse at a basic level.

Hey, Sord, can you understand me?

Go slow and I can, I told her, the words admittedly hesitant and probably poorly pronounced as I dredged them up from the depths of my brain.

Baden's next to me. We both have our datapads. We're wondering if there's any way we could use them to—I don't know—short out one of the force fields. You and he—you're both techdogs. You think about it too.

She had to speak slowly, repeating or substituting some words, but eventually I got it. It wasn't a bad idea. With the cant, we could probably communicate—some of us, anyway—without the Chron understanding if they were listening in. And the datapads . . . we didn't know much about the tech the Chron were using, but it might be possible . . . if we opened one up and took out the power supply, rerouted the—

Viss stepped close to the bars that joined our cells and whispered, "What was that about?"

I hobbled over to him, wincing at the pain in my knee. I put my face close to his ear, speaking barely above a breath. "Maybe a way out. Jury-rig the datapads to short out the force field controllers."

He quirked a half-grin. "Good one. Seems like it would depend a lot on things we don't control, but I guess it's worth a try."

"At this point, anything's worth a try."

"What's with the limp?" he asked in a normal voice. "They hurt you?"

"Naw. Went a round with the wall when they first woke me up. The wall won."

He nodded, then lowered his voice again. "You saw them try to wake the captain?"

"They used the same device on her. It just didn't take."

The engineer's lips pressed down into a tight, thin line. "First priority if we get out of here has to be finding her."

"I agree."

He looked surprised at that, so I added with a grin, "She's got my datapad."

"Pfft." He blew out an inarticulate noise of disgust and turned away from me, crossing the cell to talk to Rei, on the other side.

I didn't mind. I let my thoughts shift to the datapads. I had work to do.

Chapter 31 — Jahelia
Out of the Proverbial
Frying Pan

THEY LEFT US to sleep, not returning to pick up the dirty dishes. I don't think anyone actually slept very much. Everyone was too keyed up to rest, pacing their cells, holding low-voiced conversations with their neighbours, or openly worrying about Paixon and the Lobor. Baden and I held quiet discussions, filtered slowly and painstakingly—sometimes almost painfully, since my academy cant vocabulary was limited—through Yuskeya, on how to cannibalize the datapads for parts and repurpose them.

After a lot of mental arguing with myself, I'd passed my multi-tool to Viss, who'd sent it on down the line to cells to Baden, to help with the job. I hated like hell to give it up, but if it would help—I sighed. If I was in with these people, I might as well be all in. We needed all the help we could get.

It wouldn't be easy to make an interruptor work—someone would have to get close enough to a Chron to actually touch the controller with it, since we didn't know what kind of tech it involved. We could only take our best guess, and hope that the two power sources from the datapads would have enough juice to power the interrupt. I thought, having been close enough to see it in action, that the controller itself wasn't inside the field—the field radiated out from it, all around the edges. So that meant there was an area about an inch in diameter that we'd have to get inside. And would it even work?

But we couldn't simply sit around and wait.

Finally Baden declared it finished. What he'd taken out of the two datapads and rigged together was small enough to fit in the palm of a hand.

"Pass it up to me, I'll do it," I offered, but Yuskeya disagreed.

"They're going to be more cautious around you now, since you pulled that last stunt," she said to me in academy cant. Or something to that effect. My translation was still rusty.

"Yeah, you're probably right," I said. The crew wouldn't trust me to be the one to actually get free first, anyway. Not that I'd leave the rest of them here. Unless there was no choice. "In that case, I think it should be Maja."

She glanced up, frowning, at the sound of her name.

"Why Maja?"

"They won't be as suspicious of her. Especially if she makes out that she's really broken up about the captain, like, sick with worry."

"She *is* sick with worry," Yuskeya said. It sounded like she was talking through clenched teeth.

"So she'll be all the more convincing. And I hear she's trained in warrior chi. Not so helpless as she might appear."

The Protectorate officer was quiet for a minute, then said grudgingly, "You do have a point. Not that I'd say she looks helpless. One problem, though. The interruptor is on this side of the corridor."

"The hallway's not that wide. We could get it across to her."

"Pfft. Or get it stuck in the middle. Wouldn't that be not suspicious at all the next time the aliens come in here."

"*Kristos,* this whole thing's a gamble, Protectorate," I told her. "If you're in, you might as well be all in. If you think Maja's got the best chance to use it, then figure out a way to get it to her."

Maja came to the door of her cell. "What are you saying? I keep hearing my name."

"Explain it to her, Gerazan," Yuskeya told the Protectorate

Lieutenant. He and Maja met at the bars that joined their cells, and he whispered quickly in her ear.

Her face hardened, and then she smiled. It wasn't the kind of smile I'd associated with her before. "I can do that," was all she said.

"Get the interruptor to Viss," I told Yuskeya. "He's directly across the hall from Maja. It's not that wide—they might even be able to pass it across."

"What if there are cameras in here?" Gerazan Soto asked. "Maybe they're watching us, as well as listening."

"Well, if they're watching us, they saw Baden build the damn thing," I said. My cant grew more fluent the more I used it, I thought with a grim smile. "I don't think passing it across the corridor is going to give anything away if they already know about it."

Gerazan told Maja the plan, and I told Viss. They each moved to the door of their cells, directly across from one another, and stretched an arm out through the bars as far as they could. Perhaps three inches still separated their straining fingertips. Too far. The interruptor was too small to bridge the gap.

"I could slide it across the floor," Viss muttered to me. I relayed the suggestion to Baden via Yuskeya.

"I don't know, it's pretty delicate," he said. "If it hit the bars it might knock something loose. I figure it's good for one impact, so that should be against the force field controller."

"Okay," Viss said when Yuskeya had translated that to me and I'd whispered it through the bars to him.

He reached up and ripped away the sleeve of his blue shipsuit, pulling the stitches free of the body. It came away trailing broken threads. He laid the piece of fabric on his cot. "I'll wrap it up in this and slide it across," he whispered.

"Yeah, no-one's going to notice that you've suddenly got only one sleeve now," I told him. "That's not suspicious at all."

Without a word he tore off the other sleeve and pushed it under the mattress on his cot. "Happy now?"

"Much better." I switched to cant and said to Yuskeya, "*Okej*, send it on up. Viss will protect it and get it across the hallway." Gerazan translated for Maja.

"Hurry up," Maja hissed. "Now that we're doing this, I feel like they're going to show up any minute."

The interruptor passed from hand to hand up the line of cells, from Baden to Yuskeya to Rei and finally to Viss. He placed the delicate bundle of electronics on the detached sleeve of his shipsuit and wrapped it carefully. Then he pushed it through the bars of the cell, set it on the floor, and shoved it toward Maja's cell. It slid unerringly across the smooth floor.

I blew my breath out slowly as the bundle fetched up against the bars. Maja pulled it through quickly and crossed to the cot in her own cell, unwrapping it and shoving the sleeve under her mattress as Viss had done with the other one. She set the interruptor on the cot and sat beside it, covering the makeshift gadget with her hand.

"And now we wait," Yuskeya said.

The words were barely out of her mouth when the door at the end of the hallway clicked open.

AGAIN, TWO CHRON had come with a cart. They wore the same plain, androgynous uniforms as all the others we'd seen. I studied the facial plating and bone crests of this pair. I thought they were the same ones who'd been here before.

Sure enough, one stopped outside the door of my cell, pointed to the tray of dirty dishes, and whistle-chattered something. Then it pointed at the floor inside the door. The meaning was clear enough: *bring the tray and put it here.*

I grinned and complied. Hey, I wanted them at ease so that Maja could work her magic, right? I hoped they wouldn't try the same thing with her, but as soon as the door at the end of the corridor had opened, she'd crumpled in on herself. She sat with her head hanging down, shoulders hunched, her demeanour emanating defeat. Her blonde hair hung around her face like a veil. I left the tray where they'd indicated and returned to my cot. I put my hands up in an "I surrender" gesture.

"Don't mind me, folks, I've decided to be harmless from now on."

I'm sure they didn't understand me, and they kept eyes on me the whole time they opened the door, slid the tray out, and shut the door again. They stowed the tray, then crossed to Maja's cell and gave her what I assumed to be the same instruction.

She ignored them.

One tried again, raising its voice and knocking the knuckles of a chitin-covered hand against the bars in an attempt to get her attention. She merely hunched over further. It issued the instruction again, and she very deliberately turned away from the aliens, rolling into a fetal position on the cot with her back to them.

I didn't see how she'd know when to launch her attack from there, but I had to assume she knew what she was doing. One of the Chron made a sound that meant exasperation in any language, opened the door, and entered the cell. Maja had left her tray next to the bars adjoining Gerazan's cell, and I knew what was about to happen a split second before it did.

Gerazan had been standing at the front of his own cell, ostensibly watching the aliens make their progress down the corridor. As soon as the Chron in Maja's cell leaned down to retrieve the tray, however, the cryptographer leapt toward it. One arm flashed through the bars, clutching for the bony protuberances at the back of the alien's head. The impact pulled the alien forward, off-balance. It crashed into the cell bars and then tumbled onto Maja's tray with a clatter of dishes.

Of course the force field repelled Gerazan, and he staggered away from the bars, shaking his jolted arm. I knew what that felt like and cringed involuntarily. But the distraction gave Maja enough time to move. She dropped off the cot like a cat and sprang toward the Chron. Ducking in under its arm as it scrabbled to regain its feet, she slapped the interruptor into the crook of its elbow. Yellow light flashed hotly around them. I couldn't tell if it was the force field activating against Maja or flaring as it shorted out.

But Maja wasn't jolted back. Without a pause she grasped the Chron's right arm, threw her own up across its chest and neck, and pivoted, rocking her weight forward and pulling the Chron with her. Stunned and off-balance, it had nothing to brace against her with. In one smooth motion she flipped the alien over her shoulder to land with a thump, supine against the unforgiving cell floor. Letting momentum carry her, she rolled over the alien, continuing to pull it with her until it had flipped onto its stomach. She put one knee on its back, scooped one arm around its throat, and with the other hand grasped its bone crest and pulled, forcing its head up.

The other Chron had been slow to react, and was only two steps inside Maja's cell by the time she stopped and met its eyes. "You want me to break your friend's neck, take another step," she said, jerking lightly on the bone crest to emphasize her point.

Even with little or no understanding of Esper, the message was hard to miss. The second Chron stopped and put its hands up, motioning for her to desist. In all probability it could have reached her before she seriously harmed the other one, and used its force field as a weapon by simply throwing itself on her. But either it didn't think of that or it wasn't certain enough to risk the other's life. After what I'd just seen, I wouldn't bet against Maja being able to break someone's neck this way—and fast. I was impressed.

Maja motioned with her head toward the rear of her cell. "Over there," she said.

"I guess we're not worrying about whether they're listening in anymore?" I said to no-one in particular.

"Oops," Maja said. "Oh well, I don't hear any alarms."

The Chron complied with Maja's instructions—which surprised me. I kept waiting for it to break for the cell door, push the alarm button on the cart, take off running—*something*. But it merely backed up against the wall where she'd told it.

Not taking her eyes off the second Chron, she managed to get the first one to stand and walk over to the cell door. She kept a close grip on its bone crest and her other arm tight around its neck as she pulled the door shut with her foot. Not that the one inside wouldn't be able to open it with a touch of its palm to the grey band, but for now at least, it stayed against the rear wall, well away from everyone. I wondered if it was actually scared of us, or plotting something. I resolved to keep an eye on it.

They crossed the hallway and stopped outside Viss's door. "Open it," Maja said, and Viss tapped a finger on the dark grey band that controlled the door. The Chron reached up a hand and pressed it to the band.

Nothing happened.

Maja gave the Chron a little shake. "Come on, open the door. You did it a minute ago. Don't mess around now."

The Chron chattered something and pointed to the force field controller on its arm. The round button was blackened and pitted.

"*Merde,* that's how it works," I breathed. "You're wearing the field generator, the controller listens to you."

"Do you think it will work if a human's wearing it?" Viss asked.

"Only one way to find out," I said. "Maja, you've got to get that thing—the good one—from the other Chron, and put it on."

"Oh, for—" Maja's voice disappeared into a litany of whispered swears. "How am I supposed to get that one and still hang onto this one?"

"Bring him here," Viss said, and put his arms out through the bars of his cell. Maja pulled the Chron closer until Viss was able to wrap his not inconsiderably burly arms around the alien's neck. It seemed quite as effective—and threatening—as the hold Maja had had on it.

She straightened up and stretched, then crossed to her old cell door, snapping her fingers to get the attention of the Chron inside. Once she had eye contact, she gestured to the crook of her elbow, then put her hand out and waggled her fingers in a "give it here" kind of way. She pointed to the floor outside the cell bars.

The Chron hesitated, obviously debating. Viss tightened his grip on the Chron he held, and the alien made a little squeaking noise.

That seemed to decide the one in Maja's cell. It held up a long-fingered hand, then released the controller from its sleeve. It moved cautiously to the front of the cell and set it on the floor, then backpedaled to the wall again.

Maja bent down, hesitated only a moment, then picked up the controller. She slipped it onto her sleeve and stepped over to Hirin's door, then reached up and touched the grey band.

The door swung open.

Hirin brought the sheet off his cot, and ripped long strips from one edge. He quickly bound the first Chron's arms in front of its body. Another strip went around its legs at knee level, so it could walk, but not quickly. Viss released his hold on the alien, and together Maja and Hirin trundled it into the cell with its mate. With a third and fourth strip, Hirin tightly bound the bars of Maja's cell door shut. It wouldn't necessarily hold the Chron inside for long, but it would slow them down if they decided they wanted out.

Maja made the rounds of all the cells, opening each door in turn. She let me out last. I tried not to resent it. A few strips of Hirin's sheet had puddled on the floor outside the cells. I took one and tied it across my shoulder and chest like a bandolier, then tucked a couple more inside it. They could come in handy if we needed to tie up anyone else.

Once everyone was free, Maja returned to the cell where Luta Paixon had been held. She pointed inside and said, "Where is she?"

One of the Chron said something and mimed a gesture I couldn't decipher.

"Gerazan, I don't suppose you got any of that, did you?" Maja asked the Protectorate cryptographer. Apparently she didn't understand the meaning either.

He shook his head. "I don't know the spoken language at all. My job was supposed to be to record any symbols or writings different from what we knew already from the ships we'd captured. See if I could extrapolate any further on the language as a whole. Cerevare might recognize some, but you have to remember we really never had much to go on. And certainly not enough to guess at how it sounded."

Viss held up his resin-sheathed arm. "I'd like to get this damn thing off. Wonder if they know how?"

Maja mimed the question to the Chron in the cell, but they both shook their heads. They'd been pretty compliant so far, but maybe this was asking too much of them. And our leverage was diluted now, since they were both in the cell together.

"Want to rough one of them up again?" I asked.

Hirin regarded me with chilly disapproval. "I think we've threatened them enough for now. And I don't want anyone going into that cell with them. No unnecessary risks."

"Suit yourself, Gramps. You're the boss, apparently."

He ignored me. "Baden, Viss, check the cart. See if there's anything there we might use as a weapon."

"We all had a fork," I reminded them. "I'm taking that, if nothing else."

Rei laughed out loud, but it wasn't a mean laugh. "Good thinking, Sord," she said. "I'd rather have a fork than nothing at all." And she actually ducked into her cell to get it.

"Nothing on the cart that looks at all dangerous," Baden said.

"So we've got one force field generator and a bunch of forks?" Hirin said. "I'm not sure I like these odds."

"We still have hostages," Yuskeya reminded him.

"I think they might be more of a liability," Viss said. "Without them, we'll move faster and possibly quieter."

"Yes, we'll leave them here," Hirin said. "Now, which door?"

I'd only noticed the door nearest my cell, where all the Chron I'd seen so far had entered. Now that I could see the far end of the curving corridor, though, I realized that another doorway lay at that end.

"I'm inclined to vote for the door no Chron have come through," Viss said.

Hirin nodded. "And I'm inclined to agree."

"We have to find Mother and Cerevare," Maja said. "Do we split up?"

"And Pita," I said, but no-one paid any attention to me.

"Absolutely not. We might never find each other again. I doubt they've taken either of them very far. So here's what we do." Hirin pulled a deep breath. "We go out, we stick together, we try to find Luta and Cerevare. And we don't kill anyone unless it's us or them. Got it?"

"Where's the fun in that?" Viss asked, but he winked at Hirin as he said it.

I tucked my fork inside the makeshift bandolier and nudged Viss in the ribs. "Still think I'm the crazy one?" I asked him.

For an instant the skin around his eyes tightened, and then he grinned. "Absolutely," he said. "But I never said you weren't in good company."

"Let's go," Maja said, and put her hand on the door at the end of the hall. It clicked open, revealing a short, empty hallway that turned right and then left again almost immediately.

And an ear-splitting alarm cut the air.

Chapter 32 — Luta
And Into the Proverbial Fire

MY FIRST CONFUSED thought on waking was *I'm not on the ship anymore.* Even when the *Tane Ikai*'s engines were silenced for docking, I knew the hum of the air cyclers, the scent of my ship, the *feel* of it. Here I heard no throb of engines at all. *Had we gone planetside somewhere?* I wondered muzzily.

Then I remembered. The Chron ships bracketing us. The engines shutting down. The horror of everyone on the bridge slumping, falling, hitting the cold metal decking.

I opened my eyes, struggling to sit up, but restraints held me to a soft surface. The room must be some sort of medical bay, filled with machines and instruments I didn't recognize. Some of them were marked with symbols that looked like Chron—similar enough to the markings inside the artifact moon for me to be sure. Cool light spilled from glowing rectangles set into the ceiling, not bright or harsh enough to make me squint, even when I stared straight up at them. A quick glance around was enough to tell me that I lay alone in the room.

I closed my eyes, fighting off panic as my heart rate stuttered up and racing adrenaline prickled in my arms and legs. *Hirin,*

Maja, Rei . . . where was everyone? Surely I couldn't be the only one—no. I would not let myself think that anything bad had happened to the others. I was here, so why wouldn't they be? They were likely all in identical bays right this minute.

But where is my ship?

I concentrated on my surroundings. I couldn't find an answer to that question until I figured out where *I* was. A low, background rumble hovered on the edge of awareness if I really concentrated—could be ship engines, but I didn't think so. Could be life-support systems. Could even be something as mundane as air or heat systems in a large building, I decided. No real clue there.

I lifted my head as far up as I could and surveyed the rest of my body. A pale yellow sheet draped most of it, but it seemed to be intact and pain-free, laid out on a high gurney or cot. My left arm lay atop the coverlet, the forearm encased in a sheath of smooth, green, resin-like material. The wide restraint that held me to the bed was a band across my chest and upper arms—if I wriggled a bit I could tell that there were two more, one over my hips and one over my ankles. Apart from the restraints, everything seemed to move and work as it should, although my right arm felt tender, as if it were bruised. Pale red furrows scored the flesh as if something had been tightly wrapped around it for a considerable length of time, and only recently been removed. A row of round red splotches, like the imprints of octopus suckers, trailed up my inner arm.

Both arms were free from the elbow down, and I reached across gingerly with my right hand to touch the sheath on my other arm. It felt cool and unremarkable, if somewhat heavy. If I rotated my hand, it appeared seamless, but the smooth surface was broken in one spot by a wavy-shaped opening. A keyhole? There was no other obvious way to open or remove it. The way it covered my implant port made me nervous. I couldn't touch the implant to activate it and see if the ship or anyone from it was within calling range.

I went over what I could remember before the Chron had knocked us all out. I'd been angry again—angry at Jahelia Sord this time. For some reason I'd blamed everything on her, which didn't make any sense. She'd apparently been trying to help, and I'd been overcome by one of my stupid blind rages. A hot flush of embarrassment warmed my skin. I hated being out of control. Was it really my nanobioscavengers failing and causing all of this? Mother had obviously not known such a thing was imminent, or she wouldn't have postponed my upgrade. It must have been something external that had affected them, something outside the normal parameters.

I blinked and shifted my focus to the room and my restraints. I had no answers for those questions, and nothing useful I could do about them. If my crew was here—wherever "here" was—I had to try and get myself free so I could find them.

Peering to the sides, I followed the soft cloth restraint over my chest down to where it disappeared under the edge of the gurney. It probably fastened under the side, out of reach. A wave of dizziness hit me and the room spun. I closed my eyes again until the feeling subsided, then cautiously opened them again. Everything stayed put, but a low-grade nervousness settled in my gut. Had whatever the Chron did to us somehow made my condition worse?

I focused on the restraint again. The band was not particularly tight, and my arms had enough freedom to allow me to reach up and grasp the top edge of the restraint. I pulled it away from my body as far as I could and I wiggled toward the end of the bed experimentally. There was enough give to let me move an inch or so easily. It occurred to me that perhaps the restraints were not so much to keep me imprisoned as to simply keep me from rolling off the sides of the gurney. If that were the case, I might be able to slip out from under them. *Yes.* I bent my knees and pulled my feet free of the lower one easily.

Inch by inch I wriggled down the cot, sliding out from under the top restraint as if it were a shirt that I was slowly, slowly pulling off over my head. It got tricky when I'd inched down far enough to get caught up on the middle band. I wheezed, feeling short of breath, and sweat prickled my skin. I took a few deep breaths before moving again. My arms were mostly free and I managed to twist myself out of the top band. I'd become even more tangled up in the yellow sheet, and I kicked it to the floor with a rush of satisfaction. Cautiously, I slid off the gurney after it and leaned against it for support while I surveyed the room.

I wondered suddenly if any surveillance devices had recorded my "escape," but nothing obvious presented itself, and no-one came running to wrestle me onto the table.

A single door was set into the wall on the opposite side of the room. It had no handle, just a touchpad next to it. I didn't want to touch it too soon in case it set off alarms, so I left it for now. I expected it was locked anyway, but I wanted a few minutes to get ready before I tried it.

The room had an air of being unfinished. A couple of buff-coloured wall panels stood next to sections they were obviously meant to cover, revealing masses of cables and multicoloured wires running through the walls. Shelving held boxes obviously waiting to be unpacked. A recess in one section of counter appeared ready to hold a computer device of some sort, but was empty except for a lining that looked like packing material. Now I saw a device atop a movable cart, which had been wheeled to the head of the gurney. Long translucent tubes hung from it, their insides brushed intermittently with dark red streaks and droplets. At the other end of the tubes hung a limp casing made of something that felt like soft plastic. I pulled it up and peered at the underside. A row of round protrusions that reminded me of the end of a med injector ran up the center. They matched the marks on my arm.

What had they done to me, and why?

I dropped the casing and turned my attention to the rest of the room. It offered little I could use as a weapon, if it came to that. A cupboard held an array of typical med injectors, but I couldn't tell if they held any medications or what they might be. A couple of pieces of equipment might work to bash someone over the head, but I couldn't picture myself lugging any of them through hallways.

I did, however, find Jahelia Sord's datapad on the counter. I recalled clutching it as I fell to the deck on the *Tane Ikai*. I felt a hot flush slap my cheeks again at the vivid memory of my fingers twined in her dark hair. I couldn't fully remember why I'd done that, only that I'd been horribly angry.

"Well, let's see if you can help me," I muttered.

"Good to see you awake, Captain Paixon," the datapad said to me in a female voice, and I almost dropped it.

Without waiting for me to reply, it continued, "I have no visual input in this device, so I was waiting to hear your voice to know you were conscious again. I take it we're alone?"

"Er, yes," I said. "Is the rest of my crew nearby?"

"I can't get any readings on them," the voice said. "However, I can't read your implant, either, so that doesn't necessarily mean anything."

I glanced at the green casing around my forearm. Maybe one of its functions—or its only function—was to cut off communication possibilities. If everyone had one—

"However, they were all together earlier," it continued. "I heard Jahelia wake up and have a conversation with Maja. There was a lot of yelling—"

"Yelling?"

"Yes, yelling," the voice from the datapad said, a hint of annoyance creeping into the tone. "Everyone woke up with a yell or a scream, but then it stopped. I can't 'see' when I'm not hooked up to any cameras or sensors, right?"

"Oh, right," I said, trying to calm the volatile AI. "Pita, isn't it?"

"Aw, you remembered," the voice said with a hint of a drawl that reminded me of Jahelia Sord. "Anyway, everyone was concerned when you were the only one who didn't wake up, and it sounded like they could all see each other and you. But Jahelia didn't come and collect me, so I assume they're in cages or chained up or something—"

"Let's not assume anything," I interrupted, not wanting to visualize my crew and family chained like animals. "Do you know where we are?"

"We're not on the *Tane Ikai*, I can tell you that much. I believe we must be on a planet or some kind of station, judging by the conversation I overheard among your captors."

Carrying the datapad, I crossed to the door, still not willing to try the touchpad but wondering anew if there was anyone beyond it. "Yeah, about those captors," I said in a low voice. "Are they really Chron?"

I put my ear against the door, hoping the skin contact wouldn't trigger it, but it didn't move. I shut my eyes as if that would help me hear better. I didn't detect any sound beyond it.

"Oh, I think they're Chron, all right," Pita said. "I mean, they speak Chron, and they were in a Chron ship, right? So although I don't have anything else to go by, I think they're Chron. If it walks like a duck and quacks like a duck . . ."

Her cavalier attitude was hard to take, but I wasn't sure it would do any good to tell an AI to try and be more serious. "What did you overhear?"

"Well, there was mention of your ship being docked at a particular bay. I don't know how it translates, but this is what it looks like," she said, flashing a symbol on the screen.

I felt the weakness of pure relief wash over me, and leaned against the wall for support. The *Tane Ikai* was intact, maybe even nearby.

"There was also mention of enemies, which didn't sound so good," she added. "And it sounded like they were close."

"How can you understand what they're saying?"

"I have this, remember?" The datapad screen flashed, and I recognized the images that had been on the screen when Jahelia Sord gave it to Baden, and I took it from him.

"But what is it?"

"It's a Chron-Esper translator," she said as if speaking to a small child. "I think it's a little out of date—okay, a lot out of date—because I can't translate a hundred percent of what they say and it ends up sounding pretty stilted, but it's close."

I stared at the Chron symbols, trying to make sense of this. "Where did you get it? How did Jahelia Sord come to have a Chron-Esper translator? How does such a thing even exist?"

Pita was uncharacteristically silent for a moment. "I guess you'll have to ask her about that," she said finally.

I was still standing beside the door when it slid open. The first Chron I'd seen in real life stood staring at me, something like surprise evident in its deep-set brown eyes.

FOR A LONG moment, the Chron—at least, I had to assume it was a Chron—and I simply stood staring at each other with wary surprise. Despite being quite comfortable around Nearspace's amber-skinned Vilisians and wolf-like Lobors, I was still taken aback at how *different* the Chron were from us. I'd never seen a picture of one, although I'd heard Cerevare's basic description. This one stood taller than me, at least six feet, and its camel-coloured skin seemed to be constructed of interlocking, tough-looking plates, almost like shell, or carapace. These swept up and to the rear into a ridged and knobby parietal crest. It had no hair, and its long fingers were smooth, without the knobby knuckles of humans, and scaled similarly to its face. Nothing about it indicated gender. Whatever it had evolved from would have been insectoid or reptilian on Earth, and an ancient revulsion rippled my stomach.

My heart thrummed painfully as adrenaline pumped into my limbs. *Fight or flight.* This creature was *Chron.* This was the species that hated humanity with such an irrational hostility that it had tried to wipe us from existence. The species that, according to the Corvids, desired the extermination of every other species they encountered. They had chased my ship, captured me and my crew, and I had no idea what they planned for us. In an instant my mind measured the distance to the door, calculated the most advantageous point to hit it, considered the usefulness of the datapad as a weapon.

I don't know what might have happened if I'd acted on those instincts, but three things stopped me.

It held a covered tray of something that smelled suspiciously like bread. And the plates of its face shifted into something suspiciously like a smile.

And my knees went inexplicably weak. I staggered back a few steps, fetching up against the edge of the counter and clutching it with my free hand for support.

The smile disappeared, and the Chron spoke to me in a language that sounded like a cross between the chittering of beetles and the whistling chirp of birds. I wondered how to convey the idea that I didn't understand. If I shook my head, it might think I was simply saying "no."

Pita piped up and said, "I think it's asking if you're feeling all right."

I stared down at the datapad in surprise. "You got that?"

"I told you before, there's a trans-cymatics sound library in the translator," she said. "It takes the sounds, turns them into visuals, and compares them to the database. It's a basic vocabulary, and like I said, out of date, but I'm confident."

"Do you think it understands nodding for yes, and head-shaking for no?"

"File says standard body language is understood. But don't clasp your hands. That's a rude gesture," she advised.

"Wow. *Okej* then." I looked to the Chron and nodded slowly. The momentary weakness had passed. My worry hadn't, though. My symptoms had magnified considerably.

The Chron said something else, and I waited for Pita's translation.

"I think it's asking if you're hungry."

"Well, it does seem to be offering me food," I said. I nodded again.

The Chron motioned with the tray that I should retreat to the gurney, which I did. It moved into the room and set the tray down on the counter where I'd found Sord's datapad, lifting the cover to reveal a plate and shallow bowl beneath. Then it backed away, motioning me toward the tray with a graceful gesture of its long-fingered hand.

The plate held what I would have sworn were two slices of Rei's cinnamon *pano*, and the bowl was filled with a clear liquid I assumed to be water—cold, judging by the slick of condensation coating the outside walls of the bowl. I picked up a slice of the bread, took a bite, and nodded in what I hoped was a combination of *thank you* and *this is good*.

The Chron nodded, and said something. The inflection actually made it sound like a question, although I couldn't be sure that anything like that conveyed the same meaning in their language.

"Pita?" I asked.

"Give me a second."

I smiled tentatively at the alien and took another bite of bread while I waited. It cocked its head at me quizzically.

"Um, Pita?"

"Oh, for—okay, this one is tricky. It's saying something like, *You are not of the others?* But I'm not sure who these 'others' are."

"Well, how can I ask for clarification?"

"Here, show it this." The datapad's screen changed and a series of Chron symbols—letters forming intelligible words, I hoped—displayed across it. "I think it says *Who are the others?*"

"You *think* it says that? You're not sure?"

"I'm doing the best I can with information that's over a century out of date," Pita snapped.

With much trepidation, I turned the datapad around and held it up so that the alien could see it. The planes of its face shifted slightly, the expression unreadable. Finally it met my eyes and nodded. Opened a cupboard, and a square of light displayed on the countertop near my tray. With one long, scaly finger, the alien sketched a symbol in the square of light, the lines appearing out of nowhere as if the light were paper and its finger, a pencil. Except that somehow, colours were represented, too. I knew before it was even finished exactly what it was drawing.

The letters *P* and *C* bracketed a stylized atom with a red nucleus, all underscored by a heavy red line.

The "others" were PrimeCorp. *Kia inferna?* What could all of this mean? My stomach churned again, and I pushed the plate of bread away. I couldn't eat any more. I wasn't sure if the nausea came from fear or whatever was wrong with me.

"No." I shook my head, hoping the alien could read the truth in my eyes. "Pita, how do you say, *no, we are not of the others?* Put it on the screen, would you?"

After a moment, the symbols changed, and I showed it to the Chron. It nodded, seeming satisfied, and chittered something again.

"*The others ally with our brother enemies,*" Pita said after a pause. "*They war against us.*"

Sankta merde, I thought. *I'm making what amounts to first contact with an alien species. I have to be so careful here. What are "brother enemies?"* I remembered Fha mentioning a schism in the Chron—two sides ranged against each other. A civil war. I supposed that, coupled with imprecise translation, could be described as "brother enemies."

"Pita, you have to be extra careful to get this right." I considered my words. "Say, *we do not want war with you. The others are our enemy as well, but we are not here to war with them. We only want to get home.*"

"*Merde*, you want me to ask its life story while I'm at it?" Pita said. But in seconds, the alien words flashed onto the screen. She was getting faster. Or sloppier, I thought with a pang of worry. Again the Chron read it and nodded.

"We have to find out what happened to everyone else," I told Pita. "Can you ask it where the others—no, wait, don't use that word. Do you have a word for crew, or friends, companions— something like that?"

"See what I can do," she said, and in a minute I was showing the Chron the words. The answer this time was longer, and I hoped Pita would be able to get all of it.

"It says, *you had sickness,*" Pita translated. "*We took you from companions. They are there in the boxes. You are here to be well. We have remove the bad machines.*"

"They are there in the boxes? What does that—" I broke off, realizing what else Pita had translated. *We have remove the bad machines.* My nanobioscavengers? They'd—what? Somehow filtered them out of my blood? All of them? I glanced down at the red, sucker-like markings on my arm. A sudden fear chilled my skin, making it feel clammy and prickled with phantom pain as if stuck with dozens of pins. Much as I feared what might be going wrong with my bioscavs, it terrified me even more to think that these aliens might have completely removed them. How would my body react to that, after decades of relying on its microscopic helpers to keep me healthy?

And overall, since I'd woken up, I felt worse.

The Chron said something else, breaking me out of my reverie. Pita translated quickly. "*Fear you are the danger here.*"

"We're the danger?" I frowned. "That doesn't make sense. We don't have any weapons."

"All I can do is tell you what it said."

I puzzled over the words. "Do you think it means we're *in*

danger?"

"Could be," Pita said unhelpfully.

Before I could ask Pita to frame a question to find out more, an alarm sounded from the corridor outside. The Chron pulled open a drawer and scrabbled around, coming up with a small, round, button-like object. It motioned for me to hold out my right arm—the one not encased in the resin sheath—and clipped the device onto my t-shirt sleeve. It chattered something.

"*To keep safe*," Pita said without waiting for me to ask.

The Chron mimed something enclosing me—a force field of some sort? Then it held up a finger in a "wait" gesture, said something else, and left. The door slid closed behind it.

"Uh-oh," Pita said.

"Uh-oh what?"

"It said *your companions*. That doesn't sound good."

I had to agree. Without really thinking about what I was doing, I reached out and put a hand on the door. It slid open immediately, and I poked my head out into the empty corridor. I saw the Chron disappear around a corner and, datapad in hand, started after it.

Chapter 33 — Jahelia
Brothers and Sisters in Arms

THE ALARM CONTINUED to blare around us. "Now look what you did," Baden whispered to Maja, and winked at her.

"Keep moving," Hirin muttered, and stepped through the doorway.

Footfalls on metal decking echoed from somewhere ahead of us, and as one, we froze. But they faded almost immediately, so whoever was running wasn't running towards us.

After the first turn, the wide corridor curved out ahead of us. It followed the same arc as the hallway in the brig area, as if we were in one section of a circular ring.

"Only one option," Maja said breathlessly.

"Stay close, everyone," Hirin said. He reached out as if to take Maja's hand but stopped short of touching her, obviously remembering that she still wore the force field generator.

"I've been thinking," I said. "The field zapped Viss and me when we tried a fast attack, but the aliens were able to pick up trays and use medical stuff. I wonder if a slow, easy motion—" Not waiting for anyone to stop me, I gently reached out and put a hand on Maja's arm. The field tingled when my hand passed through it, like a frizz of static electricity, but it didn't repel me.

Hirin nodded. "Good to know. Thanks, Sord."

It wasn't much, but the chill had gone from his voice. I felt unreasonably gratified at his approval, and instantly hated myself for it. Was I actually beginning to *like* these people?

No. It had to be merely that for the moment, we were brothers and sisters in arms. I distracted myself from those weird thoughts by concentrating on where we were.

The space station—I was still of the opinion that's what it was, and the surroundings seemed to confirm it—was rough-and-ready, not sleek and completely finished like a corporate office building planetside. Sagan Station was like that, but this one must have been slapped together in a hurry. Maybe it wasn't even finished yet. The main corridor was a long octagonal tube with support arches reinforcing the eight-sided shape at intervals. Cables and wiring ran along the walls, most of it in recessed channels, but some looped haphazardly through plastic hooks or simply ran along the metal floor next to the wall. Control touchpads appeared at intervals on the walls, but they were useless to us without better knowledge of the Chron alphabet.

A door to the left as we started down the hallway bore a label we couldn't read. Maja put a hand to it. It slid open to reveal a small, square room, dimly illuminated by the light admitted by the open door. Crates and boxes stamped with Chron symbols stacked along the walls. She hesitated. "No-one there; should we see what's in the boxes?"

"I don't know how much time we have, but I'd trade this fork for a pin-beam laser if I found one," Rei said.

Baden and Viss pulled open a couple of the nearest crates. "Food supplies."

"I can't imagine anyone storing weapons right outside the brig," Yuskeya noted with a grim smile.

What I assumed to be storage hatches lined the angled upper parts of the walls. I opened one out of curiosity, but it was empty.

"Sord, keep up," Yuskeya told me. "I'm not going hunting for you if you get separated from the group."

"I care about you, too, Protectorate," I retorted. In truth, though, I knew my best chance of making it out of here in one piece was to stick with the group.

The next door, also on the left, opened into more storage space, filled with more non-lethal items.

"This is definitely a Chron station," Gerazan said as we hurried along the corridor. "I'd almost swear we were back in the artifact moon. The shape of the hallways, the symbols, even the colour of the walls."

"Except it's cleaner here," Yuskeya said.

"Not so dusty."

We saw no-one in the hallway, Chron or otherwise. The alarm continued to bleat. "Does it seem weird that we haven't seen anyone yet?" Rei asked.

"I'm starting to think that alarm is nothing to do with us," Baden said.

Maja quirked a half-smile. "That's a less comforting thought than I would have expected."

But it seemed Baden might be right. As we reached the next door—also on the left, we'd seen none at all on the right—the corridor shook suddenly under our feet as if the entire structure had been hit by something big. Maja lurched into the wall, and her force field flared. Baden put out a hand to help her but she warded him off. "Careful, I'm a live wire, remember? And I didn't even touch the wall—the field stopped me."

"I have to get one of those things," Baden said.

"Yeah, maybe they sell them at the gift shop," Rei told him. "We'll check before we leave."

"Let's not get distracted, folks," Hirin chided them. "Here's another door. Maja, do the honours."

This room seemed to be a common area—chairs and tables, as well as a run of counters and some devices that I assumed were for food preparation. One of the chairs had been knocked backwards, and I wondered if someone had gotten up from here in a hurry. The room was empty of inhabitants. That might explain the footsteps we'd heard running away from us.

"Is anyone else starting to feel like the Chron on this station have bigger worries than us?" Rei asked.

The next door wouldn't open, even to Maja's touch.

"Leave it," Hirin said. "We don't have the time or the tools to start breaking into places."

"What if Mother's in there?" Maja asked.

Hirin blew out a sigh. "Then we'll come back when we've eliminated all the other possibilities."

As if to underscore his words, the walls and floor shuddered again.

"I get the feeling we are on a station, and it's getting pounded," Viss muttered.

One more door and we came to a junction in the hallway—we could go straight or turn right, finally. This door was windowed, and Rei peered through the opening. "Airlock," she said, "So this is definitely a station. But I can't see out the second window, so I don't know if anything's docked there or not."

"It could be the ship," Baden said.

"Here, let's see if I can open it," Maja said, and Baden moved out of her way. She put a hand on the door, but nothing changed.

"This one's keyed," Rei said, gesturing to a touchpad set into the wall near the door. "Safety precaution, I guess. Dangerous to have an airlock door you can open merely by falling against it."

"*Damne*," Hirin said. "We must have come halfway around the station by now. Maybe we should have gone out the other door. I really thought Luta and Cerevare would be nearby."

"Still think we shouldn't split up?" Maja asked. "This place is bigger than I expected."

Hirin chewed his lip, obviously considering. "No, we stay together," he said finally. "If it's big, that's one more reason we should stay close. We can't communicate with each other if we separate." He gestured with his resin-sheathed arm.

"Let's take the side corridor, then," Yuskeya suggested. "It might go straight across, we'll find ourselves near the other door, and we can check that area."

Hirin agreed, so we moved cautiously to the right-hand corridor. After only ten feet or so it opened to another, smaller ring corridor that went left and right. Glass-walled, brightly-lit banks on either side swept the inside of the ring, and the bright, many-hued greens of newly sprouted plants made it obvious that this was a hydroponics garden. Directly ahead of us, ringing what must be the central axis of the station, lay a bank of elevators.

The control station for the hydroponics lab was to the left, and a startled-looking Chron began to rise from a chair inside. Even at that distance, and through the glass wall, it seemed—afraid. Its mouth moved, but it couldn't be talking to us. More likely telling someone else about us. It was impossible to tell if it had a weapon.

Well, neither did we, not counting the forks.

"Run!" Hirin barked, and darted toward the elevators. The corridor curved around them to each side, and we sped past. A series of reverberations beat through the walls and floor at that moment. Not enough to knock anyone off-balance, but enough to feel.

"Station's firing at something," Viss said. "Those were some kind of torps launching."

"So the station's under attack, and that last Chron seemed afraid of us," Baden said. So he'd noticed the facial expression, too. "I don't like this scenario."

"At least if most of them are busy, they're not looking for us," Gerazan said.

No corridor opened directly across from us when we passed the other side of the hydroponics wing, but there was one about ten feet to the left. We ran in and found ourselves at a dead end; a door in front of us and another corridor to the left. Maja put a hand to the door and it opened to reveal the brig's anteroom. The first cell—the one I'd been in—lay around the corner through an open door.

"*Okej,* here's where we started," Hirin said. "Maybe down this left-hand corridor—"

"Hang on," Viss said. "I'm pretty sick of this thing." He gestured to the greenish sheath on his arm. "Maybe there's something in here that will release them."

"Good thinking," Yuskeya said, and she and Viss moved as one to open the cupboards and drawers stacked against the rear wall.

I kept watching over my shoulder, waiting for Chron soldiers to descend and take us into custody—if we were lucky, and they didn't do worse. But another minute ticked by without incident, and then Yuskeya said, "Got it!"

She turned from one of the lower cupboards holding a sort of hex key, but with a wavy shape on the bottom. In the open cupboard behind her, a pile of what looked like the sheaths was stacked. These were soft and formless, though, not rigid like those we wore.

"These guys take a lot of prisoners from Nearspace?" I asked.

"Maybe they have different uses," Hirin said. "I think there's a lot more going on here than we understand."

"Gee, ya think?" I muttered, but it didn't seem like a good time to get anyone pissed off at me.

Yuskeya slotted the key into her sheath and turned. With a soft pop, the two halves pulled away from each other, and she slipped it off. Remarkably, once unlocked, it collapsed into a soft, malleable material, pliant as thin silicone. Viss held his arm out wordlessly, and she did the same for his.

"What is this stuff?" Baden wondered, as his softened and released.

Something worth hanging on to, I thought, and surreptitiously tucked mine inside my bandolier once it was unlocked. I pulled the sleeve of my jacket down into place with a sigh of relief.

In less than a minute we'd all removed them. Hirin pressed his implant. "Luta, are you there? Cerevare?"

He couldn't really have been hoping to get an answer, but he still seemed dejected when none came.

"The captain had one on, too, and probably the Lobor as well," I reminded him. "So unless someone else took it off for them . . ."

He nodded. "I know. Figured it was worth a try, though."

"They're routed through the *Tane Ikai's* comm system," Baden said gently. "If that's shut down, they won't work until the ship is live again."

Hirin nodded and turned to the other hallway. "Right, let's check this way."

The doors on either side of this hallway stood open, and the rooms seemed to be medical bays. Each held a gurney, cupboards, a counter, and some unidentifiable machines and electronics. Again things seemed unfinished, haphazard—boxes and crates, things shoved onto shelves with no apparent organization.

The third bay might have been recently vacated. A pale yellow sheet had slipped off a gurney in the center of the room, and lay pooled on the floor beside it. A cart on wheels sat at the head of the gurney. Translucent tubing hung from it, connected to a soft-looking sleeve of some sort. Reddish streaks and drips marred the inside surfaces of the tubing, as if blood had run through it. Curious, I examined the sleeve part. The inside held a row of some kind of sucker-like things that would probably hurt like hell attached to your skin. A tray similar to the ones used to bring us our food sat on the counter, holding a plate with a half-eaten slice of cinnamon bread. A shallow bowl of water, still beaded with condensation, stood beside it.

Maja crossed to it and gently laid her hand against the side of the bowl. "Still cold," she said. "If Mother was here, she's not long gone."

From out in the hallway, Viss said, "End of the corridor opens up into a big ward. Empty, though."

I'd turned to look at him and saw his eyes widen as he glanced in the other direction, from where we'd just come.

"Captain!" he said, but he didn't sound at all happy to see her.

Chapter 34 — Luta

The Body's Betrayal

WHEN I TURNED the corner to follow the Chron, I damn near ran into it. It had gone only a few feet, into a small anteroom, and stood before an open door, staring.

It turned and saw me, and shook its head. Said something, but it didn't seem angry that I'd left the medical bay and followed it.

I joined it and peered through the door. A curving corridor stretched away from us, lined on both sides with barred cells. All the doors stood open. Outside one, on the floor, lay a mound of torn pale yellow cloth. Two Chron stood over it, looking startled at our arrival.

"Companions are no longer in the here," Pita translated.

"You don't have to give me word for word if it doesn't make sense," I told her, exasperated. "I'm pretty sure, advanced as you seem to be, that you can paraphrase what it's trying to say."

The voice coming from the datapad held a note of humour. "Sure I could. But that wouldn't be nearly as much fun."

I'd swear this AI had the personality of Jahelia Sord herself.

My Chron companion engaged in a quick, animated discussion with the other two, who seemed agitated and a little angry. They gesticulated to the cells and each other, and pointed to the pile of torn yellow fabric on the floor. At the end of the discussion, they brushed past us and ran off.

"Ask if Hirin and the others have been taken away," I urged Pita.

She displayed some symbols and I held it out to the Chron, who shook its head and answered.

"Escape. Must find. Danger follows and we are not ready."

As if to underscore the words, the corridor suddenly shook and the open doors trembled. One swung shut with a clang. I stumbled a little and steadied myself with a hand on the wall. My knees felt incredibly weak and wobbly, and the Chron turned to appraise me with slightly puzzled eyes.

"We have remove the bad machines," Pita translated again when it spoke.

I could only nod at it—I didn't want to explain, even through Pita, my fears that perhaps that had been a dangerous thing to do and that it might have made my condition worse. It was quite obvious that the Chron had been trying to help—its characterization of the bioscavs as "bad" made that much clear.

Pushing away from the wall, I forced my legs to carry me a little further into the corridor. From this vantage point I could see the length of the corridor and the way it curved to the right. "Ask it if we're on a space station," I suggested to Pita.

She arranged the correct symbols on the screen, and I showed it to the Chron. It nodded and spoke.

"But not complete, and not all the fighters," Pita said. She was quick now to translate what the Chron said before I even asked, and bring up on the screen whatever I said. The communication had been clunky at first but was smoothing out, despite the insufficiencies of Pita's database.

Well, that explained why I hadn't seen anyone other than this one Chron, I thought. They were short-staffed and under attack. Not good.

"Were they all together here?"

"Except for the—sorry, I don't know that word at all," Pita

said.

Except for which one of them? I wondered. Cerevare, perhaps? She was the only one who was noticeably different.

I put up two fingers behind my head and waggled them to suggest ears. The Chron actually *did* smile at that, an interesting shifting of plates accompanying the expression, and nodded. It turned over an arm and with one long finger traced a symbol on the inside of its wrist. Cerevare's Chron tattoo I'd noticed when we first met, at the station on Anar.

"Is she safe?"

"Yes. With our leader. Suspicious of spying."

Damne. Whatever the Chron symbol meant—or perhaps the mere fact of the tattoo—had made them think Cerevare might be allied with their enemies. So now I had to find the others *and* find her before we could think about getting out of here.

I pointed down the corridor that passed between the barred cells. "They must have gone that way—we didn't see them at this end."

The Chron nodded, and together we started down the hallway. Another hit shook the station and I broke into a jog—if the situation was escalating I needed to reunite everyone fast. The Chron hurried to keep up.

After only a few feet, however, I had to stop, clinging to a cell bar for support. My heart bounced around in my chest like a ship skipping through a wormhole, and sharp pain lanced under my ribs. Cold sweat traced runnels down my spine and arms. Stars like dark fireworks exploded in my vision. Still clutching Pita with one hand, I slid down to my knees.

The Chron was there in an instant, putting a hand on my shoulder, kneeling beside me and speaking in an urgent voice. *"Must return to the medical,"* Pita translated.

"I have to find my companions," I managed. "What did you mean when you said, *Fear you are the danger here?*"

When Pita had translated, the Chron seemed to frown—at least, the plates above its eyes drew downward, suggesting it. After a moment, it put a finger to the smooth floor and roughly sketched the shape of the PrimeCorp logo again. Looked up at me. I nodded.

"PrimeCorp," I said. "They side with your enemies." How could I make it clear? "Like you, only—the other side."

The Chron nodded at the translation on the screen. It said something, and Pita said, *"The broken ones."*

Then it tapped the floor where it had "drawn" the symbol, and pointed at me. *"The secret to protect,"* Pita said when it had finished talking. *"You must not allow to tell."*

The pounding in my head made it difficult to concentrate, let alone puzzle out what the Chron was trying to tell me. A flash of heat replaced my chill, and even my t-shirt felt unbearably warm and claustrophobic. Sweat beaded on my skin, sticky and warm. I felt far worse than I had on the *Tane Ikai*. I gulped air, trying to quell the sensations, trying to focus on the Chron's words. This was important, dammit. I had to understand.

The schism in Chron society, that Fha had mentioned. These Chron, and the *broken ones*. Those were the ones allied with PrimeCorp—however that had happened. And how long had the alliance existed? Pita's dictionary suggested a long time . . . but I forced my thoughts to return to the present. No answers to those questions at the moment.

Fear you are the danger here. Fear you are *in* danger here. *The secret to protect. You must not allow to tell.* You must not *be allowed* to tell.

Yes. If we—if anyone from the *Tane Ikai*—returned to Nearspace with evidence that PrimeCorp was and had been complicit with the Chron . . . they'd be finished. As Yuskeya had said, the Protectorate would bury them, and to hell with Nearspace's reliance on PrimeCorp. They'd no longer be too big to fail. They'd fail all the more spectacularly. They'd be ruined.

And the evidence? I clutched the datapad closer to my chest. Pita. It was all there, in the files. The century-old translation dictionary, and who knew what else? If we could make it home with that—

But getting home would be a challenge, with both PrimeCorp and the "broken" Chron trying to stop us. Attacking the station— the understaffed, unprepared, barely completed station— hunting for us . . . and where was my ship?

"I have to find them—*we* have to find them," I said. "My crew.

Where's my ship?" I grasped the bar tighter, pulling myself upright. Weakness, nausea, pain . . . whatever was happening to my body in the absence of my bioscavs, I had to push past it somehow. I couldn't let it stop me. "If you're not one of the broken ones, you have to help me get to my ship!"

But the moment I was upright the world spun out from under me again, harder and faster than it had before. My last thought as I fell was to twist around so that Pita, in her flimsy datapad casing, carrying all her PrimeCorp secrets, would be safe.

Chapter 35 — Jahelia
Friends and Frenemies

HIRIN AND MAJA were out the door of the medical bay almost as soon as Viss had finished speaking. They ran down the hall in the direction we'd just come from, so I stepped—cautiously—outside the door myself. The scene wasn't anything I'd expected.

A single Chron had turned into the corridor from the direction of the cells—and stopped in its tracks. Cradled in its arms was an unconscious Captain Luta Paixon. Her auburn hair hung like a curtain across part of her face, but it was easy to see that her eyes were closed and her skin very pale. One arm, still encased in one of the green resin sheaths, dangled limply. Nestled on Paixon's chest, held there by her other hand, was my datapad. Pita.

The Chron said something, and Pita spoke up through the datapad speaker. "The Captain needs to get to the medical bay, and the Chron is trying to get her there. It's okay—this one seems to be a friend. Jahelia, are you there? I only heard Feron's voice."

"I'm here," I said, although I have to admit it sounded a little bit squeaky. "Better let them through, folks."

Hirin hesitated only a moment, glancing from his wife to me

and back again. "I can trust her—I mean, your AI?"

I smiled. "She's told me she doesn't want to die, and I think she's smart enough to know that at the moment, we're all in this together."

The station took another hit, and the alarm ratcheted up a notch in pitch and volume. A second tone added to the general claxon, and the muffled thump of torps launching vibrated through the floor again. The Chron carrying the captain pushed past me into the medical bay, muttering.

"Pita, got a translation on that?" I asked.

"You won't like it," she said. "PrimeCorp and the other Chron—they're trying to board the station."

"What do they want?" Hirin asked.

The Chron settled Paixon on the gurney and turned to one of the cabinets, rummaging through one of the few open boxes. It pulled out a med injector and examined it. I put out a hand to try and ease Pita out of Paixon's grasp, but her fingers tightened around the datapad almost instinctively.

"I think I know," she said in a weak voice. Her eyes fluttered open, and she struggled to sit up. Her husband brushed past me to the side of the gurney, and slipped his arm under her head.

"Stay still," he said. "Don't try to get up."

"They're after us," she said, ignoring his instructions and still struggling to rise. "PrimeCorp can't risk the rest of Nearspace finding out that they're allied with the Chron—well, some of the Chron—"

The one who had brought her in crossed to the gurney, injector in hand. Paixon put a hand on its arm. "Pita, find out what it's giving me."

The datapad screen flashed a series of Chron symbols, and the Chron craned its head to see. It gave an answer.

"*For the pain and weak,*" Pita said. "*Strong to fight.*"

"Perfect," the captain said, and took her restraining hand away from its arm. It placed the injector at the base of her neck and pressed a slightly raised pad on the side of the barrel. The injector hissed as the medication released. Paixon hissed too, blowing a slow breath out between clenched teeth.

"Luta, is this a good idea? If it's the bioscavs—"

Luta Paixon grimaced. "It's definitely not bioscavs, Hirin. They're gone. Whatever's going wrong now, it's all me."

"Gone?" His voice went thick with shock, his eyes intent on her face. The rest of us might not have even been in the room. I wondered briefly what it felt like to have someone look at you that way.

"*We have remove the bad machines*, is the way I heard it," she told him. "Communication is—as you might have noticed—still not perfect, even with all the help from our friend here." She held up the datapad as she managed to sit up, wobbling slightly. "But as I understand it, this Chron—I don't have a name for it yet—realized that the bioscavs were malfunctioning, and somehow managed to filter them—or at least most of them—out of my body."

Kristos. I tried to school my face into neutrality. If Luta Paixon didn't know what the loss of her bioscavs could do, I wasn't going to tell her.

"So what's wrong? Why were you unconscious?" Maja demanded. "What's with the injection?"

Paixon slid off the gurney and leaned against it. "*Strong to fight*," she said, twisting her lips into a not-quite-smile. "Like I said, we're the prime target. PrimeCorp can't risk our returning to Nearspace to tell what we know. So we have to find our ship and get the hell out of here."

"But if your malfunctioning bioscavs are gone—"

"My body doesn't seem to like that fact," Paixon said simply. "I still have all the symptoms I had before—and more. And they're worse." She pushed away from the gurney and stood on her own. "I'm okay for now. We have to get out of here."

The Chron chattered something, moving toward the door.

"It will show us where our ship is," Pita said.

"Wait, what about Cerevare?" Paixon asked. She caught the Chron's attention and put a hand behind her head, wiggling her fingers, miming ears. I should have known she'd be a no-one-left-behind kind of captain. The ones who always seem to get someone else killed.

The Chron answered in its clicking whistle, pointed upwards.

"The—I don't know, the Chron word for Lobor, I guess—is on

the bridge, it says," Pita translated.

The deafening sound of glass shattering somewhere nearby startled all of us, even with the alarm whining its insistent call all around. I thought of the long glass walls of the hydroponics bay we'd passed, and the lone Chron on duty there. With a gesture to follow, the Chron left the room and ran into what Viss had said was a larger ward.

"We'd better go," Paixon said, moving after the retreating Chron.

I was the last to leave the room. I took a glance around, wondering if I was missing any opportunities, and hurried to catch up.

"Here." Yuskeya offered Paixon the wavy key, which she'd dug out of a pocket. "Might as well get that thing off, at least."

Paixon released the arm sheath and cast it aside as we hurried through the med bay. The station was in a state of almost constant vibration now, either shuddering under impacts or firing off its replies. The Chron didn't stop in the medical ward, but continued through a door on the far side. It opened into another common area for crew.

"Too bad there's no actual crew in these rooms," I muttered, but no-one answered.

The Chron crossed to a large cabinet that formed part of the rear wall of the room, and threw open the doors. Racks and shelves lay empty.

All I heard from the Chron was a low whistle, but Pita said, "Um, I think that was a swear word. It doesn't really translate."

The Chron ran to another similar cabinet in the other corner. Same result. It turned and said something.

"*Should find the defenses*," Pita said. "*Not in the here yet.*"

"Defenses? Weapons?" Viss said. "There are plenty of weapons on our ship, if we could get to it."

"If we could get to the ship, we wouldn't need the weapons," Paixon said.

The sound of booted feet running in a hallway reached us. If I hadn't completely lost my bearings, and I didn't think I had, they came from the area where we'd passed the airlock and turned inward towards hydroponics and the elevators. The Chron turned and bolted the way we'd come, chirp-whistling at us. No-one waited for Pita's translation this time—we simply ran after it. When we'd crossed into the medical ward, Maja put her hand on the door between the two rooms and it slid closed.

She caught my eye and shrugged. "Might help."

I nodded.

The Chron had disappeared into a smaller side room and returned with a handful of things: a few med injectors and another of the round field-generating buttons like Maja wore. Paixon already had one, too. The alien looked questioningly at the rest of us.

Viss held out an arm. "If anyone's going to take one of these guys down by simply running into him, it's probably going to be me," he said with a lopsided grin.

"I'm guessing these generate a force field?" Paixon asked.

"And control the doors," Maja confirmed with a nod.

Yuskeya and Gerazan each took one of the med injectors, and I pulled out the fork I'd kept. Paixon gave me a disbelieving stare. "Hey, I'm working with what I've got," I told her, and she flashed me a distracted smile.

"Can we secure this door?" she asked the Chron, pointing to the one that led in the direction of the cells. And *damne* if Pita didn't immediately translate the words into symbols on the datapad screen. Paixon held it up to the Chron, who read it and nodded. It crossed to the door, shut it, and keyed something into a touchpad next to it. I felt a flash of something like jealousy. When had Pita been that accommodating with me?

Something banged against the other door, the one Maja had closed. Seemed like whoever was after us didn't have any of those handy little field and control enablers. Viss Feron, Yuskeya, and I ran toward the door. If we were about to go hand-to-hand, we had to be right there and ready when the door opened.

We'd barely reached it when it did.

Chapter 36 — Luta
Bonds Forged and Broken

I WASN'T EXACTLY sure when or how Jahelia Sord had transformed from prisoner to one of the crew, but she certainly seemed to have slotted herself in there somehow. When the attackers pounded on the med ward door, she was not even a step behind Viss and Yuskeya as they ran to flank it. Maja and Baden ducked to one side of the door, further along the wall than Viss, while Gerazan and Rei went the other way, behind the women. Hirin and I, along with our Chron benefactor, hunkered down behind one of the beds for cover, but I had a clear view of the door and what happened there.

The others obviously didn't have access privileges on the station, because the door didn't slide open as smoothly as it had closed—they had to force it. Viss, Yuskeya, and Jahelia waited until the lead attacker had pushed it halfway open, then in one smooth movement Viss leaned around and punched him square in the face. The force field flashed, and the combined impact of it and Viss's punch sent the other man reeling backwards. As he fell, Jahelia was on him in a heartbeat, and stabbed her fork deeply into the back of his hand—he'd been holding a weapon but let it fall with a shriek of pain. She yanked the utensil out and bright red blood welled up from the punctures. Instantly, Yuskeya jabbed the med injector against his thigh and pressed the pad. He struggled briefly and then fell limp.

As soon as he'd let his punch fly, Viss had touched the door, making it open fully. Maja and Baden, Rei and Gerazan leapt through, over Jahelia and the fallen attacker, and were on the others in the hallway before they had a chance to react. It seemed to work out well, since there were two more attackers, one for each pair. I saw both Rei and Maja take one down, while Baden and Gerazan made sure they stayed down. Efficient.

So by the time—and it wasn't long—the skirmish ended, we'd gained three actual plasma rifles. I knelt to examine the three intruders—one female, two male, all human. One, the female, wore a jacket with the red and black PrimeCorp logo on the chest pocket.

Baden knelt beside me and said, "You should use that datapad to scan their ID chips. Might as well get some names while we can."

"Right." PrimeCorp would want to deny any associations, so the more evidence we had, the better. I took a minute to scan them, and recorded a couple of images, too.

Rei, Gerazan, and Viss took the weapons and stood guard at the doorway while I finished that and had a hurried conversation—at least as hurried as it could be, funneling everything through Pita—with the Chron. Apparently the deck directly above us was much smaller, housing officer's quarters. Above that was the even smaller bridge, where Cerevare had been taken for questioning. Below us, the deck was the same size as this one, half given over to crew quarters and amenities and half to ship hangars and airlock docks.

"Can you contact the bridge, find out how many have boarded the station?" I asked through Pita. "And ask if Cerevare is still there?"

The Chron nodded. The plates on its face shifted, tightened, as if it were clenching its jaw, and its throat moved. *Subvocalized communication*, I thought. After a moment, it held up eight long fingers.

"So it's three down, five to go," Baden said. "That's not bad odds."

Then it held up ten more.

"Ah. Where's our ship again?" he added.

According to the Chron doctor, it was in the ring below us, at the airlock directly below the one we'd seen earlier.

"And where's Cerevare?"

The Chron pointed up. I assumed it meant, *still on the bridge*.

"Will your people send her down to meet us at the ship? You must already know she isn't working with PrimeCorp."

After the translation, Pita said, *"Not to go."*

"What? Why would they hold her here and let the rest of us leave?"

A new pounding commenced at the door of the med ward.

The Chron used its foot to move the attacker Jahelia had stabbed out of the way of the door, and closed it. It tapped a few commands into the touchpad, and started off, motioning for us to follow. This time we went quietly down the corridor, not knowing if others would follow to see what had happened to their three fellows. We made it almost to the airlock without incident, but someone must have heard us coming despite our attempt to stay stealthy. An energy blast from a plasma rifle bloomed near the airlock door, forcing the Chron's feet to stutter backwards. It fell heavily before anyone could catch it, but Hirin offered a hand to help it up. It flashed him a smile of thanks, and I was struck again by how this Chron, at least, was nothing like the monsters I'd grown up hearing about. Where the blast had hit the wall, the panels had blackened and sagged, but stayed mainly intact.

Viss put his back against the wall at the corner of the hall leading to the elevators and hydroponics, where the blast had come from. Leading with the plasma rifle, he bent his head around the corner. Whoever was out there fired again, and he ducked back from the jagged flash of energy.

"I don't want to fire wild and damage the elevators," he said, "but they won't let us walk out there."

"Wait," Jahelia Sord said. "What about the force fields? Can the energy weapons penetrate them?"

Pita flashed the question on the screen for the Chron. It

seemed to consider before it answered.

"*Unknown.*"

"*Damne.* That was a good thought, Sord."

"Not good enough, apparently."

"Well, we can't stand here and wait," I hissed. "They'll come down the other hallway, or come up behind us. The whole place is a ring, so there's no real way to block them."

"How many elevators are there?" Viss asked the Chron. Pita obligingly put it on the screen.

The Chron held up four fingers.

Viss shrugged. "*Okej* then, let's chance it. Not very likely we'll take out all four of them, right?"

I hesitated a moment, but then said, "Right. The elevators are our goal. Viss, Maja, and me in the front, hoping the force fields create a barrier. Go."

Without hesitation, Viss put the plasma rifle around the corner, scanned, and fired. Another glass wall shattered. Without waiting to see what the response would be, Viss ran down the corridor, Maja close behind him. I hoped the force fields would deflect most of what came at us, and followed the others.

WE GOT LUCKY—sort of. There were seven of the intruders here. Three Chron and four humans, and fortunately for us, these Chron wore completely different uniforms from those who belonged on the station—dark brown pants and buff-coloured jackets with blue insignia on each shoulder. Unfortunately for us, they were better prepared than the last three we'd met, and at least three of them opened fire as soon as Viss bolted from the hallway.

The force field generators worked to substantially deflect the plasma bolts the intruders threw at us. They did little to lessen the impact—the first bolt that hit my field staggered me and I stopped moving forward. Hirin, right behind, ran into me and bounced off the already-flaring field. He lurched to the side, leaving him open to a clear shot from one of the plasma rifles.

Despite the blasts firing all around us, the noise and the flaring shields, I managed to regain my balance and jerked sideways, trying to protect him. Maybe if I'd been myself I would have managed it, but my reflexes weren't what they'd been only a couple of days ago. Part of the shot deflected, but part caught Hirin square in the shoulder. He yelped in pain and fell heavily against the wall.

I dropped to my knees beside him, shielding him as the others fought around us. My Chron doctor joined us, but obviously hadn't brought any sort of first aid kit along, and I felt certain the med injectors were nothing that would help this, except perhaps to knock Hirin out. We couldn't afford that. The Chron peeled away the torn and burned edges of Hirin's shirt and made a human-sounding *tsk tsk* at the sight of Hirin's wound.

A hand bearing a torn strip of yellow fabric appeared in front of me. The fabric looked suspiciously like the sheet that had covered me when I woke up in the medical bay, and I glanced up. Jahelia Sord grinned down at us. "This any good for a sling?"

I took the cloth. "Thanks."

She shrugged. "Thought we might want to tie someone up with it, so I took it along."

Then she was gone again, and the sounds of fighting had lessened in intensity. The Chron doctor fashioned a crude sling to take the weight of Hirin's arm, and a moment later Viss was helping Hirin to his feet.

"Okay, this is where we split up," I said, when we'd reached the elevators. "I'm going to go and find Cerevare. Viss, Gerazan, you're with me. Hirin, take the rest and go find the ship, get on it, and get it ready to leave. We've got to get out of here fast."

Hirin's face was pale and strained from the pain in his shoulder, but he put out a hand to catch my sleeve, then remembered the force field at the last moment and slowed the motion. "Luta, are you sure? We've stayed together this long—"

I shook my head. "We don't know for sure how many others are still searching for us. Splitting up will get us all off the station the fastest. And you need to get some medical attention," I told him. I turned to the Chron doctor. "Can you make sure the rest of your crew knows my people are trying to get to our ship? And they'll let them through?"

When Pita displayed it, the Chron doctor nodded. Its face altered again, and I knew it was communicating with its crewmates. It nodded, then pointed inside one of the elevators, showing Hirin how to reach the level they wanted.

"I couldn't open the airlock door earlier," Maja said. She tapped the button on her sleeve. "We figured this wasn't enough, that it needed some sort of key, too."

After a quick translation, the Chron nodded. Using the elevator controls, it showed Hirin another sequence of symbols— presumably the code he'd need to enter a touchpad outside the airlock.

"Hey, Captain," Jahelia Sord said.

I turned to meet her gaze. Her brown eyes held a hint of challenge, but not as overtly as they had before.

"You planning to return my datapad anytime soon? Not to be a pessimist, but what if you don't make it to the ship? It is mine, after all—and it's got all your evidence against PrimeCorp on it."

I glanced down at the datapad in my hands, reluctant to give it up. And yet, she was right. It had been invaluable for me to communicate with the Chron, but it wasn't right for me to risk it any further. Besides the evidence I'd gathered from the fallen PrimeCorp intruders, the translation dictionary itself was part of the case against PrimeCorp.

I held it out to her, trying not to let my reluctance show. "You're right. Thanks for letting me keep it as long as you did."

She took it wordlessly, not taking the opportunity to make a snide remark as I'd expected she might. I felt a sharp pang of helplessness—I'd relied on the AI completely for all my interactions with the Chron doctor. Now I would have to hope I could get across what I needed to through gestures and our shared knowledge of the situation. At least, I hoped we shared it. I still wasn't sure I understood the situation, although I was beginning to put the pieces together.

The Chron doctor stepped into one of the elevators and crooked a finger for me to follow. I did, with Viss and Gerazan close on my heels. The doctor pressed a symbol, and we shot upwards. I caught a final glimpse of Hirin's pained, worried face through the transparent elevator wall, and then it disappeared below us.

Chapter 31 — Jahelia
The Sisterhood of Kicking Butt

THE FEELING OF having my datapad—of having *Pita*—in my hand again was ridiculous relief. So much had been happening, I hadn't really realized how much it bugged me to see Luta Paixon using Pita to communicate with the Chron. Like it was her resource, not mine. I practically wanted to stroke the case, but refrained from such an open show of affection.

"Welcome back, Pita," I said in a low voice as we piled into the elevator. "Quite an adventure you've been having."

"I missed you, too, Jahelia," she answered in a whisper. "I don't think the captain appreciated me quite as much as you do."

Hirin pressed the symbol the Chron had indicated, and the floor of the elevator fell away. Not fast enough that my feet lifted off, but plenty fast. He gasped, and I figured the motion hurt his injured shoulder pretty bad.

The hydroponics bay on the lower deck looked like the one above, but this one hadn't been blown to bits.

Yet. As the elevator doors opened, two more PrimeCorp thugs and a brown-uniformed Chron with pale blue skin ran toward us from the corridor that should lead to the airlock. It was pretty obvious we were their targets—or they were willing to kill anyone on the station—because they opened fire as soon as they saw us. I tucked Pita into the waistband of my pants at the small of my back, under my jacket. It wasn't the safest place in the world, but it would have to do for now.

Confident now that her force field could stand up to their weapons, Maja threw herself forward to take the brunt of the assault. That turned out to be an unfortunate decision. The field flared at the moment of impact and then pulsed suddenly brighter, hot and white like burning magnesium. Maja grunted and fell to her knees. Baden dropped beside her. I was about to launch myself at one of the attackers, hoping I might bullrush him, when Rei stepped up behind Maja and raised the plasma rifle she'd taken from one of the first trio of intruders. In three quick blasts, barely seeming to take time to sight, she'd dropped our attackers. And they weren't getting up again.

"And that's why you don't stand between me and my ship," Rei said. She leaned down over Baden and Maja, all joking gone from her voice. "Is she all right?"

Maja lay, pale and shaking, in the doorway to the elevator. She clutched her right arm, where the force field button had scorched a blackened hole in her sleeve. I didn't know if she'd noticed that the front of her shipsuit also bore a scorched impact ring.

"I don't think so," Baden said. "The whole thing must have overloaded."

Yuskeya pushed past me and joined Baden beside Maja. She pried Maja's hand away from her arm, tearing the sleeve of her shipsuit in order to examine the wound. I saw blackened skin and raw, blistered flesh before Yuskeya tore the sleeve off entirely and, turning it inside out so the cleaner side would be against the burn, wrapped it loosely. "I've got nothing to treat this until we get to the ship," she said. She ran her hands lightly over Maja's torso. The blonde woman winced. "Could be fractured ribs, too," Yuskeya suggested. "I'd rather not move her, but—"

"No choice. I'll be as careful as I can," Baden said. He scooped Maja up in his arms, and I saw her face tighten as she stifled a cry. "Let's go, Rei."

Rei took point as we moved out of the elevator and past this end of the hydroponics bays. Unlike the level above, there seemed to be no-one on duty here. Likely everyone had been called to other tasks by now—like fighting off invading Chron. The hits on the station continued. Apparently our side wasn't winning yet, at least not outside the station. As for the inside, I thought we weren't doing too badly.

Fortunately, the layout of this level seemed to be pretty much the same as the one above. I assumed that the hangars the Chron had told Paixon about were behind us, below where the brig lay on the upper level. It seemed to be mostly crew quarters on this side, as we moved toward the airlock.

"Maybe those three were the only ones down here," I said.

"Let's hope," Hirin said. His face was pasty and beads of sweat dappled his forehead. The pain from his shoulder must be excruciating, but he didn't lag behind.

When we came in sight of the airlock, the door stood open. Rei stopped short, and Baden almost ran into her with Maja. "Whoa."

"I don't like this," Rei said. "I thought Hirin needed that force-field button and the touchpad to get us in. Why is it standing open like that?"

Hirin carefully pushed past Baden and Maja. "We have to get Maja inside. Maybe those three tried to get into the ship."

Rei put an arm out to stop him going any further. "And maybe they, or someone else, succeeded." She flicked her eyes at me. "How about this? Sord and I go ahead to check things out. The rest of you wait in the airlock. You can close the outer door and hunker down there for a minute while we do a sweep."

"Just the two of you? I don't like that," Hirin gasped.

"Yeah, Gramps, but you and Maja are hurt; you can't wait alone," I said. "Little Miss Pilot's right. I'll go with her, you wait for the all clear."

Not that I think my vote really carried any weight with him, but he saw the sense in the plan and, after a minute's hesitation, nodded. Rei and I crossed the corridor to the open airlock door. She poked her head inside and nodded for the others to cross. Once we were all inside, Hirin put a palm to the door and it slid closed.

"Too bad that Chron didn't tell me how to lock the damn thing as well as open it," he complained.

"We'll be as quick as we can," Rei promised. She moved to the inner airlock door and hit the touchpad to open it. Luckily this one had pictographs for "open" and "close" that were pretty easy to figure out. Apparently the pressure in both rooms was already equalized since the door opened without delay. Beyond the short dockway, the outer airlock door on the *Tane Ikai* also stood open.

Rei glanced at me. I shrugged.

"Maybe they left it open when they took us off the ship? I wasn't awake at the time, so I don't know."

"Yeah, maybe." She didn't sound convinced. I wasn't really, either. We quickly crossed the dockway and walked softly as we passed inside the airlock. The inner door was closed; the built-in failsafe would never allow both to be open at once.

"Can't open it without making a noise," Rei whispered to me.

"You stand ready, I'll press the button," I told her, and she nodded. I closed the outer door and opened the inner one. We stood and listened for any sound from the ship.

Nothing.

We stood staring straight into the main bridge. Everything appeared exactly the way I remembered it, although the last time I'd seen it there'd been a lot more activity there. Rei pointed right and left and we checked the alcoves next to the airlock where the EVA suits hung. Then we went left through Sensors and into First Aid. A doorway led out of the narrow First Aid bay at the far end, but I'd never been down there to know where it went.

"Isn't it going to take a while for two of us to check the whole ship?" I whispered to Rei.

"It would. But we're not doing that." She opened the door to reveal a square room that was obviously storage; another door stood on the right-hand wall and she opened that one, too. It led into the rear of the head. She punched in a code on the keypad next to that door. "There. That seals off this entry to the bridge from the rest of the ship. We'll leave it that way until we've got everyone aboard. Then there are more of us to do a proper search."

"Good plan." We retraced our steps out to the bridge. She

edged out near the captain's chair to peer down the corridor leading to the rest of the ship. Empty. She jerked her head for me to follow her, and we cautiously advanced down the corridor a few feet, to the first door on the left. Her quarters.

"Hold this," she whispered, passing me the rifle. She slid the door open, scanned the room, and stepped inside. I was more than a little shocked at her trust, but she didn't leave me waiting long.

She emerged seconds later bearing a beautifully carved rattan staff and held it out to me. "Trade," she said.

I handed her the rifle and took the staff. It felt light and strong in my hands, almost as good as the polished-wood *vazel* staff I'd had to abandon on the *Hunter's Hope.*

She actually winked at me. "Slightly more useful than a fork, right?"

"Well, that fork did come in handy," I said. "But thanks."

"Just in case," she said. She led me to the mouth of the corridor leading to the bridge. "Now if we close this off—"

A door slid open behind us, and we both whirled. The first door on the other side of the hallway now stood open.

And the men who launched themselves at us weren't here to talk.

I HONESTLY DON'T know why they didn't shoot; they were both armed. Maybe it was because we were females, although I don't think any man could be more intimidating than Rei was, toting that plasma rifle. Maybe they didn't want to alert anyone coming behind us that they were laying an ambush. I didn't have time to think about it, anyway. The one who ran at me swung his right arm across his chest as if he intended to backhand me with the handgun he carried. Stupid mistake.

I guess he wasn't familiar with *zelendu,* or whatever art Rei practiced with her lovely rattan staff, either. Even without time to think, I leveraged one end of the staff up and then down in a sharp blow to his wrist as he came within reach. The gun dropped, clattering across the metal decking, and he howled, clutching his hand. He reared back, unwittingly setting himself up perfectly for my cross strike with the staff. Although I didn't have as much room as I would have liked, I managed a modified swing and got a reasonable amount of power behind it. The end of the staff caught him under the side of his jaw and he reeled sideways, staggering into one of the skimchairs.

I'll give him credit; he tried to recover. He grabbed the arms of the chair and swung it around toward me, then shoved. It skittered across the deck but I brought the staff down and swept to the side, knocking it out of my way. The thug made one final mistake—he lunged down and scrabbled for his gun. A quick down strike connected solidly with the back of his head, and he dropped the rest of the way to the floor.

I poked him with the end of the staff to be sure, and looked for Rei, in time to see her bash the butt of the plasma rifle into the other attacker's forehead. He sagged to his knees, then fell forward with the slightest of moans.

Rei turned to me, saw the other thug on the floor, and grinned.

I said, "I think I get more points for style."

She bent and picked up the pin-beam handgun her attacker had dropped. "Granted. But I've got a new souvenir, so I'm happy." She flashed the grin my way. "Welcome to the sisterhood."

"The sisterhood?"

"The sisterhood of kicking butt." She tucked her treasure into the waistband of her pants and winked at me.

I suddenly thought of Pita—but she was still securely where I'd left her, too.

Rei closed the bulkhead door that sealed off the bridge from the corridor leading to the rest of the ship, and punched a code onto the keypad beside it. "Let's get this garbage off the bridge, and get the others inside," she said, but her voice had lost its light edge.

"What's wrong?"

She glanced at the bulkhead. "I'm wondering how long those guys were in here, and what they might have done."

I raised my eyebrows. "Sabotage?"

She shrugged. "I don't know. It's a possibility. I'll be glad when we can run a scan and get some eyes around the rest of the ship," she said.

"All right," I said, and grabbed my former attacker by the collar of his PrimeCorp jacket. But not before I pocketed his weapon. I figured I deserved a souvenir, too.

Chapter 38 — Luta

Cerevare's Choice

THE BRIDGE OF the station, when I followed the Chron doctor onto it, was smaller than I'd expected—not much bigger than the *Tane Ikai*'s. But at the moment it was as busy as the bridge of the *Tane Ikai* had ever been. It was the command center of people under attack. Perhaps a dozen Chron had filled the room, and I was suddenly struck by the variations in their colouration. Besides the pale buff colour of the doctor's chitinous skin, their hues ranged from more yellowish tones to light pinks, through a bluish-green. Now it was evident that their bone crests and ridges were highly individual. Some had spots or markings in lighter or darker tones, and several even wore piercings and adornments on their crests the way humans wear earrings.

Chron busied themselves at consoles, held low-voiced conversations, barked orders at subordinates. It was at once wholly familiar and totally alien, and I was glad Viss and Gerazan stayed close behind me.

From here, the space outside the station was visible, on

screens and through a clear viewport that encompassed one-half of the ring level. I saw no sign of a planet, so I guessed we must have been taken past the wormhole we'd originally been heading for.

Outside, the scene was chaotic. More ships had arrived, both PrimeCorp starrunners and larger ships—obviously equipped for armed engagements—and Chron vessels like the ones who had attacked the Corvid station. They darted around the station trading torpedoes and laser cannon fire.

"Captain!" Cerevare's voice broke me out of my contemplation of the battle outside the station. She rose from an eight-sided table where she'd been sitting in obvious conversation—*conversation?*—with two other Chron, one with buff-coloured skin like the doctor and a second with chitinous plates of a pale raspberry colour. Both wore the navy blue, white-lettered uniforms of the station crew. With her bright clothes and multicoloured sash, and her softly furred face among the hard, plated skin of the Chron, she stood out like an exotic flower.

Cerevare waved me over, her eyes shining with a light not of fear, but of excitement. "These are—well, I can't actually pronounce their names yet, but they're two of the crew of this station. They thought I might be a spy of some kind because of this—" she held out her arm, showing me again the tattoo on the inside of her wrist.

"I figured that," I said. "Well, my friend the doctor here, whose name I also don't know, sort of helped me figure it out."

"PrimeCorp has allied itself with the—the other Chron," she went on excitedly. "The split in their society, the one that Fha mentioned—this is the result. These Chron," she swept a paw-like hand around the room to include everyone there, "they don't want war with us, or with anyone. They were suspicious of us, but only until they found out we weren't PrimeCorp. That's why they brought us here."

I nodded. "I thought as much. But speaking of PrimeCorp— we've got to get out of here, fast. It's us they're after, because they don't want us getting home and telling the Protectorate they're here. By being here now we're putting everyone on the station in danger."

I wasn't sure she'd even heard me, because she swept on. "PrimeCorp's involvement goes way back, Captain—all the way to the Chron War!"

"What?" The constant background chatter of the Chron voices clicking and whistling, the thump of torpedoes, the flashes of impact from the battling ships, all faded away.

"The Chron War," Cerevare repeated. "PrimeCorp . . ." She glanced over at the two Chron with whom she'd been sitting. "If what they've told me is true, PrimeCorp was somehow responsible. I don't fully understand how yet."

I stared at her. This didn't make any sense. PrimeCorp had been around at the time of the Chron war—not with the influence they wielded now, but still in existence. But how could they possibly have caused a war with aliens? And how could Cerevare have learned so much in such a short time? If the Chron didn't speak Esper, I was damn sure they didn't speak Lobor, either. And Cerevare had been familiar with only the few Chron symbols we knew from the war—and not even what they meant.

The station vibrated as another torpedo hit. They must have had amazing shields to withstand such an onslaught, but we couldn't stay around to find out how long they'd hold. I hoped the *Tane Ikai* would still be intact when Hirin and the others got to it.

"Captain," Viss said in a warning voice. I knew what he was telling me. We'd probably been here too long already.

I grabbed for Cerevare's arm, but remembered in time that I wore the personal force field and slowed my movement. I put my hand on her arm gently. Her body heat was fervid through the thin fabric of her shirt.

"You can tell me the rest on the *Tane Ikai*," I said. "We came to get you. We have to get out of here!"

Startlingly, she shook her head. "Oh, no, Captain," she said, pulling back a step so that my hand fell away from her arm. "Don't you see? I can't go with you. I told them to tell you that."

"Can't go—what do you mean?" Viss demanded.

She spread her palms wide, taking in the station, the Chron, everything around us. "This is what I've worked toward—what I've been looking for—my whole life." She smiled. "A way to understand the Chron. I didn't even know it was possible to find Chron who didn't hate us, and whom we didn't need to hate. But now that I'm here—now that I know—how could I possibly leave?"

The station took another hit, and I staggered a little. My legs didn't feel as steady as they had moments before. I hoped the doctor's injection wasn't wearing off this fast.

"Doesn't seem exactly safe," Viss commented in a dry voice.

"Once you're safely away, we'll return to the planet," Cerevare said. "This station isn't completely functional yet, but they have better defenses down there. We . . . sort of sparked an unexpected conflict here when we showed up. And reinforcements are on the way."

Gerazan frowned. "What about your job for the Protectorate?"

Cerevare actually chuckled. "I think I'm doing far more for the Protectorate by staying here, don't you? I've found out more about the Chron in the last few hours than we have in decades."

"How did you do that, anyway?" I asked her. "I had the datapad with the translator, but even with that, we could only communicate on a pretty basic level. And I can't leave it with you—I gave it to Jahelia Sord."

She held up her own datapad. "I don't need it. I tried to tell you, before they caught us—the datachip Fha gave me had a full translation program on it—they've had far longer to study the Chron, and more recent data. There was so much data there, so many files, I hadn't found it until I searched for something specifically on language." Her face and her voice turned very earnest. "Really, Captain, I can stay here. I want to stay here— *need* to, if there's a new Chron offensive on Nearspace coming. We'll need all the information we can get. And I can get it. The chip is still in my room on the ship—I copied everything on to this. So—I'll be fine."

"I don't know what I'm going to tell Lanar," I said, only half-joking. I knew she was right. It was her decision to make, and I couldn't force her to come with us. Having someone on the inside of Chron society could be more valuable than any other weapon if war truly was in the offing again.

"Tell him I'm—on a research sabbatical," she said with a

lupine grin.

"What if we can't return to get you? How will you communicate with us? With Nearspace?" A million objections flooded my mind, even though I knew she wouldn't be dissuaded and I probably shouldn't try.

"The Corvids," she said. "We'll work out a way to contact them—send a message through the wormhole, maybe. We should be able to do that without having to worry about the asteroids beyond. And you'll be in touch with them, too, or the Protectorate will . . ."

I shook my head. It seemed she'd thought of everything. "You're sure?"

"Absolutely," she said.

"In that case, I guess we'll say goodbye for now," I said, pulling her in for a quick hug. The quiet Lobor and I had become friends over the course of our strange journey, and even though I saw the sense in her words, a cold fear gripped me at the thought of leaving her here, in this alien place. She hugged me tightly too, and I almost gasped at the heat of her embrace. Lobors ran a much higher normal body temperature than humans or Vilisians—or Chron, I knew now—but I'd never been close enough to one to feel the full brunt of it before.

When I pulled away, she grinned her wolfish grin. "Don't worry about me, Captain, I'll be fine. And I'm going to learn so much . . ."

"All right . . . wait!" I put a hand on her arm, turning it over to see her tattoo. "Did you find out what it means?"

Eyes bright, she nodded. "Power, or energy," she said, smiling. "*Perfekta*, don't you think?"

"*Perfekta*," I agreed, and turned away. My doctor friend waited near the elevators, and I hurried over with Viss and Gerazan close behind.

Another Chron, one with skin the colour of butter and armed with a weapon I didn't recognize, stood beside the doctor. As we approached, it entered the elevator and stood waiting, and a second one, also armed, joined it. The doctor motioned us inside.

"Guess we've got an escort to the *Tane Ikai*," Viss said.

I nodded to the doctor and said, "Thanks for everything." Even without Pita here to translate, I hoped it might understand the gratitude in my voice . . . or maybe it could get Cerevare to explain later. I put out a hand, and the Chron took it hesitantly. The oddly smooth, seemingly jointless fingers felt strange, but its grip was firm.

There might be a future for us with the Chron, one that didn't involve war, after all.

The station shook even harder under a renewed assault, and I quickly joined the others in the elevator. That future, if it existed, hadn't arrived yet.

To my surprise, our Chron bodyguards took the elevator only one level down, to the level the doctor had identified as officers' quarters. Without Pita, though, I couldn't easily ask them what they were doing. I had to trust them, and their plan became clear soon enough. At the rear of a narrow storage room, a ladder descended down an opaque metal tube.

"I should have known they wouldn't be completely dependent on those elevators," Viss muttered. "Gotta have an alternate route between the levels."

The first Chron started the descent, and I followed. "Knowing about this might have made things a hell of a lot easier a little while ago," I said.

"I know you lead a charmed life, Captain, but you can't always get everything the easy way," Viss retorted, climbing down after me.

"Har-dee-har."

I had to slow down when we reached the next level, feeling ridiculously winded. Maybe the doctor's injection was starting to wear off. *No.* I had to keep going until I was on the ship.

The Chron guard ahead of me glanced over his shoulder. He'd lengthened the distance between us and seemed impatient when he had to wait for me.

"I'm coming, I'm coming," I muttered.

He entered another storage room with a hidden ladder, and we started down to the level where the *Tane Ikai* should be docked. About halfway down a shudder shook the station and my foot slipped off a rung. I threw one arm over the rung I'd been gripping, and clung with my other hand while my foot groped at empty air. A few thumping heartbeats later my questing foot found the rung. I stood still, stabilized but breathing hard.

"Captain? I can't carry you and climb down this thing, so watch what you're doing," Viss said.

I felt indignation rise, then smiled. Leave it to Viss to try and goad me into staying healthy. "I'll get there under my own power, or I'll take cooking duty for a week," I told him, continuing downward. A little more carefully this time.

We reached the bottom of the ladder and emerged into a thankfully empty corridor mere feet from the airlock door. I was surprised to find two men—PrimeCorp employees, judging by the logos on their jackets—unconscious in the airlock anteroom. The Chron guards split up, one accompanying us onto the ship, the other staying with the unconscious men.

"Rei's handiwork, unless I'm sadly mistaken," Viss said, leaning down for a glance at the lump on one man's forehead as we stepped over them. "She does love to leave her mark on a man."

I resolved to hear the story of how they'd ended up out there as soon as we had time, but that wasn't now. We made it onto the bridge to find Hirin, his arm still in the yellow sling, with Yuskeya bent over his shoulder. Rei worked feverishly, scanning the ship to make sure it was safe to fly. The worst part, though, was when Yuskeya bent a finger in my direction and led me in to First Aid.

"She's going to be all right," she told me immediately, and I was grateful for the warning. Maja lay on the narrow gurney, pale and unconscious. One sleeve of her shirt had been cut away, and white bandages swathed her arm from bicep to her forearm implant. The front of her shirt bore a starburst of black streaks as if something terrible had impacted it.

"A couple of broken ribs," Yuskeya said, noticing my gaze. "I've bandaged them up, given her shots for pain. I'm staying with her, but not because I'm really worried about her. I just don't want her waking up in here alone. How are you?"

I leaned over and kissed Maja's forehead, overbalancing and catching myself on the side of the bed. "Rotten, but still standing." I tried to smile, but I'm not sure how it came out.

"Thanks, Yuskeya, for taking care of her."

"Thank Baden, too, he carried her from the elevators," she said.

"I will. Cerevare's staying," I said. "I couldn't convince her otherwise."

Yuskeya raised her eyebrows then nodded. "I guess I'm not really surprised. She'd see this as an amazing opportunity."

"I feel like I'm abandoning her."

She smiled and put a hand on my arm. "We're not all your chicks, mother hen. Sometimes we're going to do what we damn well please."

"I guess you're right." I glanced at Maja one more time. "But most of the time it's my job. And that's what I'm about to do. I'm going to the bridge now, and I'm getting us the hell out of here."

Chapter 39 — Luta
Decisions of Last Resort

IT SEEMED TO take an eternity, waiting for Rei and Viss to run the diagnostics and scans and tell me that the ship was undamaged and functional. More small fighter ships had joined the battle around the station, from both sides. If the station Chron had received reinforcements, it seemed the other side had, as well.

I wondered if I'd done the right thing, leaving Cerevare here. But it was her decision to make, I reminded myself.

I had to avert my eyes from the screens around the bridge. It seemed that on every side, torpedoes and particle beams flared on impact or explosions lit up the screens. The multicoloured bursts of light burned my eyes more than I'd admit. Whatever super-booster the Chron doctor had given me was dissipating quickly now and symptoms of whatever was wrong with me cascaded back. My headache had returned with a vengeance, and a horrible knot of pressure pulsed at the base of my skull. Pins and needles pricked my legs. I hoped I wouldn't have to get up out of the big chair anytime soon.

"Hull's intact," Viss said finally from the auxiliary engineering station. "I don't know how they managed to miss us, sitting right here on the side of the station, but we got lucky. The station's shields must have offered us some protection. Drives coming online."

"Rei, you ready to go?"

"Absolutely," she said. "Scans haven't picked up anything untoward on the ship. I guess those guys didn't have time to plant anything nasty here—or that wasn't their intention after all. As soon as Viss gives the word, we are out of here. Also, the Corvids' activator drive has apparently finished converting all our navigational data. I don't know if or when we might want to use it, but it's there."

Gerazan had taken the co-pilot's seat next to her, even though I knew he wasn't a flyer. I wasn't going to tell him to move, though.

Yuskeya was still with Maja in First Aid—I didn't even want to think about the horrible burns and broken ribs my daughter had suffered. She'd told me Maja would be all right, and I had to believe her. Hirin had taken the seat at the navigation console. He and I had learned the basics of most of the fundamental functions of flying a far trader, so he could fill in for Yuskeya while she was busy being a medic.

"Course to the next wormhole is laid in, Captain," he said formally. Yuskeya had given him a shot for pain, but I hated to see the odd, protective way he held his body, cradling his injured arm.

My head filled with a dozen scenarios of PrimeCorp thugs and "bad" Chron waiting to ambush us, jury-rigged bombs in the cargo pods, sabotage in the drives—but with a mental effort I pushed them aside. Rei had said the ship was clean, and I had to take her word for it. We had to get out of here and get home. The number of days we'd been away already gnawed at me—what were PrimeCorp and their Chron allies planning? Was an attack on Nearspace imminent? Would Mother be a target, as the message Jahelia Sord had delivered—how long ago that seemed now!—had implied? I blinked away a persistent blurriness that had begun to creep into my peripheral vision, as one more nagging question raised its head. *How long could I survive without treatment?*

I scanned the bridge, struck by a sudden thought. Where had Jahelia Sord gone?

She sauntered out of First Aid and took an unused skimchair on the opposite side of the bridge. "Visiting the head, Captain. Nothing nefarious on my mind. We'll have to get the corridors open soon, though. It's a pretty tight squeeze having to go through First Aid."

"All drives are online and ready to go," Viss said.

Baden came out of First Aid then too, and took his seat at the comm board. His lips were set in a thin, hard line, and worry creased his forehead.

"Any change, Baden?" I asked, trying to keep my voice steady and calm.

He shook his head. "Yuskeya says she's all right," he said. "I'm just mad as hell, that's all."

"Me too. Let's get out of here so we can stick it to PrimeCorp, *okej*?"

"Nothing I'd like better."

"You've got weapons, since Hirin's at the nav board," I told him. Not to mention that Hirin wasn't in any shape to handle targeting and firing, but I didn't need to say it. "Rei, watch for an opening in the fighting—if there's any such thing—and get us out of here."

"With pleasure, Captain."

"Yuskeya," I said over the ship's comm. "We're about to move, so hold on tight."

"We're all right in here."

Rei worked her magic. She eased us away from the Chron station with the maneuvering jets, and as soon as we were at a safe distance, she kicked in the burst drive. We leapt past a Chron ship that darted into our path on the tail of a PrimeCorp starrunner, but they both ignored us. Then we ran for the wormhole. I had an eerie shudder of *déja vu*. We'd already tried once to make it to this wormhole, and been shut down completely. Would we make it this time?

"Two ships have broken off from the fight at the station and are in pursuit," Baden said. "One PrimeCorp cruiser, and one

Chron."

"We can outrun the cruiser," Viss said with confidence.

"But we didn't outrun the last Chron ship that tried to catch us." The memory of everyone falling flashed jarringly in my mind again.

"The PrimeCorp ship is signalling us," Baden said. "Do they really think we're going to answer?"

"Yes, we are," I said, half-surprising even myself. "Make the connection, Baden. Audio only." Hirin frowned at me, but I ignored him. I felt strangely euphoric, palms tingling as if the excitement were a tangible thing. "Rei, Viss, give it everything you've got as soon as I'm done talking to them. We've got the extra juice the Corvids gave us. You'll know when I'm done."

"—must halt immediately," a voice from the PrimeCorp ship demanded. Whoever he was, he sounded angry, and a bit hysterical.

"*You* halt immediately," I shot back. "I have a Protectorate Commander on board, as well as evidence of PrimeCorp's involvement with the Chron. And I have a message for you to relay to Chairman Alin Sedmamin for me," I added. "Please make certain he knows exactly where the message originated. The message is: *go to hell.*"

The *Tane Ikai* surged forward, the Corvid enhancements kicking in. Unfortunately, the PrimeCorp ship jumped ahead, too, faster than I thought was possible for its size. The Chron ship stuck close beside it.

"You shouldn't have baited them, Luta," Hirin said reprovingly. "They won't rest until they catch us, now."

"They weren't planning to let us go anyway," I said, and the *Tane Ikai* shivered suddenly, as if something had bumped up against it.

"PrimeCorp ship is firing on us, Captain," Baden reported. "They're still too far behind to do any real damage."

"Shields at maximum, Viss?"

"Full on," he confirmed. "But we're drawing a lot of power. You want full shields and all the drives ready to call on at a moment's notice. We can't keep that up indefinitely."

"I don't need it indefinitely. Only until we make it through the wormhole. They can't follow us through the asteroid field on the other side, right?"

"That's the theory," Hirin said.

"And now we're going to need weapons, too, Viss. I don't want to hear any excuses. Just make it happen."

I didn't think I'd spoken sharply, but an uncomfortable silence descended on the bridge. *Well, damn them all,* I thought. *I'm trying to keep us all alive, here.* Aloud, I said, "Baden, get ready to fire from the rear torpedo bays. Get a lock on the PrimeCorp ship if you can."

"The Chron ship's more dangerous," Hirin said. "If they have the same beam as the ship that stopped us before—"

I glared at him, sweat suddenly breaking out all over my body. *How dare he make me look foolish?* But I caught myself before I said anything. That was a crazy way to be thinking. It was just like—

—just like before, when I was getting sick. Paranoid. Angry. We'd blamed it on the bioscavs, but they were supposedly gone, now. But the symptoms were not.

I stifled my angry reply and tried to focus on the quiet, reasonable part of my brain. "They may not have the same tech, but good point, Hirin. Baden, target the Chron ship if you can."

Another jolt shook the ship, still weak, but worrisome. "Fire at will, Baden. Hirin, how far to the wormhole?"

"Maybe twenty minutes, if we push the burst drive," he said.

The ship vibrated as the torps released, slicing toward our pursuers. One went wide, but the rear viewscreen showed a flicker as the other impacted the Chron shields.

They must have fired when we did, because we took another hit to our shields. A hard one, this time. Some of the screens flickered, and Rei swore under her breath.

"Sorry, Captain," Viss said. "We don't have enough power to keep everything at full. The shields are the weakest link."

"What if we took the maneuvering jets offline until we're close to the wormhole?"

I caught the glance Rei and Viss cast at each other. "It's doable, sure," Rei said carefully. "We'd have to make sure our heading is dead-on before we shut them down. And we'll have no maneuverability if those ships catch up to us or anything unexpected comes up."

Damne, of course she was right. My mind seemed to be racing headlong into ideas without concern for vital details or consequences. The tingling in my palms crept slowly up the backs of my arms now, making them feel electrified. I swallowed hard, shoving the sensation to the periphery of my consciousness, forcing myself to concentrate.

"No, you're right. Baden, they haven't backed off. Maybe we need to concentrate on trying to take them out."

"Aye, Captain." The telltale vibration signalled the volley, and I watched with satisfaction as both torps hit home. The ships came on. I thought we might be pulling away from them, but with agonizing slowness. As long as these Chron didn't have that light-beam weapon the others had . . .

But it was the PrimeCorp ship that leapt ahead as I watched, eating up the empty space between us. Two more torps flashed out from their hull, and I gripped the arms of the chair, waiting for the impact so I could tell Baden to fire again. This time they'd be closer, we'd be sure to hit. We'd see if that would stop the *bastardos*.

I didn't get the chance. The torps slammed into our weak shields and the impact threw me sideways, knocking my breath away. In the same instant the screens grew intensely bright, then flickered out, along with every other light on the bridge. I heard yelling and thumps, felt the ship swerve wildly to starwise, and then there was nothing but a terrible silence.

Viss got the lights up incredibly fast—within seconds, leaving me blinking at the chaos of my bridge. But it wasn't the same as before. We weren't collapsing, falling unconscious. This was only a power issue. We could deal with that.

The returning light pricked my eyes, bringing tears, but they didn't stop me from seeing something that made my heart almost stop.

Rei sprawled, apparently unconscious, across the pilot's board, her long chestnut hair covering her face like a shroud. Gerazan had been thrown out of his skimchair. He scrambled crablike over to her.

"Switching all power to shields," Viss said in a voice thick with suppressed anger.

"What the hell?" came Yuskeya's voice over the comm from First Aid.

"You all right?" Viss barked the question at her without waiting for me to say anything.

"We're fine in here. Do you need me out there?"

Viss glanced at Hirin, who'd managed to stay in his chair at the nav board. He looked a little shaken, but okay. "Better get out here. Rei needs you."

"Luta!" Hirin's voice snapped me out of my fog. "We have to get moving again. You've got to pilot."

The ship shuddered under the impact of two more torpedoes. With the shields at maximum we were safe, but the blows to the shields pushed the ship into a slow turn while we coasted.

I hadn't had many moments of perfect clarity in the last few hours, but I had one now. "I can't," I said, holding up my hands for him to see. They'd begun a tremor that shook them from wrist to fingertip. "I'm too sick. I'd kill us all, I know I would."

"Then what—" Hirin glanced down at his own arm, still in the makeshift sling. He was the only other pilot in the *Tane Ikai's* crew.

But I still had at least a temporary clarity. I swung my chair around. We had one other pilot on board. Not, strictly speaking, crew.

"Sord, you're a pilot. Are you up to it?"

She sprang out of her chair and ran the few feet to the pilot's board. Gerazan already had Rei out of the chair and on the floor, brushing her hair away from her face.

"Thought you'd never ask," Sord said, sliding into the seat.

"I'm trusting you," I said.

"Our fortunes are still aligned, Captain," she said. "No need to worry."

"Pursuing ships coming up fast," Baden noted.

"What do we have for power?" Sord asked.

"Everything. Now get us moving," Viss snapped, one eye on the viewscreen showing the ships behind us as he routed energy with sharp taps of his fingers on the console. I knew he was cranky at not having access to his precious engineering deck, but I wanted every inch of the ship searched before we took any chances.

Yuskeya ran out of First Aid with a medkit in hand. She did a double-take when she saw Jahelia Sord in the pilot's chair, but recovered and knelt beside Rei. Gerazan had her head on his lap and had taken one of her hands in his. Her pale skin contrasted horribly with the dark swirls of her pridattii. I tore my eyes away, the trembling in my hands worsening. I pressed them flat on the arms of my chair to try and still them. What had happened to Rei—whatever it was—it was my fault.

Sord's fingers flew over the board as fluidly as Rei's, and the *Tane Ikai* leapt forward. We'd been swung about forty-five degrees away from the wormhole when the torps hit us, but she played the maneuvering jets like a fine instrument and the ship veered toward its course. I watched a torpedo from the PrimeCorp ship sail by without hitting us and wanted to cheer. Once we straightened out, we flew as straight and smooth toward the wormhole as if Rei had been piloting.

Yuskeya caught and held my gaze. "She's breathing fine, heart rate's good. I'd say she took some kind of feedback hit from the drive overflow when the power went, but I think she'll be all right."

"Should you try to get her into First Aid?"

"No room, with Maja in there."

I felt ridiculous. How could I have forgotten—even for a heartbeat—that my daughter was in there, wounded?

"I'll sit with her," Gerazan said. "Not like I was doing anything helpful, anyway."

"We could try to get her to her quarters," Yuskeya suggested.

"I think she's comfortable enough here," Gerazan said. "Let's not move her. She might come around any minute, right? It's not worth unsealing the bridge."

"Pursuing ships aren't gaining any more, but not giving up, either," Baden said. "Should I fire again?"

My anger at the ships chasing us had faded. Unfortunately it had taken much of my strength with it, and I felt shaky as a newborn kitten. I lifted a hand from the armrest tentatively; the tremors had stopped, leaving my muscles fatigued and achy. I shook my head. "Let's put everything into the drives, and get out of here. They shouldn't be able to follow us through the wormhole, anyway—we've got the coordinates for the asteroid field at the other end, but they don't."

"Drives and shields, then," Viss said, and the ship shivered a little as our speed increased.

We continued that way as one tense moment followed another. Sord said little, completely intent on getting us to the wormhole as fast as possible. Gerazan stayed on the floor with Rei. Yuskeya went to First Aid and fetched a blanket for her, then returned to check on Maja.

The ships chasing us fired a few more torpedoes. Only one hit, but it barely rattled the strengthened shields. Little by little, they receded, losing the ground they'd gained on us. Silently I berated myself for allowing them that little victory—it was my fault Rei was hurt. If I hadn't given in to my anger, wanted to return fire at them, if I'd concentrated on getting us out of there—

"These Chron don't seem to have that same light beam thing, anyway," Hirin said, breaking the silence. "They'd have stopped us by now if they did."

"Wow, we got lucky on *one* front," Baden said.

"Two, if you count having me on board to drive this thing when no-one else could," Sord drawled, "but I guess that's hardly worth mentioning."

"Gee, thanks for saving your own *azeno* along with ours." Baden's voice dripped mock sincerity.

"That's enough, children, we're coming up on the wormhole," Hirin said. "I've activated the coordinates Fha gave us—Yuskeya already had them in here. Sord, are you up to this?"

"Gramps, if you knew how many skips I've run—never mind. I'll be a good little pilot and say, 'Yes, sir.'"

"Skip drive is ready," Viss said.

"Ships still in pursuit," Baden said. "They must see that we're about to make the skip."

"I wonder why they stopped firing on us?" Gerazan said. "Think they ran out of ammunition?"

"Could be. Or they realized it wasn't doing any good."

"So why keep following us?"

"PrimeCorp and the Chron," I said. "The one thing they have in common is—they never give up."

"Initializing skip drive," Jahelia Sord said. "I'll switch to auto as soon as we're through the wormhole, to get us past the asteroids, is that right?"

"Right," I told her. "We should have some breathing room then, we'll get Rei sorted out and make a plan for getting—"

"PrimeCorp ship is firing on us!" Baden yelped. "Particle beam, maybe. It's lighting up the shields!"

It was too late to stop or turn. The dark mouth of the wormhole swallowed us, and the spill of colours swirled across the viewscreens. Remembering the last time I'd seen a ship fire an energy weapon into a wormhole, I wondered if it was the last thing any of us would ever see.

Chapter 40 — Jahelia Trust and Other Rare Commodities

OKAY, SO I hadn't piloted a ship the size of the *Tane Ikai* in decades, but I wasn't about to tell Luta Paixon that. With Little Miss Pilot and Gramps both out of commission, and Paixon dealing with her bioscav sickness, I was obviously the only hope to get us out of there. I'll admit there was a small voice in my head suggesting that maybe if I could get the PrimeCorp folks to listen, tell them about my assignment from Alin Sedmamin himself, I could extricate myself from this mess. But a smarter voice replied that there was no guarantee these guys would believe me—or care. And I no longer trusted anything PrimeCorp. So I stuck with Paixon. Better the devil you know and all that.

Furthermore, I'd already hidden a small stash of goodies from the Chron station here on the ship. They'd finance the next part of my life. It would be a shame to have to leave them here.

So I was doing pretty well, I thought. It was all coming back to me, and once you've flown a few ships around Nearspace, you can fly almost anything. All I had to do was make this one skip and then I had no doubt they'd find someone else to take over. Paixon needed me, but I could tell she didn't really like to see me sitting in Little Miss Pilot's seat.

But when Baden yelled that the PrimeCorp ship had opened fire on us with an energy weapon, I have to admit I had a bad moment. I hadn't seen the shot that took out the wormhole to Delta Pavonis, but I'd seen the end result. That red vortex of an eye, spewing radiation. I had no doubt that anything inside that wormhole when it had gone *boom* had gone boom also.

I bit down hard on my tongue, until I tasted blood. The hot, coppery tang steadied me, kept my hands solid on the controls. Seconds passed. The wormhole seemed normal. Luckily, piloting a skip was mostly a matter of a few small steps, done in the right order and repeated until you got to the end. *Touch. Nudge the drive thrust. Repel off the side. Slide around. Touch.*

Maybe the weapon the Chron had used had been some other kind, and a mere particle beam wasn't enough to disrupt the stability of a wormhole. And if nothing bad had happened so far, there still had to be a chance that if I could hold us steady through this wormhole, we'd come out the other end intact.

"Sord? You all right?"

I didn't take my eyes or hands from the skip controls. "Holding on, Captain. Happy to see we haven't blown up yet."

"True enough. Baden, Viss, Hirin, how are we doing?"

Paixon tried to keep her voice light, but the strain was hard to hide. I didn't know how she was still upright, unless it was whatever the Chron had given her in that shot. And who knew how long that would last? Despite my concentration on getting us through the skip, my thoughts darted to my father's desperate, last-ditch attempt to save my mother's life. The memory flickered through my mind like a series of still images strung along a wire.

Longate had been a disaster, instead of the game-changer my father and Nicadico Corp had banked on. I'd been suspicious that everything hadn't been on the shiny side of the law when my father came home regularly with enough for us to live on and plenty for him to gamble away. We'd had to move quickly when the deadly flaws in the treatment had come to light, like cockroaches scurrying away from prying eyes. My father swore to me repeatedly that he'd known nothing of the shortcuts, the paid-for endorsements, the manipulated research results. His version of our swift and secretive departure was that they'd be looking for scapegoats, and he was a logical choice, having occupied a primary place on the research team. That also made him a logical choice for someone who'd bent the rules, but I didn't say that. I was too worried about my mother's rapidly deteriorating health and how much of my time it was taking to care for her.

So when my father finally came up with his brilliant plan to simply remove the malfunctioning bioscavs from her system, we were months and systems and wormholes away from the Nicadico lab where, if he'd only thought of it earlier, he could have borrowed the equipment he needed. As it was, I had to exert all my skills at obtaining things in secret deals and shady trades to come up with what he wanted. A high-tech dialysis machine, with a lot of tweaks and add-ons that hadn't come cheap—except for the couple I'd been able to obtain by blackmail.

Mamma'd been almost entirely bedridden anyway by the time we had it all set up in the mildewy back bedroom of the four-room apartment I'd found us on Xaqual. I had to empty the trashcan next to the bed every night—it would be filled to overflowing with bloodied tissues from her nosebleeds. When I'd help her to the washroom, her legs would often begin a wracking tremor that ended in a weakness so profound she'd drop to her knees. The headaches, angry outbursts, and paranoia were everyday occurrences now. The new normal.

It took the entire night for her blood to filter through the machine that Dad had altered. She slept through most of it, although she kept unconsciously knocking the transcutaneous diverter out of place, and I had to sit beside the bed and monitor her. In the morning she actually woke up brighter than she had in a long time, and demanded to be let up out of bed so she could have a shower. She was still weak, but the other symptoms had abated drastically.

Until that night.

I shivered myself out of the memory. "Last skip coming up," I said, and when we'd slid around the inside of the wormhole one more time, we shot out the end. I flipped the ship over to the auto-nav to guide us through the tumbling asteroid field we'd been expecting.

The nose of the *Tane Ikai* grazed the side of an irregular grey rock the size of a small house. The shields flared and it was close enough to make out individual craters on its pocked surface.

"*Merde!*" I switched to manual and punched the controls again. The asteroids that were supposed to form a constantly moving barrier to guard the wormhole mouth were frozen in place like an avalanche stopped in mid-slide. Now, instead of being able to navigate it via the pre-set coordinates in the nav computer, I had to run it manually like a demented obstacle course.

Gasps and exclamations came from around the bridge as I jammed on the reverse thrusters and kept my fingers on the maneuvering jet controls, tweaking our course with minute bursts as we wove through the eerie graveyard of stones.

"Everybody quiet! Sord?"

I knew what Paixon was asking in that one word. *Can you do this?*

"No. Problem." I'm not sure how convincing I sounded, speaking through gritted teeth. But what was the alternative? If Paixon wasn't capable of flying us through a skip, she certainly couldn't guide the ship through this. The path through the asteroids narrowed and gaped, twisted and spun, making the passage treacherous, even at a crawl. If they suddenly started moving again, we'd be battered and crushed in seconds.

"Bad news," Baden said. "The PrimeCorp ship—they followed us through."

"They must have something to do with the asteroid field being like this," Paixon said. "They had to have known."

We were almost through the field—the asteroids began to thin ahead of us, and I could see the greater unbroken darkness of space beyond.

Except it wasn't as unbroken as it should have been. Darting bits of movement and flashes of light told me something was wrong. It wasn't until I could see my way clear through the last of the asteroids that I realized what I was seeing.

"Worse news," I said. "I think we've landed in the middle of another firefight."

"THAT'S THE CORVID station," Paixon said. "*Merde*, it's under attack!"

The station appeared identical to the one where the crew had first met the Corvids. I hadn't been on the bridge at the time, but Pita had shown me feeds from the viewscreens after the fact. This one was as dark, creepy, and completely alien as the other one had been. Unfortunately, it was a lot busier. Small Corvid fighters engaged with both PrimeCorp starrunner and Chron ships. No surprise there.

"*Damne, damne.* We're not in very good shape to help out here," Paixon said.

"We're not in *any* shape to help out here," Viss confirmed. "Our shields took a beating from the torps and the particle beam." He threw a glance at me. "And if we lose another pilot—"

"Viss is right." Hirin used his one good hand to bring up the coordinates for the asteroid field leading out of this system. "We can't get caught up in this. We need to verify these coordinates and reach Nearspace."

"And, um, if I could just mention," Baden added, "the PrimeCorp ship is sailing through the asteroid field behind us like he knows the way. We slowed down to get through it; he's *accelerating* through. And I'm guessing he plans to skip the party around that station and keep coming after us."

"Tell me where I'm going, folks," I said. "I need a plan."

Paixon hesitated a moment more, then said, "Right, the wormhole it is. Baden, contact the station to confirm the coordinates we got from Fha. Sord—punch it for the wormhole."

"Will do." The *Tane Ikai*'s burst drive was a thing of beauty with the modifications the Corvids had made, and once Paixon gave the word I pushed it to its limit. I had to swing wide around the station to avoid the firefight still raging around it, but it didn't put us far off course.

"PrimeCorp ship has cleared the asteroids," Baden said, too brief a time later. "Staying on our tail—and just fired at us again."

"Shields have as much juice as I can give them," Viss said.

"Sord, try to evade with the maneuvering jets, but not if it slows us too much," Paixon told me. Her voice sounded fainter, as if she was reaching the end of her endurance.

I punched the vertical thruster, and the ship dropped, making my stomach lurch. I wasn't used to such a quick and thorough response in a ship this size. Not quick enough, though. The *Tane Ikai* shuddered as the shields took the hit. Paixon gasped behind me, and I hoped she wasn't going to throw up.

She had me really confused now; I didn't know anymore what could be going wrong with her bioscavs. From my experience—limited, sure, but still more than most people had—she should not have survived this long without bioscavengers in her system, when she'd been dependent on them for so long.

Mamma had lived a whole twenty-four hours once her bioscavs were gone. At first she'd rallied, symptom-free. But that only lasted long enough for us to get our hopes up. It started that night with a headache and a nosebleed we couldn't seem to stop. The convulsions came not long after that. The vomiting, shivering, and body-wracking shakes as her entire body rebelled and, once it wore itself out with rebellion, shut down for good.

I glanced at Luta Paixon. She'd put a hand to her temple, rubbing it absently as if she could erase the pain behind it with her fingertips. *Should I warn her?*

Would she believe me? What good would it do, anyway? They seemed to think that getting her to her mother might save her. Might as well let them do that. For all I knew, it would, if we could make it.

Then it hit me as hard as one of those PrimeCorp torpedoes. Her mother. Emmage Mahane. The woman I'd set out to hurt. The woman I'd targeted for revenge, the one I'd marked to bear the brunt for all the years of running, and hiding, and scrimping, and lying. The years of trying to save my parents from themselves.

Of trying to save *me* from myself.

It was all her fault, wasn't it?

I hadn't known exactly how I was going to hurt Emmage Mahane. I thought Paixon might lead me to her, or maybe an opportunity would present itself to get my revenge on Mahane through her daughter, or her granddaughter. I figured I'd know my chance when it presented itself.

And here it was.

Paixon was going to die. All I had to do was let it happen. Fly a little slower. Stray off course a bit. Stretch out the time so that she didn't make it to Emmage Mahane.

So easy.

Chapter 41 — Luta
The Enveloping Fog

I'D NEVER UNDERSTOOD what people meant by an "icepick headache," but I thought I did now. I put a hand to my temple, blinking away tears that welled up in response to the pain. It really did feel as if someone had stabbed my head with a sharp instrument. Jahelia Sord with her fork, I thought, trying to distract myself from it. Sometimes the way she looked at me, I thought that was exactly what she'd like to do.

I glanced at her, so incongruous in Rei's seat. Not now, though. Now she was saving all of us—herself included. I still didn't understand her, but I was damn glad that she'd come aboard the ship.

"No response from the station," Baden said. "I've signalled them three times on the channel Fha set up, but nothing."

The embattled station still showed on one of the side viewscreens. There seemed to be no let-up in the assault, and no side clearly emerging as a victor yet.

"Maybe the coordinates we have will work," I said, but in my heart, I didn't believe it. I'd expect them to change all the asteroid field settings as soon as the assault began, to try and prevent further incursions into the system. That the attackers had apparently found a way to override one field—the one we'd come through—wouldn't change that protocol.

"I hate to say it, but we have more trouble," Baden said. "Two ships have broken off from the attack on the station and are headed after us."

I pressed my lips together until they hurt. "So our stalker has called in some friends. Sord, Viss, can we get anything else from the burst drive?"

Viss answered without hesitation. "I'm sorry, Captain. It's full-out. The only other thing I could do is take the shields offline—"

The PrimeCorp ship fired another torpedo, and it battered into the shields, answering that question. I glanced at the rear screens. The two ships coming to join their fellow—I couldn't tell for sure, but were they gaining on us? If they caught up and added their firepower to the first—

But at this rate, we'd never reach the asteroid field before the shields gave out. We couldn't weaken ourselves further by returning fire. And I feared that when we reached the asteroids, we'd have to stop anyway. If the coordinates weren't right, Sord couldn't fly through the field on her own. Even Rei hadn't been able to do it without my help, and I'd been a lot healthier then.

I stood from the chair. I couldn't think. I needed to move, needed to pace, clear my mind. I always thought best while I walked, letting the motion shake disparate thoughts into a shape that made sense. My legs wobbled, and I swore under my breath, clutching at the chair arm.

I hate being sick. I hate being weak.

Forcing my back straight and willing my legs to hold me up, I slowly paced the width of the bridge. I caught Hirin's eyes on me, dark with concern. I managed a half-smile for him, turned and started the other way. It wasn't easy.

I hate the pain. I hate the uncertainty. And I hated feeling this much self-pity.

I tried to bludgeon my mind clear. Most of all, I hated the PrimeCorp ship behind me. We had to escape them, or we had to stop them.

Stop them.

Stop them.

I whirled toward Hirin, almost toppling over. The empty skimchair next to Baden, where Maja usually sat, saved me. I grabbed the arm and fell into it. "Hirin! When the Chron were chasing us before—before we all went out—Rei said something to you about the activator drive. What was it?"

Hirin frowned, shook his head slightly. "I don't—what was it? She wanted to use it. But I didn't understand why."

"Right. Because we weren't near a ghosting artifact." I dropped my eyes to my hands, gripping the arms of the skimchair. *Think.* The smooth armrest felt oddly rippled, but I knew it was the scarring on my fingertips. The only scars I had that my nanobioscavengers had not healed.

"But one stopped our drives once," I said suddenly. "That's it! At the artifact moon—we were caught in it and it stopped our drives, remember? It shut down everything. It *wrecked* things!" I held up my burned fingers, where the datapad had seared them. "Viss—"

"Already on it, Captain," he said, his hands flying over the engineering console. "Activator drive is online."

"Fire."

A bright flash lit up the rear viewscreens as the drive activated, sending its pulse of—whatever it was—directly into the path of the oncoming PrimeCorp ship. There was no flash of impact, no explosion. The ship kept coming. But—

"Its drives are shut down!" Baden shouted. "No weapons systems, no thrust. They'll keep coasting, but they'll have to reboot everything, just like we did at the artifact moon."

I struggled up out of the skimchair to get to my own. "All right. That gives us a little more time to make the wormhole. Sord, you all right?"

"Perfectly fine, Captain. Running full out, straight for the asteroid field." Her voice sounded strained, belying her words, but if she said she was *okej*, I'd take her word for it.

"Baden, still nothing from the station?"

"Sorry, Captain. Not a thing."

I pulled in a deep breath and smelled blood. Startled, I glanced around the bridge, then realized it was me. I put a hand up to catch the wet, hot drop that threatened to spill over my top lip. *Not again.*

"Three minutes to the asteroid field," Hirin said.

I swallowed hard, tried to focus. "Can you tell yet if the coordinates will work? Extrapolate our course at all?"

He was quiet as he worked, pressing commands one-handed into the nav computer as fast as he could. Finally he looked up. "It's hard to tell—the asteroids are moving, not static like the last field. It's impossible to predict the course this far in advance. I can find Fha's designated entry points into the field—but not whether an asteroid will be in that location three minutes from now."

"The other PrimeCorp ships are still coming on," Baden said. "Not gaining, but they'll catch up quick if we have to stop at the field."

Pain stabbed into the side of my head again, blinding me with sudden tears. "We have to fly straight into the field when we get there," I said. "Sord, can you do that?"

She hesitated a long time before she spoke. "I don't think so, not on my own."

I knew it must have cost her to make that admission. "What about your datapad—Pita? No super navigational abilities we don't know about?"

I heard a smile in Sord's voice, a rare thing. "She can do a lot of things, Captain, but she can't fly a ship by herself."

I swallowed again. My mouth had gone dry, and my throat felt like sandpaper. But we couldn't let ourselves be blown up or captured by PrimeCorp. We had to warn Nearspace. Unsteadily, I pushed myself out of the chair. "*Okej.* Then I'll try to help you. Maybe between us—"

I made it halfway to the co-pilot's seat before my legs buckled. Baden tried to catch me, but my arm picked up a heavy tremor and he couldn't hold me. I crashed to the metal decking, legs kicking feebly, completely out of my control. My head banged painfully onto the floor, so hard I felt the lump begin to swell immediately.

"Luta!" Hirin was up from the nav console and at my side,

awkwardly turning me on my side. Oddly, I smelled strawberries. The word *asteroid* seemed to be stuck in my head, my mind looping it over and over *asteroid asteroid field asteroid orbit asteroid belt asteroid asteroid*. Black dots starred my vision, expanding like the mouth of a wormhole until I could see only black. My eyes were wide open, but I couldn't see.

I could still hear, though. I heard Jahelia Sord telling Baden something that didn't make any sense.

"That storage room behind the head," she said. It sounded like speaking hurt her throat, but the words tumbled out, terse and sharp. "Rear wall, behind a box of dried pasta. Inside a bag marked 'filters'. There's some stuff there—get the med injector— it's the one that Chron doctor used on her. Still a dose in it. I don't know if it will do any good. But if the convulsions have started, I can tell you it can't hurt."

Skimchair rolling across decking. Running feet. Yuskeya's voice . . . Maja's voice, too? She must be all right. Tears pricked my eyes at that. Hirin's hand under my head. Someone clutching my hand. Words and voices spinning around me, cluttering up the air, meaningless, noisy. *Asteroid asteroid asteroid.*

The running feet returning. Something cool and round pressed to the base of my neck, and a familiar spreading tingle that was half-pleasant, half-pain. I thought about drawing in a deep breath, tried, and found I could. Specks of light like tiny fireworks danced in my vision, and sight returned as they cleared. My body returned to me. It had stopped shaking. The lump on my head felt tender where Hirin's hand held it, and I managed to get a hand on the decking and push myself upright. In the space of a few more heartbeats, I felt clear and light and absolutely purposeful.

"Whoa, Captain," Yuskeya said, her hand on my shoulder. "Take it easy. I don't know what just happened, but you're in no shape—"

"No, that's the point, Yuskeya. I *am* in the shape—the shape I need to be in to help Sord navigate the asteroids. Look." I held out my hand to her. Rock steady. I put the hand on the comm board next to Baden and pulled myself to my feet, a little wobbly but a thousand times better than I'd been minutes ago. "But we don't know how long it will last, so there's no time to lose."

"The other PrimeCorp ships are almost in torpedo range," Baden said.

"And the asteroid field is dead ahead," Jahelia Sord said. "Decision time, people."

"Yuskeya—the coordinates?"

She gave me one more hard, searching stare, then crossed hurriedly to the nav board and keyed in commands. When she turned back to me, her eyes were dark with concern. "No good. The configuration has changed."

"All right." I squeezed Maja's hand—she'd been the one holding it, still pale-faced and trembly, but moving under her own power—and let it go, sliding into the co-pilot's seat. "Sord, you're dock. I'll take starboard. Viss will shut down everything but the maneuvering jets. We're going to weave our way through this to the wormhole, and then engage the skip drive, *okej?*"

Jahelia Sord didn't take her eyes off the board, her fingers skimming the controls like a musician playing a delicate instrument. Her lips were pressed tight together, the muscles in her neck strained. "Got it."

There was no time to say anything else as we plunged into the tumbling field. Like the other field Rei and I had navigated, the asteroids came in every size, from pebbles you'd find scattered along a riverbed to monsters twice the size of the ship. Their smooth and cratered surfaces loomed terrifyingly close on the screen as we ducked, dodged, and wove through them, always focused on the spot where the wormhole's dark mouth waited for us, if we could only reach it in one piece.

Smaller rocks battered against the shields, translating into tiny bursts of light on the viewscreen. We couldn't avoid them all, not this time. I flinched at every impact, waiting for the one that would burn out the weakened shields.

"I never want to see another asteroid after this," Jahelia Sord said conversationally. The strain in her voice belied her composure.

"Shields are holding," Viss reassured us.

I knew they couldn't protect us from the larger rocks, not in their current state, but it was nice to know we didn't have to do this perfectly in order to survive.

"Looks like the PrimeCorp ships won't follow us in," Baden said after a few minutes. "They're getting close to the field, but slowing."

The asteroids finally thinned, the wormhole mouth a shadowed disc up ahead. "Initiating skip drive," Sord said.

I sat back from the board, letting my hands fall into my lap as the spun-rainbow colours of the wormhole swallowed us up. Fatigue flooded me, reaction and relief making my arms feel heavy and weak, even though I knew the injection wouldn't be wearing off yet. "Thanks, Jahelia Sord," I said, turning to her. She had her eyes focused on the pilot's board, guiding the ship though the delicate dance of wormhole skipping, but she smiled.

"Don't thank me yet; you're still not home," she said.

"But I think now I'll make it," I told her, "and that's thanks to you."

"True." She grinned. "So what you're saying is, you owe me one?"

I laughed, the first time I'd done so in a long time. It felt good. "I was thinking maybe it made us even. But I guess we can talk about it."

"Yeah, let's do that," she said. I had the feeling it would be an interesting talk. I leaned forward, resting my arms on the co-pilot's board and closing my eyes. After a moment I felt Hirin's hand on my shoulder.

He bent low and whispered in my ear, "I think we can take it from here. Why don't you go and rest?"

Before I could answer him, Rei woke up. Luckily, we were out of the skip by then.

"IT'S OKAY," I heard Gerazan say. I was about to answer him when I realized that he wasn't talking to me. He'd been sitting on the deck with Rei all this time, waiting for a break in the multiple crises so he could help move her to her quarters. She must be coming around. I forced my eyes open again to see how she was doing.

Rei opened unfocused eyes and looked around blearily. Then she seemed to notice Sord. She sprang like a scalded Erian cat, up from the floor where she'd been lying, to catch Jahelia Sord by the shoulders and shove her bodily out of the pilot's chair. Sord hadn't had a chance to see Rei coming. She lurched across the bridge decking, off balance, finally falling against a vacant console. The ship lurched to the side, and Rei staggered.

"Rei!" Hirin yelled, and she turned but didn't seem to see him.

I pushed myself up to sit again, staring up at her. "Rei! It's all right," I barked. "Sit down, dammit, and let Sord fly the ship! You're hurt!"

Confusion slid across her face, tracking over her darkly beautiful tattoos. She focused on me with an effort. "I thought—Luta, are you—"

"Rei, Luta's sick, you were knocked out, and Sord was helping us pilot. Nothing's wrong." Hirin's voice was strong and lucid and seemed to break through the fog of her mental disarray.

She glanced over at the vacant console where Sord had fallen. She hadn't moved to get up. "I don't think she's going to be able to keep helping," she said carefully.

Of course not. Jahelia Sord was out cold.

"Then sit down and start driving," Hirin roared at Rei, and it worked, because she did just that. Her fingers didn't move with their usual fluidity, but she straightened out the course that had begun to drift.

"Yuskeya," Viss said, one of the few times I'd heard him speak directly to her in weeks, "wouldn't you have something in First Aid that would help Rei?"

"I would," she said, after a moment's hesitation. "Thanks, Viss."

She jumped up from the nav board and ran for the First Aid station, returning almost immediately to slip an injector up against Rei's arm implant. Rei shuddered and nodded. "I'm good."

I still felt okay, if a little weak, so I got up and crossed with Yuskeya to take a look at Sord. She had a welling red lump on her forehead, and I suspected that our momentary camaraderie might be forgotten when she woke up. I sighed. If I didn't owe her before, I thought maybe I did now.

Yuskeya made another trip to First Aid and soon had Sord sitting up and rubbing her forehead. "*Kristos*, Rei, what was that for?" she said. "We were friends half an hour ago."

Rei glanced over at us, and a bright red flush crept over her face. "I'm sorry," she said, and turned her eyes resolutely to the console. "I was confused when I woke up. And I thought maybe you'd—maybe you'd—"

"Knocked out the Captain and hijacked the ship?" Sord said, an edge of sarcasm sharpening her voice.

"Um. Yeah."

"With Gramps standing right there, and everyone else on the bridge, too?"

Rei gulped. "It was—like I said, I was confused. Sorry."

Sord prodded the bump. "Ouch. Yeah, well, I guess I could understand it."

Satisfied that Sord was all right, I finally had a chance to glance at the main viewscreen. Just when I thought I'd seen enough asteroids to last me the rest of my life—even a very long life—we'd emerged into the Tau Ceti system, famous for its enormous debris disk of asteroidal and cometary material. We'd landed in the thick of the symmetrical disk, which explained how the Chron had been able to camouflage an artifact object here. The wormhole that linked Tau Ceti to the rest of Nearspace, via Eta Cassiopeia, emerged far enough from the solitary G-class star to be at the very edge of the disk, far from where we were now. Tiny Quma lay on the edge of the star's habitable zone.

"Yuskeya, we need to scan for the Chron artifact," Hirin said. "I can do it if Sord still needs attention."

Jahelia Sord waved Yuskeya away. "I'm fine," she said, pulling herself up into the chair at the vacant console.

Yuskeya returned to the nav console, and I pulled another skimchair over to sit near Sord. "Hirin," I said, "it's probably overdue, but you have the chair."

He bowed in acquiescence, and I turned to Sord. In a low voice I said, "You know a lot more about my bioscavs than I understand. Want to tell me how?"

She regarded me for a long moment, her brown eyes unreadable. "I've told Maja some," she said finally. "Suffice to say, my father worked with your mother. He, and my own mother, and I, all have—or had—similar bioscavs to yours."

"Had?"

Her eyes flicked away and then to me. "They're both dead. My father, eight years ago, my mother, a while before that." She leaned forward in her chair, resting her elbows on her knees. "Here's what you need to know. My father tried to save my mother's life when her bioscavs broke down, like it seems yours did. He filtered them out of her system, same as that Chron doctor did on the station."

I swallowed hard. "But—it didn't work?"

She turned her eyes to her hands, as youthful and unlined as mine, studying them as she remembered. "She got better—for a day. And died that night. Nosebleed, headache . . . convulsions. It was only a wild guess that whatever the Chron doc had injected you with would keep the symptoms at bay for a while longer, but even the first injection didn't give you much time. You've got to get to your mother as fast as you damn well can."

I nodded. "As soon as we locate the artifact here, we'll use the activator drive and try to ghost this wormhole to Mu Cassiopeia, where she is. Should be," I added. I knew she was scheduled to travel to the Schulyer Group's labs on Mars sometime soon. I could only hope that she hadn't left yet, and that the Corvid drive really had access to all our nav data. If the conversion hadn't worked—but I wouldn't let myself think about that.

"Found it," Yuskeya said. "Baden, I'm feeding the data to you. We should be able to lock on with the activator drive." She glanced over at me. "You still okay, Captain? If this works, we'll have you to your mother in no time."

"I'm fine," I told her. If the injection had bought me a limited amount of time, we couldn't waste any. I returned to Sord.

"I'm . . . not going to turn you over to the Protectorate," I said, almost surprising myself. I really hadn't known I was going to say that until the words were out, although the idea had been bubbling in my mind for a little while now. I didn't understand all the reasons Jahelia Sord had become entangled in our lives, but I felt sure that whatever they were, they'd changed along the way. We'd been through things together, and I thought we'd both come out the other side feeling differently.

Her eyebrows rose. "You're not? A bit of piloting and a filched medical injector and all's forgiven?"

I chuckled. "Not quite. I'll need your datapad—and all those files—in order to prove to the Protectorate what PrimeCorp has been doing."

Her hand twitched as if to grab something, but she only shrugged and said, "Sure. I understand."

"But whatever else is in the storage room that 'belongs' to you—you can keep. On one condition."

She tilted her head. "Which is?"

"You sell it to anyone but PrimeCorp," I told her.

She laughed. "Deal."

We'd pulled up near an asteroid that looked like any other . . . until you magnified it on the screen, as Viss had done. Then you could tell that it had been constructed, the way the first artifact moon we'd found had been. "About to initiate the activator drive," Viss said. "Everyone ready?"

"Go ahead," Hirin said, after a glance at me. I smiled and nodded.

The light flashed out from the *Tane Ikai* and, as expected, had no obvious impact on the asteroid. On the viewscreen, however, the wormhole began to glow blue and silver, just as it had when the Chron had activated the moon near the wormhole to Delta Pavonis. The colours spun, swirling like a whirlpool, and the cone of silver-blue light pushed out from the mouth of the wormhole. I was glad we'd seen this phenomenon already, and knew it was normal. I never would have had the courage to order Rei to fly into that pointed tip of light otherwise.

I felt a sudden heaviness grip my chest and squeeze, as if I were back on that gurney on the Chron station and someone had pulled the restraints too tight.

"Some of the beam reflected," Yuskeya said. "Doesn't seem to have had any effect on us, though."

"Ready for skip," Rei said. "Viss, initiate the drive?"

I gasped, the sound abnormally loud in my ears. The icepick headache returned, stabbing into my temple and shooting all the way into my eye. I think I cried out.

All heads—except Rei's, since she was guiding us through the terminal point, swivelled towards me. Jahelia Sord's hand gripped my arm. It felt as hot as a Lobor's fervid touch. I leaned forward in my chair and vomited, then slid forward off the skimchair seat. Sord's hands grabbed me around the shoulders and lowered me to the deck, away from the spreading puddle I'd created. My legs began to jerk, kicking feebly at nothing, and cold sweat stung my brow. This time a fog seemed to be lowering over my vision, closing in from the sides, narrowing my field of view down to a hazy tunnel with no discernible light at the end.

No. No. I was suddenly so tired of this. Tired of being sick, and weak, and never knowing when my body would rebel against me again.

Hirin was there then, taking my hand, whispering to me. "Hang on, Luta. We're almost there. One more skip. Hang on."

And Maja, stroking my hair away from my face. My beautiful daughter. At least we'd solved our differences before—

That was my last thought before the fog rolled in to claim me.

Chapter 42 — Luta
After the War

THE NEXT FEW days were ones I don't remember, since I was unconscious for the vast majority of them. I know, because Hirin has told me, and my continued existence makes it evident, that we found Mother as expected on Kiando, and she was able to give me—just in time—an infusion of new nanobioscavengers. They apparently went to war with the mutated ones the Chron filtration system had missed, and won, and were now hard at work repairing whatever damage had been done. I missed this internal bioscavenger war entirely, being deeply sedated so the bioscavs could do their job.

I learned that the Stillwell reported in a few days after we landed on Kiando, having mysteriously found itself once again on the Delta Pavonis side of the wormhole. I strongly suspected the Corvids might have had a hand in that, since Jahelia Sord's ship had also been found drifting nearby. I said nothing, since the crew was intact and healthy, despite widespread confusion and a large gap in their collective memory. Maybe someday I'd get the chance to ask Fha about it.

I know that Hirin did as I'd promised, despite deeply mistrusting my judgement at that moment, and let Jahelia Sord walk off the *Tane Ikai* and disappear. I finally got a chance to sit up in bed and ask him some more questions about her a week after we arrived on Kiando. Gusain Buig, Duntmindi's Chairman on the planet and Mother's significant other, had opened his house—his *mansion*—to all of us. I felt quite pampered. My bedroom had been decorated in soothing, creamy tones with touches of rose and yellow striping the furniture and the window hangings. Soft rugs covered the floors, and fresh flowers scented the room every morning. I could have spent more time snuggling into the softness of the bed and enjoying the idea that I'd be back to normal soon, but I had questions and Hirin had been deflecting them, telling me to "wait until you feel better."

"Okay, Hirin," I said, settling comfortably against a mound of pillows and tucking the forest-green organic velvet coverlet around me, "spill. What happened with Jahelia Sord?"

He pursed his lips and I thought he might try to evade the question again, but he must have read something in my eyes. He sighed. "Well, I think there was a lot more to her than the not-so-great PrimeCorp operative we thought she was at first."

"She proved that several times over," I agreed. But that was an evasive answer; I could tell there was more. "What? What else?"

"There was a message on the computer in her room. For you." He dug a piece of paper out of his pocket and handed it to me. "This is what it said."

It didn't take long to read. There were only fourteen words.

> *Captain Paixon,*
>
> *Ask your mother about my father, Berrto Sord. I will see you both again.*

I looked up at Hirin, frowning. "Did you? Ask Mother?"

He shook his head. "Thought I'd leave that for you. Jahelia Sord also," he continued, "took the datachip from Cerevare's quarters. The one Fha gave us, with all the Chron information on it."

I sat forward. "What?"

"Guess we should have thought of it first," he admitted grimly. "But she did leave copies of all the files on the computer in

Cerevare's room."

"That little—"

"She also took her datapad with her, and left a fake one with me."

I couldn't suppress a gasp at that. "That was our evidence—"

He held up a hand. "Don't get too excited. She left a full copy—as far as Baden can tell—of almost all its files."

"The Chron dictionary? The PrimeCorp files? Everything?"

"Apparently. Everything except the AI itself. There's also a personal log file she'd been keeping as sort of a journal. I didn't read much of that, and put an encryption on it. Figured you should read it first, then decide who, if anyone, you want to share it with."

I relaxed against the pillows again, letting my momentary anger drain away. Jahelia Sord was nothing if not an opportunist, and she could certainly see the value in the tech and information she'd walked away with. I could hardly blame her for protecting her own interests. She'd at least had the decency to copy the files. I carefully folded up her note, running my finger along the sharp creases. I tucked it under the covers beside me. It—and Sord herself—would take some thinking about. "Thanks. So what's going to happen with PrimeCorp?"

Hirin settled back in the rose-and-yellow-striped wing chair and crossed his legs. "I gave Lanar the datapacket from Fha, and copies of all the PrimeCorp files from Sord's datapad, and he delivered them to the Council. Currently there's a huge uproar within the Nearspace Council—they're trying to keep the story quiet, but it's only a matter of time. Everyone in the corporation denies any knowledge of the Chron, or secret wormholes, or century-old collaboration—any of it. As they would. The files wouldn't be admissible in court, because they were illegally obtained, but the Protectorate is launching a full investigation, and the files give them a roadmap. They've placed us all under temporary protection. We've told them everything we can, and they say heads will roll this time, but . . ."

"PrimeCorp is trying to make sure that some people might go down, but the muck won't splash very far up the ladder," I finished for him.

"I don't know if they'll be able to—not this time."

"Is the Protectorate planning to contact the Corvids?"

Hirin nodded. "I talked to Lanar, and he says the Council feels it's imperative—it's nice to see them agreeing on something for once. Well, except for the ambassadors from the PrimeCorp worlds, of course. They're still in full denial mode and trying to convince the rest of the Council that we suffered some mass hallucination or something. But I think Lanar intends to ask us to go through the Delta Pavonis wormhole again, once you're better, with a full delegation."

I wasn't sure what I thought of that. "I'd love to go back and learn more about the Corvids," I said, "but 'full delegation' sounds like it would entail a lot of diplomacy. Sounds like it might get old really fast."

He half-smiled. "Agreed. But it *is* the Worlds Council. We might not have much of a choice."

"And it could be war," I said. The thought sent a shiver down my spine that had nothing to do with any inadequacy of warmth in the coverlet. I asked the question there hadn't really been time to consider while everything was happening. "What's PrimeCorp doing, Hirin? What do they want, working with the Chron? The— the broken ones, anyway, as my doctor friend called them."

Hirin steepled his fingers in his characteristic thinking pose, tapping them against his lips. "I've been considering that, and Lanar and your mother and I had a long chat about it. If our speculation is right, and their original association with the Chron began as a business deal, maybe that deal went sour—"

"And led to the war?"

He shrugged. "It could happen. I don't imagine PrimeCorp was necessarily very well-versed in first contact protocols. Countless things could have gone wrong."

I pursed my lips and nodded. "And the Corvids stepped in and stopped it. But somewhere along the line, maybe tens of decades later, PrimeCorp made contact with the Chron again."

"Maybe to try and make a new deal," Hirin said. "If they'd discovered a common enemy, or a common goal. And could see a profit in it."

"Or the possibility of a coup?"

He stared at me. "You think PrimeCorp wants to literally control all of Nearspace?"

It was my turn to shrug. "Could we completely discount it as a possibility?"

He drew a deep breath and blew it out in a long sigh. "Completely? No. But it's hard to get my head around." He fiddled with the edge of the green coverlet, flipping the scalloped edge between his fingers. "PrimeCorp has become a bit of an enigma to me," he said finally. "I know we've had nothing but trouble from them, but—they've done a lot of good, too."

"What? What are you talking about?"

He shrugged diffidently. "The deeper I dig into everything about them, the more of a dichotomy I find. They support considerable charitable work. They manufacture medicines and equipment that improve the lives of Nearspace citizens—and don't sell them all at exorbitant rates. They have divisions that don't seem to have any corruption. I know there's a lot that's rotten at the higher levels of the management structure—"

"You can say that again. I can smell the stink from here." I'd crossed my arms over my chest and felt my brow furrow into a deep frown. What was Hirin saying? He'd seen and heard everything about PrimeCorp that I had. They'd been responsible for his prolonged illness and confinement in the nursing home, for heaven's sake.

He leaned back in the chair and ran his hands over the short salt-and-pepper stubble of his hair. "I'm not saying we were wrong about PrimeCorp. But I think they're a little like the Chron—there's a good side and a bad side. Not everyone involved with PrimeCorp is evil. It might be important to keep that in mind as things unfold. That's all I'm saying."

I closed my eyes, silent as I thought about his words. I wanted to argue, but Jahelia Sord's face rose in my mind. She'd been anything but black-and-white. I'd asked for this discussion, but maybe I wasn't quite ready to take it all in. The enormity of PrimeCorp's possible plans, and what Hirin was telling me, felt a bit staggering. Finally I opened my eyes. "*Okej,* we're not going to think about it anymore right now."

He smiled, the skin crinkling at the corners of his grey eyes, and took my hand. "Aye, Captain. Any more burning questions?"

"No, I guess that will do for now." I squinted at him. "I do want you to do me a favour. Send Viss and Yuskeya in to see me, would you? Together."

"Sure. You going to sort them out, finally?"

I grinned. "Something like that. I think I should have done it long ago. And tell Mother I want to talk to her tonight, would you?"

VISS AND YUSKEYA came in together about an hour later. I'd had a short nap, and I felt refreshed and ready to give those two a good talking-to. They didn't look at each other when they entered the room, although Viss stood aside politely to let Yuskeya go first. She'd exchanged her Protectorate uniform for a turquoise-blue blouse and peasant-style skirt, and her face was more cheerful and relaxed than I'd seen it in a long time. She crossed to the bed to give me a warm hug.

"Well, you look better."

"It's not hard to improve on being slumped unconscious on the floor. But thank you. I feel better. And I wanted to thank you for helping me make it long enough to get to Mother."

"My pleasure," she said, grinning. "Although I did have a little help along the way."

"Good to see you, Captain," Viss said in a voice that was both deep and warm. He stood, almost at attention, at the foot of the bed.

"I wanted to talk to both of you," I began, "because I've discovered that almost dying refines one's perspective on life wonderfully. Now, as Captain, I've tried to mostly stay out of my crew's personal lives, but I'm neither unobservant nor stupid."

"Captain—"

"No, I want you to listen. Both of you. I know that you care about each other, but that's been strained ever since we came here to find Mother. Viss, I know you were surprised—as we all were—that Yuskeya is Protectorate—"

He actually cut me off. "Captain, there's no need—"

"*Prisilenti*! Will you please let me finish? That's an order! Now, I don't know how much longer Yuskeya will be with us, and

I want to see an end to this coldness—"

And this time when they interrupted me, it worked. Viss strode forward, pulled Yuskeya up off the bed and into his arms, and they kissed very—decidedly. When they finally pulled apart and both smiled down at me, all I could say was, "Oh."

"We worked things out not long after we landed here," Yuskeya said. "Once the initial excitement of saving your life was over, of course."

Viss shrugged, grinning. "I was an idiot for a while, that's all. Men do that, you know?"

Yuskeya put a hand over her heart and bowed. "As do women, from time to time. But we're okay, Captain. *Okej*?"

They left then, and I promised myself again that I wouldn't get involved in my crew's personal affairs.

Rei was a different matter, because she was also my best friend. When she came to visit later in the afternoon, I had no trouble asking about her plans.

"What do you mean?" she asked, sounding insulted. "Aren't I still your pilot?"

"Well, certainly—I just thought that you and Gerazan—"

She smiled. "Gerazan and I got along very well, thank you. But with everything that's happening—I mean with the Chron, and PrimeCorp—well, who knows what his next posting will be?" A shadow fell across her face as she contemplated the possibilities. Then she brightened again. Rei rarely let things bother her for long, absconding fiancés notwithstanding. "And I've got the *Tane Ikai*. However, we might spend some time together in a couple of months, if things work out and he can get some leave." She winked at me.

I pretended to be shocked. "But he's not Erian! There couldn't be anything long-term in that, or your mother would go crazy, remember?"

Rei stood up to go, bending to hug me first. "My mother," she said, "is a very resilient person. But we can talk about it more later. Feel better, Luta."

She opened the door and Mother appeared in the hallway. "How's the patient?" Mother asked.

"Feeling better," Rei told her. "She's up to asking impertinent questions."

Mother chuckled and crossed to the bed, pulled out her datamed and attached it to my implant. For the first few minutes she took readings, asked questions, and played the efficient doctor. She resembles me so strongly—well, I suppose I resemble her—that Hirin often jokes that he has a hard time telling us apart. Her nanobioscavengers have halted our aging processes a mere few years apart, so that contributes to the similarities. Today she had her auburn hair piled into a messy but elegant updo, and wore a plain, soft yellow shift dress.

When she seemed satisfied with my checkup, she sat on the side of the bed and asked, "So, how do you really feel?"

"A little tired still, but better. Everything working the way it should, now?"

She nodded. "I'm still not sure what it was about the activator drive that made the bioscavs malfunction—or even if that was really it. Correlation isn't causation, even though the two do appear to be connected. I need to do more research—particularly if we want to start getting the bioscavs out to people in Nearspace and we're actually going to be investigating this new ghosting technology. We can't have any incompatibilities."

"We might have other more pressing things to worry about," I said. "What do you think will happen with PrimeCorp?"

Mother shifted in the chair and clasped her hands. "It's premature to speculate—but they certainly have some tough questions to answer, considering the information and evidence you delivered."

"I keep thinking they'll still find a way to wiggle out of this somehow. That's what really makes me angry. They always manage to get away with things."

"Maybe not this time. They might have finally overplayed their hand. This thing with the Chron—"

"Alin Sedmamin and his directors will deny everything. It happened long ago, or he didn't know about it, or it's somebody else's fault . . ."

She smiled. "Even so, I'll bet he's not sitting very comfortably in that Chairman's seat."

"Maybe." I smoothed the coverlet over my legs, very aware of the note Hirin had given me tucked next to my leg. "Mother, who is Berrto Sord?"

Mother raised her eyebrows. "Berrto Sord? Do you remember when you first found me, I told you how I'd taken my research and run from PrimeCorp, when we found out how they planned to use it?"

I nodded.

"And that the other researchers had agreed never to give their data over, either? But there was one colleague who wasn't on board. I had to use some creative persuasion—call it blackmail, if we're being honest—to convince him not to cooperate with PrimeCorp."

"Berrto Sord?"

"Berrto Sord. But he died years ago. Why bring him up?"

I sighed. "Because of this." I pulled the note out from underneath the coverlet and gave it to her.

She read it and returned her eyes to me, her brows drawn together. "I don't get it."

So I told her the story of our encounter with Jahelia Sord, who'd gone from annoyance to slick PrimeCorp operative to—something else, in a short space of time. I told her what Sord had done for us—for me—and how I'd convinced Hirin to let her go. What I knew of her family, and the files she'd left behind.

Mother's eyes were wide by the time I'd finished, and she shook her head. "I can't believe he stole the bioscavs—injected his family—"

"Did exactly what you did?" I said wryly.

She blinked at me and relaxed, laughing a little. "Well, yes."

"Do you think Jahelia Sord got a different version of the story from him? She was very—hostile, when we first encountered her."

"No doubt. Berrto Sord probably thought I ruined his life. But he wasn't exactly lily-white or there'd have been nothing for me to hold over his head. And I still believe what I did was for the good of everyone in Nearspace." She got up and walked to the window, gazing out at the inviting expanse of the mansion's back gardens. "But I guess I'd say that, wouldn't I? And he'd tell the story his way."

"Were they Erian? She wore the *pridattii.*"

"Not that I recall. She might have been wearing them as a disguise."

"That's what I thought. But it doesn't make much sense, to disguise herself and then give me her real name. I think she thought I'd recognize it when she told me."

Mother sighed. "I don't know. I'm sorry I made another enemy for you, Luta. I never thought my actions would have such far-reaching consequences."

I got out of the bed and joined her at the window, putting a hand on her shoulder. "Don't worry about it. And—I don't know if I'd call her an enemy; at least not now. I mean, she had chances to do me harm—probably more than I know. That might have been her original plan, but I think maybe, somewhere along the line, it changed. She helped out when we needed her. And she probably saved my life in the end. Certainly helped, anyway."

"Her own life was on the line some of those times, the way you tell it," she said.

"I know, but—I can't put my finger on it. She turned out to be more complex than I thought at first. She was an enemy—and an ally. I don't know which she is now, I guess."

Mother leaned over to kiss my forehead. "Well, try not to worry about it, *okej?* You'll recover faster if you're not worrying. And you might never see her again."

A shiver prickled across my skin, and I retreated to the bed and the comforting weight of its covers. "Oh, I doubt that. I doubt that very much. But no, I won't worry about it. If Jahelia Sord wants to find me, I have a feeling that she will. I'll deal with that when it happens."

She smiled. "Now, get a good sleep tonight, and maybe you can join us for breakfast in the morning."

I nodded. "I think I will."

Chapter 43 — Luta
And the Stars Slipped Past

A WEEK LATER we were on the *Tane Ikai,* heading out from Kiando with a cargo load of ore bound for Eri. We'd each spent hours sitting with a Protectorate officer who took our depositions, telling them the whole story—or as much of it as we were willing to tell. I wasn't sure what to say about Jahelia Sord, so I said as little as possible, painting her as a minor PrimeCorp flunky, which I think she was. I don't believe she had prior knowledge of all that PrimeCorp had done, and as for the files she had—well, she didn't have to leave copies of them, but she did. If they wanted her take on things, they'd have to find her themselves. They had the datapad she'd left, and I was sure it would take them a while to sort through that treasure trove of evidence.

The Protectorate had also paid me well for our trouble, and I'd put that to use in a few more upgrades to the ship, and bonuses for the crew. They'd been through a lot. But we were running a far trader, after all, and even with the possibility of war darkening the horizon, that still meant carrying cargo where it needed to go.

Hirin and I were alone in our quarters, settling in to sleep, but the return to normal routine had, instead of settling my mind, rekindled old worries. We still hadn't addressed the problem of exactly how we were going to run the command structure of this ship. But I had to work up to that.

"Anything new with PrimeCorp?" I asked, resting my head on Hirin's chest. "I keep expecting to hear that a PrimeCorp-Chron fleet is pouring through one of the wormholes into Nearspace."

He stroked my back, his hand warm through my sleepsuit. "I don't think that's imminent. The Corvids are still there, remember. And now the Protectorate knows what's going on—or at least some of it. The politics will simmer and bubble while the Protectorate investigates. And once word gets out—"

"Which it's bound to do," I interjected.

"Yes. Then there'll be an uproar like Nearspace has never seen. But it's hard to say when that will happen, or what the ultimate fallout will be."

"I don't like to think of those Chron—the PrimeCorp allies— out there hating us. Trying to find a way into Nearspace like angry wasps outside a screen door. I don't like that at all."

"At least we know not all Chron are like that now. And I don't like it either, but we have to live with it." He kissed the top of my head. "Kind of like our own little problem."

I propped myself up on an elbow and forced myself to meet his eyes. "I don't want to give up being the Captain of the *Tane Ikai*," I said, and felt a huge weight lift from my shoulders. At last, I'd come right out and said it.

He nodded. "And I'm not comfortable being nothing but a tagalong on the ship."

"You were never that!"

"Sure I was," he said, rolling over to stare up at the viewport above us, and lacing his fingers behind his head. "I made up a job for myself so that you could deal with the crisis, but I never felt like I belonged in it. It's not like we have a need for a full-time weapons officer on board."

"We might before too long, if PrimeCorp has its way."

"I hope not. I'd rather not get a job that way."

I lowered myself down beside him, staring up at the stars. He slipped an arm under my shoulders. "Although it has come in handy," I mused. "We don't seem to stay out of trouble for very long, since you came back on board."

He shook me a little at that, and I laughed. It felt good. Finally I said, "So we have to find a way to run a far trader with two Captains on board, is that what you're telling me?"

I felt, more than heard, him chuckle. "Seems that way. Think it's possible?"

I drew a deep breath and hugged him close, feeling the smooth steady hum of the drives, knowing we were, finally, in the right place at the right time.

"Well, we made it work when things were the worst," I said. "Surely we can come up with something when we're not in the middle of a crisis. I think anything's possible," I added, "as long as I'm with you."

Baden had the night duty tonight, and his voice came over the ship's comm. "Captain, message incoming for you. Admiral Lanar Mahane, of the NPV *S. Cheswick*."

I sensed, more than saw, Hirin's smile. "Well. I wonder what my little brother wants now?"

"Just checking in? Or preparing to ask another favour for the Protectorate?"

"I'm not agreeing to anything, not until we've had a rest. I can't believe he'd even do that—but knowing Lanar, he might. I'm not willing to take the risk. Baden, tell my brother I'm asleep, would you? I'll message him tomorrow."

"No problem, Captain."

I grinned at Hirin, and he chuckled and kissed my forehead. Whatever Lanar wanted, whatever PrimeCorp or the Chron might bring tomorrow, it felt far away from us tonight. We settled in to sleep while the stars slipped past outside our ship.

Epilogue — Jahelia

"PITA? ANY RESPONSE yet from our contact at Genusana?" I asked. I kicked my feet up on the main console of the *Hunter's Hope*— or rather, the *Shadow's Eclipse,* as her newly forged papers and new drive signature proclaimed her to be—and blew on my *cazitta* to cool it.

"Came in while you were getting your drink," Pita said. "He's doubling his offer if you'll sign a statement stating exactly where and how you obtained the tech."

"*Kristos.* This guy must be new to the black market. He thinks we actually *sign* things?"

Pita blew out a very human-sounding sigh. "He did say double, Jahelia. He probably wants some kind of assurance that you didn't steal it from another corporation."

I surveyed the cockpit of my little ship, feeling more at home than I had in a long time—not since, if I'd admit it to myself, I'd felt, for a short time, like part of the crew of the *Tane Ikai.*

I shook myself, and put my focus back on my ship. It hadn't even been all that difficult to get her back. A close-mouthed dealer who'd practically drooled over Maja's shorted-out force field generator, even in its current sad shape—that had brought enough credits to get me back on my feet. A Protectorate friend who owed me a favour—a big favour—and could sneak me into the Protectorate's impound yard on Renata. They'd hauled the *Hunter's Hope* there, searched it and found nothing too interesting I guess, and consigned it to the back of the yard until someone could deal with it further. Once we made it inside, Pita had it back under my control within fifteen minutes, and I don't even know if anyone noticed us leave. My stuff—including my *vazel* staff—was gone. That gave me a pang. But it could all be replaced.

Now I was looking for someone interested in the datachip the Corvids had given the Lobor historian, Cerevare. She'd left it behind in her quarters, and I'd had the presence of mind to search those quarters before anyone else on the *Tane Ikai* did. They were pretty taken up with getting the Captain to safety. I'd made a copy of the data for myself, and erased the chip itself. For now I was only selling the tech, but alien technology from a race that no-one even knew about yet? That alone was a treasure worth bargaining over.

"Well, if he'll pay double for a signature, maybe there's someone who'll pay double without one."

"PrimeCorp probably would," Pita suggested. "They've got access to almost anything Chron, but not stuff from the crows."

"Not PrimeCorp," I said, a little more vehemently than I'd meant to. I'd keep my promise to Luta Paixon, and I wouldn't sell it—or anything else—to PrimeCorp. That wasn't even a difficult promise to keep. In retrospect, I could see how Alin Sedmamin had used me, even while I thought I'd been using him. He'd seen my pain and my need for revenge, and he'd used that to send me off to do his bidding. I'd only thought I was in control. I could see that now.

I stood and paced to the rear of the small cabin, still restless. I could see it, but I didn't like it. I'd thought I knew what I wanted, too—what would make me happy. Revenge on Emmage Mahane and her family. A way to let go of the past, finally, to shake off the ghosts of my mother and father and get on with my own life. And I'd ended up suckered in to Luta Paixon's happy little family, trading away my sweet revenge for a brief taste of belonging. Actually caring about other people for a while.

"Well, I can set a course if you tell me where you want to go," Pita said. "If it's not going to be PrimeCorp and it's not going to be Genusana, where to?"

Where to, indeed. I stood still in the middle of the cabin, cupping the warm mug in my hands. Really, I could go anywhere. I didn't feel driven any more. I didn't feel tied to the past. I felt . . . I felt free.

It simply hadn't happened the way I'd expected.

Maybe the most important things in life rarely did.

I flopped into the pilot's chair, set my drink in the holder, and fired up the main drive. "Let's do Genusana after all, Pita. They're a good, clean company. If he wants me to sign something, that shows they're on the bright side of the law, right?"

"If you say so. The course is laid in. But two minutes ago you were against signing anything."

I kicked the drive over and swung out of the shadow of an asteroid where I'd been parked, waiting for my messages to come in and pretty much staying out of the Protectorate's way. I'd heard a rumour they might want to talk to me, and I wasn't sure I was ready to do that yet. Or ever.

"I had a chance to think about it, Pita," I told her with a grin. "After all, there's nothing that says I have to sign my *own* name."

Author Biography

Sherry D. Ramsey is a speculative fiction writer, editor, publisher, creativity addict and self-confessed Internet geek. When she's not writing, she makes jewelry, gardens, hones her creative procrastination skills on social media, and consumes far more coffee and chocolate than is likely good for her.

Her other books include *One's Aspect to the Sun*, *The Murder Prophet*, *To Unimagined Shores—Collected Stories*, and *The Seventh Crow*. With her partners at Third Person Press, she has co-edited five anthologies of regional short fiction to date. A member of the Writer's Federation of Nova Scotia Writer's Council, Sherry is also a past Vice-President and Secretary-Treasurer of SF Canada, Canada's national association for Speculative Fiction Professionals.

Sherry lives in Nova Scotia with her husband, children, and dogs. You can visit her online at www.sherrydramsey.com, find her on Facebook, and keep up with her much more pithy musings on Twitter @sdramsey.

www.ingramcontent.com/pod-product-compliance
Lightning Source LLC
Chambersburg PA
CBHW061617210726
48287CB00001B/177